Author of *An Unseemly Wife*

E. B. MOORE

STONES
IN THE
ROAD

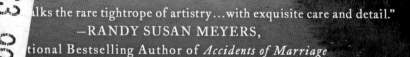

"...alks the rare tightrope of artistry...with exquisite care and detail."
—RANDY SUSAN MEYERS,
...tional Bestselling Author of *Accidents of Marriage*

continued . . .

ALSO BY E. B. MOORE

An Unseemly Wife

STONES
IN THE ROAD

E. B. Moore

NAL NEW AMERICAN LIBRARY

New American Library
Published by the Penguin Group
Penguin Group (USA) LLC, 375 Hudson Street,
New York, New York 10014

USA | Canada | UK | Ireland | Australia | New Zealand | India | South Africa | China
penguin.com
A Penguin Random House Company

First published by New American Library,
a division of Penguin Group (USA) LLC

First Printing, October 2015

 REGISTERED TRADEMARK—MARCA REGISTRADA

LIBRARY OF CONGRESS CATALOGING-IN-PUBLICATION DATA:
Moore, E. B. (Elizabeth B.)
Stones in the road/E. B. Moore.
p. cm.
ISBN 978-0-451-46999-1 (softcover)
1. Young men—Fiction. 2. Amish—History—19th century—Fiction.
3. Domestic fiction. I. Title.
PS3613.O5553S76 2015
813'.6—dc23   2015013929

Printed in the United States of America
1   3   5   7   9   10   8   6   4   2

Set in Stemple Garamond • Designed by Elke Sigal

To my mother,
who kept the old stories alive,
and for my children,
Brad, Cally, and Sarah Moriarty,
may they pass down stories of their own.

ACKNOWLEDGMENTS

I am ever grateful: to Alice Tasman at the Jean V. Naggar Literary Agency for her continued belief in my stories, and to Tracy Bernstein at New American Library, who dared sign up for my second novel sight unseen. With vision and tact, she encouraged me to dig deeper levels within an expanded plot.

To my constant first reader, Priscilla Fales; my children, Brad, Cally, and Sarah Moriarty; and "All-body," the group of vacationing friends, for ignoring my immersion in writing at the expense of swimming the frigid Maine waters, beaching, card playing, Ping-Pong, and pool.

To my treasured whole-novel group, for their loving commitment to my future, for their devotion to craft, and for the fortitude to read and reread whole drafts on demand: Nichole Bernier, Kathy Crowley, Juliette Fay, and Randy Susan Meyers.

To the many people at the Joiner Center, especially those in my long-term poetry group who saw this book through its narrative poem stage: Susan Nisenbaum Becker, Ann Killough, Frannie Lindsay, and Christine Tierney.

To the many at Grub Street Writers, starting with Jenna Blum, who lured the long poem into its current permutation, and to the Novel Incubator community for their unending support.

To my weekly Cambridge Writers, who continue to hold my feet to the fire, seven pages at a time: Lallie Lloyd, Frances McQueeney-Jones Mascolo, Louise Olson, Deb Peeples, and Sandra Shuman.

To the Vermont Studio Center and Yaddo for uninterrupted writing time peppered with delicious breakfast, lunch, and dinner I didn't have to prepare or clean up.

To my copy editor, Michele Alpern, for her sharp eye catching grammar slips, my disastrous spelling, and occasional time warps.

And finally, I'm indebted to friends and strangers who have bought *An Unseemly Wife* and taken the time to rate and write reviews on Amazon, Goodreads, and social media of all sorts. For you, my grateful thanks, and I hope you enjoy *Stones in the Road*.

One generation passeth
away, and another generation
cometh, but the earth
abideth forever.

—*Ecclesiastes 1:4*

STONES IN THE ROAD

PART I

The Road

CHAPTER 1

The Graveyard

Joshua urges his horse through the iron gate. Hoping to find his father's headstone, he dismounts at one slab not yet covered with lichen and reads the name. It's not Father's. He reads it again. Hand to his beard, he compresses his lips. The name is his own.

He never imagined this welcome, or the chiseled inscription: *Beloved Boy, 1872.* The year he ran from Father and the farm.

Beyond disquiet, he lingers on the hill overlooking his family's stone house and white barn, the rebuilt woodshed, all at peace as it should be, no hint of demolishing flames. Only birdsong greets him, and air fresh with the tang of falling leaves.

Quiet surrounds him, the shouting over long ago.

He lets himself revel in the spread of quilted fields, this Amish land woven into the chambers of his heart along with Mama and his sisters. They draw him, but he stays in the graveyard. His horse crops the grass.

A runaway no more, after ten years and six thousand miles, he has returned ragged in brown castoffs, his beard matted. He shakes off hesitation.

Gathering the reins, he girds himself against Father, the

Deacon of their Plain Fold, the one who propelled him, eleven and alone, into the arms of *English*.

In their Gomorrahs Joshua resisted what frightened him most: the advent of hate. Yet try as he might, he fell from grace, another man's blood on his hands.

At twenty-one, he has come to reclaim the boy he once was. He wants to earn the Plain jacket, pants, and hat, black as Mama's blackberry jam. He wants his family. But first comes Father. Face-to-face.

CHAPTER 2

Where the Road Began

Tucked in his narrow bed, Joshua listened to Father slam through the kitchen. Father, back from prayer in the barn, head full of God; on his breath the liquid of visions, the smell sharp as a snake's tongue.

As if in the room, Joshua saw him, smelled him, coming through the dark. Father but not Father, shoulders hunched, wet hair streaming into his collar, dripping off his square beard. His boots squelched with rain, and he kicked the logs stacked for the morning fire. Joshua heard them roll onto the hearth, and, *clang*, the iron fork fell on stone. A great clomping followed. Father kicked at the oak table. Its legs chattered along wide-board floors. He tripped into the parlor, shoved a straight chair, and lurched to the steps. Stomp on the first—stomp, the second—his knee hit the third. *Slap, slap*, his hands on the sixth, the seventh, he dog-paddled to the landing.

Joshua knew the sounds. He'd seen Father, how he would slide his bulk up the wall, shoulder first, legs wobbly, pushing himself up the last steps to the hall.

"Isaac." Father's voice hoarse. "Where are you?" More and

more nights, he wasn't himself, and Father called Joshua Isaac, though he'd been Joshua all his eleven years.

Pulling a patchwork quilt over his head, Joshua prayed, *Please, please, let me be but a mote in his eye,* ever hopeful that this time Father would stagger past the door. But he paused. His boots regrouped at the top step.

Silence. Then, along the wall, Father's hand slid toward the bedroom. Joshua peered from under the quilt. Father pushed the door and pawed the opening. A waft of manure filled the room, and big as a tree, he toppled onto the bedside.

He sank to his knees. "God." Father struck the mattress, his left fist a finger's width from Joshua's head, his breath a slap. The bed shook. Joshua inched to the farthest edge, belly to his backbone, eyes squinched.

Father wept. "Dear God . . ."

And it seemed God answered, as He would, Father being Deacon.

"Yes," Father said. He and God agreed. They were as one, and Joshua less than crumbs under their table. He knew because Father had told him often enough. Crumbs. Though he strove to be the whole loaf Father wanted, a slice would have done.

Breathing heavily, Father gripped Joshua's shoulder, raised one knee, and, dragging his boot beneath him, heaved to his feet. He yanked Joshua's arm, the shoulder fit to pop, and hauled him off the bed, his legs tangled in the quilt.

At the end of the hall, Father took the steps two at a time, Joshua's bare feet bumping the treads, down, down, through parlor and kitchen, his knees cracking against chair legs, the table leg, and out the door into the blowing rain.

Father had him by the hair, head pressed against Father's jacket sharp with sweat and the stench of wet wool. Joshua's nightshirt clinging like a second skin, they splashed across the dooryard.

Wild with what might come, he drove his heels into the mud, plowing crooked furrows. "Oh please," he whispered.

Father wrenched him toward the woodshed. Joshua yowled. Luke yowled in return, the black dog latched in the toolshed.

Luke, Joshua's confidant, a ready ear those nights after Father beat him in the woodshed. "Why does he hate me?" he'd ask as he curled on the dog's bed, and the dog would lick his face.

Luke whined and scratched against his confinement, until Father, dragging Joshua, slammed the woodshed door, the world shut out.

One-handed, Father pushed aside the chopping block, an oak stump with the hatchet whacked in the end-grain. Blood and feathers marked the morning slaughter.

The speckled rooster had run headless circles, unaware the worst was over. Now gutted and plucked, he hung in the rafters by yellow feet, the shed smelling of blood.

Father lit a candle on the stump next to the hatchet. With a black boot, he kicked the floorboards free of kindling, and knelt, saintly in the candle's radiance. From nowhere, he held a quart jar brimming with clear liquid. "Communion cider," he always called it. "Pray with me, boy."

Hard fingers dug into Joshua's elbow, hauling him to his knees, and Father lifted the jar to his lips. He took a long swallow. Another, and he grimaced, lips off his teeth.

The liquid didn't look like cider. Didn't smell like the cider Joshua and his sisters tapped from the barrel outside the pressroom. Only Father went inside to the press; his job alone, the making of cider.

"Lord forgive this boy," Father said.

And Lord only knew, Joshua wanted forgiveness. He needed forgiveness for reading books beyond the Bible, for woolgathering when he should have been working.

But the other faults? *Soggy fields, seed rot, rain—?* If those powers were his, surely he could loosen Father's grip, rise, take up his fright, and walk from the woodshed.

Looking like Sunday, Father intoned a prayer, the man upstanding as a white board fence, hair trim at the earlobes, his marriage beard square, upper lip razored smooth—all according to the Ordnung. He kept to the Plain rules.

His fingers bit the back of Joshua's neck, while the other hand held fervently to the half-empty jar, and through the window, distant as someone else's life, the house stood outlined in the dark: the steep slate, high chimneys, Joshua's bedroom dormer, his sisters' dormer. If he listened intently, he might hear their sleep and Mama's.

On the first floor, no lamp on the table, no square of window glowed orange. There'd be no light or way to bed for him.

Father's grip loosened as his prayers droned, ". . . for I am Yours unto the flesh of my flesh, my Isaac, should You ask."

Isaac again. But would God stay Father's hand as He'd stayed Old Testament Abraham's? That son saved before the knife descended.

As Father's grip eased, Joshua shifted sideways. But a quick twist of his ear brought him to his back on the floor, the jar by his head.

Father patted the floorboards beyond the candle's glow. His hand came up empty, the usual apple switch not found, and this fault *was* Joshua's. He'd burned the switch that morning.

Father searched with the other arm. "God bless it." And for a moment Joshua seemed forgotten in the candle's flicker. The blade of the hatchet glinted.

Joshua spidered backward, arms cocked, palms down, feet under his rump. One outflung foot caught the jar. The remaining liquid ran rat-quick under the dry woodpile.

Father bellowed. He lunged for the jar and missed as an unsplit log rolled beneath his foot. He landed hip first, his face so close, Joshua could have kissed his cheek.

Father had him by the shirt; in the pit of his eye, no hint of reprieve. Joshua saw only his own reflection: the open mouth, panicked eyes. Even God Himself couldn't stay this Abraham's hand.

Joshua closed his fists in Father's long beard and pushed. Straining against Father's chin, his arms shook, but Father's grip wouldn't loosen.

Letting go, Joshua flung his arms above his head, fingers locked together. He wrenched side to side, frantic to break Father's grip, and *oh God,* his locked fists slammed Father's face.

Together they jolted against the chopping block. The block wobbled.

Above their heads, the candle toppled and rolled onto the blotchy floor. A whoosh of blue flame leapt around them, yet Father's grip fiercened. Joshua's shirt tore.

The flames leapt up their clothes. A hand passed Joshua's lips, and he turned badger. All tongue and teeth, he bit. In the Devil's own rage, Father lifted Joshua out of the flames and threw him through the window, shoulder first, head bent, shattering mullions and glass. He landed in a sea of mud.

Searching for breath, he curled on his side. The dark house shimmered.

He wiped his eyes. The woodshed wall sheeted with flame, and from the door came a separate conflagration like a burning bush. *Dear God.* And there in the midst of the burning, what did Joshua see? *Father? God the Father?*

The apparition fell, groveling in the wet. Just a man, he beat at his clothes, splashing until the flames snuffed, and he lay quiet in the roar of the woodshed.

A bell rang, a rapid *clang-clang, clang-clang.* Someone—it had to be Mama—whipped the rope, the clapper slung rim to rim.

Locked safe in the toolshed, Luke yowled high, keening among the shouts of the faithful as they ran over the fields and down the lane, buckets clunking. Fast they came, rousted from bed, running in answer to the iron bell, the insistent clangor sounding fire.

Father stirred. He rose to hands and knees, hair plastered to his head. Smoke billowed, and he pointed a shaky finger. "You!" Father reared, hands reaching.

Joshua's head filled with its own clangor. *Run, run,* and, jumping to his feet, he ran behind the barn, flying across the harrowed fields, hedgerow to hedgerow.

He hadn't meant to hit Father. He hadn't meant the candle to fall. Yet who would believe him over the word of their Deacon?

Out of the fields and into dark woods, he entered the slap of branches, his chest filled with a white fire at every breath, his legs weak as a new lamb's.

"Oh, Mama." Eyes and nose leaking, he stumbled through windfallen limbs.

Father thundered in Joshua's ears, long after the voice faded—*He'll find you.*

The moon slid from banked clouds. And there they were waiting, tall shadows by a road cutting the woods, as if Father's Flock knew right where he hid.

CHAPTER 3

Miriam

Peace without end, a blessing Miriam had been too blind to fully savor. It came unquestioned with her Plain faith. Until contentment ended, she'd never thought to look for hints of ruin.

That spring, rain had lashed the windows and soaked the farm's hundred acres. In occasional sun, the big chestnut spread shade between house and barn, the massive trunk at the center of their circling lane. Lush oaks edged the narrow way, but the once slow creek crowned, overflowing its banks. Mosquitoes whined in the lowlands as seedlings drowned, a time so wet, Noah would have risen, taken up adze and mallet, and built himself an ark.

Of the Old Order, she'd lived Plain in black. Along with Abraham and the littles, she'd bent her back to the land. Pledged never to raise a hand against another, they dwelt in post and beam, fieldstone and mortar, keeping separate as the Ordnung demanded. Separate and safe in Abraham's Flock, the outside world a mystery best left to itself.

Joshua's last morning, Miriam had slaughtered a rooster for supper and they all—Adah, strong at thirteen, Emma, Mary, and little

Rebecca—spent the day in the side field, mud to their ankles, draining puddles of standing water. Abraham, Miriam, and Joshua dug trenches, and the girls swept brown water into the hedgerow, their black clothes spattered with mud.

By evening, quivering with exhaustion, they rinsed off at the pump. They ate pickled pig feet and yesterday's corn mush, no time or inclination for more. They could cook the rooster another day.

Miriam tucked in the littles, hung damp clothes and her white prayer cap on a hook. She changed to a white nightdress, then unwound her lifelong hair, plaited it in a single braid, and fell into bed. Sleep swamped her before Abraham finished bedding animals in the barn.

Raccoons screeched through her dreams. Wind knocked at a loose door. She tossed under the spring quilt and, with a jolt, woke from her dead sleep. It felt like all the mud she'd moved that day now thickened her legs. She sat up and sniffed. "Smoke."

They hadn't cooked, so— She reached for Abraham's shoulder. "I smell—" Her hand fell on the cold sheet.

She swung her feet to the floor, and a flicker of yellow launched her to the window. The woodshed.

She jammed her feet into boots, not bothering with laces. *He should have woken me.*

"Joshua," she shouted as she ran downstairs, white nightdress rippling at her legs. "Fire! Everyone up."

Out the door, she dashed to the iron bell, rain in her eyes. She hauled on the wet rope, and the night filled with clang. Flames rose over the woodshed roof; the barn would be next.

"Abraham!" At the pump? No. "Joshua!" Where were they? She'd work the pump herself, but the bell—she had to keep the neighbors coming. "Joshua?" she shouted into the rain. Her braid slapped across her back. Loose strands stuck to her face.

"Mama." Adah joined her on the pull. "I'll do it."

"Me too." Little Rebecca tugged at the knotted end. Mary and Emma, like their sisters in braids and white nightdresses, crowded ready.

Miriam fled across the dooryard. "Faster," she shouted at Adah. And the rain came faster.

Mud beneath her boots, Miriam slid to a stop at the trough as her closest neighbor thundered in on his horse, a bucket in each hand, reins flapping.

"Whoa, boy." Before the horse stopped, Zeke swung a leg over the animal's neck and slid to the ground. Together, he and Miriam scooped the buckets full and ran, water sloshing their legs. At the shed, they flung what was left at the flames.

Behind them more neighbors flooded in. On horseback, they came shouting. They came in carts, on foot across the fields, down the road, buckets clanking. "Here," one called, "line up."

"You pump," another yelled above the din, and grabbed Miriam's bucket. She worked the metal handle, water in the trough barely keeping up with the long brigade. She thought she saw Joshua, a flash of yellow hair, at the other end of the line. *He'd be with Abraham in the cluster of black-clad men.*

"Inside," a man called. "Douse the inside—we're gaining."

Women in white prayer caps stationed themselves by the barn doors ready to get the animals out. Their worried faces glowed orange above black dresses.

Breathing hard, Miriam kept her eye on the smoke. Through dark billows, sparks danced like fireflies, until the smoke paled to white, the flames tiring.

Hands pulled her from the pump while others set to on the handle. "It's Abraham," Hannah said. "Zeke's with him." She pulled Miriam around the corner of the shed toward a group kneeling in the mud, their backs to her. Hannah's husband motioned her over.

Miriam searched the backs, none as big and square as Abraham's. The men parted, their pale faces turning her way.

She no longer heard the bell, the shouting, the roar of the fire. She didn't see the flames or feel the rain. She saw only the mud-blackened shape, square and solid, lying on the ground.

"Abraham." She rushed to him. One of his eyes opened, the white bright in the mud-dark face, the pupil darting. His lid clamped shut. A cough racked his body.

"He's burned," Zeke said.

Miriam knelt, her hands wandering above him, unsure where to start. "Water," she said, and tore the sleeve from her nightdress. Zeke held out a bucket. Miriam squeezed the cloth, dribbling water over Abraham's face, mud running off his bubbled skin. Wincing, she dipped the cloth again. "More."

Zeke tilted a slow stream, which Miriam guided through Abraham's melted hair, over his forehead, and neck. Hannah opened his burned shirt. "Let's get him inside."

Abraham struggled to sit. "No, I've got—"

Two men slipped arms under his and lifted him to his feet. He howled. They retreated from his flailing arms, and his legs buckled, bringing him to hands and knees. "Find—" He gagged. "Save him—" His back humped. He wavered, tipped, and splashed on his side.

At the worktable in the crowded kitchen, women doled food off platters they'd brought from home. They kept their backs to the dinner table, where the men had laid Abraham, his body doused and dripping. Hannah and Miriam worked at his clothes, cutting and lifting burned strips, baring his mottled skin. Miriam sluiced the yellow blisters on his chest and rinsed char from the cooked flesh. Down his belly and legs, meaty patches gleamed red.

He moaned, his voice hoarse, words more and more disjointed. He shouted for Isaac. *An angel, perhaps, who'd flown through a window.* Abraham did have visions.

"It's the burns," Hannah said. "I've seen it before. He needs liquid inside as much as out. A wash in chestnut tea." Hannah took a lantern from the sideboard. "Collect leaves," she directed one of the women, and to another, "In the cellar, we need potatoes. Lots. I'll make a poultice."

"No, no." Abraham struggled. His leg dangled off the table.

Hannah blocked his fall, and three of the servers grabbed ankles and wrists. Pinned to the table, he shrieked.

Miriam steeled herself against his cries and tweezed bits of black skin along with shreds of cloth resistant to water. The tiniest scrap or drop of mud could kill if left buried in raw folds under his arm, behind a knee, in the curl of his blackened ear. She bent closer, and more candles appeared, held high without being asked for.

Thank heaven for Hannah and the Flock's many hands. One family, they belonged to one another the way pieces of grain gave themselves to be bread. Hannah and the Flock would take care of them, the way Miriam and the Flock had taken care of Hannah and Zeke when their first infant passed. No one had to ask, no one beholden.

A thudding of logs sounded in the dooryard. Someone had planned ahead, a place where her thoughts wouldn't have gone, not until the cook fire dwindled and she remembered the woodpile, another thing they'd lost along with the shed.

God had been watching out, and God would see Abraham through. He had to. The Lord and Abraham had each other's ear. They always did.

Abraham's faith drew people to him, had drawn Miriam, not just his full lips and the dent in his chin now covered with his marriage beard.

Grateful for blessings, she felt her eyes well. She pursed her lips, cleared her vision with a shake of her head. This was no time for tears.

She poured more water from a pitcher over the ravaged side of Abraham's face. She dabbed gently with a wad of lamb's wool, working around the puffing blisters, the features blurred as if she'd stuffed him in a sausage skin. "Oh, Abraham," she whispered. "What happened?"

He twisted under the women's muscular arms, no sign of hearing, and with greater care yet, Miriam dabbed where he had no skin at all. He gave another agonized cry.

The girls burst through the door, pressing in beside Miriam. Bending over Abraham, Rebecca choked and turned away, then back, her palm cupped over her nose and mouth.

Until then, Miriam hadn't noticed the smell of burned hair and, worse, the scorch of meat. Emma ran from the room followed by Mary.

"Adah," Miriam said. "Take Rebecca upstairs." This was no sight for a four-year-old. "Get everyone to bed."

"But—"

"I'm seeing to Papa. I'll come later." Light would likely come first, for dawn already seeped at the edge of eastern fields.

"Where's Joshua?" Adah paused at the bottom step. "Bed for him too?"

"I'm sure he's with the men," Hannah said. "Clearing the fire." She waved the girls up the stairs. "Off now."

Abraham moaned. "Hurt—he's—"

"Shhh, Abraham." Miriam blinked hard. She'd do anything to ease his writhing. How could tea help, the burns so deep, so wide-spread?

"He needs a pallet down here," Hannah said. "He can't be up-stairs."

Abraham struggled onto his elbows. "No." Swelling lips muffled his words. "Find him." His elbows slid, slamming his back to the table. One eye stretched wide, the brown center rolling under its lid, left a sightless white pebble. His body went slack.

A rosy glow filled the parlor's east window while the women grated mounds of potato. One by one, the men, having knocked down the fire, came for breakfast. They ate hurriedly, and collected their wives, except for Hannah, who continued grating.

"I'll tend the animals," Zeke said.

Miriam looked up from bathing Abraham with cooled chestnut tea. "Bless you," she said. She could hear impatience in the cows' lowing. "Joshua must have started by now."

"I didn't see him." Zeke rubbed his beard. "Not at the fire either."

Miriam frowned. *Hadn't she seen him in the line?* "He has to be there. He wasn't in his room." Looking from face to face, she gripped the edge of the table.

"Go," Hannah said. "We'll set the poultice."

Miriam threw a black shawl over her muddy nightdress and ran. She cut across the circling lane, Zeke behind her, both of them calling, "Joshua." His voice low and rumbling, hers growing higher and higher.

Cows in a line at the barn's side door turned their heads expectantly. Joshua wouldn't be inside if the cows were out; he hadn't started. She called again, her voice a squeak.

Luke barked. *Of course, he'd be with Luke.* She flung open the toolshed door, and the dog shot out. He circled the lane sniffing.

By the charred woodshed, he stopped under the shattered window. He whined, sniffed the air, sniffed the wet ground in widening circles, and returned to the window.

"Zeke," Miriam said. "Abraham must have thrown him from the fire—that's what he meant. We have to find him. He's hurt."

She ran to the bell again, ringing in the neighbors. By full light, they'd gathered, black figures fanning out across the fields and into the hedgerows.

"He can't have gotten far," Zeke said. He and Miriam parted the brush and peered for any hidden sign. "Not with burns like Abraham's."

She pushed his words away. "I'll try the barn."

She passed the waiting cows and opened one stall after the next, praying she'd find Joshua feeding the horses.

In the lofts, she turned over hay while Zeke saw to the cows. She headed behind the grain bins. He wouldn't be there past the hexing of pitchforks, but maybe. She had to look everywhere. Uncrossing the pitchforks, she leaned behind the bins. Nothing but a line of corked jars. *Where is he?*

Outside again, the girls, now in black day clothes, gathered to Miriam. They latched on as a drowner would, clutching her. Rebecca wrung Miriam's nightdress.

Men and women called, "Anything?"

Others answered, "Nothing here." "Nothing here." "Nothing here."

"Try by the yearling pen?"

The girls followed her to the pens behind the toolshed. "This one?"

"No. Not here either?"

They swung back to the lane. "Where next, Mama?" *Where indeed?*

The barn, as if Miriam hadn't checked every loft and corner. The edges of her vision darkened with panic. She used to wonder how horses could be so senseless. Having been led from a burning barn, they'd return to the flames if they weren't blindfolded. She closed her eyes. *Think now.*

She'd been looking for her boy in black. He'd be wet, limping, sitting perhaps, cradling a broken limb.

No—what was she thinking?—not in black. Like herself, drawn from bed, he'd be in mud-soaked white, if his shirt hadn't burned away, his body bubbled and torn like Abraham's.

"Abraham." She ran for the house.

No, Hannah would have him in hand. "Girls, help inside. I'll be in in a minute. Go."

They'd seen Abraham, and she didn't want them finding anything worse. She dreaded the glimpse of cloth in a hedgerow, a charred knee poking from behind a fallen log, yet any sighting would be better than none.

All day in her nightdress, hair unkempt, Miriam ran circles. Centered on the huge chestnut, she veered off to the beehives behind the shed of yearling sheep, back to the tree. If only she could climb it and see the whole of their land.

Off to the barn. A third time? She might have missed—something, anything.

The cider room? No, Joshua wouldn't. The room sacred, only Abraham allowed.

She unlatched the door, the room a jumble of barrels and jars, the big press and odd equipment, things *her* father had never used for cider. But no Joshua.

Out the door, she ran to the henhouse, to the old well. The stone slab, too heavy for one person to lift, lay firmly atop the hole. A small relief.

In the hedgerows with her neighbors, her mouth a fearful desert, she searched more slowly. God bless Zeke and the Flock taking her chores on top of their own. Bless Hannah shooing her out to search. Hannah, her elder by four years, had a steady hand on the girls and Abraham.

The sun fell behind the grave-covered hill, and dark closed over the farm. Lamps glowed through the kitchen windows. On her way to the house, Miriam, in a last look across the fields, watched her neighbor's torchlights bobbing near the woods.

So like lightning bugs the littles loved to chase on balmy summer nights. If only those lights were lightning bugs, she'd be sitting on the porch amidst the day's harvest, hulling peas and

limas or shucking corn, a wealth of food for winter. By fall she'd
have a cellar full of jarred vegetables of every color. If only this
could be last summer.

She hated the thought of Joshua lost in the trees, fear and the
night chill adding to his pain.

She swayed, her legs gelatinous. Zeke hurried across the lane
and took her arm. "Inside now. You need rest." They entered arm
in arm as others came out.

"We'll keep looking," the men said.

The murmur of voices went quiet. Her girls threw arms around
Miriam as neighboring women loaded more plates and passed them
to the crowded men who stood, hasty forks making quick work of
their meal. And finished, they put their plates in the washtub,
touched Miriam's shoulder in passing, and headed out again.

Hannah sat on a chair close to Abraham's pallet. She'd set it in
a corner away from the hearth, a cup and a pitcher of water by her
feet. "I think he sleeps," she said. "You should too. I'll keep watch."

All eyes followed Miriam, the center of this unwelcome world
of attention. She led the littles to the stairs. Murmurs followed
them to the second floor.

In the girls' room, Miriam left a burning candle on the windowsill, and lit a stub in her own room. Maybe the light would
draw him. Or maybe *she* needed the light.

When he was small, Joshua liked having a candle, the way
shadows flickered on the walls and ceiling. He saw Noah's animals, giraffes grazing in the treetops, lions stalking in long grass.
The teacher, Frau Lentz, had filled his head with a peaceable
kingdom that lit the dark so feared by other children.

But now, Miriam couldn't see his kingdom. She saw the plain
walls boxing her in, the room no longer a place of comfort. Lying
on her back in a dry nightdress, she stared at the ceiling above her
like a plaster lid, and below, her black dress and apron hung limp
on their pegs. Lifeless, the dress mocked her.

When she finally dozed, Joshua haunted her dreams. He called, *Mama,* and she followed his faint voice. His pleading drew her down a hall of locked doors. Finally setting her shoulder to one, it opened and—*oh, Joshua*—there he stood, nightshirt in shreds, his body weeping with burns. She reached for him, gathered him in her arms, relief throbbing through her.

Mama, he said, and dissolved. She woke gasping, a sheet clutched to her breast.

On the windowsill, the pooled candle guttered to nothing. She shifted under her patchwork quilt, the straw in her mattress doing nothing to shush the stampede in her head. The moon cast dim shadows.

Miriam threw off the covers. She took clothes from the pegs where she'd hung them before the fire, and dressed, a shawl over her shoulders. Tiptoeing, she passed the girls' room and down the stairs and into the kitchen.

Hannah sat by Abraham, her eyes closed, head leaning against the wall. The others had left. Miriam should send Hannah home, but she knew she wouldn't go.

Continuing to tiptoe, Miriam slipped outside, closing the door softly behind her. She held a lamp, the light bathing her hands, her skirts, and a small pool of ground around her boots. The light made the surrounding dark even darker.

Alone, Miriam probed the night.

CHAPTER 4

Sweet Chariot

J oshua tripped. With each painful step, tangled brush gave underfoot. Panting, he fell. Twigs dug at his burned legs. He shrieked.

The men waiting by the road, surely they'd seen him cowering in the woods, but the shadowy figures didn't move. "Take me. Be done." He waited for their crashing footsteps through the woods. It didn't matter. Only the pain mattered. His head buzzed, eyes filling with an ocean of silvery minnows, and darkness swallowed him back to his bed.

He heard Mama's voice from down the hall: "Abraham, Jesus waits." As if Jesus stood in the room, tapping His foot; she with a braid to the waist of her long nightdress, Jesus beside her, His hair loose to His shoulders, robes to the floor, ready as Mama to turn the other cheek. Forgiveness. Joshua snuggled in, forgiveness deep and soft as straw ticking.

But the ticking heated hotter than a frying pan, hot as the forge. Was he shaping horseshoes in bed? Coals tipped onto his legs.

He lurched to his feet, shying from his mattress of sticks.

Home, his bed, the forge, gone, yet fire stuck to his legs. He staggered in the dim morning woods till he touched the smooth road and remembered the men.

About to run, he saw at the road's far side not men at all. Nothing but a windbreak of cedars.

A rumble came from around the curve, the beat of hooves, and a wagon broke into view. Joshua jumped for the trees, Father's voice in his head—*He wants you.*

God wasn't his worry. Father was.

Fearful of eyes seeking a burned boy, Joshua hobbled on, hair in his face, torn nightshirt, bare feet bleeding. Drizzle started. A vine snared his ankle, and falling, every briar in the woods pounced, vicious as hornets.

Days and nights floated together. In sun and rain, in patches of moonlight, dusk and dawn he startled at the snap of sticks.

Eyes closed, he ran. Trees ran with him, harsh breath in his ear, heart-hammered chests fit to crack. Trees and boy, limbs waving, sap flowing. Visions of Father high on a lathered horse pressed him onward.

He ran dizzy, ran dark, ran sun, the fields as strange as the roads he'd never seen. Though not expressly forbidden, he had never ventured past the ridge. For all he knew, he could be in Egypt. He, like all the Plain, stayed separate, uninfected by rabble *English* living in their run-down farms and godless Gomorrahs.

Joshua's head overflowed with he-devils and she-devils in flame-lit finery, a seething mass dancing around a pen of stray children fattened for roasting. Yes, far-fetched in the light of day, yet the images haunted him.

The only sure thing: dawn at his back, the day setting in his face, and another fitful night of burning legs.

Worry of all he'd left undone swamped him: Mama at the plow, at cooking, baking, sweeping, hauling water from the pump to the house, chopping wood, driving the hay wagon. Adah mucking and milking.

Never look back. Joshua knew he'd turn to a pillar of salt, and still he cast back to last Sunday, how his sisters had teased him, chirpy and laughing, while setting up benches for service, their turn hosting that week. Adah had said, "You're too pretty for a boy." The girls, miniatures of Mama except for their black prayer caps, laughed and twitched long skirts. "You should wear these."

"Nooo," said Mama. "Too much muscle for a girl." She'd brushed yellow hair from his eyes and kissed his forehead. He wrapped his arms around her, holding to her softness, the smell of stew and corn bread in her clothes.

She gave a hug to each of the black-capped girls. "Hurry now, it's time to ring the bell. Rebecca, your turn. Remember, slowly; you're calling the faithful to church, not a fire." No fire, how he wished it were true.

Forget the house. Forget Rebecca cheeping like a fuzzy chick. Forget Emma and Adah shaking rain from their skirts the way ducks shiver water from their feathers. And Mama, forget her teasing smile, the safety of her arms.

Joshua had no horses to feed, no sheep to shear, no barn peeling in the heat. Those burdens theirs, all he needed was another puddle to sip, a few twigs with bark new enough to chew.

He thought himself all cried out, but his cheeks stayed wet.

At a scabby farm scratched into the hillside, Joshua dared not test for kindness. Not this farm or the one before it. The lighted windows spoke of home, but these English were no kin to him. And if kin lived there, worse yet.

His legs burned as if the flames that took the woodshed licked him to the bone.

Another day, and shivery-hot, Joshua found a place so neglected— a gaping roof, fences down, the gate cockeyed on one hinge—it had to be abandoned. Vines choked the porch; a plow rusted in the field; a wagon missing a wheel tipped on its axle. He couldn't imagine what lash would put an entire family to flight.

Joshua sidled clear of the house. Maybe English lived like that.

Crouched low, he came behind a mossy trough, looked left, looked right, before dipping his cupped hands. Water dribbled. His head jerked at the noise.

All was quiet. He leaned on the trough and pressed his lips into the heavenly water, gulp after gulp till his belly could hold no more. He splashed his legs. Mud flowed down his shins, exposing char and yellow blisters. Dizzy, he hunched over the trough edge, so like Father had after a night in the woodshed.

Father had smacked the reflection with the flat of his hand, groaned, and dunked his head. He came up, his hair dripping, and from a bucket, he'd taken a bristle brush. He scrubbed his face, scoured hard on the back of his neck, under the beard, over a shoulder, and down each arm. While he scrubbed, he chanted hymns of suffering, how the bodies of Old Order ancestors had been stretched on the rack. He scrubbed until he was clean and pink as a newborn pig.

Joshua tried the barn door. It wouldn't budge, the door too heavy on a rusted track. He crept around to the other side.

At the back, once-red boards curled, leaving a slip-space big enough to wedge his head. He wormed on through, careful not to let his legs touch the boards.

Inside, open beams rose to a roof where light shone through. Slanted rays full of dust landed on burlap sacks piled in a corner. Mice rooted for a few remaining oats. He shooed them and plucked each grain, popping the dry morsels in his mouth. Cow on a cud, he chewed, forcing himself not to swallow until the grain turned pulp.

He spread the sacks on a skim of straw. Cold and hot at once, he covered his chest. The rough cloth fell against one leg. He howled and sank again into glimmering minnows. So many fish, it had to be Frau Lentz's California, his beloved teacher's land of plenty.

Hordes of mice burrowed under his back, and raising him, they carried his white and naked body into unbearable brightness. *God's face?* One look could mean blindness.

A sound sweeter than birdsong filled the air. "Swing low, sweet chaaaa-riot." A dark figure on either side carried him from the barn.

"Watch his head."

"Oh—" A jounce. "Jesus!"

"Bet that hurt."

They backed up and started again.

"The sack don't work. 'S too small."

"Wish we had a litter."

"I wish we had fried chicken, grits, and redeye gravy."

"No hope there."

Hope—food for the living. And being in heaven, Joshua had no need. *This had to be heaven.* Maybe not Father's, that gate too strait for the likes of this son.

The spirits passed his body through a mess of rooms. Paint curled off the walls, chunks of ceiling on the floor. They stomped up a flight of complaining stairs.

"Careful now. Watch the rail." They gentled him onto an iron bed of twisted white flowers.

In the bedroom, the figures came clearer like dark angels, a great white wing between them. Waving it, they cooled the boy, these angels with brown faces and hands. Close to black. *Heaven for the burned?*

Or some other burning place, said Father's voice. And he saw Father with his Lord in tow. It seemed they sat at the foot of the bed. God in white robes made a throne; Father in his usual black sat in the Lord's lap.

Father's beard, gray as God's own, wagged with each word, a sneer to his smooth upper lip. *Heaven's not for you, boy. Let me tell your angels the murderous truth.*

And Father told Joshua's angels about the fire. Told it in sorrow. He rode on a sea of humble regret, looking to be the gentle man his Flock knew, a man selfless in the service of others.

"No," the boy cried.

Yes. On purpose, you tipped the candle. You burned the woodshed. Tried to murder your father.

"Nooo!" The body on the bed thrashed. "Not on purpose."

Oh yes! Father's accusations tore the room, but the angels reached right through him as they worked.

". . . trouble," the big one said, and scratched short curls tight as a black lamb's. The small, ropy-haired one said, "How can you tell? He sleeps."

They waved their shared wing.

"Good Lord—you saw his back."

Keepers at the Gate saw things even mamas missed. At home he'd bathed alone since the age of nine, never let Mama see the welts.

And there she was, Mama standing at the foot of the bed, Father's arm locked through hers, his other around her shoulders. In black, one body, two heads.

Come home, Joshua, her head pleaded. *You didn't mean the fire. A moment of anger is all. And your father forgives you.* Father could make her believe anything.

Abraham. She strained at his arms, her eyes red rimmed. *Please, Joshua, your sisters need you. I need you.* Father shut her in the folds of his clothes.

A new fear racked the boy. Who would collect Father's wrath? Luke? Joshua's sisters?

Mama had questioned Father once. "What prayers take you to the barn at night?" she'd said. "Is God deaf in the day?"

"Tend your tongue," Father had told her. "God's word is my command."

Mama struggled beneath his cloak. Father gave a wolfish smile, and drew God's beard around their shoulders. The boy kicked and screamed.

The rope-haired one sat on the bed beside the boy's body and dispersed Father with a wet cloth. "Yes," she said to her husband. "I saw his back. I saw the scars. So like yours, and were you trouble?"

He rubbed the top of his head. "So they say."

"Did I believe them?"

"Best damp the curtain. He still feels hot."

Hotter than August, Joshua floated in a cloud of stinging insects, no more smell of soup, no visage of God too bright for mortal eyes.

"We'll take him north," she said.

"He's trouble, I tell you. He stays here."

Where's here? At the window, a half curtain hung in shreds.

"Trouble or no, he's not ours. Someone's hunting him, and if he's found, we're found. On that day, Georgia will look like paradise."

She laid a cool hand on Joshua's forehead. Another at the back of his head, and a cup to his lips; thirsty as he was, his mouth wouldn't answer commands. Water dribbled his chin and neck.

Joshua wanted to meet their eyes, that they might know his gratitude. His lids stayed shut. His stomach growled.

"One day, we'll have our own boy," the man said.

"And you'd abandon this one?"

"We've no choice. He's too sick to move, and too little food for us, much less him."

"May as well lay him in the road," the higher voice said. "Let the crows have at him; all out of his mind, he'll never know." Feet scuffed the floor. "With luck, his hunters will find him while he still has eyes."

"What luck is that?"

"You think on it."

"I've thought," the deep voice said low as if soft words would soften the message. "The boy can't walk, and I can't carry."

"And if we leave him?"

"It's up to God."

She dampened the curtain again, and laid it on Joshua's legs. She filled a tin cup by the bed. The man brought a chunk of crust.

She said, "All of it. We'll find more." Her lips mothering-soft, she kissed Joshua's hair. The man slung a sack over his shoulder.

"May Jesus keep you," she said.

The stairs creaked. A door swung shut, and Joshua dreamed of Mama ladling corn soup in a bowl. He dipped his spoon, sipped. After chewing tender kernels, he washed them down with milk, and banged his empty cup on the table.

Silence like a person in the room, Joshua rose on one elbow and blinked. A torn curtain waved in the wind from a broken pane. He smelled lilacs gone by. A tin cup rested on its handle in the dust of the bedside table, no noises from downstairs.

In need of the night-jar, he threw off a moth-chewed blanket and sat on the side of the bed. He gasped, pain shrieking up his rag-covered legs. The dizzies spun him.

He waited, propped on scabby arms, and when he could lean without falling, he retrieved the night-jar from under the bed and used it. Clearly he hadn't always managed, the mattress rich with his mistakes.

At the foot of the bed lay clothes neatly folded and smelling of the outdoors. Sliding a crusty arm into the stained shirt, he balked at buttons. The frayed pants had them too, and a hole in one knee.

He mustn't wear buttons, though these hadn't so much as a hint of the fancy. Nothing prideful about them, two broken, the rest chipped, one missing completely.

His choice came down to buttons on clothes or a fig leaf. Not that he could find a fig tree or even a needle and thread to sew the shirt closed. Buttons it would have to be.

Unaccustomed, he fumbled each one through the opposite hole and closed the shirt. The pants more difficult, he slipped them over rags sticky with salve. The sharp smell of herbs came off the bindings as he worked. Fortune smiled. The pants big around, and once they were pulled up, the hurt lessened.

Rag boots showed below the too short pants. He held the wide waist and hunted for rope, the blanket slung over his shoulder.

Downstairs, he kept an eye out for food as well as string or anything else useful. A few broken dishes sat on a doorless hutch. Ashes in the fireplace cold.

He turned and turned in the middle of the room, and stopped facing a washstand with a bowl and pitcher empty except for a dry cloth. It would have to do.

Tearing it in three strips, twisting and knotting them, he tied the cloth around himself, tight, with the top of the pants folded over. He could then walk without holding on.

Alone in the house, yet he called through the rooms. Warm sun streamed in the windows, lighting the curled paint. Striped wallpaper spoke of long-gone care, the stripes milky and faded.

If it weren't for the bandages, he'd have wondered if his angels had ever been there, their squirrel soup and gentle touch pieces of dream.

Thirst drove him from the house. He stood on the porch in the shade of leafed-out roses, the buds just starting to open. By the look of the flowers he'd been weeks on the bed.

He hobbled down three rickety steps to the trough, the burns on top of his feet nothing to the stab in his legs. Slurping from the trough, he craved signs of his dark angels, but a searching eye found only the fallen fence and the weed-grown lane.

He'd starve if he stayed, so he took to the afternoon road, blanket under his arm, sun in his face. He was Daniel in a den without walls, Daniel waiting for the lion.

CHAPTER 5

The Lion's Den

Father's reach stretched. Joshua had to put Pennsylvania between them.

The first day from his angels, he hobbled, maybe a mile. None the second. Half a mile the third. By the fifth, maybe a mile and a half, but where was he?

He pictured the schoolroom map. Frau Lentz had drawn Pennsylvania and pinned it to the wall, rivers in squiggly lines, mountains full of triangle trees, black circles for Philadelphia, Lancaster, Harrisburg, Pittsburgh. A tiny dot for New Eden, just west of Lancaster. She hadn't drawn California, but it was in his head, a heaven she had given him. The place he went when Father's switch cut his back and his legs, a land of year-round sun, a farmer's dream. No matter what Father had said, Joshua *was* a farmer.

Before dawn, his last morning at home, Father had caught him reading on his bed. Dressed only in a shirt, Joshua wished he could shrink into the mattress.

"Wastrel." Father strode across the bedroom. "You'll never make a farmer."

Joshua gripped the book Frau Lentz had slipped under his arm after school. *How could reading make him not a farmer?* When plowing, he angled the team across crest and swale, never a rill after he finished. He reveled at earth between his fingers, the planting of corn in rows, wheat seeds scattered. Joy came with the greening fields.

Father had grabbed the book. Now Frau Lentz would never loan another. There'd be no more showing maps, thrilling him with stories of the outside world. No more telling him her secret dream: California, a place where summer never ended.

"*The Inferno*, is it?" Father said with a grunt. "Inferno it shall be." Pages fanning, he flung the book into the fire. The paper curled black at the edges.

Eyes closed, Joshua thought on the shimmering West, where he could walk in sun, raise sheep in lush pastures, sit beside the still waters. Father couldn't burn those.

Surely if he made it to Pittsburgh, almost three hundred miles across Pennsylvania, he'd be safe. Or prayed he would.

Hills rose. The Susquehanna lay behind him, where a wide ford had been deep to his chest. After another week, maybe more, the hills might be the start of the Tuscarora. They gobbled the summer sun. Cold stones waited sharp in the shadows and bit through his tattered bandages. A two-day thirst nagged him.

Joshua's ear, usually bent for the rumble of wagons, now listened for water, and once again, leafy hardwoods hung over the road. A light breeze picked up, and on it the sound of peepers. They talked water, and he could smell it.

Funny, at home the creek had been a cheerful burble, good for cooling milk in the milk house. The fish he caught, a nice change from dinners of chicken or lamb.

Around the next bend, he followed a whisper into the woods. Blessed water, and down on his knees on the bank, he buried his face in the flow and drank.

He stretched on the ground in a moment of well-being, before his stomach complained, water no substitute for food. He returned to the stream, hoping he'd find minnows or a low-lying catfish.

One hand propped on a rock, he took a breath, held it, and with the other hand swept what he prayed was a catfish bedroom. His fingers clamped on a wiggly soft something. Quick out of the water, he slammed it on a rock. No more wiggle, and he held dinner up to the fading light. A frog hung from his fingers, its belly smaller than his big toe, limp legs, its tadpole tail not quite gone.

At first, chomping raw flesh put him off his feed, but hunger ended squeamishness, and he dropped the frog, legs and all, into his mouth. One quick chew and he swallowed, then another to get the toes down.

Sitting on the bank, he picked at his bandages. The dirty cloth stuck as he unwound the strips. Underneath, new pink skin rippled around red centers.

Road dust muddied the water as he scrubbed the cloth between his fists, a sorry wash for shreds serving as bandage and boot. He wrung them and laid them on branches to dry. If they lasted the week, he'd be lucky, not that he knew the end of one or the beginning of the next, all his attention on water and food and his slow-healing burns.

At home, time had been told by hungry sheep, or tolled by the school bell, or Mama on the dinner bell. His sisters announced mealtime with the clatter of forks, spoons, and knives as they set the table.

He missed Father's sermons ending the week. How strange. He missed Sunday dinner at the long table, the buzz of the Flock's talk, friendly visits on Sunday afternoons.

He rested his head on his knees. No use crying; he'd think on California. But home insisted on creeping in.

At dusk, Father would be bedding the horses, Mama peeling the last squash from the cellar, cutting it into the evening's stew.

The littles and Luke might herd sheep, penning them for shearing the next day, now long past warm enough. He worried about who would tip the full-grown ewes and drag them to Father on the shearing platform.

Adah was quick, but not strong enough. Mama would have to do it. Emma could tend dinner. Mary probably kneaded the dough. Poor Rebecca had to collect eggs, even reaching her little hand under the red hen, the one with fierce yellow eyes and a beak sharp enough to draw blood. He should be there.

But if he went home, he knew he'd find Father in the lane, scythe ready, the blade sharp. He'd never see Mama or the littles. Father would cut him down.

It hadn't always been so. Father and Joshua had worked the land together, Father teaching the motion of tools, the blessings of rich earth, and its care. They pulled horses through colic, birthed calves and lambs, mourning the ones they couldn't save.

Each year he could remember, Joshua had ridden Father's shoulders downstairs for a birthday breakfast, piggyback when he grew too big. And he'd grown big for his age, and strong, he and Father a team sharing the notion of years to come, as it should be, world without end, amen. And yet now, he couldn't go home.

Each day Joshua's feet hardened a bit more. He didn't mind the road, but in the woods, his legs suffered the branches. He wound the blanket around his middle like a skirt. If they saw him, oh, how his sisters would laugh.

Weeks and weeks of the same shirt, the same baggy pants. *Thank heaven* they couldn't see him, all filth and stink. Worse yet, the colors and buttons.

Hunger wouldn't quit, not on roots and ferns and bark. In those scraggy foothills, he needed a working farm.

The ground steeper by the day, the nights grew cold, mountainous roads narrower, the woods thicker. Late afternoon, a wagon scared him into the trees, and again a quick wrap in the blanket. His pace slowed; no wonder girls didn't run in the woods.

Something skittered. A ground squirrel? A snake? Turning, he found a farmyard showed through the trees. He crept closer. Not really a farm, just a patched cabin and a split-rail fence surrounding a garden. His prayer answered.

The cabin squatted in a circle of beaten earth where chickens scratched for bugs. A shed tilted at the circle's edge, and beside it a stack of logs fell into knee-high weeds.

Near as he could tell, two more hours of light. A thief in the night had to wait for night. He waited.

Dusk hung in the woods when the cabin door opened. An old man, as run-down as his home, stepped out. He limped toward the woodpile and stopped. Peering into the woods, he raised his nose like a dog sniffing the wind. Joshua stooped in the underbrush.

Scanning the woods, the man shook his head, lifted a small log from the pile, and split it with a hatchet. Thin slivers fell under his weak strokes, slivers he gathered in the crook of one arm. He shuffled to the cabin, and kicked the door shut.

Soon a plume of smoke drifted from the chimney, followed by the smell of frying eggs. Joshua chewed his tongue in a covetous fit he knew would make the Devil smile.

Patience, he told himself, *be the old catfish at home in the creek.* That fish knew how to wait, taking nibbles of worm, while younger fish gulped Joshua's hook.

The evening air filled with little black insects. They flew up his nose, bit in the crease behind his ears, drowned in his eyes. Up his pant legs, they bit his burns, sending him into a frenzy.

You deserve it, Father's voice in his head, *stealing from the infirm. You're a vulture feeding on the living.*

No, Joshua was the body being eaten.

The old man came out of his cabin. A bag in hand, he called, "Come, chicky, come." Six hens rushed to his feet. He talked to each as he might to a daughter. A few kernels of corn taken from the bag, he offered the treat on his flattened palm. The birds craned their necks, red combs wobbling, and gently pecked. He chucked a finger under their beaks and headed for the shed. They followed through a half door. The top half, off its hinges, leaned against the outside wall.

In order to steal, Joshua had to dislike the old man, overlook his kindness, see him as unworthy, this English who took no care of the blessings God gave him.

Joshua did what Father had done to him, picked at every little fault.

His last soggy spring, Joshua had hitched Goli to the plow. As the horse pulled, the coulter cut sod. The share dug, but when the earth should have curled in a wave off the moldboard, mud glommed, forcing a halt every few paces, the furrow crooked as a dog's hind leg. Father shouted from across the field, "Hold the line."

Joshua had tried, but his feet slipped, boots covered in mud mittens. The reins loose around his neck, he held the wood handles, muscles bunched and pushing.

"Come on, boy, lean into it." Father's voice rang with hate.

Wood handles at his stomach, Joshua had pressed all his weight, one stone more than a stunted sheep, but the blade jumped the furrow and bounced along the ground.

If the handles had broken, Father wouldn't have waited for the woodshed.

Joshua smelled the old man, distant as he was, rank as a billy goat. Or was the stink his? He felt the beam in his own eye as he cast about for the codger's mote.

The fellow blew his lamp, and Joshua finally set two hands on the fence rail. He hiked both feet sideways and vaulted into the garden, landing light as a fly on meat.

He trod carefully, steering clear of tomatoes. The dim moon wouldn't tell him how green they were. Even pink tomatoes gave a mean case of the collywobbles.

He slid his hands through strawberry leaves, feeling for the slight give of the hidden fruit. Since the rains of spring had dried to summer drought, the berries felt small. Still, nothing had ever tasted so good.

Using both hands, he stuffed his mouth. Joy blotted out all else, and on that note of greed, he picked the biggest berry of all, soft and succulent. Just short of his mouth, he felt the slime. Oh, comeuppance, a slug fat as his thumb curled on his palm.

"Ach." He flung it and wiped his hand on his pants, ready for spinach, then peas.

At the second beanpole, he stubbed his toe on a dropped tool, the handle of a hoe, thankfully not the blade. God's hint, time to work for his dinner.

Joshua swung into familiar rhythm, loosening the earth at the base of the poles. He pulled weeds between rows. The strawberry patch had to wait for the old man.

The shame of thievery washed off with sweat, and he ate more, not watching his footing. Midmouthful, he tripped on a bucket. Falling with a clatter of poles, he took down beans and tomato plants in a tangle of twine.

A door slammed, and, *bang*, a mix of shredded bean bush and dirt showered him. His arm stung.

"Gotcha, you varmint." And *bang*, the whole plant above his head blew away, tomatoes and all. He flailed at poles strung with a cat's cradle of twine and, finally free, leapt the fence, retrieved his blanket, and streaked for the trees.

He stumbled blind through the woods, till his fright eased and the sting in his shoulder took his attention. He probed through the torn shirt to a flesh wound less severe than the whipping he deserved.

With every step, his legs throbbed, and giving in, he cleared a circle of deadfall. Deadfall himself, he collapsed in dry leaves, his head pillowed on the blanket of food, and dreamed of sweet melon, its yellowish insides the color of winter nights in the parlor, the white walls of day softened by a glowing fire. Surrounded by Mama, his sisters, and the smell of supper to come, he heard himself read verses where shepherds found their lost sheep as they should.

Hunger drove Joshua garden to garden, like a groundhog picking someone else's hard-grown peas. Dirt stuck to every part of him as if he truly lived underground.

Father's ever-present voice boomed: *A thief, boy? I'm not surprised.*

Run though he might, Father followed, wielding his God and the Ordnung with its rules, rules Joshua believed in, but couldn't seem to keep, starting with "Thou shalt not raise thy hand against another." He'd never imagined he could raise such a hand. But he had.

He'd raised both hands. *And if thy hand offend thee, cut it off.* Would God ask Joshua for both hands? Then would the Flock forgive him? And what use would he then be?

Guilt salted every strawberry. He remembered thefts in his own garden, the anger on mornings he'd found a groundhog's destruction. The animal always chose the juiciest tomatoes, the ones he'd hoed and manured for weeks as they ripened. The morning he planned on picking, the groundhog took a mouthful out of each. The waste of it!

He'd stomped around the house, Mama reminding him, "He's one of God's creatures." She never showed anger, just cut out the bite marks, and saved what was left.

Uncountable days through the mountains, and eventually the land leveled. Farms came closer together. Moonless nights forced his thefts into the light of dusk. Success made him bold, and he dared a wide sunlit road.

Leaving the trees, he took the smooth way. A wagon rumbled and he dove in a ditch. Watching the driver's back grow small in the east, he crawled to the verge, hooves echoing in his ears. He turned west, straight into the face of an oncoming buggy. Heart knocking his ribs, he stood rooted to the roadside as the driver passed, arguing loudly with his passenger.

The buggy spat dust and wind enough to whip hair across Joshua's cheeks. He pressed the matted strings behind his ears, yellow ends almost to his shoulders. The men took no notice, as if barefoot boys wandered ragged every day.

More carts passed, and no one seemed to mark Joshua as a thief.

He pressed on, his steps lighter. More roads angled in and out. Small farms gave way to houses crowded beside the road. People and people came at him, their clothes in every color: so many English, he'd drown in their fancies.

CHAPTER 6

Helpless

Daylight knocked at Miriam's closed lids. Warblers had arrived and in full throat, they'd started the day without her. Spring no time to be lazy.

Half-asleep, she stretched her legs. Leather heels skidded the floor, a ratcheting sound in tune with a hacking cough. She wasn't in bed.

Her eyes popped open, and the fourth morning fell on her. No Joshua.

In a chair, fully dressed from the day before, she gulped for air as she sank into her quicksand world. Sun streamed through the window—*how could it?*

At her feet, Abraham whimpered on his pallet, his body scorched scalp to ankles, the worst covered in cheesecloth. His long toes curled and uncurled. No hint of red marred his pallid feet, boots having saved them. Thank God for small favors. Inside her shoes, Miriam's toes worked in unison with his.

His bandages had to be changed. Cheesecloth, chestnut tea in a bowl. *But Joshua.* She hurried to the window overlooking the lane, the barn, and out to the fields. She leaned on the table with the dishpan. Closer to the window gave a wider view. She wanted to be out there, *but Abraham.*

He writhed. He cried out, the cry gagging in cough after cough. The sound tore her.

Joshua's absence dragged her in the opposite direction, wife and mother splitting her where once smooth dovetails kept her whole.

The girls rattled above, and hesitant steps brought them to the kitchen. They clustered at the foot of the stairs. Shocked from their routine, mouths open, they cast about as if needing a map to this new land.

Abraham ranted on his pallet. His words a slur, the girls stared. In and out of himself, next he whispered secrets to God and shook his bandaged hands. Miriam hurried to him and knelt. If only she could put her arms around him, give him comfort. She could use some herself. Their touch had always been the answer.

Now her embrace would add to his misery. She must let him heal, and heal herself alone. Hannah helped, but great as her comfort was, and it was great, it couldn't measure up to Abraham's gifts. His touch, the way he knew her thoughts before she spoke, could finish a sentence if she be lost in the middle. Safe with his body curled around her in bed, warm on winter nights, or just the touch of his little finger against her arm when August hung the air too thick to breathe.

Though truth be told, it had been different in recent months. At first nothing she could voice or hold in her hand, a fog she'd been too busy to look at, until his sickness came on.

Just like the littles, so cranky, and Miriam would wonder what had gotten into them. The next day they'd be down with fever.

Abraham didn't have fever, just grumbles and the nighttime onset of something eating his belly. He'd weather his sickness in the barn, but she smelled vomit in the morning, his eyes red and hooded. "It's nothing," he'd say.

It looked like a lot of something the morning he came late for breakfast. Miriam had finished cutting raw lamb and scraped it into the cauldron. He slouched in his chair, a boneless rumple in yesterday's shirt. One suspender looped at the knee; one clung over his shoulder hitching stovepipe pants, dead-animal breath near licking the littles to tears. Them frozen in their ladder-back chairs.

And no wonder; his red-laced eyes half-shut, he looked like a different person. He scratched at splinters caught in his shirt, one cheek lined as if he'd slept on the floor.

"What on earth?" she'd said.

He sighed. "Reasoning with the Lord." He stabbed a fork in the headcheese.

"All night?"

"Yes!" He ran his fingers through snarled hair. "The Lord is demanding."

"Looks like the Devil's work," she said, covering worry with a teasing smile.

She swung the iron arm over coals poked ready for an all-day simmer and came behind him at the table. Rubbing his shoulders, she aligned his suspender.

"Leave me be." He flung himself from the table and mumbled his way outside.

By midday, after scrubbing himself at the trough, he'd been fine, if more distant, more lost in prayer.

Painful as it was, she had to touch his burns. She peeled the covering from his chest, legs, and hands. He tensed. She hated inflicting this torture, but she had to clear the potato poultice, wash him with tea, and slather on honey.

"Sweets for the sweet," Abraham had always said when he brought honey from the hives behind the barn, jars of honey she'd thought they'd never finish, and now they needed every drop.

. . .

Miriam held Abraham's head with one hand, a cup in the other.

"No—," he croaked. He lay under a sheet on his pallet.

"You have to," she said, and tipped the cup to his swollen lips. The girls leaned as one, as if they too tipped the cup.

"Hannah says it cools the fever." Hannah had said more, said, "He's the patient now, not your husband. This time, *he* obeys you."

But husband he was, the man Miriam honored and obeyed, the man she loved, not like some men she knew who needed a push in the right direction. He never needed—well, yes—*once*, she'd given him more than a push.

He'd been out of sorts for days before Luke appeared. Joshua, all a-dither, had run in the house. He couldn't hide his excitement. Ten years old, Joshua was, and the dog had found him, had wormed lovingly into his skin the very first day. She could see it before he spoke. That's how he was with animals.

Respectful as he could be, Joshua said, "May I keep him?" He held his arms at his sides, but they rose on their own, almost praying. "Please, Father, I'll—" And before he could stammer it out, Abraham snapped at the boy. "No!"

No reason, and Joshua twisted his foot on the floor. He wanted to be good, accept his father's decree, though clearly he couldn't resist another try. Abraham rounded on him and swung his palm, just missing his face when Joshua spun away. "Not another word."

Joshua bolted. The rest of them, the girls in the kitchen too, stood like stalks, and breathed through their mouths. Abraham could be gruff, but never this.

Other men smacked their children's rumps. No one wanted a spoiled child, but they didn't use rods or hit a face, and Abraham wouldn't either. There was never a need with their littles; a disappointed word was all it took.

As startled as the rest of them, Abraham had bent his hand

against his chest as if to take the strike back. The littles fled to their chores.

"How could you?" Miriam said. "He's a little boy, and you a Deacon."

"He's not too little to listen when I speak." She'd never seen her husband like this. He smoothed the hem of his jacket.

"You lead the Flock in peace. Is your son less than they?"

He flushed. "Don't be questioning me, not in my own house."

"I do question *this*," she said, chin high, her arms stiff to her fists. "I won't have it. You'll not strike him—"

"I didn't—"

"And you won't." She'd stepped closer. She couldn't believe her willfulness. "Not ever."

Everything about him had sagged. The color in his face ebbed, and he bowed his head. "I want *him* to hear me," he whispered. "I don't know what to do."

Miriam touched his hand on the back where a thick vein ran blue under his cuff. "Joshua hears every word. He's a fine boy—"

"That's not what I—" Remorse glistened before Abraham closed his eyes. He gave a wan smile. "Yes, he's a fine boy; next to God, the treasure of my life." He let her take him in her arms.

He'd always been a good man, a loving father.

Miriam spooned honey into the cup, added more water, and stirred. "You *will* drink this," she said, and he did.

The seventh morning, a tapping came at the door, and Hannah, the broker of peace between Miriam the mother and Miriam the nursing wife, entered. She poured chestnut tea in a bowl and gathered clean cheesecloth, preparing the change of Abraham's dressings. "We'll manage here," she said, motioning Adah and Mary over to the pallet. "Go, Miriam." With both hands, she shooed her from the hearth. "Rebecca, have you fed Luke?" Scraps from dinner and breakfast sat on a plate next to the dishpan.

Going into the second week, a reminder of chores helped tame everyone's wandering focus. Miriam kissed Hannah on the cheek, took a shawl from the hook by the door, and rushed out, grateful not to feel as guilty as usual. Leaving the girls to watch over Abraham didn't feel right. She'd always changed the dressings herself, but they twisted their fingers and glanced around the kitchen, so she knew it made them uneasy. Hannah calmed everyone. Miriam's closest confidante, and all the more after Miriam's mother had died. Her death suddenly seemed a blessing. She didn't have to live through this.

Would her faith have carried her? Her mother capable of the instant acceptance Miriam should have mustered by now. Hannah could. Her other friends waited for calm to prove her acceptance instead of this fishlike struggle as she clung to the possibility of life.

Through the first weeks, Miriam's neighbors had taken turns searching farther and farther afield. Today, at the end of the second week, she continued unstringing hedgerow vines, parting the tangle of brush, unmindful of scratches and bruising. If anything, the blood made her know she was alive in this repetitive searching.

She took advantage of Hannah's oversight and stayed out until midday dinner, more stew simmering and ready for the ladle. Stew someone could stir occasionally, nourishing yet needing little attention, making do with an occasional swirl, the long-handled spoon left for anyone passing. Rebecca often took it on herself, unlike Emma and Mary.

Back in the house, Miriam washed blood-speckled hands and mixed flour into the dark lamb gravy, bringing it back to a thick boil. She ladled a bowlful for each of the girls, then set about chopping the soft meat, carrots, turnips, and potatoes for Abraham. She'd learned the hard way, spoon-feeding Abraham went better when she thickened the gravy. Not so much dribble into what was left of his beard.

Through the afternoon, she hovered over him as she had with her babies, this giant infant in a motionless cradle, one she couldn't pick up or cuddle, or walk the room with, no way to soothe his distress.

In the chair, her night's sleep light, she still woke to his slightest sound, but to what end? Helplessness swamped her. All she could do was keep him company when he woke, and what good was sitting in the chair above him? She needed to be lower. She'd get her mattress.

Everyone asleep, she stretched her stiffening limbs and climbed the stairs. In her bedroom, she changed to her nightdress, sat on the bed, and took off her shoes. Her achy bones could do with a night stretched flat.

She hung her clothes on the wall pegs, and shame for her selfish comforts flooded her. What respite did Abraham have? And then again, what good would her discomfort serve? She looked at the big bed, high headboard above the ticking thick with straw. Lifting the corner told her no—too big and unwieldy. There wasn't space downstairs.

As she passed Joshua's empty room, his small bed carefully made, star quilt over the pillow, his young voice said, *Take mine, Mama.* She gathered the bedding in her arms, the scent of her boy there as if she hugged him. Her sweet lamb.

Standing in the middle of his room, she let herself drift, lost in those nights when he'd had a nightmare and on his bed she'd held him, yellow cowlicks at her cheek, until he slipped into happier dreams. Stifling a sob, she remade the bed. She couldn't squander the scent on everyday use.

Pulling the big quilt from her own bed, she carried it down, and spread it beside Abraham. He moaned. "Where were you?" he slurred through puffy lips. "You're never here."

She settled on the patchwork beside him, his honey smell mixed sharp with burned hair. "I'm here now." Her head close to his, she talked low, of the farm, the planting, shearing sheep, his healing burns, anything to let him know he wasn't alone.

"You're always out," Abraham said, his words clearer after the fourth week. This refrain filled with irritation she tried to ignore. She finished changing his dressings.

"Adah will be down in a minute." Miriam opened the door. Mornings brought a glimmer of hope she wanted to capture, quick before it faded. "One more look. I'll be back soon."

"With Zeke?" he said as she opened the door.

"Most likely, and God bless him," Miriam said. "Hannah too. You should be thankful." Both had been at Miriam's elbow keeping her head above the overwhelming waters.

"Mama, Herr Kauffman's here," Rebecca called from the stable.

Zeke paused in the dooryard with his team and two others. "Thought we'd do a late planting," he called. With plows and a harrow, they set off to the languishing fields.

For two weeks the neighbors had dotted the land, black figures of every size spread to the ridge, but family by family, they returned to their farms. The call of their own work long ignored. Joshua's death an accepted fact, they mourned for him, and Miriam knew they mourned for her as she would have mourned for any one of them. But she wasn't ready to mourn Joshua.

After washing the night-jar, and freshening Abraham's bed, Miriam fed him chicken stew she'd mashed and cooled. His hands still wrapped, he couldn't hold a spoon. She washed the dishes and set the girls to kneading bread.

"He's not out there," Rebecca said, her mouth down, "is he?"

"Zeke?" said Abraham. He bristled at the name.

Foolish man. Miriam foolish herself to be irritated. Abraham couldn't feed himself—of course he resented it, but he couldn't take it out on her or the friends who kept the farm limping along with no end in sight. She wouldn't let herself snap in return. That wasn't fair either.

"No, not Herr Kauffman." Rebecca pushed down on the dough. "Joshua."

"We just haven't found him," said Miriam.

"Mama?" Rebecca divided the smooth lump in two loaves. "Did Joshua run away?"

"Why would you think that?"

She hung her head. " 'Better off dead,' Frau Gruber says."

"No, Rebecca, he wouldn't run away."

"So he *is* dead."

Miriam kissed the top of Rebecca's prayer cap. "We don't know."

Adah thumped her piece of dough. "Frau Gruber says it's enough to unhinge anyone."

"What's 'unhinge'?" Rebecca asked.

"Nothing to worry about." Miriam set six loaves to rise in the dough tray, covering the box with its long wood lid.

"Frau Kauffman told her, 'Close your mouth.' She said the other foot wouldn't fit."

Unhinged. Is that how they see me?

Well, let them. She wouldn't leave the smallest stone unturned.

"You're not carding wool," said Abraham. He sat propped against pillows on his pallet. "You haven't done the shearing. What have you been doing?"

She wanted to shake him. "How can you think about wool? For Lord's sake, Joshua's gone. I want to know where. What happened?"

Tears welling, Abraham turned his head to the wall. "It sickens me, every minute of every day." He gasped for breath. "I can't—"

Too heartsick to talk. How could she press him? Not yet.

She *should* be thinking of wool, and she had, the crops too, her garden, the animals. Abraham might never recover. Then where would they be?

"The shearing's already done." She couldn't keep it a secret.

It had taken days. Miriam, Adah, and Mary herded the flock of fifteen sheep inside the barn. They hadn't done the spring cleanout, so the winter pen had months of straw and manure soft underfoot. It slowed the chase as they cut one white-faced sheep at a time from the flock, Mary and Adah chasing, Miriam diving for the catch. She sank her fingers in the thick wool. The hornless animal struggled to escape, but pulling hard, she tipped it off slender legs with her knees, and once it was on its rump, she dragged it to the shearing platform.

Zeke crouched finishing the first, the one he'd caught. It sat docile between his knees and he bent, working the shears with powerful hands, snipping down the final length of the body to the last leg, the whole fleece folding in one continuous piece. He worked fast, his only respite when he sharpened the blades with a whetstone he kept in his boot top.

Abraham might never shear again, not with those hands webbed in slow-healing scars.

They'd had a good yield. She might as well admit it. "Zeke sold the wool," she said. "We need money, a hired hand till you're strong." Strong, a bright side she held out like a carrot for Abraham. *Would he ever be strong?*

"The Flock's not helping?" he asked.

"Yes, but—"

But she needed more, someone with a sharp eye, a ready nose, two ears. Abraham couldn't see or hear rain invading the hayloft, and if Miriam heard it, she feared climbing rafters to know the damage. She did it so mildew wouldn't set in and take a winter's worth of fodder.

She did what she could, leaned on Zeke and the others for now, but she'd let money into their lives. It had to be. Hers the last word, a woman's place or not.

CHAPTER 7

Gomorrah

T he city glittered before him. Cliffs rose across the river, and from the heights, giant houses overlooked black water snaking under bridges, the long spans linking the cliffside to the flat city streets, clogged by wagons and carts and buggies and people endlessly pushing and shouting as they loaded and un-loaded low barns where no animals lived, only forges spitting out heat and smoke. The dying sun, reflected in windows, gave houses the look of a conflagration. The Devil's own home.

Wide skirts billowed in waves around Joshua, skirts worn by women with laughing red lips, women in bonnets that weren't bonnets at all, but piles of cloth twisted like entrails. Joshua swam among swinging arms and sharp elbows, his hand shielding his eyes.

He'd seen English before, but small numbers, not this hellish crowd, its rising stench—this inferno, Dante's hell made flesh. The godless, as Father would have said, for how many hearts could God know? In this herd of Pharisees and Sadducees, he hoped there'd be a willing Samaritan.

Sticky with late summer heat, skin coated in dust, he itched on the outside, while hunger ate his innards. He stepped off the walkway and onto the cobbled street among horses and wagons. Even in great numbers, these animals were less daunting than the people.

"Hey." High on a cart, a puffy man raised his whip. It cracked close to Joshua's head. "Out of the street."

They called the place Pittsburgh, but Joshua knew better. This had to be Gomorrah, one of the many Father warned of, as far back as he could remember.

Leaving the crowd behind, he worked into smaller streets, where houses with swaybacked roofs leaned together. Men in shirts without sleeves sat on stoops; snot-smeared littles in short pants and no shoes screamed around the corners, chased by mothers in full cry, "You lazy good-for-nothing sons of—"

Come night, he slipped between houses and into their trash-filled yards. They offered little more than gnawed bones and the slimy leaves of something once green.

He sneaked up one street and down the next, toward the center of the city. The houses grew higher, two floors, three, four. He found one yard with a pit good as a bowlful of dinner. How low the English had brought him, a fisher of garbage.

The pit overflowed, lettuce still green, carrot and potato peels, moldy bread, a partially eaten chop, the edge of taint overlaid with mashed potato and pudding. A feast. One handful after another, he wolfed so much at once that swallowing came hard. Yet swallow he did until his belly stretched tight as Mama's sausages.

He paused for breath and sat leaning against a fence to the next yard. And rested, he couldn't resist stuffing in more. When he was too full to take another bite, he relived each swallow, thankful and groaning with joy.

In time, his groans changed to moans. He shifted position,

straightened one leg, the other cocked at the knee. Then switched legs, no position better than the last. Potato and pudding aired their grievances.

Shortly, spasms took hold. Standing, he held to the dooryard fence, feet back, head sunk between his arms. He heaved up rivers of muck and retched till the bile of earlier hunger crossed his tongue. The price of gluttony.

Joshua's third night in the city, it rained. He wandered a street of stores. Dark canvas overhung the windows, and he walked beneath, out of the wet, the blanket heavy on his shoulders.

A large man crossed the street, advancing on him, crowding him. "Off with you," the man said, and waved a heavy stick. The brim of a hat shadowed his face. He tapped the stick against his leg. "You're not wanted here."

"I'd as soon not be here," Joshua said truthfully.

The man swung the stick and slapped the end into his palm. "Keep a civil tongue or it's the jug for you."

The jug? Clearly something to be avoided, but Joshua didn't know what.

He didn't risk the question and moved on, bare feet splashing puddles in the cobbled street. Lamppost to lamppost, he walked through pools of light, the man waving him on when he looked back. The lights ran out, and blanket over his head, Joshua bent into the dark. If he had a tail, he'd have tucked it between his legs.

Not wanted in Gomorrah. *Imagine.*

Joshua pressed into the chill, blanket clasped under his chin. Shelter, he needed shelter, and out of the mist, a bridge took shape. Huge arches spanned the water, between them a metal floor held up by blocks of stone. He walked to the middle and stopped. His hands on the cold rail, he leaned over. The river flowed south as if it knew where to go.

"Hey." A deep shout, and out of the mist two grinning boys

bounced against him. The bigger one gripped the rail with fingerless gloves. "Lookin' to swim?" With his hip, the boy knocked Joshua into the friend, who wore torn sweaters. Rain flattened their hair.

"Too wet to swim," said the sweatered one, voice breaking as he wrung his hem.

"Yeah, time for a fire. Come on." Fingers hooked Joshua's sleeve. Sweater took the other arm. So friendly, and a fire sounded good.

They ran to where the bridge floor joined the street. A steep path cut down the embankment. They slid, arms out for balance, and turned left under the bridge to a dirt patch at the edge of black water.

There, another boy squatted by a small fire. "You got food?" he snarled without looking up. He rubbed his hollow cheek and tucked his knees to his chest. Long pants covered his toes, his feet with the look of a ragged duck.

"Better," Fingers said as he settled on his haunches and stretched hands to the flame. "You look cold," he said to Joshua, his smile showing teeth as brown as his clothes. He tugged Joshua's arm. "Come, warm yourself."

The duck-footed boy looked up as Fingers pulled the sopped blanket off Joshua's head. His yellow hair swung. The boys grinned.

"Oh, Christ," Duckfoot said, his eyes alight. "Lookie what you brung."

Christ on his lips, not a godless English. Joshua couldn't believe his luck. Friends, they made the chill more bearable, theirs the first smiles he'd seen. He squatted, hands to the fire.

No doubt he looked like them, with clean streaks on dirt-crusted faces, but his was smooth where theirs sprouted soft hair. Fingers had the most. A thin fringe curled over his upper lip. The hair on his head, like the others, was dark and rough cut above the ears. Besides being older, they weren't so different, Joshua as tall as Fingers. They could have been brothers.

"Ah, the fire's warm," Joshua said. "Good of you to share."

"Good—oh, that's us." Sweater screwed a little finger into his nose. "Good and kind." He extracted the finger, surveyed a nugget on the tip, nodded, and ate it.

"Sure 'nough, we're sweethearts." Duckfoot's grin looked to split his face.

"Are you brothers?" Joshua asked.

"Cousins." Fingers shook the water from his hair.

"Yeah, kissin' cousins, and now you are too." Sweater giggled.

"Shut up." Fingers tipped the boy over with a blow to the head.

"Hey, that hurt."

"So shut up or I'll dip you in the river."

"All right, all right, hold your water."

Joshua had never seen the like of such cousins, but he wasn't ready to move from the fire. The flicker lit their faces, hands, knees, and feet as they squatted, Fingers solid on worn boots, his rump on his heels. Sweater shifted, unsteady in his too long shoes cracked across the top where his toes ended.

Mud dried on Joshua's feet. Fingers patted the ground. "Here," he said. "Come closer. I'll warm you proper."

The boys all grinned wider as they cozied up, Fingers to Joshua's left, Sweater to his right, Duckfoot on Sweater's right. They rocked on their heels, rubbing hands at the flame, while rats skirted the water's edge, dragging thick tails and sniffing.

Stones aplenty underfoot, Fingers pelted the rats into retreat. Joshua could still see their eyes, small dots of fire in the dark. They watched from under the trusses.

Overhead, a world away, wheels crunched. Hooves clattered the metal. Dirt rained through to Joshua's scalp. The rats' eyes disappeared.

"Someone's in a hurry," he said.

From rain-dark nights on the farm, he knew the race for shelter, reins flapping across the horse's rump, and the "Haaaa!" as droplets forced their way deep into clothes.

That lucky soul on the bridge, he probably clutched his hat, hearth waiting with an applewood fire, a cup of warm cider beside a wedge of shoofly pie. *Someday, he'd have a roof and a warm bed. Maybe in Monte Rey.*

Rain pocked the river. Sweater passed a handful of bread. "Here you go, cutie."

The blessing of stale bread held Joshua's attention. He broke it and ate, licking every crumb from his palm. Little did he know until then the value of crumbs.

"Now, that's better," Fingers said. He put an arm around Joshua's shoulder and slid a hand down his thigh. "Hungry, are we?" His eyes stayed on Joshua as if Joshua were a platter of lamb.

Sweater offered a bottle they'd been passing between them. It smelled of woodshed fire and brimstone. Joshua could hear Father, *Pray with me, boy.* He shied from the bottle. The boys laughed and poked one another. "Beats food," said Duckfoot.

"Too good for us, are ya?" Fingers pushed the bottle's mouth at Joshua.

"No, I—"

"Then drink up."

Still squatting, Joshua cleared hair from his face and took a swallow. He choked and sat hard on his rump. Fingers pulled him close, clamping his neck in the crook of an arm. "Another swallow." He pressed the bottle to Joshua's lips and upended it.

Joshua sputtered. The boys rocked back and forth, screaming with laughter, their eyes afire as they elbowed each other. "Another. Another," they chanted.

"No." Joshua's belly churned. "Please, I can't."

"Aw, you're no fun," said Fingers.

"It smells of Communion cider."

"Now, there's a new one." Sweater pulled his sleeves over his hands. "My daddy called it hooch. But then he called me shithead."

"At least you got a daddy." Fingers slapped Sweater and looked at Joshua. "What's your daddy call you, cutie?"

That word again. "Well—" An odd warmth crawled in Joshua's innards, and he found he wanted to tell them. "Father's a Deacon and he—"

"Well, la-di-da," said Duckfoot.

"Sometimes he calls me Isaac, as if I was the son of his dreams." He wiped his mouth on his sleeve.

"Son!" they laughed. "We're sure glad you're not."

"If I were Isaac," he told them, "God would smile on Father." He wanted his new cousins to understand. "Maybe if God smiled on him, Father would smile on me."

The three of them looked at one another with raised eyebrows. Duckfoot touched a finger to the side of his head. The others nodded. They weren't listening.

Joshua talked louder, leaning into Fingers' face. "The son of Abraham has a—"

"Blah, blah." Sweater yawned.

"No, listen. Let me—"

"Don't bother," said Fingers. He poked the fire and offered the bottle again.

"No, truly, I can't."

Fingers' face went hard. "Come on, bitch."

Joshua looked for a dog. The others leapt to their feet, ganging like his sisters about to tickle him breathless.

Sweater hauled on Joshua's collar. Fingers' lips twisted to a strange smile, and he slid a hand under Joshua's shirt. Duckfoot, from the side, jammed his hand down the front of Joshua's pants and, with a bark, yanked it out. "Son of a bitch." He flailed his hand in the air as if he'd been burned. "She's got stones."

"What?"

They stared. "Son of a bitch, and I do mean son."

"So, cutie." Fingers sneered. "You're Isaac after all."

He drained the bottle, wiped his nose on a sleeve, and broke the glass on a stone. "You bugger." He slashed, and the bottle flew.

Joshua ducked the sharp points, a feathery touch catching his cheek. They all waded in, fists at his slippery face, his ribs, his stomach. They shoved him, one to the other, hammered his head, shoulders, and neck.

Reeling, he coughed. Liquor-soaked bread splashed at their feet. The boys scrambled away, hands above their heads.

"Aw, cripe." Duckfoot shook his leg. "Upchuck."

Joshua heaved again, hands on his knees. Nothing spilling, they came at him, kicking him to the ground, Fingers' boot the worst.

"Hell with this." He kicked Joshua onto his belly. Straddling his back, Fingers pinned his arms. "Gimme your knife, Ralph." Fingers wound his fist in Joshua's hair, yanked his head back, neck exposed like a lamb at slaughter.

CHAPTER 8

June

With each passing day, Abraham's blisters had deflated, crusted, and peeled. The scarred eyelid didn't rise past half. No matter, the eye below had clouded blue and useless. His breath gurgled deep in his lungs.

Obsessed, they said, and maybe Miriam was, but she had to find Joshua. Yesterday, she'd been south; tomorrow would be west again. She'd let everything go except feeding the animals and tending Abraham's bandages.

Out from the house, she and Luke started north. They'd already searched each degree, yet somehow—

They skirted the edge of field after field, the cloudless sky arcing above them. Sun the only witness, no one to frown at her lack of acceptance. She couldn't believe God had willed this.

By noon, they neared woods on the western rise, the only possible place left in their sheltered valley. And beyond the woods? She shivered. Pushing the thought away, she imagined Joshua in a stick house of his own making, trapping rabbits, a hermit boy, not knowing what had happened or who he was. *Silly woman, a clutcher of straws, that's what you are.*

Alive or dead, if only she could find him.

With burns as bad as Abraham's, he would've been found by the first field. He'd have been saved, easily. . . . She fell on her knees, face in her hands.

Her girls at home where they couldn't see her, she let herself cry.

Luke prowled into the woods, and when she didn't follow, he circled back. He whined and hunkered beside her bent legs, pushed his nose between her hands and her cheek. He leaned against her side, tipping her until she wrapped her arms around his neck, her face in his ruff.

"You miss him too, don't you, boy?"

Wiping her eyes, she could see the leaves lift on the warm wind. She yearned to feel its balm.

Enough, now. You can't kneel in dead leaves forever. She stood and Luke danced farther into the woods, a ready companion, never tiring of the same ground, sniffing at the same dead log a little too long, making her heart jump. "Luke?" He'd look up and wag his tail and go on to the next pile of leaves, any scent of Joshua long since washed away.

Briar-torn stockings hung on her legs. Abraham would know she'd been far afield. Perhaps beyond the bounds deemed allowable. She backtracked to the woods' edge overlooking the fields. Daylight drained from the sky. Candles in the windows invited Miriam's return. Only if he came with her. She prayed it would be so. Be soon.

"Look at you." Abraham scowled from his pallet. "Enough now. Someone would've come forward if they'd seen him."

"In the Fold, yes." Miriam opened jars of carrots and peas, dumping them into thick rabbit stew bubbling over the fire. The girls had been busy. "Not English; they wouldn't know who he was."

"You'll not ask," Abraham ordered. "Not English." She knew she shouldn't. He didn't have to bark.

He seemed out of sorts, more every day, the soup too thin, the stew too thick, too hot, too cold. Shouldn't he be less miserable with his burns improving?

Maybe not. With healing, he couldn't help but see what would never regrow.

In any event, she wouldn't argue in front of the girls. They sat at the supper table, heads bent over chalkboards lined with numbers. Adah, out of eighth grade and through with schooling, helped Mary and Emma, while Rebecca pretended, her numbers in a scatter. They looked busy, but Miriam knew their ears collected every word.

English. The idea of walking across foreign fields or driving a buggy up their lanes made her knees quiver.

The more she thought on who could have seen Joshua, the more she knew she had to ask, no matter what Abraham said, or how shaky her knees felt. Every step had to be taken.

Anything to find him. And the English may have. They might bury him not knowing who he was, no way to tell in his nightshirt.

Surely a simple conversation wouldn't put her at risk. Amish came home from trading at market none the worse for seeing fancies and frippery. But who was she to test it?

She lay awake nights on the floor next to Abraham, listening to the gurgle of his breathing. Every day putting off further search meant less chance someone would remember a shadow in the night, a cry in the woods. Stray bones. She swallowed a sob. Abraham coughed.

Taking advantage of his nap the next morning, Miriam pressed her Sunday dress. She tied a black bonnet over her white prayer cap, her face hidden in the depths, and harnessed Goli into the shafts of their one-horse buggy.

At the ridge, they entered shadows of the western woods, leaving their quilted valley behind.

Goli slowed on the unfamiliar road. Miriam's heart sped up.

"Come on, boy," she said with a flick of the reins. "Don't be scared."

It seemed like hours before the woods opened to fields again, a rough brown house and a red barn in the distance. Her stomach tightened.

At the lane, she turned in, Goli walking slower and slower. "They don't bite, Goli. Move along." She didn't flick the reins.

As she stepped from the buggy onto a path to the house, a great baying arose. Seconds later, two black-and-tan hounds cornered the house and rushed her. She clamped her arms straight at her sides, knees locked. The brim of her bonnet trembled. English might not bite, but English dogs—? They stopped short, lips curled in a show of white teeth.

"Pay no attention." The cheery call came from the house. Miriam swiveled her eyes, the rest of her unmoving. The caller, in a wrinkled blue dress, waved. "They're glad to see you."

Of course, all fangs, why hadn't she guessed? Miriam stayed where she stood.

"I promise, they're smiling."

Attempting a smile of her own, Miriam lifted her lip, no doubt as convincing as the hounds.

"Come in, come in." The woman held the door wide. "Push right past."

What was the use? Joshua would have heard the dogs and fled.

"I'm sorry," Miriam said from the path. "I'm looking"—she clasped her hands—"for my son, but your dogs—" She swallowed. "He's eleven and—"

"You're Amish, aren't you?"

The hounds snuffled around her feet. One licked her hands.

"We heard a boy went missing, shouldn't be hard to find, all in black. I'm keeping my eye out."

Miriam didn't have the heart to say otherwise. In black or in white, it didn't matter. The woman would have noticed.

Miriam took a right fork, and a left through woods again. *Think, which way would he go?*

Another track, nearly overgrown, curved to a house with a wide porch covered in vines, and behind the house a swaybacked barn. Abandoned. She felt it before she saw the broken windows, and yet she reined in, stepped from the buggy, and mounted the porch.

Knuckles to the door, her knock echoed lonely in the silence. She peered in a sidelight. Dust covered everything, dishes on the table, a knife propped on a plate, fork on the floor, as if the owners had been whisked away.

The weight of their loneliness on top of her own, Miriam fled to the buggy and drove. Huddled in the seat, she envied Hannah, the grief she could hold, her baby gray in its crib, certain and solid. After that time with Hannah, the viewing, the mourning, Miriam imagined nothing could be worse than the death of a child. Now she knew better.

Another lane, treelined, the fencing straight—she drove to an immaculate white house and barn. The place teemed with sheep in the pasture, horses with their heads over the barnyard gate. A farmer deep in a field cultivated a fine crop. All heartening.

At the door, the farmer's wife answered. She bent forward, intent on Miriam's words. Saying her mission again exhausted her. It all seemed futile. She'd gone against Abraham for nothing.

"You look done in." The farmer's wife in a dark blue dress took Miriam's elbow. "Come, we'll have tea." She guided Miriam in and down a hall hung with jackets. "A cookie or two should perk you up."

Miriam took off her bonnet as they followed a sweet smell into the kitchen. On the table, racks of yellow cookies cooled.

"Can't say as I've seen hide nor hair, Amish or no," she said. Bringing a second cup from its shelf, she poured black liquid and added more to one on the table. Steam rose, the smell pungent. "From China." She offered a bowl and a spoon.

Miriam sipped the liquid. Her face twitched. She couldn't help it, and set the cup on the table. Bitter as an unripe persimmon, it must have gone bad in its travels.

"You might want sugar." The woman smiled, indicating the bowl of white granules.

The look of salt. Miriam hesitated. She didn't see any honey and wouldn't dream of asking.

The woman spooned in two heaping scoops and stirred. "Try again. Sugar makes all the difference, in the butter cookies too."

Miriam dared a sip hardly big enough to touch her tongue and waited for her eyes to squinch. She pulled in a little more, discovering a sweetness beyond the ripest persimmon. With her cup in one hand and a cookie in the other, Miriam settled on a straight-backed chair by the hearth. Except for the tea, this could have been Miriam's kitchen, this woman, Susan Jackson, with kind eyes, a friend. Susan pulled another tray of cookies from the oven. "I've many, too many," she said. "You must take them to your children."

English, who'd have thought? When Miriam said Joshua's name, Susan didn't flinch, and Miriam didn't want to scream at her the way she wanted to scream at her neighbors, who urged, "God's will, you mustn't fight it."

But she did fight it, slipping from the Plain way she'd always found a comfort. Her friends, forever there when needed, now seemed to be drawn into a wary bundle she couldn't penetrate. Their confused hurt made her shy.

She had to try harder, be a grain of sand as they were, matching their thought and deed to one another. Her edges already sharpening, she'd become prickly in their gentle midst, while here in this English kitchen, her prickles flattened. Miriam less foreign in this most foreign of places.

Visiting her neighbors next Sunday, she'd have to work harder. And Abraham, what would he do if he discovered where she'd been?

Sunday, this time visiting Frau Hubler's place. On the way, as she drove Goli on the rain-washed road, a reddish flutter on the verge made her slow. The flutter stopped and sank from sight. Nothing moved.

She'd stop for anything, wouldn't she? Putting off the moment of walking in Frau Hubler's door, her neighbor's welcome a little too hardy; the pause after, a little too long.

By the side of the road, burdock leaves spread, inviting as rhubarb. She'd made that mistake when she'd been a child wanting to surprise her father with a pie.

That early summer day, she'd hiked her skirts and walked out to the farthest hedgerow, where she'd spotted the leaves earlier that morning. Long green stems. She wished they'd been red. They would have made a prettier pie, but some rhubarb had only green stems. No bristly heads in evidence or she would have known. It takes a while for them to develop.

Sawing with a knife, she'd cut a bundle of stems, stripped the leaves, and left them to mulch the rest of the plants. Back in her mother's kitchen, she took out the cutting board from the shelf under the dishpan and chopped the stems with a cleaver. A hatchet might have been easier. This should have been a hint.

She boiled the pieces, boiled and boiled with honey until the juices thickened, and baked them in a lattice crust crimped at the edges. So pleased, she brought it out after Mama had cleared the supper dishes.

Everyone *mmm*ed and smacked their lips. Papa cut a big wedge and dug in.

His appreciative grin stiffened. "A new recipe?" he asked with his mouth full, and wiped his lips using a whole napkin. "Practice makes perfect." He patted her head. "And the crust is perfect."

"What's in it?" her brother had asked. "Kindling?"

Miriam pawed among the leaves at the roadside. Farther on, the fluttering rose out of the heart-shaped leaves. It grew more frantic as she approached.

A female cardinal, caught by its wing on a clump of burrs, flapped and flapped. The bird beat itself to exhaustion, and its weight bent the stem till the bird flopped on a broad leaf.

Miriam cupped the little body in her hand and gingerly separated one feather at a time from the burrs. She could feel its heart racing as she worked.

By the time she finished, the cardinal lay still on her palm. How many days had the little thing been there fighting the sun and the rain and the hooks digging deeper with each attempted escape? A slow and useless death.

How many times had riders passed by the spot and not seen the bird hidden under the leaves? If only Miriam had come along sooner.

How many times had someone walked past Joshua in his hiding place? How close to seeing him before his heart gave out?

CHAPTER 9

The Heights

Under the bridge, Joshua waited on the knife. He'd seen enough slaughter, the ear-to-ear slash, the spurt, and how as the carcass drained, the eyes went dull.

"You'll not fool no one no more." Fingers brought the blade across, not Joshua's throat, but sawing across his hair, gouging his scalp from crown to neck. Nothing more to cut, he dropped Joshua's face in the dirt. "Hey sissy boy, you look good."

"Blood becomes him, don't it?"

Through the blood, he saw their feet. Clumps of hair littered the ground.

Fingers climbed off. "Now get out."

Joshua wobbled onto all fours, and Fingers gave him an encouraging kick. Head heavy, Joshua dragged a knee forward, a hand, the other knee, and crawled into the dark.

"We should kill 'im," Duckfoot snarled.

"Go ahead." Fingers' voice. "Here's yer knife. What-cha waitin' for?"

Joshua, at a quick shuffle, scurried into the drizzle, past low buildings by the water, then uphill away from the river on a switchback through woods. The shallowest breath stabbed his ribs. A sticky mess clouded his right eye. He didn't touch the other; that eye wouldn't open.

The sound of footsteps shoved him faster onto the ridge, where houses huge as barns overlooked the dark cliff. Below, lights sparkled as if the world had turned upside down, the stars shining up.

He crept behind the bigger houses, feeling along solid board fences for an open gate. He had to hide.

At one house, the gate gave, and he tripped into the yard. Woozy with pain, he bent double in the walkway leading to the back door. He listened.

No sound. The house stayed dark, and he dared to look around. A shed in the corner of the yard offered shelter, and to his relief, the door stood ajar. He slipped his fingers in the opening. Rusty hinges squawked.

Using one finger, he eased the door and slipped inside, pawing his way among shovels, rakes, a fork, a hoe. The scent of earth and manure lulled him.

Moving like an old man, he cleared tools and lowered himself to the floor. His body retold the hit of each boot and fist. His left eye throbbed, but the dirt floor warmed away the shakes, and finally he slept.

Joshua opened one eye with a start. The other refused. Aching at the marrow, he remembered where he was, the toolshed. A squeal of hinges, and the shed door opened. Sun poured in around a shadow filling the doorframe. Joshua squawked in fright. The shadow shrieked. Its arms flew high. Tools clattered as he shrank against the wall.

"Good Lord." Slowly the arms came down. "What have we here?" The figure stepped into the shed.

Shielding his eye, Joshua crouched farther into the corner. The shadow advanced, and light filled the shed. A gray-haired English, pink dress, buttons down the front, bent over him. "You poor child," she said, and knelt at his side. He averted his face.

"Don't be afraid," she said with a hint of laughter.

English laughing, not a good sign. He drew his knees to his chest. *God, it hurt.*

Serious now, she took his hand in both of hers. Soft hands. She slid one to his elbow. "Up you go." She pulled him to the door. He clung to the frame.

"There, there." She patted his hand. "I won't hurt you."

So she said, but could she be a sweet-talking spider, and he the fly? He had to admit, her blue eyes looked gentle.

No prayer cap—her gray hair swooped from her face and wound in a marbled loaf on top of her head. "I'm Mrs. Biddle," she said. "What's your name?"

"J-J-Joshua," he said, towering over her.

"It's all right, J-J-Joshua. Come with me." She led him shuffling down the garden path, his head head-and-neck above hers. The brick path wended amidst small trees and broadleaf bushes, surrounded by yellow, white, and red flowers, ending at the red-roofed house. Up three steps, they entered the kitchen. The hearth at the other side of the room had no fire, but the room was warm. He stood stiff by the door.

She tugged gently on his arm. He winced.

"Oh dear, I *have* hurt you." She pulled a chair from the table. "Here, sit."

He sat and stared at a loaf of bread on a board in the middle of the table. A knife lay beside it. He worked to tear his eyes away.

She moved to a metal box on legs. A black pipe joined it to the wall. From on top of the box, she lifted a copper kettle and poured steaming water in a bowl. A drop fell on the metal where it bounced and hissed and disappeared. *Some devilish trick.* He lurched in his chair. She came at him, a white cloth in one hand, the bowl in the other.

"Poor wounded bird," she said. "So much blood. Now hold still. I have to wash that eye." She grimaced as she took a closer look. "Tip your head." He tipped toward the ceiling. She dabbed the left side of his face, and he gasped, the shock driving hot slivered light through his head.

"I'm so sorry." She frowned at her work.

Like raccoons, do devils wash their dinner before they eat?

Water ran down his neck. With each squeeze of the cloth, the rinse darkened.

"That's quite a gash, Joshua. Oop." She held the cloth with both hands spanning from under his eye to his ear. "Bleeding again. You'll have a scar." She wrung the cloth, held it tight to his cheekbone, and put his hand over it. "Press hard. I'll get fresh water."

His good eye went to the bread. For an instant, hunger squashed fear.

She picked up the knife. He stumbled off the chair and headed for the door.

"Joshua, stop." One hand on the loaf, she cut a thick slice. "Here."

He sidled back to the table. Would she cut him if he reached for the bread? She held out the slice. A sharp twinge in his ribs made him grunt. A tear squeezed between the folds of his swollen eye.

"No, don't rub it," she said. "Wash your hands." She sounded like Mama.

With the bloody rag, he scrubbed his hands. She emptied the dirty water in a stone trough. With a glug, the water disappeared. When she turned a handle above the trough, water flowed, and she swept it down a hole.

"This will do for now, but you need a bath," she said. "And those clothes—but first—" She opened a cupboard lined with metal. "Butter?" she said. He'd already swallowed the bread.

"You're starved, aren't you?" She cut more slices and spread butter crust to crust.

He crammed in the second slice.

"Enough, you'll make yourself sick." Her eyes searched his, hers kind. She slid the last slice to the other side of the table, and lifted the cloth off his face. "Bath first. Then we'll see about bandages," she said. "Rest here. You look peaked."

Joshua heard water splash. Mrs. Biddle bustled room to room gathering towels, a washing cloth, and clothes.

"These are Mr. Biddle's, God rest his soul. They won't exactly fit, but they'll do." She took the armful into the other room and returned.

"For dinner, we'll have chicken. How nice to cook for someone again. It's been over a year."

He sat at the table and focused on the bread, praying it wouldn't disappear. In the other room again, she splashed more water. "Come in the bathroom," she called.

He went to the doorway. "Good Goshen," he said. The room billowed with steam. He sniffed for the Devil's sulfur. None, yet he dared not enter.

"Come, come, you bathe, and I'll make dinner."

In the kitchen, she hummed at her work, clanking metal, the thunk of logs. Dishes clattered. He heard chopping, the sizzle of meat. He smelled onions. "You like chicken?" she called.

"Mmmm." He could have eaten a coop full.

"Bath," she said. "Sit right down and soak a bit."

Sit? At home he stood in the round washtub. Luke was the only one small enough to sit in it! But this metal trough on claw feet was plenty big.

Joshua undid the last button on his bloodstained shirt, stripped the torn cloth, and dropped it on the floor, unknotted the rag around his waist, and stepped out of what was left of the pants. Muscles he didn't know he had complained.

He held the wood edge of the tub and stepped in, ooh-oohing as the hot hit his burns. Rump quick in the water, he lifted his legs to the rim. Water sloshed. Every nick and cut stung.

After a few minutes, the sting lessened. Heaven or hell, he could have stayed forever.

She called from the kitchen, "Soap's in a dish on the floor. You want me to wash your back?"

"No!" He sat up fast. A wave sloshed the edge of the tub.

"Don't worry. I won't come in."

And calmer, he said, "No, thank you." No one saw him bathe. No one.

He looked for a brown block, and found only a white egg in the dish. He dipped his head, and gingerly rubbed the egg on what was left of his hair. Sweet-smelling bubbles fell in the water.

He soaped himself, sniffing through his clogged nose as he raised more bubbles. Then low in the water, he rinsed, rubbing until the slipperiness disappeared. He climbed out.

The towel, soft as it was, felt harsh on angry patches of blue and black and red. He didn't touch his healing shins.

Once dry, he pushed his arms into Mr. Biddle's collarless shirt and worked at buttons, thinking more of the meal to come than damage to his soul. Tan pants too wide at the waist; the legs short, he showed a bit of ankle. He stepped into the kitchen.

"That's better." She shook her head. "You were a sight in the shed, you with your one good eye ready to pop." She laughed. "No one's ever been afraid of *me*."

"I was," he whispered, his eye at her feet. He wasn't exactly over it.

"Pish-tosh." She hurried from the room, coming back with suspenders and socks.

"Now, shoes," she said. "Too big's better than too small."

After months of bare feet, what she gave him did nicely.

"They belonged to Robert, my son," she said. "He's in Iowa." Her mouth compressed. The room seemed dim as if the sun had gone under a cloud. "When I live with him in Iowa, I'll miss this house."

She looked around the kitchen and out the window to the yard. Flowers swayed in the breeze. She took a deep breath. "When I was little, I played in the garden." She let the breath out. "The gardener taught me flowers. Cook taught me arrangement." She waved in the direction of the window. "You could pick some, if you're up to it." Her smile returned. "Chrysanthemums," she said. "Yellow and white, my favorite. A few red will brighten the others." She handed him scissors. "When you come in, I'll see about that hair."

Outside, brisk air carried sweetness. He cut the stems, and laid the flowers, one at a time, across the crook of an elbow. Flowers in the house, who would have thought?

Mrs. Biddle propped the flowers in the trough and cut the stems to different lengths. She put them in a tall container with water and set them next to the bread. Joshua wanted another slice.

"Now, your hair." She threw a towel over his shoulders, and picked up the scissors. *Snip snip snip.* The bits of hair Fingers had left on his head fell on the towel. She scooped them into a bucket, and went to the tub room, bringing out a looking glass.

"Dear Lord." The reflection came clearer than off the clearest water, his hair shorter than fuzz on a caterpillar, and below it, sharp bone under yellowish skin, a stranger's face looked at him. All nicks and bumps, the nose swollen and pushed to one side, the gash open and meaty, he looked like a plucked chicken. And the clothes! Nothing left on the outside marked him as Plain.

"By the time I leave for Iowa," she said, "your hair will be respectable." Her shoulders sagged at the word *Iowa*, and she busied herself with towel and scissors.

She would leave, and what then? Starvation gnawed.

"Iowa, that's west, isn't it?" he said.

She nodded.

"I could help you get ready." He chewed the inside of his cheek. "I'm strong, a hard worker."

Her eyes brightened. "That's something to ponder."

But before she pondered, her forehead creased. "Where is my mind? Your mother, she must be worried sick."

"No. No," he said. His good eye darted around the ceiling while he tried to find the right words, as if they might be printed there.

"Mama doesn't expect me. I'm . . . I'm on my way to—" To where? "Goshen" popped out of his mouth.

"Goshen?" Mrs. Biddle's frown deepened.

"I'm going to my uncle's," he said. One lie primed the pump, and more gushed. "Since I've finished school, I'm to help on his farm. Mama and Father have me on loan."

"And where are Mama and Father?"

Another twinge of panic. *Would she tell Father?*

"Home," he said.

"And home is where?" she asked, her look more curious than suspicious.

"Lancaster." Too taken with her own worries, she wouldn't find New Eden easily.

"That's German country." Her frown disappeared. "Now I place you. Your accent, you're Pennsylvania Dutch."

She could think that. She didn't need to know he was more than German; he was the plainest of Plain, Old Order Amish.

She smiled. "A good people, Mr. Biddle used to say. Hardworking, trustworthy."

Her eyebrows shot up. "You walked all the way from Lancaster? Alone? That's two hundred miles. A lot for someone so young."

"I'm not so young."

"What are you, sixteen?"

He didn't tell her eleven, no, twelve; his birthday had come and gone without a cookie, much less a cake.

"Not alone," he said. "I stopped at family farms." He had stopped, and they were family farms, just not his family. In the stream of big lies, why justify the little ones? But he felt compelled.

"What will your uncle do if you stay here?"

"He won't need me yet. The fall hay is in already."

If Joshua thought it would help, he would have knelt before her. She said no more about it, and he resigned himself to leaving after the chicken.

A large pot bubbled slowly on the stove. Steam seeped from under the lid.

"Mmmm!" He took as deep a breath as he could, ribs squawking. At least he'd eat well today. The smell of chicken made his tongue sweat.

A bell tolled. He tensed, but Mrs. Biddle stirred the stew without concern.

"Fire!" he said, and bounded for the door. Ooh, his ribs.

"It's the cathedral, the noon bell. Dinnertime." She pointed at the hutch. "Forks and spoons in the drawer," she said. "You can set the table."

He jangled utensils in his hurry.

"Bowls," she said. "Napkins too."

No end to the preparations—he thought he'd expire. Mrs. Biddle brought the pot, and ladled broth with chunks of carrot, potato, onion, for herself. She put a scoop in his bowl, broth with one small piece of meat.

"Usually I make it thick," she apologized.

"So does Mama," he said.

"Thick wouldn't sit well."

At the table, they dipped their spoons. "Slowly," she said, and rested a finger on his hand. "Enjoy the flavor, the last of summer thyme."

They ate in silence. Joshua rolled every spoonful on his tongue, and near finished, his body turned heavy. With the last swallow, his suspicions drained. He slumped in his chair.

"You need a rest," she said.

From the kitchen they took the narrow stairs. "That's the door to the second floor. We go to the third."

Off the third-floor hall were three rooms, each big enough for an iron bed painted white, a small bureau, and a washstand covered in dust.

"These haven't been used in years," she said.

Each room had a dormer looking over the city with its triangle of land where the river split, and crossing the river the bridge of boys. He hoped never to cross it again.

"Look, the cathedral," she said. "I love the spire." High above surrounding buildings, it pierced the sky. "I missed today's service. We'll go next Sunday."

He sat on the mattress, relief flooding in. He'd be there at least a week.

Mrs. Biddle gave him a mothering smile and lifted his feet onto the bed. She untied his shoes and slipped them off before covering him with a blanket.

"Sleep as long as you like. You need it."

By the time service came, his aches and pains would have quieted. He thought about Sundays at home. Three hours of service had made him rooch around, but he couldn't after a night in the woodshed. He didn't squirm then, his backside too tender. He'd sit on the edge of the bench, looking forward fervently to the end of service. Father most likely thought he saw the fruits of his midnight labor.

The house dim and quiet, Joshua woke to the bliss of being in a bed. He sat up, shattering the bliss. Every inch of him hurt.

He could have sworn he creaked as he laced his shoes and felt his way downstairs. The smell of chicken stew filled the empty kitchen, and he looked for more. Not that he would take it. He just wanted to know where it was.

"Joshua?"

He flinched.

"In here," she called.

He followed her voice through a room with a long table, then into a hallway, a room in itself with lots of doors and wide stairs going up.

"In the morning room." She laughed. "I know, it's evening, but this is where I do my letters." She laid down her pen and faced him. "You should write your father. And your uncle, I don't want them worrying. Use Mr. Biddle's desk." She pushed back her chair. "Come, I'll light the lamps."

She led him across the hall and through another door. "His study." She twisted a knob on a wall lantern. It hissed, and she touched it with a match, a great light blooming.

Pictures hung centered in dark wood panels. They showed men on horseback chasing dogs over fences. In the middle of the room, a wide table with drawers down the sides and one across the middle faced a huge fireplace.

He lowered himself in a leather chair, his knees neatly tucked in the space below the center drawer. The tabletop, smooth beneath his hands, glowed, the grain in swirls like dark and light water—fancywork by God's hand, how confusing—framed in plain wood by an English hand. A glass dish holding pens and nibs in separate compartments sat above a square of dark green paper, a bottle of ink beside it.

Mrs. Biddle laid white paper on the green. She ran her hands lovingly over the swirling wood. "I wish I could take the desk," she said. "Mr. Biddle loved the burl. He spent Sundays here writing letters." She put her hands on Joshua's shoulders.

"Before the end," she said, "he sat here well into the night, every night. I'd wake and find him slaving over columns of numbers. They wouldn't come right, and he couldn't bear it." She gave Joshua's shoulders a squeeze. "Enough of that. Write your father."

Joshua didn't want to write. He didn't want to think on Father. "Father won't care," he said to Mrs. Biddle.

September

Father,

I write because she wants it. The Widow Biddle says family is everything, so write your father. So I write. I am fine.

Your Son,

"Two lines?" she said, and clicked her tongue. She nudged his shoulder. "Then write your mother. Worry's a terrible thing."

With no intention of sending the letter, Joshua did as Mrs. Biddle asked. If he sent one, Father would appear on Mrs. Biddle's doorstep, take him home, and kill him where Mama could see. That would be much worse than her worry now.

October

Dear Mama,

I am well. I talk to English. Even here in Gomorrah there are blessings. Thank God for the Widow Biddle. She cooks chicken not little children. Tell Father.

Your Loving Son,

It felt good to write. It brought Mama close. Joshua could see her holding the paper as she read, her lips moving. He saw her put it behind her back when Father came in the room, saw his anger, saw him crush the letter and throw it in the kitchen fire. Joshua saw tears. He was right not to send it.

November

Dear Mama,

Mrs. Biddle will keep me. Her God is gentle like yours. You would like her even in flowered dresses with buttons. She has bright colored rugs too. Heavy cloth hangs beside the windows and across the top too. Cheesecloth covers

the glass. Mirrors framed in gold stand on stone mantels.
All this and nothing of the Devil about her.
   Be glad for me.
   Your loving son,

On reading this, Mama would faint. Joshua might as well tell her he'd gone to hell in a bucket. Another reason not to send what he wrote.

He took his letters along with Mrs. Biddle's across the river to the post office, keeping watch before he ran over the bridge of boys, and the same on the way back, his mouth dry. Letters to Mama stayed in his pocket.

After a stint of organizing, Mrs. Biddle napped, and Joshua headed for the library. He passed through the dining room. Strange, only three in the family and they sat at a table for twenty.

Did they sit close and talk, or silent, she at one end, Mr. Biddle at the other, Robert lost in the middle? Mrs. Biddle and Joshua ate in the kitchen.

In the library, his favorite, she kept books on shelves that stretched floor-to-ceiling. He had a choice of chairs, three soft with wide arms covered in leather, two with high backs and blinders. Wing chairs she called them.

His first time in the library, he'd chosen a leather chair with the best view of the books. He wanted to read every word in the room.

He would touch spines, and spoke the gold titles aloud. One shelf had Bibles in every size. He slipped out the smallest one, so like Mama's. He tucked it in his pocket to look at when he wouldn't be interrupted.

On the shelf below, he found more books smaller than his hand. He tipped one out, *Sonnets* by Shakespeare, and next to it, equally small, *King Lear*. And best of all, one he never thought to find again, *The Inferno*. He turned the onion-thin pages, the leather binding soft as the skin on his thigh.

Now in the winged chair, another title caught his eye, *Paradise Lost*, a title Frau Lentz had once promised him. He took it off the shelf and the book beside it, *Paradise Regained*.

Could he regain Paradise? Living with Mrs. Biddle seemed close.

He started with Dante. *Having lost his way in a gloomy forest . . . conducted by Beatrice into Paradise.*

Heart full of gratitude, his head against one wing, he closed the book on his first finger. He'd been to hell, and now he heard his own Beatrice call. "Joshua, we'll work on the linens, come."

Joshua left books piled by the chair for later and silently mounted the rug-covered stairs. The banister rose smooth under his hand, the close-set spindles with the look of braided wood. On the second floor, five bedrooms opened off the hall. So many beds for three people, two beds in each room. He wondered, were the Biddles bereft of more children?

At the top of the stairs, graven images hung boldly on the wall. The eyes of fierce-looking men in high collars followed him. Mrs. Biddle's father, his eyes kinder than the others, his gray beard below a wide mustache falling to his collar.

The day before, in the back hall, Mrs. Biddle had cried in front of a small painting of her mother holding a little dog. "How she loved that dog," Mrs. Biddle had said aloud.

When she noticed he stood beside her, she said, "Oh, this is silly. My mother died fifty years ago." Mrs. Biddle blew her nose on an embroidered handkerchief she kept in her sleeve. "I was fourteen, and still I cry."

Joshua didn't know what to do. He'd never seen a grown woman cry.

.   .   .

"Here, Joshua," Mrs. Biddle called. "In Robert's room." She had the drawers of one bureau pulled open. "Everything on the bed."

He stacked sheets, blankets, quilts, and put them in wobbly piles. On the other bed, Mrs. Biddle laid out boy's clothes in ever increasing sizes. Of all, only one pair of pants and a shirt looked as if it might fit him.

"You could use these. Here." She passed them. "Put these in your room and get a crate from the yard. May as well pack the easy things now."

The back stairs too narrow, he brought the crate up the front, careful not to nick the paper-covered walls curving beside the stairs. With the house not yet sold, it wouldn't do to scar the stripes. It wouldn't do, no matter what.

"We'll take bedding just in case." She separated sheets and blankets.

February

Dear Mama,

Christmas has come and gone. I saw nothing of Baby Jesus. He must have been with you.

Now snowdrops pop up in the garden.

Here I have everything I could ever want.

Your Loving Joshua

Everything he could ever want, a lie he'd like to believe.

CHAPTER 10

Clearing Out

Mrs. Biddle's garden bloomed in tulips and jonquils, the air heavy with flowering crab apple. "I don't make crab apple jelly," she said. "The trees just look pretty."

Planting to no purpose—Joshua couldn't understand it.

After he washed the breakfast dishes, Mrs. Biddle said, "We'll pack the kitchen last. Today we do the dining room."

Mrs. Biddle wandered around the table. She looked lost. "Ah well, it's a new day." She tipped open drawer after drawer of the sideboard. "Even if the bailiff didn't take it all, what would I do with linens and silver tea sets in Iowa?" She held an imaginary cup and sipped air, her little finger extended.

Stopping at one drawer with silver serving pieces, she said, "These are plate, but the bailiff will take them too." She felt deep in the drawer and brought out a slender spoon with a long handle. "I hid this one." She gave Joshua a sly look. "A present from my mother when I learned to stuff a turkey. Father was furious, too menial. I should have been learning piano." She shut the drawer. "It's time to ask forgiveness, at least for me." She slipped the spoon in her apron pocket and started upstairs. "We both need church clothes."

"It's fine today. We'll walk to church," Mrs. Biddle said. "Save the price of a hansom."

They turned down the steep hill to the bridge and crossed, taking in the Monongahela with its many bridges upstream and down. Joshua felt safe with Mrs. Biddle, odd, she being so small.

Almost there, she breathed hard. "I'm going to need a cart to get home. I don't care what the neighbors think."

April

Dear Mama,

 Mrs. Biddle's God lives in a redbrick house. Every piece has a name. Buttress abutment pinnacle spire. The towers touch heaven. Every week she shows me the nave and transept vaults higher than the highest hayloft. A man in a dress swings a box of sweet smoke.

 The windows have color pictures of Jesus. The sun comes through and splashes everyone. No one minds.

 A woman in black scrubs the floor after service. She reminds me of you.

 I wish I were home.

 Your most loving son,

If he were home, he'd be on the hill, at rest among his Ancients and the stillborn.

Joshua savored times when Mrs. Biddle napped, time away from fetching and carrying, from pruning, weeding, and transplanting bushes only to move them yet again. The garden would help sell the house. It had to be perfect.

In those stolen moments, he haunted the library. Curling into the red wing chair with Dante, he walked the levels of hell, submerged in love's confusion.

Joshua wasn't the only one confused. Mrs. Biddle too, but her God steadied her.

She'd told him, "He stands beside me in the kitchen, apron at His waist. He fries chicken, the same God as your father's."

"The same?" Joshua had laughed. "Your God doesn't make you wear black. You go where you want, talk to whoever you want."

"You do too."

"It's true," he said with a pang of regret, "but I'm not supposed to."

In the garden working over the flowers, he caught Mrs. Biddle crying. She weeded around her hollyhocks. "I hate leaving," she said, and dabbed her cheeks with the cuff of her glove. He knelt and weeded beside her.

"There's so much I'd like to take," she said. "These lilies, I love the red; they're rare." She smiled to herself, the way Mama did over a baby. "I'd like—" She shook off the rest. "Don't set your heart on possessions, Joshua."

With a hand fork, he loosened the dirt around a budding dandelion and ripped it out. He threw it on a pile of weeds. Small white hairs on its taproot wilted in the sun.

"This leaving," she said, "it's a death."

Sitting on her heels, she took off a glove. "Some days, I feel dead already." She pulled the handkerchief from her sleeve and blew her nose. "With Robert grown, I'm not a mother anymore. With my husband gone, I'm not a wife. What good am I? No better than a dandelion."

Joshua slid closer. His knee touched her skirt, his shoulder to her shoulder. "You'll always be a mother," he said. "Remember in the hall, looking at the portrait?" She nodded, and he went on.

"She's been dead, how many years? And isn't she still your mother?"

Mrs. Biddle took his hand and kissed it. "If I was your mother, I'd miss you."

It was his turn for tears. She put her arms around him.

He wanted to tell her the truth. But what if she said, "Wicked boy, you don't belong here. Go home"?

July

Dear Mama,

The house is sold. We leave early in August. Her son Robert says his house is small. She need not worry, the bailiff will take most everything. She looks like a kicked dog.

Your Joshua

After dinner Mrs. Biddle spread a map on the kitchen table. Her son sent it, the route marked west from Pittsburgh. She left his letter on the table, *I'm glad a trusted man will drive you.*

She'd planned on a boat, riding the Ohio to the Mississippi, but in the end couldn't afford the ticket. He told her, bypass Springfield, too expensive and not safe. He'd meet them north in Port Clyde.

He'd divided the route in segments with way station stopovers, the first stop East Liverpool, Ohio, then Canton, Wooster, Mansfield, Marion, stopping many times again before skirting Indianapolis to Springfield, and finally north beside the Illinois River. About forty days if all went well, four times the distance Joshua had come on foot.

July had come and gone with Joshua's thirteenth birthday. He'd been away from home almost a year and a half, nearly a year with

Mrs. Biddle. She claimed he grew like a weed. He'd rather be her tree, tall and strong enough to keep.

It pleased him that she thought him a man, but being a boy, how would he keep her safe? As if she read his mind, she said, "I have a present for you. Something for the journey." She placed a bundle on the map, the wrapping stained and pungent. Joshua unfolded cloth layers, each more oily than the last, down to glistening blue-black metal.

"Mr. Biddle's sidearm," she said, and picked it up by the wood handle. Its weight dangled, and she slipped the metal nose into a leather case. "Here, try the holster." She held the ends of a strap. "Stand up," she said. "Now turn."

With his back to her, she hugged him around the middle and buckled the leather low on one side. His hips too narrow, the strap slipped, and the thing hit the floor. He stepped out of the loop while she got a reamer. "You need another notch, son."

Did she call me son? Did she really? Son, the word like syrup on dry toast.

August

Dear Mama,

 Haulers left us a cart. No space to stow a mouse. The seat takes room and the water barrel. Mrs. Biddle has two carpetbags. I have a change of clothes paper pen ink. May the stopper not leak in my satchel. In a few days the big mattress goes on top.

 We leave soon.

 Your loving son,

He tucked all the letters in his satchel, as if taking Mama with him.

. . .

The fluted glassware had gone, the linens and the silver. He didn't know what she'd done with the stuffing spoon. The clothes dealer came next.

A rap at the front door resounded through the house. "Let them in," she called.

Joshua turned the key in the brass lock. Beefy and rumpled, the bailiff pushed through the door. Behind him came a man in new-looking clothes, whites bright, a sharp crease to his dark pants and long jacket, no rag-and-bone man. His minion followed.

"If Mr. Biddle were alive," said Mrs. Biddle, "they'd never enter the front door."

To keep the men out of her bedroom, she'd had Joshua bring the clothes downstairs. He'd laid them over the dinner table.

In the dining room, the dealer waved at the mound. Mrs. Biddle picked up her red dress with the enormous skirts, her favorite at three-wine dinners. The dealer raised a finger, and his minion snatched it. He hurried out the front door and returned for the next item, the blue with a lesser skirt.

Mrs. Biddle lifted dress after dress, then on to her husband's pants. She turned them front and back before the dealer, ten pairs and fifteen shirts all laid across the minion's arms.

The dealer turned up his nose at the rest, the pants too shiny, a button missing from shirts, the whites not white enough, the off-whites too off. He dropped them one by one at her feet, turned on his heel, and left. His minion followed.

"I'll take those," the bailiff said, pointing at the pile on the floor. "Rag-and-bone man might give two bits. Box 'em up, boy." Joshua gathered them. In his arms, the clothes felt limp as a body.

The next day, books, then furniture. Mrs. Biddle watched in a fog as she stood in the front hall, hands behind her, leaning on the newel post. She wore a faded print, the material buttoned from her chin to below the waist, hung thin to the hem. Tendrils of hair trickled from her bun.

Joshua had packed the books in crates, except the smallest Bible, and as he nailed the crates shut, three burly haulers in open shirts, sleeves rolled, tromped into the library. Two to a crate, they carried them out the door and down to the wagon. The third man watched; they took turns until all the books were out. The loss so keen, the books could have been Joshua's. He'd transferred the Bible from his drawer to the garden shed. What kind of a believer was he? *Thou shalt not . . .* and of all things, stealing a Bible.

Next, the dinner table. Mrs. Biddle's jaw worked as each piece went. Dry eyed and stiff boned, she looked out the window when they laid hands on her husband's desk.

They emptied the downstairs rooms, leaving dust bunnies snuggled at the baseboards. In the study where the desk once stood, a fallen button lay next to a quill pen and three pennies. The bailiff picked up the pennies.

"Upstairs too," he said. "Third floor first." The bailiff led the way. The haulers ran dirty hands on the curved wall. The smaller bedrooms cleared first, iron beds, small mattresses, the bureaus, then the second floor with the sleigh beds and bigger bureaus.

The last morning, in Mrs. Biddle's room, the haulers propped mattresses against the wall, unscrewed bolts of her canopy bed, then Mr. Biddle's heavier mahogany.

Down and up the front stairs, the men sweated and hawked, two to a headboard, two to a footboard, one to each rail. They waited until they were outside to spit.

"Thank heaven," Mrs. Biddle sniffed. As the haulers reached for the final mattress, "No, that one stays," she said.

The haulers looked to the bailiff. "It goes."

Mrs. Biddle stood wilted by the door. "The lawyer promised," she said.

The bailiff crossed his arms. "They told me everything."

Her small voice rose. "Please, you can't." She moved to the middle of the room, her eyes first on the bailiff, then the haulers. "Please."

"Everything goes." The bailiff wouldn't look at her.

She bent forward, hands clasped at her waist, fingers locked together. "We need it for the trip," she said. "I can't sleep on the ground."

He stood with feet planted wide. "Everything means everything."

Mrs. Biddle stayed bent. No one moved.

Slowly she straightened. Her eyes narrowed. A calm took her, and her words came hard as the iron bedsteads. All eyes shifted to Mrs. Biddle.

"Everything?" she asked. "Then I suppose you want the boy's pants. They were my husband's, after all, and you might get a penny for them."

The bailiff looked confused.

"You said everything." She drew a breath through her nose. "Joshua," she commanded, "give the man your pants."

"Now?"

"Now," she snapped.

He dragged suspenders from his shoulders, and twisted the first of five buttons.

Her eyes drilled into the bailiff. She reached for the tiny button tucked in the neck of her dress. "Everything it is," she said.

The bailiff's jaw loosened. He retreated.

"Yes, the dress." She twisted the second button. The third. As the notch in her throat appeared, the bailiff's cheeks grew pink. His neck bulged as he swallowed.

Joshua worked the last button on his pants.

"Take them off," she said, and twisted at her fourth resistant button.

Joshua hooked thumbs in the waist of his pants and pushed. No one watched him.

Her words like razors, Mrs. Biddle said, "My apologies for being slow. Small buttons are hard on old hands."

Joshua stepped out of his pants. She worked at the fourth button.

CHAPTER 11

Widow's Weed

On to the fifth button, Mrs. Biddle gave a glimpse of collarbone. The bailiff coughed. Joshua stood, pants in hand.

The bailiff fidgeted with his vest, slid a watch in and out of the small pocket. "Now, ma'am, I—"

"No, no, just a few more. It won't take long."

"Ma'am, that won't be—"

"Oh, but it *is* necessary. You said so yourself."

"Please," he said, his face red enough to burst. "St-stop."

He shook his watch at her. "I've no time for this." He rammed the watch in his vest. "We—we have what we need. Let's go, men." He made for the door.

The men dropped the mattress and hustled after the bailiff, leaving the door open. Joshua stepped into his pants.

The kitchen man came and went. Mother Biddle swept the bare rooms. Joshua itched to start. The empty house made him want to cry.

A four-wheeled cart waited in the alley. The mattress loaded, Joshua stashed foodstuffs in a corner for easy access: potted meat, fresh carrots, peaches, pears, bread. Oats for the horses.

He hung an ax and a cast-iron pot on hooks fitted to the side-boards, then retrieved treasures from the shed. As well as his Bible, he found the portrait of Mother Biddle's father, behind the little one of her mother.

"Can we make room?" she asked as she held open the door. "I'd rather them than food."

He'd do anything for Mother Biddle. "I'd rather not go hungry."

"We won't," she said. "We've porridge aplenty, and we'll dine at way stations."

Traces in order, Joshua swung onto the seat, took up the long reins, and rippled them along the horses' rumps. "Hup, boys." The wheels crunched cinders in the dirt.

Mother Biddle rested a hand on his knee. "It's a new beginning." She patted his cheek. "We're blessed."

"Without a doubt," he said.

Heads high, they drove out to the street and followed the ridge past neighboring mansions. Not a wave good-bye or a face in a window marked their departure. The late start worried him.

On the far side of the hill, the houses grew smaller and smaller, then thinned to fields and woods. The sun hot, the sky clear, a welcome breeze came off the river.

West through fields, the heat increased. Then with small relief, the road cut into woods toward East Liverpool, and Mother Biddle passed him a thick slice of bread with a swipe of potted meat.

"I'm ravenous." He'd like to eat the whole loaf, but he wouldn't squander food.

They rode in easy silence, keeping to their own thoughts, the road stretching before them. From hauling this route, the horses knew the way. They knew when to pick up speed for a hill, to slow at the crest without being told, but when dusk overtook them, the Liverpool Inn lay miles farther.

"We have a choice," he said. "Get off the road in daylight, or trust the horses for another three hours."

She frowned. "Travel blind? I'd rather sleep in the woods. We have a mattress."

Joshua scanned the verge for another half mile. "There, at the curve, see?" A narrow track cut into the woods. "We'll be out of sight." He tightened the reins. The horses resisted the turn. "Hup now, come on, boys."

Off the track, he unhitched them, and tied their halters to the tailgate. They bobbed their heads and touched noses.

Joshua and Mother Biddle ate dinner by lamplight, a repeat of lunch. And following a trip to the woods, he untied the cart's canvas. Still in her clothes, she stretched on the mattress.

"Big enough for two," she said. "You lie right down. I won't bite."

"I know that now," he told her, and she laughed. "But don't worry," he said. "I've slept on the ground before."

"Not this time," she insisted.

He gave her as much room as possible, and kept the pistol in easy reach, though he'd no idea how it worked. Like a talisman, its very presence warded off danger.

"Good night." She blew out the lamp.

Tired as he was, sleep wouldn't come. He heard her chortle in the dark.

"Sleeping with someone takes practice." He could hear her smile. "Robert would think me improper," she said. "Sharing quarters with a young man."

"And no bundling board," Joshua said.

Of course, they weren't courting, but still. He crawled toward the seat. "I'd best sleep under the wagon."

"Joshua, no. There's nothing improper. God knows, and that's what counts."

The dark freed them to speak in ways the light wouldn't allow. "It seems like you and Robert don't agree," he said.

"Mmmm, sometimes, that's true." She rolled on her side. "He assumes the worst," she said, "and often finds it."

"You look for the best," said Joshua.

"There's goodness in people, though sometimes hard to find. The bailiff for one. He wouldn't let me undress."

"Would you, if he'd let you?"

"All my life I bent to others, and for a moment, I had no bend left. A small victory, and I rather enjoyed it."

"When you live with Robert, will you enjoy that?"

"Growing up, he saw me bend." She paused. "And expected his wife to do the same. Now she's gone to her mother's, the children with her." Mother Biddle squirreled to another position. "I'm old now, and bending's not easy."

She lay quiet. He thought she'd fallen asleep.

"Would *you* like living in Iowa," she said, "if—"

For an instant, he thought she'd invited him.

"If you were me?" she asked.

"Well," he said, all caution gone in the dark, "I'd live anywhere with you, and like it."

"I know I'd be pleased if you were in Iowa."

What he wouldn't do to bridge that *if*, though he knew it could never happen.

"Will you like being with your uncle?" she asked.

"Anywhere is better than being with Father." He hadn't planned this honesty.

"Why is that?" she said.

"You say there's good in everyone. Does it work the other way?"

"What way?"

"Father looks for the worst in me and finds it, if it's there or not."

"Maybe it's you." She laughed. "Something hidden and mean."

"Maybe," he said. "I worry about that."

"No, no, I'm teasing you. You couldn't be mean if you tried."

"I wish that were true," he said, remembering his badger self.

"Now put that thought out of your head. Sleep is what we need, and we better get to it."

Not yet light, and he'd been lying awake. Had he said too much? Had she? With the light, would they be shy, one to the other?

He inched his way over the seat, trying not to wake her.

"Joshua?"

"Yes, I'm off to hitch the horses."

A glimmer of dawn sneaked among the trees, and Mother Biddle made her way to the thickest underbrush.

"I'll get us some breakfast in a minute," she said. At least she was talking.

"We should eat under way," he called, "or we'll never make Canton tonight."

A few hours out, they passed through East Liverpool without stopping. Through the morning, the land rose and fell with the buzz of cicadas. Sweat stood on their faces. The sun not yet at its zenith, Mother Biddle pulled a bonnet out of her bag behind the seat and a hat with a mouse bite out of the brim. "You'll need this," she said. "Mr. Biddle used it touring the mines. The smudges won't come off."

In comfortable quiet through the day, they made no reference to the night before. By evening, the sun behind the hills, a slight cooldown took hold. They pushed on, though dark crawled out of the valleys.

Knowing they neared Canton, he gave the horses their head. He knew the surge of a horse headed for the barn, or, in this case, the way station yard.

They arrived after dark to a lot full of wagons covered in

canvas, their loads chained, dogs on top, snarling. He unhitched the horses by the light of a lamp and led them to a long shed, joining others tied to a manger. Mother Biddle went into the station.

The horses settled, he carried her bag inside. He found her standing at a long table lined with empty glasses, the room low and dim, heavy with the smell of mutton too long on the hoof and too short in the pot.

". . . one room," said a sour man behind the table.

"No, two," Mother Biddle said, a tired edge to her voice. "I need two rooms."

"Got one," the man said. "Take it or leave it."

"She'll take it," Joshua said, and to her, "We've no chains and no dog. I best sleep on the cart."

"Food?" the man asked.

Trail-roughened haulers crowded small tables. They watched in silence, the dim light not dim enough to hide the dirt.

"Fellas'll like that." The man snickered.

"My son and I will eat in my room," she said, her words tart.

"He's extra."

"I'll take your bag up," Joshua said, "and eat outside."

"Room three." The man pointed at a flight of narrow stairs.

Joshua dropped the bag inside the dirty little room with its small bed, table, and chair. He opened the window, hoping to rid the air of its last tenant.

"Do you want the pistol?" he asked.

"No, you might need it."

The man came in with a steaming bowl. The downstairs aroma mixed with upstairs mildew and sweat. "Yours is downstairs," the man growled.

"I'll see you in the morning," Joshua said. "Push the table against the door."

"Good idea." The man winked.

. . .

The way stations, each worse than the last, and Mother Biddle never complained. The cart may have been dusty, and their clothes damp under oilskin capes, but clean dirt, the damp fresh.

Forty days and forty nights on the road, raining much but not all of the time. The city of Springfield had been rucked-up, even the outskirts, with little care taken to stop washout.

They passed it by, and were pleased to do so. Again the horses resisted, clearly thinking they saw the end of their journey.

Rain kept the dust down, but soft spots waited in the deeper ruts, maneuvering around them impossible. In the fields, grass bent to the sun. Trees by the side of the road offered a minute of shade as they passed, leaves curling at the edges. They jolted along, hoping for an afternoon breeze.

"Shouldn't it be cooler? It's September." Mother Biddle stretched her back and fanned her face. "My bones are fit for soup."

At the word "soup," he heard a pop. The wagon jolted.

"What was that?" Mother Biddle looked around.

Joshua pulled off the road, and the horses began a return to the city. "Whoa, boys, this is a wheel check." He hopped down and examined wheel to wheel around the cart. The wood looked sound until the left rear. One of ten spokes had snapped in the middle.

"A nuisance, not a calamity," he said. "Best fix it."

"How?" Mother Biddle climbed down.

"Sistering. I need three pieces of oak and twine. It's like splinting a bone. We should be in Port Clyde tomorrow."

"We camp now?" Mother Biddle asked.

"Yes. We'll pull further off, once the wheel's fixed. I'll hunt oak; in the toolbox you'll find the twine."

He took the ax from the cart and scouted through the trees. Finding the right wood was the hardest part. After an hour, he spotted a black oak, the bottom branches old and gnarled. Higher up, the new wood grew straighter.

He hooked the blade in his suspenders, swung onto a low branch, and climbed to the highest one strong enough to hold. He braced himself and swung the ax. One bad swing and Mother Biddle would never know what became of him. She'd be frantic if he disappeared.

He cut three branches long as his forearm. He'd save the trimming for later. Mrs. Biddle was his responsibility, and he would protect her just as he would his mother. As he walked back, he thought about his real mother. Wasn't she frantic when he left? Why wasn't she his responsibility?

But Mother had Father and the littles, the farm, and more work than she could do. She had no time to think of Joshua. Besides, she might have another son by now. He tightened his fist on the sticks.

Why should that make him angry? Hadn't he replaced Mama with Mrs. Biddle?

The whisper of a breeze chilled him.

Joshua dropped the branches by the wheel. He sat and shaved one side free of bark, the wood underneath flattened.

Kneeling, he squeezed the sticks over the break. "A hand, please," he said. With the twine, Mother Biddle knelt beside him.

"Hold here," he said. She held where he had, and he wrapped the twine in a smooth sleeve, the splint complete.

Away from the cart, Mother Biddle had a fire burning. The iron pot bubbled. Joshua sniffed.

"Porridge," she said, and stirred with a long-handled spoon.

"Good, I'm starved."

"You can eat till you burst."

Their stomachs full of porridge and strips of dried meat, he tucked extra strips in his pocket for the road tomorrow. They watched coals settle in the fire. Mother Biddle sat on a log with her legs stretched, boot toes up. Close to the fire, his legs still hurt, so he knelt, his shins tucked safely under his thighs. The lamp stayed unlit by the log, the dark a comfort.

"What a toll on my old bones." Mother Biddle sighed. "But I wish we could keep going, just run away." She brushed dust from her sleeves. "When Mr. Biddle was young, he used to say he wanted to join the circus. Now I know how he felt."

"What's a circus?"

"A traveling menagerie where people go to forget their worries."

"Did Mr. Biddle ever run away?"

"No. Dying was the closest." She adjusted her skirts over her legs. "I thought I'd die myself." Her eyes rested on the last of the coals.

"And Robert? Did he run away?"

"His wife did the running, not that I blame her. He inherited my family's high expectations and his father's disdainful ways. Not a good combination."

"You don't want to go, do you?"

"I must, though I wonder if he'd just as soon I didn't."

"Why, then?"

"Robert's alone."

"What about you?" he asked. "What do you want?" And Joshua, what about what he wanted?

She put her hand on his knee. "You said I'd always be a mother, and you were right." She patted his thigh. "Robert loves me in his way, I love him in mine, and that's what we have."

The dark had descended, and he couldn't see her face. "It sounds a bumpy ride."

"It's like your sistered spoke," she said. "This fix will do for now." She drew her feet under her. "The worst part is leaving you." She struck a match and lit the lamp. She leaned over and kissed his cheek, the touch of a dry leaf, and looked him in the eye. "Is it the circus for you? Or will you go back?"

"Back?" he said.

"To your family. You can't leave them. They're the only ones you have, and running away isn't the answer."

"You know?"

"Your tongue shaded the truth. Your face never lied. I knew, but I wanted you with me. I persuaded myself you needed me as much as I needed you."

"I still do." He took her hand. He knew he was making it harder, but he had to make her listen.

"No, you *have* a family." She squeezed his hand. "You're good at sistering. Please, tell me you'll try."

When she slept, he took up his pen.

Dear Mama—

He went no further. What was the use? Letters got him no closer to Mama. He should throw them in the fire. But, no, tenuous as it was, they tied her to him.

They followed the Illinois River north to Port Clyde. There, he and Mother Biddle would have to part.

After forty-seven days on the road, nothing Joshua wore looked presentable, not Mr. Biddle's best pants or Robert's abandoned yellow shirt, the collarless neck crumpled.

What did it matter, in this one-horse town, as Mother Biddle called Port Clyde? Just the one street with its flat-front buildings connected one to the next, wood walkways in front, and everything covered in dust.

A tall figure stalked the road, his lips moving.

"That's Robert." Mother Biddle sighed. "He argues with himself."

So tall for having such a short mother. Arms akimbo, Robert squinted in their direction, his face set hard.

"He does hate to wait," she said in Joshua's ear, and waved a cheery hand. Despite Robert's grumpiness, her smile was enormous. "Hellooo, Robert."

"You had me worried," he shouted. At least he cared enough to worry. "I had to sleep in that so-called church." He lifted his chin toward the one peaked roof in the line of stores. A cross, nailed under the peak, threatened to fall on the steps below. "Cost me an arm and a leg and a sore back."

Joshua stopped the horses. With no effort Robert hopped onto the seat beside his mother. "Hey, where's the driver? A trusted man, you said."

"Robert, this is Joshua, my driver and friend."

"He's a boy!"

"Please, Robert, he's a fine young man."

Joshua wanted to crawl away.

"Fine indeed! That scar, the crooked nose? I bet he got those in church."

"Now, Robert."

"And he's wearing my shirt. Why is he wearing my shirt?"

"It—it's—" Her voice began to rise. She looked from Joshua to Robert, and then calmed. "It's not your shirt, dear; it's Joshua's. I gave it to him." Robert stared as if looking at a stranger, not the woman of his childhood, not the bent grass Mr. Biddle left in the field. She had risen as storm-flattened grass never did. Someday, Joshua hoped to have even half her fortitude.

In front of the church, he tied the team to the rail. A saddled horse lazed with one leg cocked, saddlebags packed for travel.

Robert unfolded his legs and jumped from the wagon, raising a hand to help his mother. Once on the ground they hugged. He folded his arms around her, protective as wings. "It's good to see you," he said. Joshua believed him, but it didn't mean he liked him. Mother and son hugged and hugged, she smiling through tears.

"Ma, we've got to go." His back to Joshua, he said, "I'll take her from here."

He untied the saddled horse, hurried it with a yank, and retied the reins to the cart, then climbed the seat. "Now," he commanded, reaching for his mother's hand.

"No, Robert, Joshua needs his things. They're behind the seat."

He pulled out a blanket and satchel with the sidearm set on top. "What's this?" Robert said, and waved the pistol in its holster. "It's Father's."

"Your father doesn't need a sidearm now. Joshua does."

"I need a pistol," said Robert.

"Yes, and you have one on your hip, so not another word."

He dropped the satchel and sidearm on the ground. "Now?" he said with a scowl.

"In a minute, Robert." She kissed Joshua on the cheek and pressed something in his hand. He opened his mouth to protest. "I—"

"Shh," she said, her eyes filling. "Promise you'll try," she whispered. "The thought of you without family—" She pressed her lips together and shook her head.

His eyes swam, lips trembling to match hers.

She squeezed his hands, crumpling the paper, then reached for the seat. "Now, Robert," she said.

He hoisted her up beside him. Once she settled on the seat, he shouted, "Haa," and slapped the reins hard. The horses lurched, front wheels grinding as they turned into the middle of the road. They picked up speed, and a brown cloud took them.

Joshua unclenched his fist, in it a note wrapped around a fold of money. He smoothed the note.

My Dearest Joshua,

I miss you already. It started the minute I realized I could no longer pretend. I have no right to you, and would only stand in the way of your return to those who must love you. You will always be in my heart, as I hope to be in yours.

Your Most Loving,

Mother Biddle

PS I knew you wouldn't take money if offered, so please forgive my sly method. Use it for food on your way home, and think of me with every bite.

The billow of dust settled, and she was gone, Joshua in the middle of the road, nothing but a boy buttoned in dead man's pants.

CHAPTER 12

Visiting

Abraham waited in his rocker, his body sheeted from shoulders to his toes, only his grizzled head showing. He needed his midday meal, and Miriam had returned early from service, leaving the girls at dinner with the Flock.

She kissed his unburned cheek. "It's time," she said. "Everyone wants to see you. They doubt my stories of your returning strength."

He glowered. "Maybe they *should* doubt," he said. "What strength would they see?" He adjusted the sheet with bandaged hands. "I can't dress myself."

"They know your burns won't tolerate clothes. Hannah told them." Miriam talked over her shoulder as she stirred eggs into chicken corn soup.

"I don't want visitors," he said.

"Not even Claus? They made him Deacon." The squeaky young man had waylaid her. He'd begged. "He says the Flock needs you."

Twice already, Abraham had made her turn the poor soul away. "*Claus* needs you." She ladled soup from the cauldron, bowls on the table beside his chair, a plate of cold green beans to the side. "Those other visits, he knew you weren't sleeping." She frowned at him as she spooned soup into his mouth. "What worries you?" She drizzled honey on the beans. He needed every encouragement to eat.

His good eye flickered. He shut both like a child hiding.

It wasn't the food. He was quick enough to push his plate away. When he managed to consume so little, no wonder he questioned his strength.

Then what was this fear she saw?

Finally, he'd acquiesced.

"Abraham?" Miriam shook his shoulder. "They're coming." He woke groggy from a nap on the pallet.

"I remember." He heaved a sigh.

Need had been the key. For a true shepherd, his Flock couldn't be resisted.

He'd never been happier than gathering faithful from across the county, rebuilding Kruger's barn, or tending the widow Youse's garden with the littles. The new widow too distraught, Miriam had jarred the harvest, and Abraham delivered baskets and baskets of carrots, limas, green beans, beets, taken them down to the cellar and lined the shelves. Abraham, everyone's link with God, interpreter, guide in the wilderness without question. He had God's ear. This fog would dissipate as he healed, and somehow their home would be restored. Miriam had faith.

The girls upstairs, Abraham threw back his sheet. He rose nearly naked, the worst of his burns still shrouded, his nearly unscathed manhood slack and long as a horse's. He teetered when he walked, and Miriam took his arm where lesser burns had healed.

The red of his body had mottled to leathery brown, the edges of wounds crusted like ice on a windblown pond. The surface ridged in red and white.

He couldn't completely straighten his arms, his knees stayed cocked, and he shuffled like an old man, breathing as if something wrung his lungs. He coughed.

His legs softened under him, and she held tight, guiding him to his rocker. He sat on sheepskins, wool side up, and rested the back of his head on the crossbar. She slid a loose nightshirt over his arms. "Lean forward," she said, and pulled it over his head, a sheet across his lap. "Try the boots—you'll look less cadaverous."

The neighbors had seen him skinned on the kitchen table and later in the corner covered with a sheet. Constance, a woman who had helped the third day, gaped on seeing him. "Miriam, I'm so sorry. No one told me Abraham passed."

His smoky voice had risen from the corner. "If only," he'd said.

Big-eyed, color draining, Constance backed to the door. Lazarus in the flesh wouldn't have stunned her more.

Miriam had bitten the lift of her lips. She wanted to hug Constance for the piece of levity, but covered in confusion, the woman had dashed off.

The Flock's visiting wives arrived first. Seven marched through the door, hands full of covered dishes. "This one's from Constance." They uncovered the food and set plates on the table for when the men arrived.

"We've tracked in dirt," said one. "I'll give the floor a sweep." How kind they were, attending to Miriam's inattentions, never meaning to hurt her feelings.

With profuse thanks, she persuaded them to the porch. "Activity tires him," she whispered.

"How do you manage?" one said. "What strength."

Miriam had prayed her strength would come. And prayed. She felt a fraud as her innards quaked.

The men tromped into the house and for one stunned moment stood before Abraham swathed in white as if ready for burial. They stared at his face, taking in what she no longer noticed, his patchy hair, the melted ear, the bright swirl of one cheek down to a section of beardless chin.

She could see them imagining his scorched body under the sheet, the way she imagined Joshua's body. Not wanting to think on it, she found it impossible to think of anything else.

After dragging chairs in a semicircle facing Abraham, the men perched. Farthest from Abraham, Zeke sat at the end by the tamped-down fire. The women filed in, loaded plates, and passed them.

One fellow jiggled a leg; another twisted his beard; a third rubbed his palms on the sides of his thighs while he balanced a plate on his lap. Each man said his sorry. One asked, "How's—" He cleared his throat. "How's the pain?"

Abraham lifted the movable side of his mouth, the other still swollen. His good eye lit with a laugh, he mumbled, "If you scald a pig before slitting its throat, what do you suppose it would say?"

The women gasped in unison, except Hannah, who laughed out loud.

"Good to be alive," Zeke answered. Zeke and Hannah, the truest of friends.

Abraham nodded, the spark in his eye fading to truth. "Depends on the day."

The talk turned to crops and limped along as everyone forked in their dinners, declared them delicious, and, with ill-disguised relief, rose for good-byes and closed the door behind them.

Zeke, the last to leave, said, "Will we see you at service?"

"You didn't answer," Miriam said when she changed into her nightdress.

"Without pants," he snapped, "how can I go to service?"

"Are you sure it's burns holding you back?" Now she'd said it aloud.

Dark coming on, Miriam hustled from the woods. She'd forgotten Hannah and their visit to the Grubers' with a promise of shelling peas on the porch, husking corn with its hairy strands of silk embedded between the kernels. In short order all the women together would accomplish a week's worth of work and have the crop harvested before it got long in the tooth.

Elderly peas and wrinkled corn, the ruination of dinner, and eaten from jars through the winter, these meals would point at someone's laziness. Miriam's crop had been small, what with too much rain at first and not enough to follow; however, finishing the task themselves made her think maybe they could manage in the future. That didn't mean forgetting to help the others.

Stepping from the buggy, Hannah gave her a squeeze. "Another search?" she asked, an arm on Miriam's shoulder as they entered the kitchen.

"What?" Miriam tipped her head to the side. "I can't walk in the woods?"

"You don't fool me."

Miriam hadn't tried. She counted on Hannah, the one who dared say what everyone whispered. The only one who spoke without judgment.

Frau Gruber and her friends made Miriam tired. She wasn't sure which was worse, the relentless cheer or the sidelong pity from a distance. No wonder Abraham didn't like visits.

In the Grubers' parlor, cup in hand, Miriam said, "Yes, Abraham's better. You're so good to ask." She sipped warm cider and

didn't say, *By the end of the day his strength is gone and mine is too.*
"Yes, I'm well."

"You see, time heals. Didn't we tell you?"

One foot before the other. Miriam could forgive the platitudes.
She knew everyone did their best and she loved them for the attempt, but it didn't mean they weren't tiring.

"You did tell me," Miriam said. And indeed Frau Gruber had,
several times, and Miriam had learned that when some asked,
"How are you?" it wasn't always an invitation to say. With Hannah
it was.

Miriam wished she could quell the flutter in her chest. What if
her thoughts spilled from her mouth?

Hannah stood close as a calming breeze on this hot August
day, restraining Miriam from a headlong dash for their buggy in
the shed.

It had always been Hannah's hand in hers making the difference. From childhood scrapes to her reassuring touch when
Miriam choked on her first labor, Hannah five years older and
forever wiser.

"I can't do this," Miriam had wailed.

"You're stronger than you think. Just breathe." Hannah put
her broad hand on the mound that would be Adah, draining the
terror. Part mother, part sister, Hannah Miriam's ready family,
taking their places as one after the other had succumbed, her
youngest sister in childbirth, making this terror worse; her mother
and two older sisters, like many that year, had been taken by fever.
Home became a house of distracted men, Miriam caring for her
father and three brothers, yet Hannah always came with an eager
hand and an infusion of grit.

"Remember, you're the one that fell out of the tree. Anyone
who walks a mile on a broken leg can do childbirth standing on her
head."

Another pain had cut off Miriam's laugh.

"Just be glad, for this birth, you're lying down."

The tree had been an accident she vowed never to repeat. Not so with babies, ten in her future, or so she'd thought then. She'd only just begun.

In the buggy, Miriam closed her eyes, breathed in the scent of new-scythed hay, and sank comfortably on the hard seat. Hannah clicked her tongue and the horse trotted toward home.

CHAPTER 13

A World of Mischief

Standing next to Mother Biddle, Joshua had seen himself as a man. He wanted to be that man, not be this sorry possum kit dropped from its mama's pouch.

He could hear Father's hiss of disgust, Father on his throne in Joshua's head.

Joshua dragged his satchel and blanket to the church steps, adjusted the sidearm, and sat. He didn't notice the bits of glass until a sliver pricked his rump. Joshua stood and brushed at his pants, folded his blanket, and sat on it. The pistol point hit the step and the butt gouged his ribs. The discomfort nothing, yet his eyes stung. Pathetic, worse than Robert wanting the sidearm.

Joshua had left a perfectly good mother, and here he was coveting Robert's. A father as well, and not just the one clamoring in his head.

Some father. With a dull knife and a hard piece of wood, he could have carved a better one.

Wagons passed in a spew of new dust. Horsemen tied up at the rail and stomped through the swinging doors of the next building. Some curious, some hostile, they watched him where he sat. He didn't risk meeting their eyes. Fingers and his friends under the bridge had been a lesson learned.

No more tears, his nose stopped dripping. He wouldn't be a possum kit, all round-eyed and squirmy. *Those kits have fifty teeth,* he remembered. *They can eat anything.* He felt taller already. So where to go?

Monte Rey. His mind dredged up Frau Lentz's map and he reset his sights west past the river. The land opened. Crossing meant getting wet, not a good idea with night coming, and he wouldn't spend money, not until he starved. His gut rumbled a warning.

He fished the last strip of dried meat from his pocket, blew off the fuzz, and took a bite. Sniffing came from under the steps. A dog crawled out, skinny and hairless around hungry eyes. "Sorry, boy."

The dog pawed his hand. He thought on Luke and gave the dog half a strip of meat. Luke had been in worse shape when they'd found each other.

Before the dawn milking, Joshua had caught a dark shape slipping through shadows outside the barn. If it was Father, he didn't want to know.

When Joshua finished the cows, he turned them to pasture. The shadows had lightened, and there lay a black dog, his coat clotted in mud. The animal rested his head on his paws, backbone jagged. Brows twitching, he lifted tired eyes.

Joshua set down the milk pail and held out a hand. "Hey, boy."

The dog crawled forward, belly to the ground. He raised his nose and sniffed.

Rebecca hopped from the henhouse, a basket of eggs hooked on her arms. "Who's your friend?" she'd asked.

"Wish I knew."

"He looks hungry." She checked in the milk pail and, basket on the ground, ran to the henhouse, returning with a pan. Joshua poured in milk.

The dog's eyes flicked from the pan to him. Joshua knelt. "It's for you, boy." Their faces close, he stroked the animal's neck and their eyes laced together, the dog's brown pools of trust. It rose on stiff legs, stepped to the pan, and, with a quick glance from under his brows, lapped with delicate pink tongue.

"Atta boy," Joshua whispered. "Finish your breakfast."

Breakfast, good grief. He tipped more milk in the pan. "Quick. Go," he said, and rushed Rebecca, the milk, and the basket of eggs to the house.

At the door, she stopped. "We should keep him," she said.

Joshua pushed her into the kitchen. Scrapple sizzled in the pan, the air rich. Father glowered from the table. Clearly, not the best time to ask.

The stray dog pawed again. "No more," Joshua said, deep and stern. The mangy creature snorted and loped down the street.

Drizzle dampened Joshua's hair. He pulled Mr. Biddle's hat from his satchel. If desperate for cover, Joshua could crawl under the boardwalk. From next door—the sign said SALOON—a swell of laughter drifted to him along with a woman's voice.

Where was Mother Biddle? Warm and dry and cooking dinner for her son? Smiling at her son? Sleeping in a big bed? Or was she scrubbing crusted pots, sweeping the house, washing clothes, before she could start his dinner? Bending again, begging a blanket for her pallet bed.

Even bending, she had a bed. Joshua dreaded more nights like those in the Tuscarora, the sneaking and thieving, the hunger. How much harder they'd be after his time in Gomorrah.

"What's a matter, boy?" A man in black with a high white collar laid a hand on his shoulder. Joshua scooted sideways.

"You lost?" He sounded almost hopeful. Joshua slid farther along the step.

"I'm Syd," the man said, "Pastor Syd. You've come on a good

day, horsemeat for dinner, no beans." He smiled with half his mouth.

He'd been offered smiles before.

Drizzle turned to rain. Why let one man drive him off? A man of the church at that, so like the priests in Mother Biddle's cathedral, though no swinging smoke. Someone godly, the collar proved it, grimy or not.

"I can't pay," Joshua said.

"Did I ask?" The white-collar man stepped aside. "Last night's guest was a most generous man, praise the Lord." Yes, praise the Lord, and that prayer was the only one Joshua heard on *Pastor* Syd's lips, what with him too busy wheeling and dealing with hapless strangers.

With every few meals, Joshua owed another day's work. Days of clearing bat droppings from the church attic. Surprising how much accumulated, even with Joshua sleeping there.

Early in November, most likely the last of warm days, local farmers trekked to town, stocking up. That's how Sylvie and her grandpa Baylor happened into church. Also, Pastor Syd was the old man's nephew.

"Surprise," Grandpa said as they blew in the door. "Dinner smells good." He fell into an empty chair. "Shopping's a killer. How 'bout a shot to buck me up."

"A bottle and two glasses," Syd said. Joshua gave Sylvie his chair.

"Don't I get a glass?" she asked, and flicked cherry hair behind her shoulder.

"Turning into a right vixen," said Syd.

"Already turned." Grandpa sucked his teeth.

Sylvie, the same height as Joshua, managed to look down her nose at him. She wore what Syd called a town dress, fancier than everyday, but nothing like that of the woman Joshua had seen going in the saloon. Little pink flowers covered Sylvie's full skirt and up the bodice to her neck. Her face showed sun.

Grandpa wore the brown clothes of a farmer, a small attempt at polish on his boots. He curled the toes around his chair legs and tucked into Joshua's dinner, consuming half by the time Joshua came back with the bottle and a plate for Sylvie. He scooped on beans and pork, one of three meals Syd had him master right off. He stood waiting for instructions.

"How's Edith?" Syd asked around a mouthful of beans.

"So-so," Grandpa said. "Not much time to grieve for poor Bart, what with all his brothers living in the house. Sylvie helps when we can catch her. Fifteen last week, and she's hard to catch."

Sylvie poked out a full lower lip. Grandpa went on. "I got her picking dry goods over to Frasier's. Caring for five men, it's too much for Edith. They may be my boys and her husband's brothers, but they're a pissy bunch."

"Too bad, wish I could help."

Grandpa's eyes crinkled. "I could ask Crystal, next door."

"Crystal? From the saloon? Ha!" Syd slapped his knee. "You old goat. She don't know the flat of a fry pan from the handle, and you know it."

"Can't blame a goat for dreaming. Don't expect Edith would take to her anyway."

"Your boys would, till they killed each other. But you know—" Syd twisted in his chair and looked at Joshua. "What about the kid?"

"He's not as pretty." The old man gulped his drink. "And women's work is what we got."

Syd scratched his head. "The kid sets a good table. He's clean, knows how to wash clothes. I'd loan him for the price of what he's eaten. He works for room and board."

"Bed's a problem. The house's full."

"Grandpa," Sylvie piped up, "he could sleep in the barn." She snickered. "The pigs won't mind."

"You live on a pig farm?" Joshua asked. Much as he liked pigs, he'd rather sleep with horses or sheep.

"He's no stranger to barns," Syd said. "How 'bout it, kid?"

A farm. A real family. "I'd like that," Joshua said.

Two turkeys gobbled a welcome. "Better than watchdogs," Grandpa said, slowing the horses into the dooryard. "And more delicious."

"What do *you* know, Pap?" said Sylvie. "You never ate dog in your life."

"Hush your sass, girl."

Grandpa and Sylvie had picked at each other all day on the road, starting at Syd's in Illinois and winding through Missouri tobacco fields. By the time they wheeled past the Baylors' woodlot, then fields studded with corn shocks, Joshua couldn't wait to get off the wagon.

His first glimpse of the family came framed in a warm glowing window. Inside, a thin woman sat at one end of a table. Had to be Bart's widow, Edith. She tightened a blue cloth knotted at the back by her bun. Sharp nose, mouth set, she oversaw the feeding of four burly men with dark beards. They sat two to a side. Squabbling over platters piled with food, they yanked dishes from one another's grasp, hitting and spilling gravy.

"My sons." Grandpa nodded at the window. "Dead Bart's younger brothers. Mack, John, Joe, and Runt. Edith's at the end." An empty chair stood on one side of the table, another empty at the far end.

"Get out here, you louts," Grandpa yelled. He rubbed his knees. As he took breath to yell again, the door opened.

"So here you are. 'Bout time too," said Edith—Mrs. Baylor— on the top step. "With another mouth, I see."

"Now don't get your knickers in a twist." Grandpa labored up the steps. "He's here for you."

"May as well come in." Mrs. Baylor nodded at Joshua. "Dinner's hot."

"Not you, kid." Grandpa waved Joshua toward the horses. "Unhitch first."

By the time he finished, dinner was over, and the uncles pushed past him out of the house. Runt shouldered Joshua into Joe. "Grubby little turd," Runt said. His dislike prickled Joshua's skin. *What had he done to Runt?*

A stray is a stray, a thief. . . . Their look repeated Father's words. But what Joshua wanted couldn't be stolen.

They moved on to the barn, and he knocked on the open door. Sylvie's mother, dressed in men's pants and shirt, came to the sill. The table behind her overflowed with dirty bowls and plates and platters. God, he hoped they'd left a little for him.

Sylvie peeked over her mother's shoulder. "That's him," she said, and did a delighted little dance. *Was she simple?*

Up close, Mrs. Baylor looked sinewy, range-fed, more fowl than hen, her mouth down in close-drawn lines, her eyes hard. She stared at Joshua's hair, bowl cut two months past. She took in his good shirt and worn pants, then came back to his face. Her mouth tightened. He'd forgotten his crooked nose, the red line cheek to ear. She gave a cold smile as if she'd unearthed a secret.

"Help yourself." She inclined her head at the table. "When you're done, wash up. You too, Sylvie, everything." She pointed her thumb at a pile of dirty pots. "I'll find bedding."

Joshua scraped the remaining slice of meat onto the squash platter, added mashed potato, and sat in an uncle's chair. Too hungry to find his own fork, he used a dirty one. Sylvie sprawled in her mother's chair, grinning like a fool.

One eye on her, one on the food, he wished she'd stop staring, but the food was too good not to enjoy. At the last forkful, Sylvie backed out of the room with a trilling wave of her fingers. "Scraps go to the pigs." She laughed. "Have fun with the dishes."

As Grandpa had said, catching her was clearly the problem. Joshua rolled his sleeves.

Dishes, mounds of them on every surface. He unstuck each from the other, scraped, and restacked dinner plates, dessert plates, serving bowls and platters, glasses fogged with milk. It would take a while. Too bad they didn't have running water like Mother Biddle.

How fast English weeds took root. He *should* pluck them out.

Mrs. Baylor returned with blankets. "So, Sylvie abandoned you," she said. "She deserves a good smack."

"No, not on my account, please. I'll manage fine. Really." He shuffled the dishes. "Really, don't smack her."

"It's all right, Joshua. Calm down. My, my, what a tender turn of mind." She put the bedding on a chair by the door and slid her hands down the small of her back. "I hate to put you in the barn, but that's as must be."

Mama's words filled his head, *Behave like a pig and you sleep in the barn.* At dinner his sisters would chortle like crows, all the time nudging him with their eyes, while they kept their arms to their sides, feet straight below their knees under the table. None of them would think of bad behavior.

He picked up his bedding. At least he needn't wallow with the pigs.

"Pigs are behind the barn." Mrs. Baylor put the platter of scraps on top of the blankets. "Take the lamp, and mind you don't kick it over."

Was this the secret she saw in his eyes? The burning shed? Father burning?

She held the door. He balanced his load across the dooryard to the barn looming in the cold night. Not till he came close again did he notice the red color.

He went around to the pigpen and, bending his knees, set the lamp on the ground. The pigs trotted to the fence and reared, front hooves on the top rail. All six snouts tipped toward the platter. They grunted with excitement.

He tossed the leftovers over their heads into the pen. The pigs scrambled after, biting one another's legs and squealing. The biggest difference between them and the uncles was a fork.

Then came nesting. Joshua searched the barn, blanket and platter left at the door by his satchel. The lower level, dug into a bank and lined with stone, so like his own barn, had a tack room. On his entering, the clean leather smell announced the tack before his swinging lantern showed bridles and harness hung on iron hooks. Saddles rested on wood pegs.

Out of the tack room, box stalls came next, two for the draft horses, Burt and Brutus, with their heads over the half doors. Four smaller stalls for saddle horses, hardly room to turn around.

Then came three cows tied in a row on the other side of a clean gutter. The short-horned cows, brown with white, chewed their cuds and paid him no mind.

He took open stairs to the big room. Packed hay rose above his head and out of the lamp's reach, the scent of sun-dried grass thick in the still air. A lack of draft told him the Baylors had crammed the barn full to the rafters.

A small corridor led through the hay where trapdoors lifted for filling the mangers below. The warmest spot in winter would be with the horses. He preferred their scent to cows', and Grandpa's Belgians were easy with Joshua in the stall.

He hung the lantern on a peg and scooped armfuls of straw through the trapdoor, down into one end of the manger, the hay too prickly for bedding. That way the horses wouldn't eat his mattress.

Heavy eyed, he retrieved his satchel. On his return, Brutus

nickered and stomped in his stall. Joshua opened the door, Sylvie swinging out with it, her feet on the bottom brace, arms straight, fingers hooked over the top.

"Ta-da!" she sang, hair and skirts flying. He leapt back.

"Ready for bed, are we?" She jumped off beside him. "I can help," she said.

"No, thanks. I'm finished." He threw the blankets in the manger.

"I can unpack your satchel."

"I don't—"

She snatched the bag and dumped it at his feet.

"Is this all you have?"

"That's all I need."

"I could loan you a dress. More fitting for women's work, don't ya think?"

An angry shout from the house. "Sylvie!"

"Oops, that's Grandpa. Gotta go. I'll help you tomorrow."

God forbid.

Come dawn, Joshua washed at the trough and slipped into the kitchen. No one stirred. At home he'd have barn chores done by then, breakfast half-eaten.

He stood in the brightening room as sun slanted into dust-filled corners. The dinner table and the worktable had been wiped clean enough, but not the shelves. And the parlor—Mama wouldn't allow such dust.

Mrs. Baylor, in slippers, shuffled in behind him. "No time to clean," she said, "much less sit." She rubbed her eyes, drew her nightdress close at the neck, then busied herself at the hearth. "You may as well light the stove," she said. She cupped her hands to her mouth. "Sylvie," she shouted in the direction of the stairs. "Get eggs."

Minutes later, Sylvie dragged down. From a peg by the door, she unhooked a coat, donned it over her nightdress, and slipped bare feet into big boots, before slamming out the door.

The stove blazed. "Now, see to the milking," Mrs. Baylor said. "Pail's under the table."

Sylvie, with her basket of eggs, crossed Joshua's path in the dooryard. Thank heaven, too sleepy, perhaps, to see him.

Through the weeks, his job unfolded much like housework at home, except Sylvie and Mrs. Baylor didn't do fieldwork. No need with so many men. Inside work came aplenty, the usual stewing, baking, scrubbing kitchen and clothes, sweeping, making soap, dipping candles, rendering fat for lamps, mending pants, darning socks, stitching harness, and in the barn milking and collecting eggs.

He knew where to be at any given moment, but he missed the outside, the sweet ache of hard-worked muscle after a day with Goliath at the plow, or forging him a new set of shoes. He didn't miss how Father had torn into him over the last shoeing.

At the forge, Joshua had shaved wood into the firepot, added coal, and brought the pile roaring with the bellows. He lined tools on a bench, short and long tongs, a puller, hammers, square nails, a rasp, a clincher, a curved knife, and four shoes ready to fit.

He tapped the first hoof. Obliging, the horse shifted his weight, and Joshua lifted the hoof between his apron-covered legs, the worn shoe facing up on his lap. Goli nudged Joshua's side and leaned into him. "I know, I know," he said. "You could squash me like a slug." He tickled under the horse's lower lip. "Enough now." Goli straightened.

One good tug and the shoe came off. Grunting with effort, Joshua clipped the hoof wall close to the tender sole, then evened the trim with a rasp.

Father shouted, "Watch the frog, boy."

Startled, Joshua dropped Goli's hoof.

"Can't you do anything?" Father snatched the file, and took over. The horse hitched his leg in irritation, but let Father continue the already finished task. "That's how it's done. Now, get on with it," he said.

Father returned as Joshua drew the last shoe from the coals and shaped it on the anvil's horn, sparks flying.

"We'll be here all day." Father pushed the bellows on him—"Tend the fire"—and he hammered the ends. The calks bent, and one last time in the forge, he ran the color up the shoe, blue to yellowish brown. The metal tempered hard, he quenched it, hissing, in a bucket of water.

"I'll nail it," Joshua said.

"And lame him? Not on your life."

Joshua had done the other three. Why worry about this one?

The last nail in place, with a satisfied smile, Father had run his hand over Goli's hock. He fingered the neat fit of tendon and muscle, then lifted his hand and smoothed the horse's flank. "Good boy," he said. Father knew a good horse when he saw one.

Why not the good in a boy?

One day, after emptying the night-jars, washing and replacing them under the beds, Joshua collected clothes scattered over the bedroom floors.

"We're out of bread," Mrs. Baylor called from the hall. "Baking, now."

But the clothes.

"Sylvie," Mrs. Baylor said as she hurried down to the kitchen. "You too."

Sylvie popped up behind Joshua. She blew in his ear, then held him at arm's length, surveying the effect. Apparently not satisfied, she pulled him close and, to his horror, plunged her tongue where her breath had been. His face squinched in disgust. He dropped the clothes.

With a cackle, she ran after her mother, stopping on the top step long enough to watch Joshua grind the wet out of his ear.

In the kitchen, Sylvie had the barrel of flour open. She'd taken the jar of starter from the shelf above the stove and set out two freshly scrubbed basins. Mrs. Baylor measured flour into each basin, then poured warm water and the seething starter. He knew the process.

He and Sylvie rolled up their sleeves. They sank their hands in the basins and worked the mess into dough with their fingers. Joshua's came together first, and he turned it onto the floured table. He kneaded in a steady rolling motion, pushing down with one hand while pulling the dough into position with the other, the dough folding on itself.

"That's dumb." Sylvie pushed her gooey mound down with the heels of both hands, stopped, pulled it toward her, and pushed again. She leaned into him. "I'll show you how it's done."

Sliding her flour-smeared arm on his, she grunted on the downstroke, throwing off his rhythm. He had to start again. They both pumped in their own way, his three strokes to her one. His dough came smooth and elastic, ready to rise before hers lost the look of cooked oatmeal.

"Where did you learn that?" Mrs. Baylor asked.

"My mother." His neck heated under her attention. "We all learned bread."

"Show me," she said.

Sylvie stomped on his foot. "Show her, Mr. Know-it-all." And she dashed out the door, wiping her hands on his back as she passed.

He started in on Sylvie's half-kneaded mess, slowing the motion so Mrs. Baylor could watch.

"Let me try," she said. She worked while he measured two more batches, altogether eight loaves. Easier with Sylvie elsewhere. Talking came easier too.

"Your mother must be a good cook," Mrs. Baylor said.

"She is." And to his surprise, he blinked back tears. His head bent, he looked at her hands, the motion right, the dough elastic.

"That's a talent," she said. "What else is hidden in that head of yours?"

Delicious words. Embarrassing words. They made him squirm, and he wanted more. She still didn't smile, though the chill was gone.

Winter threatened gray through November, colder than January in Lancaster. Joshua wore both his shirts and a sweater, shivering when he brought wood for the morning fire. Splitting the logs had warmed him, though it didn't last, cold shaking him into the kitchen.

"Joshua," Mrs. Baylor said, "where's your coat?"

"I've not got one."

"Good Lord."

Sylvie, laying the table for breakfast, waggled her head, and in a grating squeak said, "Good Lord."

Headed for the stove, Joshua edged behind her as she set the table. She cocked a hip and bumped him. "Poor Joshua," she said. "Whatever are we going to do?"

"Do about what?" Grandpa came in. "What's the kid done?" He pulled out his chair at the head of the table and sat.

Sylvie poured milk in his glass. "Not enough fuzz to warm him." She wiggled a finger over her upper lip. "Much less the rest of his skinny self."

"Fuzz today." Grandpa frowned. "A beard tomorrow."

"Use Bart's jacket," Mrs. Baylor said. "That one, on the hook by the door. It's time I wore my own."

. . .

First Sunday of the month, they changed the sheets. Sylvie and Joshua started with Joe's bed, Runt's next in the shared room, sharp with old socks, sweat, and manure. Dropped clothes littered the floor.

Joshua stripped Joe's sheets down to the stained ticking. "Changing won't help." He held his nose. At home he emptied straw mattresses and washed the covers, then stuffed the bags fresh with the smell of sun and wind.

"These are horsehair," Sylvie said. "We turn them yearly."

Runt's bed had a trench down the middle.

"This needs it now," Joshua said.

"Suit yourself."

Joshua coughed in the surge of musty flakes. Sylvie shook out a clean sheet. He grabbed the loose end and folded it under the foot.

They finished and went on to Mrs. Baylor's room. A mysterious scent warmed his insides. He could've stayed there for hours, but Sylvie whisked him through the changing and on to her room. She folded open the bed and reclined slowly. "Try it."

"No, thanks," he said. He untucked the bottom of the bed with her in it, then the top. He untucked the side. The sheet firmly in his fists, he rolled her onto the floor.

"Hey." She scrambled up. Joshua ignored her.

Her mattress looked clean, but a sag had started. He gripped the edge and hoisted.

"No!" Her arms shot up, blocking the flip. The mattress dropped off center. There on the slats lay thin paper books with pictures on the covers. One had a young woman, her bosom big as a cow's udder swelling under her dress. She leaned backward, a knee peeking from under a torn skirt, the back of her hand held to her brow.

Joshua spread the books. Three women looked at him the way Sylvie did, their expressions saying . . . he wished he knew what.

Sylvie turned snake, head thrust forward, eyes dark and beady, ready to strike. "You tell, and I'll make you wish you died at birth."

Joshua didn't doubt her.

CHAPTER 14

Daft

F all, and frustration edged on anger. Without thought, Miriam's words spilled on Abraham as he sat in his rocker. "Where is he? You have God's ear—ask Him."

With what looked to be a twinge of pain, Abraham bowed his head. He held on to his covering sheet and shuffled to her. "Oh, Miriam." Unable to straighten his arms, he rested one bandaged hand on her shoulder. "He's with God, four months now."

"Then why can't we find him?"

"Animals crawl off to die. It's what they do." He kissed Miriam's cheek. "Remember Adah's cat? How long she searched?"

"But you saved Joshua; you threw him through the window."

Abraham dropped the sheet and spread his cocked arms. "Look at my burns."

"I've seen them." She moved to the worktable, propping herself on the edge.

"Do you think," he rasped, "Joshua could have survived this?"

"I have to make dinner." She retreated to the hearth.

"No more searching." He wrapped the sheet around himself and sat. "Go to service. Ask forgiveness."

She didn't want to go. Though service itself could be managed, dinner after took careful girding. Her neighbors had healed. They'd accepted the unacceptable, while she remained raw. Her tongue more raw every day with the biting it took to curb the questions she needed answered. God didn't talk to her directly. She had to depend on Abraham for His words. Could he hear God, with that crinkled ear?

Nothing else to distract that ear, the everyday sounds not loud enough, maybe God's whispers came through louder. *Hold your tongue,* she advised her teeth, *and let Abraham listen.*

The season's last haying and Miriam swung the scythe beside Zeke along with five other men. They watched the sun smile on their efforts, drying the long grass where it fell. Two days later, she and the girls turned it, exposing the damp underside, and fluffed where mats had clumped. They all knew the danger of fire if they stored it wet in the barn. At the very least there'd be mildew no animal would eat.

The third day they forked the hay into windrows, and the men tossed it high on the wagon Miriam drove. Seeds and chaff flew, sticking to their sweat-covered arms, necks, and faces.

Adah and Mary stomped the loose hay, compressing it to a heavier load, while Rebecca and Emma hauled water from the pump. Emma poured, while Rebecca handed it out in tin cups. The men dumped some over their heads, washing off the dust and seeds.

Abraham stayed inside despite the wondrous weather. "I can't sit on the porch while everyone works," he'd said to Rebecca when she went in to check. "I can't bear it."

That evening Miriam and the girls came in weary with a job well-done and started supper. They fried carrots, turnips, squash, onions, potatoes, and chicken in a huge double-handled skillet.

"Look at your hands," Abraham said as she spooned his plate full. "You shouldn't be out there like that."

"That's God's will too," she said. "Would you have me sulk in the house?" So unkind, making him feel worse. But really.

This time, with service at Hannah's house, Hannah had offered Miriam protection. She could slip away if she wanted. But she wouldn't; too much whispering would follow.

Accompanied by the girls, Miriam carried in a large pan of corn pudding and set it on the hearth, warming till dinner. In the women's section, her knees together, ankles touching, she sat with Adah and Rebecca on one side, Emma and Mary on the other. She kept her hands clasped, her head bowed so the other women wouldn't see her attention gallop to the rolling fields where corn shocks gathered to tepees wizened in the sun. Where pumpkins ripened orange amidst a sprawl of wide green leaves, the season unfolding as God intended, the natural flow uninterrupted by tribulations haunting her from her prayers.

She reined herself back to the sermon. "Seek the LORD. . . . Let the scoundrel forsake his way. . . ." *Am I a scoundrel?* ". . . let him turn to the LORD for mercy; to our God, who is generous . . ." *Is He? Is He GENEROUS!*

Service no place for the cranky, again her attention took to the fields, her refuge, where clouds casting shadows gave way to patches of sun.

At dinner after service, the men seated at a long table, she held the pan of corn pudding. Offering it one to the next, she brought the pan down between their shoulders. With a big spoon they scooped yellow kernels suspended in creamy custard onto their plates and continued talking.

She wished her attention would gallop off again, and yet it stayed sharp, her ears pricked the way Luke's did. The men talked, seemingly unaware a person held the pan.

Was she the grain of sand after all, fitting in, as she should? She could fool herself about tomorrow being a day when all would come clear, but was she, Miriam, a grain of sand? No, not now. She'd chalk this up to the obliviousness of these men.

Their talk, snippets about record crops, came to her ear, snippets of whose hay to cut next, and the Deacon's boy.

"—a shame, and so young. Do you think—"

"Dead, no question."

Her mouth grew tight, heart buzzing in her chest. *Of course, a question!*

"She's at it yet. She's—"

What did they know? Joshua wasn't their son. Their sons worked beside them in the field.

The man on her right said, "Daft! Of course he's—"

Daft? Daft?

"No," she shouted in his hairy ear. "He isn't dead."

The man lurched. His shoulder knocked her arm, and the pan tipped. Six servings of pudding slid, creamy and yellow, onto his black lap.

She shook the pan, and the last little bits fell on his plate. She wasn't sorry, and Deacon's wife or no, she wouldn't say she was.

The man scraped pudding from his pant legs, and a phalanx of murmuring women swooped her away.

"Did you see his face?" Hannah said as she led the group, Miriam in the middle, into the kitchen. With fingertips of both hands, Miriam rubbed her creased forehead. Her heart slowed. "So foolish," she said. "He meant no harm."

"Nevertheless," said another. "The pudding was well spent." They all laughed.

Pleasantly surrounded, Miriam smiled.

In one unguarded moment, she'd proved their point—daft, no doubt about it. She'd made a spectacle of herself, one they wouldn't forget, and neither would she.

At dessert the men watched over their shoulders as Hannah

and the others passed the peach cobbler. Some even said "thank you." Miriam thought it a good thing.

Maybe the men, wary now, didn't see it her way. Even her good things came tainted.

October. One day warm, the next cold, wilting the last tomato leaves. In the garden, they hung black on twisted stalks, the sun unable to perk them back to life.

Inside the kitchen, Miriam at the dishpan, Hannah dried a mixing bowl while bread loaves rose in the dough tray. Silent for a bit, Miriam sighed. "I need something solid."

A bubble rose from the dishpan, delicate and shimmering with color lit by in-streaming sun. Miriam popped it with her finger.

"You know he wouldn't run away," Hannah said. "You can't keep searching."

"I'm not really searching." Miriam twisted a dish towel around her hand.

"I've seen you," Hannah said, "from the road. A black figure, I know it's you."

"In the woods, I talk to him." Miriam surveyed her feet. "I suppose it's daft."

"Unhinged, some would say." They both laughed.

"I hate Joshua being alone in the woods."

Hannah pulled Miriam to her, arms around her shoulders. "I don't mean to make it harder."

"You don't." Miriam melted into her. "You're the only one I can talk to."

With a hint of a smile, Hannah squeezed her. "Besides Joshua."

"And sometimes Luke," Miriam added. "He's always ready to listen."

"You've worn yourself out," Abraham said, sitting away from the fire before supper. She didn't doubt what he saw, skin pale, cheeks hollow, but it wasn't nights on the floor or walking the woods that did it.

"What happened?" she asked, as she set the table. "*That* night?"

"God's will." He scratched at the scars on his neck. "That's what happened. The boy's dead; the girls are not."

He was right. For hours at a time she had no idea where they were. Working, but where? Adah had become the mother hen, Emma, Mary, and Rebecca under her wing. But Miriam couldn't abandon her boy.

At bedtime, she changed Abraham's dressings as usual. The raw pools on his hands, chest, and legs and behind the knees had the look of ponds in drought, the wet center all but gone, the skin a strange new landscape.

She helped Abraham into a clean nightshirt. "Tell me," she said.

He scowled, the crinkled side of his face pulling awry. "It's time you slept in a real bed," he said.

"You'd be alone."

"I mean it. Go." He settled on his pallet. "Tuck the girls in and leave me be."

Miriam retreated to the second floor, banished to listen instead of watch him writhe. The more he healed, the more pain he seemed to have. He dug his fingernails into his scars until they bled.

In the girls' bedroom, she sat on Adah's bedside first. "What would I do without you?" Miriam whispered in her ear.

"Mama," Rebecca said, sitting up in the farthest bed. "Is God everywhere?"

Sometimes, it was hard even for Miriam to remember God was *anywhere*. If Joshua made it to the woods, he was with God. She should be content.

She moved on to Emma's bed, then Mary's, tucking in their blankets and pulling up quilts. At Rebecca's, Miriam stretched out beside her.

"What's bloat, Mama?"

"You know, how sheep eat grain until their bellies puff."

"Yes, but Joshua wouldn't do that. Frau Gruber said—"

"No, he wouldn't." Frau Gruber again, of course, saying what festered in Miriam's imagination.

Miriam had seen animals in every stage of decay, from bloat to the scatter of bones. Farm animals and wild ones in the woods, Luke brought them to her attention.

"Can I keep Luke," Rebecca said, "after Joshua comes home?"

Rebecca's faith in his return hit Miriam harder than anything Hannah or Abraham had said. She saw the futility of her dreams, her hopes ridiculous.

He wasn't coming home on his own. Miriam had to find him. He needed a proper burial.

CHAPTER 15

Devilment

Joshua got used to Sylvie's taunting, but he didn't get used to eating in the barn. True, he ate himself full at every meal, but he ate alone and when he finished, a hollowness remained. Sometimes food isn't the most important thing.

He watched the family at meals as he passed the window where he'd first seen them. Not always happy, but a family. Looking felt like poking a bruise.

Was that how Luke had felt, a stray relegated to the toolshed? A lucky stray, thanks to Rebecca.

For days after Father said no to keeping the dog, the animal skulked in the hedgerows, appearing at dusk, sometimes as dawn broke. His limp worsening, he kept his body low to the ground. Joshua sneaked pans of scraps meant for the pigs, and left them hidden far from the barn.

Come Sunday dinner after service, Father sat at the men's long table, the littles clearing the Elders' plates. Talk of Father's sermon had wound down when Rebecca crawled onto his lap.

"I could be a Good Samaritan," she said, "if I had help." She looked Father full in the face. No one could miss her worry.

"He's half-dead in the hedgerow," she said. "And I can't carry him."

"Who is?" said the closest Elder. He leaned forward, placing a hand on her knee.

"A Plain dog," she told him. "He must be Plain—he's all black."

The Elders' mouths twitched at the corners.

"It's nothing to smile at," she said, her eyes shiny with tears. "He'll die."

"She's taken your message to heart, Abraham." The men chuckled in their beards. "Now it's your turn."

Father kissed Rebecca's nose. "Of course we'll take him in." Soft words for her, but over her head, a glare for Joshua.

Late that afternoon, he and Adah had filled buckets at the pump, heated the water, and, outside again, soaked the dog. He sat in the round washtub, Mary and Emma lathering him. Twice, it took, to rinse the filth.

With Mama's help, they cleaned the fester from a gash in his flank, salved it, and they took turns brushing snarls from his fur.

From then on, Luke had helped run sheep and cows to fresh pasture. He even herded chickens, and never a feather in his mouth.

"One fine day, he'll—" Father didn't finish, but Joshua knew: *A stray is a stray. A thief or, worse, a killer.* It's what strays did. But Luke wasn't that kind of stray.

To prove the Baylors just, Joshua ate unwashed like a pig. In his solitary circle of light, he rolled cheese in bread and pushed it into his mouth with the heels of both hands. He drank soup from the bowl without aid of a spoon. He licked crumbs off his shirt, rubbed dribbles of milk from his cheek, and wiped his nose on a sleeve. How quickly he'd forgotten the blessing of a full stomach.

He sat on an upside-down pail, a plate on one knee. Feeling sorry for himself, he didn't see Sylvie outside the lamplit circle until her voice came out of the dark and made him drop the plate.

"You belong in the barn," she said. "I don't know why Mama wants you inside."

"To stay?" The wild hope just popped out.

"Don't be stupid," she said. "Christmas dinner. Tomorrow." And she left.

In high excitement, he pumped buckets of water ready for a dawn bath.

Come morning, silence woke him, the windows plastered white with snow. He lay in a nest of three blankets covered with straw, cozy, just his nose in the cold. He vaulted from the manger, hurried at chores, and, after milking, carried the two buckets of cold water to the gutter behind the cows. He stripped his clothes and dumped one bucket over his head before soaping his naked self with a rag. He scrubbed every inch, the soap brown and slippery through his hair, over his goose bumps, neck to burned shins, and between his toes. Out of habit, he watched for Sylvie's peering eye, and rinsed with another bucket of freezing water. Gasping, he hopped out of the gutter and donned clean clothes.

The world outside billowed white, snow to his knees. A rock buried from sight brought him down. His arms high in alarm, he fell as if into a feather bed. Falling without hurt made him laugh. He slogged toward the house and every few paces threw himself on the snow's tender mercies.

"Are you daft?" Sylvie yelled from the open door. "What's wrong with you?"

"Does it always snow like this?" he asked.

"What, this dusting?" she said. "Wait till it really snows."

Was there no end to what he didn't know?

He reslicked his hair. Spine straight, elbows at his ribs, he crossed the threshold into the kitchen as if he'd never been there before, the house thick with the smell of roast turkey stuffed with thyme and sage. A pine tree in the parlor had been decorated with bows, and a huge fire warmed the room.

Sylvie disappeared, and Mrs. Baylor entered the kitchen. She'd changed her men's clothes for a simple dress the color of eggplant and fussed with a bauble in the middle of her collar.

"Help me with the pin." She stood before him, chin high. "Here," she said, "behind the cameo. It goes under the hook." She moved her hands so he could see a woman's face carved in an oval of gold ribbon. "My one unsold treasure." She sighed. "Bart gets the damn family out here and has the nerve to die."

Close in the center of her warm breath, Joshua fumbled with the pin. Her sigh, the warmest Sylvie's mother had been. If she were Mother Biddle, he'd have hugged her, but as Sylvie liked to remind him, he was the hired hand.

"Look at you, all cleaned up," she said. "You look nice." Mama had called him handsome. Now, no one would with his face all scars and a scattering of little red spots on cheeks and chin. He felt a flush start.

Sylvie danced into the room. "Don't stand there gawping." She shoved him. "Get to work."

"Sylvie," her mother snapped. "If you worked half as hard as Joshua, we could sit at the end of a day."

The flush climbed higher, and he busied himself peeling butternut squash.

As they worked, he became more comfortable. Walnuts they'd shelled the day before waited on the worktable. He measured flour for piecrust, added salt, cut in butter hard from the larder. A sprinkling of water, a quick squeeze, and he rolled the crust before mixing egg, sugar, and nuts.

Runt and Joe came through the door. Joe first. "Not ready yet?" His clean clothes marked the day as special, but he showed no sign of water.

"Did you bathe?" Mrs. Baylor asked Joe.

"I washed my face," said Runt. "And *you* didn't notice."

Mack came in, pushed along by John. "Found him hiding in the hayloft."

"I'd rather skip dinner than bathe." Mack shrugged.

After another hour, the turkey done, Mrs. Baylor took off her apron. "Dinner," she called. They all gathered and, with a great scraping of chairs, settled at the table.

She carried the crisp bird, setting it before Grandpa, and sat at her end, Sylvie beside her. Joshua got a short stool from under the worktable.

"Here by me." Mrs. Baylor smiled and pointed at the corner between herself and Sylvie. Joshua swallowed hard. It would be safer next to Grandpa. God only knew what Sylvie might do under the table. Joshua slid his stool close to Mrs. Baylor and straddled it. He sat a head below everyone else, his eyes level with Sylvie's chest.

Joe leaned forward around Sylvie for a better view of Joshua. The others followed suit, looking down from on high as if they'd spotted a stinkbug.

"Well," Grandpa said. "Not a very festive group." He picked up the long carving knife, the two-tined fork, and slashed them together. "Glad you could make dinner," he said to Joshua as if he'd turned down countless invitations.

Grandpa stretched his arms, and with one stroke of his knife, the leg and thigh fell from the huge bird. "That's mine." Joe held out his plate.

"Thigh's the best part." Sylvie put her hand high on Joe's thigh. He smacked it.

"Sylvie." Mrs. Baylor, half out of her chair, thumped the table's edge. "Your room or I'll tan your hide."

"What'd I do?"

"Edith, she didn't mean anything," said Grandpa. "It's Christmas. Let her stay."

"No. Upstairs now."

Sylvie stomped upstairs. Mrs. Baylor and Grandpa traded hard looks.

Grandpa stripped half the bird to another platter and passed the meat. He helped himself to mashed potatoes and sent the bowl on. The others dug in. All attention moved to the food, and without Sylvie at the table, Joshua savored every bite.

From Christmas on, by Mrs. Baylor's decree, he ate inside, the others watchful. They'd never trust someone who bathed on a regular basis. Still, if Sylvie would leave him be, he could make this his home.

Thick snow compacted. The top crust slick and glaring in the sunlight, Joshua spread ash on the paths he'd shoveled from house to barn, barn to trough, to the lambing shed and the woodshed.

"Keep the damn doors shut," Grandpa bellowed over talk at the breakfast table.

He wanted the animals inside the barn. Any foolish enough to venture out slid if they were light, landing downhill of their destination. If they were heavy, a leg might go through the crust and break. Lambs born early bounced about the inside pen, their long tails caked orange with milk-run manure.

"Time to dock those tails," Joe said. "Runt's turn."

"It's John's, not mine." Runt angled his chair from the table, stretched his legs, and locked his hands behind his head.

Mack kept his head down. Joshua worked a mop in front of the stove, docking tails not his job, though he'd done plenty at home.

His sisters wouldn't watch as he tied off the wiggly tails close to the rump and finished the job with one whack of the hatchet. Rebecca once asked how he'd like it, if she chopped his little finger. His little finger wouldn't make him sick.

Sylvie wasn't so squeamish. She'd watch anyone do anything

as long as it didn't mean work for her. Mostly Joshua managed to ignore her when she admired his ankles now showing below his pants, or mocked his voice when it cracked.

"You need new clothes," Mrs. Baylor said. "New to you, in the attic."

Joshua hoped Sylvie wouldn't come. The times her mother and he worked side by side, Sylvie out of sight and mind, Mrs. Baylor seemed warmer, yet hesitant in some way as if she didn't trust him, not comfortable like Mother Biddle.

Some evenings, they all sat in the parlor after supper. Mrs. Baylor said Joshua had a civilizing effect, that his mother would be proud. He knew it was a compliment, though his mother would be mortified to think someone thought she harbored pride.

A week later after the midday meal, the kitchen put right, Mrs. Baylor said, "Joshua, let's check the attic." She wiped her hands on a towel. "We're rich with hand-me-downs. Something's bound to fit."

"You first, Joshua." Upstairs and through her bedroom, he went first on the attic ladder, saving the embarrassment of climbing into her skirts.

In the low room they surveyed the stacked trunks, some domed, some flat topped, all strapped shut. She unbuckled several and lifted the tops. At one she stopped.

"My other life," she said, with a far-off look. "I didn't always live so rough. Not after I married Bart, that is." She lifted out a fancy white dress. "Back east we had a large house." She held the dress to her body and looked down. "My wedding dress. Bart had it made in France." She gave a slight smile. "To tell the truth, I think his mother bought it, afraid of what I might buy, left to my father's tight pocket." She compressed her lips to a line. "Boston ladies have rules about what to wear."

"Where I come from," he said, "we have rules too." He sat cross-legged on the lid of a trunk. "We wear black. Everyone the same. The only difference in our clothes is the hand that stitched them. By the time we were seven, my sisters and I knew how."

"You sew?" She set the dress aside and pulled out a blue one.

"Harness and shoes," he told her. "With four sisters I didn't need to sew clothes."

"Bart wouldn't do women's work to save his soul." She spun with the dress. "None of the boys would. When their mother died, Grandpa and Bart's younger brothers moved in. They never did live up to Grandma's standards, and it's been downhill since. Grandpa doesn't have the grit to push." She gave a mirthless laugh. "Then there's Sylvie." She lifted a small book from one of the trunks, the book smaller than the Bible Joshua kept in his manger bed.

"What's that?" he asked. Curious. No other books in the house.

"My dreams," she said, smiling, and riffled pages full of longhand. "You know what I miss most?" She didn't wait for an answer. "Friends. Not that I have the time." She closed the book and tucked it in the bottom of the little trunk. "We used to go in and out of each other's houses, sharing secrets. Now—" She scowled. "What I have is Sylvie playing at being a woman. Not what I thought life would be."

She folded the dresses. "But that's not why we're here." She opened another trunk. "No, these are Joe's. He was taller even then, and broad. You'd swim in his."

She lifted another lid. "These, Bart's when he was young. Good for something, hooked rugs if nothing else." She held up a pair of work pants, then a darker pair.

"Church pants. Hardly used. He figured every church is like Syd's." She pulled out more pants, and two heavy jackets. "You better choose or we'll be here all day with me mooning over the old days. Take as much as you want."

"Thank you, Mrs. Baylor," he said.

"I'd like to think we're friends." She handed him the church pants. "Call me Edith. I won't feel so old."

Joshua peeled down to long johns Grandpa had given him and pulled the new pants up. While he buttoned the front, she slid a black dress from another trunk. Her eyes clouded as she held the cloth to her middle. The black made her look like Mama.

Mrs. Baylor—Edith—closed her eyes. Joshua wanted to comfort her. He only knew how Mama used to comfort him, holding him pressed close and safe. Joshua could do that. He could, but he didn't move.

"So good-natured," Edith said. "Easy to talk to."

Joshua hoped she was talking about him. She could be his mother, one who confided, someone who wouldn't leave him by the roadside like Mother Biddle.

He felt favored, if not above the others—well, yes—above the others. A place in the family. He wanted to skip.

The pants fit, and he handed her the old ones. Leaning in, she took them, her eyes warm, a look for a moment like he was the center of her mothering world. She brushed hair from his forehead. He smelled the morning's corn bread lingering in her clothes mixed with a musty trunk smell. She looked in his eyes as if searching for more secrets.

She kissed his cheek, and he was back in his mama's kitchen. He threw his arms around Edith's neck and breathed her in. The corn bread was the same, but the underlying scent differed. He lifted his head, and her lips were right there touching his. Hers soft. Moist.

Surprised, he opened his mouth. Her eyes and his, so close together, widened. His muscles clenched. Goose bumps exploded all over his body. His privates poked at the new pants, and he stumbled backward.

"Oh," she said, hands up, fingers splayed. "I—I didn't—"

He slid down the ladder, hit the bedroom floor with a thump, tripped down the stairs, and staggered out of the house, his knees threatening to pitch him on the ground.

For the rest of the day, he kept his eyes on his chores. But his mind slipped off.

What happened? How did *what* happen?

He couldn't see it clearly, what he'd done, what she'd done. Wrong whatever it was, and more wrong as a piece of him fought to bring the feeling back.

That night, she made baked apples. At the table, she didn't look up from her plate. The others dug in, spoonful after greedy spoonful. He took a bite and couldn't go on, the sugaring too sweet, the apple too tart.

After dishes, he retreated to the barn. His new clothes waited in the manger. She'd been there. She'd touched the blankets. He pressed his fingers to the rough wool, breathed in, hoping for her scent. It wasn't there.

A breath of spring hung on the cold evening air. In the trees, hard buds loosened. Soon the time of birds and fireflies. Joshua missed his sisters, especially Rebecca with her eye for the birds, marking the joys he might otherwise miss.

On his way to late milking, pail in hand, Sylvie skipped into his path and ran backward as he pushed on toward the barn. "You're no fun. Work, work, work. Is that all you think of?"

He kept moving as if she weren't there, and she danced backward right into the barn. They passed the horses and on to the cows. He lit the lamp hanging from a rafter. She hovered, a gnat buzzing his head.

As he reached for the milk stool, she grabbed the back of his collar, pulled the jacket off his shoulders, and locked his arms at the elbows. A button popped. The pail bumped against his knee. She rubbed her nose on his neck.

"Sylvie, don't be disgusting."

She shoved him against the cow's manger.

His intention to ignore her gone, he pushed her with his shoulder. "Scat." Another button popped. The cow stomped her cleft hoof.

"Now look what you've done," he said in a harsh whisper. With all the kerfuffle Bertha wouldn't let down. "If there's no milk, it's your fault." He broke free, shrugging his jacket onto his shoulders. He set the pail under Bertha's udder, then sat on the three-legged stool. Before he could pull in close, Sylvie, her hand on his head, threw a leg over his knees. She mounted his lap and pressed her nose to his. "Aw," she said, "are we getting mad?"

"Yes, I'm mad." He tried to shake her off.

"All that muscle." She poked his chest. "And women's work is what you do. Are you a woman? Let's see."

She tipped the stool. He went over backward. His arms flew above his head, and he flopped in the straw. Straddling him, Sylvie pushed up his shirt.

"You *do* have titties." She grinned. "Little teeny tiny titties."

He struggled, afraid he might hit her, but she clamped his hips with her knees.

"And look at that," she said. "They're—" She flicked the nubs standing brown and hard on his chest.

"AAAAH!" Goose bumps. The fizz, and devilment bold in his pants.

"Oooooh," she said. "What have we here?"

A bellow at the barn door raised her up and standing in one fluid motion. Joshua leapt up, legs in seven stages of jelly. He righted the stool and sat at Bertha's side.

Grandpa's irritated voice came out of the dark. "Where are they?"

"I saw them go in." Joe's voice. "They're here."

Joshua looked over his shoulder at Grandpa advancing past the stalls, a lamp held high. Joe followed, then Mack, John, and Runt, fists ready.

"Why, Gramps," said Sylvie in a high child's voice, "we're right here with Bertha. Her milk won't come down."

Lordy, that girl sure could spin a yarn.

Joshua had a place at dinner, knife and fork, a plate, and little welcome to it. He didn't dare lift his eyes. Edith kept her distance. Would Sylvie?

The dinner dishes were his to wash, and after, he walked to the barn. The moon lit his world with blue shadows. He readied his bed in the manger, but before he undressed, Grandpa and the uncles pressed into the stall. John held a lamp while Runt and Joe picked Joshua up under the arms and walked him out. They sat him on the milking stool. All scowls, their faces circled above him.

"Tell me, boy," said Grandpa, his voice quiet. "What happened today?"

Joshua looked at the man's boots, the shine gone. "I wish I knew."

"Come, Joshua, you can tell me." Grandpa lifted Joshua's chin with a finger. "Did you touch her?"

"No!" he said. He looked Grandpa in the eye. "Plain people don't."

Grandpa tilted his head with a quivering smile. "They don't?"

"No," Joshua said. "I'd never. I'd never touch any—" A flush came hot to his cheeks. His eyes shifted. "The only person I . . ."

"The only person what, Joshua?" They all leaned in close.

"My . . ." He didn't want to admit his sin out loud. "My father . . ."

Their mouths fell open. "You touched your father?"

Joshua chewed at his lip. "Yes," he said, wringing his hands. "I . . . I struck him. In the face."

They all straightened, leaning away as from some vile thing, their hands high for the downward strike. Joshua cowered, eyes closed. And *slap*, he heard it, but didn't feel it. Their hoots and hollers rained down.

He opened his eyes to the circle of men smacking their thighs and gasping for breath. He looked from one to the other.

When they finally quieted, Grandpa said, "A word of advice." He staved off another laugh and clapped Joshua's back. "You're not a bad kid, but—"

Here his words trailed off, and all eyes shifted to the door, where Sylvie stood, a mad gleam in her eye. "You wouldn't think him so good if you knew the truth," she said. "I couldn't tell you. He threatened if I told, he'd—" She rushed to Grandpa, and sobbed into his chest.

"Shh," Grandpa said. "Shhhh, shh." He handed her off to Runt. "In the house." Then turning on Joshua. "You had me fooled, you little weasel. I'll make you—"

"Heeey," said Runt. "No fair, I'll miss the fun." He pushed Sylvie, who tripped against Joe. In the scramble, Joshua dashed out the door and headed for the woodlot. *No, they'd expect that*; he cut back behind the house.

From its shelter, he watched the uncles in blue moonlight, followed by Grandpa, followed by Sylvie, shouting, "Get him." They disappeared into the woods.

Joshua circled around the barn. Inside, he threw his few belongings into his satchel, blanket over his shoulder, and took off through the back door, knowing it was a matter of minutes before the others figured he'd doubled back. One stride toward freedom, and Edith blocked his path.

Gray streaks of her hair showed blue. She gave him a wan smile. "I know you, and I know Sylvie," she said. "You didn't do anything." She brushed a hand across her face as if a cobweb had fallen on her. "With you gone," she said, so soft he could hardly hear, "I'll have no one to talk to."

He made to push past her. She laid a hand on his arm. "Please, Joshua." Her eyes held his. "I'm sorry about the attic."

He couldn't look at her. The Devil's tail had been his.

Shouting came from the other side of the barn.

"Quick." She pushed him. "Run."

Seconds later, she called by the house, "Did you find him?"

Joshua ran to the nearest tree and stood straight, sucking in his belly, thin as possible, the way he'd been in bed waiting for Father to pass. His heart pounded.

"Son of a bitch." Grandpa at the side of the barn. He had to be peering right at Joshua's tree.

"You sure he wasn't in the woodlot?" Edith shouted.

"That yellow-haired rat, we'll track him."

He may as well carry a torch, his yellow hair a signal to any gathering posse. Thank God for Mr. Biddle's hat. He crushed it on his head.

Strips of ice moldered in hedgerows and died. Joshua slipped deep into Missouri, with farms, one on a rise, and miles later another nestled in a valley.

They'll shoot you, Father taunted from his throne in Joshua's head. And Sylvie was to blame, what a liar. If she stood before him, he'd whack her—or want to. Was it a sin, just wanting to whack someone?

Awake or asleep, he never took off the hat. Farmers who hired let him go after the crop came in, hay, then corn, hay again in late summer, the families nice enough. Enough food. Perfectly friendly to the hired hand. They appreciated him the way they did a good scythe. At least he wasn't crumbs.

The rolling hemp fields gone to tobacco, a bigger farm kept Joshua through auction time. After that, shelter and food would have to be borrowed, begged, or stolen.

He wouldn't be a beggar, and no one would loan him anything. He'd been a thief, and would God forgive him? Repentance was the key, and he did repent with all his heart. He couldn't steal again. Joshua might not wear black, or have the right length hair, but inside, where it counted, he held his beliefs, a core he wouldn't abandon. Forgiveness wouldn't come twice.

At the first snow, dark threads crossed and recrossed below the white surface. A mouse popped up and burrowed again, zigzagging in search of food. He wondered if he and the mouse would survive winter.

PART II

Forging Mettle

CHAPTER 16

His Bone and His Flesh

By January, whiteouts threatened. Blizzards could leave a body walking in circles, then frozen solid an arm's length from safety. Not a bad way to go, some said. Better than a posse set on stretching Joshua's neck.

With the snow, he eked a living cutting wood, though most farmers had a supply laid in. He spent a week here, a few days there. Some days he lived on sufferance alone, and it felt wrong. He should return come spring and work for free. A risk he couldn't take.

Spring took forever to come, with Joshua curled in a lean-to, or a straw-lined burrow waiting out a storm. He listened while sleet scoured the frozen land, and slept to pass the time. Dreaming of home, almost like being there.

Awake, he railed at thoughts of Sylvie. With an east wind cutting his back, anger kept him warm, and Monte Rey pulled his steps.

After two winters of living by his wits, Joshua feared the next burrow he dug would be his grave. He had to make a change, and in a good moment, his hat pulled low, God smiled on his prayers, guiding him into a group of wagons, horses, and riders. Late fall shoppers, not a posse, thank the Lord.

Headed for Westport, they said, a town on the Missouri, north from the City of Kansas. They fetched up at a livery stable on the outskirts of town. Joshua wormed his way into the foreman's graces, becoming a guard by night, stable hand by day. The men all talked of the West.

Like Frau Lentz's brother, they told of an endless summer land. They made it sound real, a land greener than home, and he imagined the crops hard work could grow.

"Come spring, things'll get a mite busy," Boss said. "Cross the river, there's where the Overland starts, a staging field for the trail, hundreds of wagons." Joshua itched to be with them.

By spring, Joshua sixteen and some, he itched all over. Fuzz turned to bristle on his cheeks, red fur on his chest, under the arms, and between his legs. But his discomfort was nothing compared with that of the fellow twitching by the stable door. Early morning and the man waited on a team of new-bought Percherons. He scrubbed at the waist of his tan pants, scratched his armpit through a pleated shirt, loosened his string tie. His fingers gouged beneath a spotless Stetson.

"You all right?" Joshua asked.

The man crooked a finger, and close to Joshua's ear, he took off his hat. "You have a doctor here?" he whispered.

"Sure." Joshua squinted at red lumps on the man's neck. The sight reared him back. "But he's out of town."

"Fleas," the man said, and scratched under the long hairs he'd brushed over his smooth head.

"Well, that's a blessing." Joshua laughed.

"Not to me. I'm bound for California, and the wife won't let me in the wagon."

A black speck leapt into his collar.

"I know a cure," Joshua said. "An old fox trick. All you need is water and a twig."

The man looked at Joshua as if he had horns. "What do you take me for?"

"Amish don't lie," said Boss from the stable.

"Fox jumps in the river," Joshua said. "No fooling. The fleas crawl to his nose, from his nose to the twig, he lets go, and the fleas float away." He spread his hands. "You'll have to burn your clothes."

"That's ridiculous." The man shoved Joshua.

"You got eggs, they'll hatch."

The fellow kicked dirt with a shiny black boot. "Forget it," he said.

"Suit yourself." Joshua went back to work, while the man paid Boss.

"And I need a saddle horse," the man said. "A good one."

"Tomorrow's best I can do."

The next afternoon the fellow came back dressed in dark brown pants, a smooth shirt, no tie. In the stable yard, he nodded at Joshua. "The name's Lewis," he said. "Captain Sedrick Lewis the Third." He held out his hand.

Captain of what? Joshua wondered, and shook the offered hand. "I'm Joshua."

"Well, Josh, your foxy trick worked. How can I repay you?"

Joshua waved away his thanks.

"Harness the Percherons," Boss said. "I'll saddle the mare."

Captain Lewis dogged Joshua as he brought each horse from its stall and buckled them into a team. "Manifest Destiny," Lewis said as if Joshua had asked a question. Lewis's voice deepened, sounding like Father at his sermons.

"What's that?" Joshua asked.

"Westward expansion, boy, by the U.S. government. As a man of standing, I'm spreading democracy. Know it or not, everyone wants it." He coughed and palmed his hair. "Not cheap. The wagon cost me a thousand, made specially big. Plus horses. Mercy, that's the wife, wouldn't drive oxen and now she tells me she can't drive horses. All she has to do is hold the reins—any fool can do it. You could do it."

"What about you?"

"A captain doesn't drive, but you know horses—you could start now."

"He can't," Boss said. "He works for me. 'Sides, you wouldn't want him—he's a street rat, not fit for a man's family." Boss's words true, Joshua's hopes collapsed.

"But you said—" Lewis squinted at Boss.

"That was Pennsylvania. This is Missouri."

Captain Lewis mulled for a minute; then his face cleared. "Oooh, you want him yourself."

"He stays. That's final. Now take your horses and git."

"Too bad," the captain said, and puffed his chest. "Mine's the biggest wagon at the field, red top-boards—you can't miss it."

Two days later before daybreak, like the street rat he was, Joshua sneaked out of the stable, satchel in hand, blanket on his shoulder once more, and headed downriver.

He caught a skiff across and watched the sky go pink as the stable grew smaller.

At the opposite shore, all roads led west. He dragged Mr. Biddle's pistol from his satchel. Strapped on, the gun hung heavy as sin. Hindrance or help, he wasn't sure.

Captain Lewis could have changed his mind. He could've stumbled on someone the Baylors knew. Joshua pulled at his hat.

Sun burned off the haze, and he claimed the new day. The open land invited him west. No more mouse-run tunnels. Joshua believed in Monte Rey.

Three miles out, the staging field spread, a brown wound in the distant green. The brown filled with white-topped wagons seething like maggots.

An hour later, he reached the edge, walking among people and animals crammed together. Animals that pulled and ones that followed, food on the hoof, all in a state of nerves too high to stand still.

The animals he could manage, but the people! Could they be his bone and his flesh? It didn't seem possible.

Harried men checked their stores, retied tie-downs, topped the water barrels lashed to their wagons. Horses shook their heads as if at unspeakable foolishness. Oxen bellowed. Women's chatter rose to laughter and spilled over in tears, their incessant babble salted with words Joshua didn't know.

He spent hours wading in this shifting herd, searching the bright-colored top-boards, dodging piles of manure ripening in the sun. He passed too close to a tailgate and a dog snapped at his neck. Others cowered under their wagons threatening his ankles.

As dusk settled, small fires popped up, and bubbling pots gave notice of coming supper. Men drifted in groups around big fires, arguing over who would lead and what route. The southern pass? North to the Platte? And then he saw him, Captain Lewis.

He stood on a crate waving a piece of paper. "We'll follow the river to Fort Bridger." A circle of men squatted below him, their attention shifting from him to a soft-spoken man in their midst, dark hair hanging over his ears, strands caught in a week's growth on his jaw. He had his own creased map. "Show me, Lewis."

"My map's official, George." Lewis lurched off the crate. "We'll supply at Laramie, and—"

"No." A young man, with hair longer and more yellow than Joshua's, bounded to his feet. "George Hastert is captain, not you."

"Looks a boozer," Lewis said. "Not captain material."

Yellow-hair brought up his fists. "Not so."

"Easy does it, Sven," said George. "Don't be a hothead."

"We don't need Fancy Pants."

Lewis turned to a chinless fellow beside Sven. "What do *you* think?"

"I've a wife and two daughters. A military man's good against Indians."

Lewis went around the circle, the men all talking at once. The only woman in the group held her enormous belly with both hands as if the baby might fall out.

"We're in a hurry," she said. Her husband put a meaty arm around her shoulder.

"I know shortcuts," said Lewis. He patted his map, then smiled at the one silent person. "Sam?"

As Sam got to his feet, a small boy broke through the circle and threw himself at Sam's long legs. "Daddy, when—?"

"Not now, James. Off to bed." He spun the boy by his shoulders, tapped his rump, and sent him out of the circle. Sam, sinewy, clean-shaven, hat rolled at the brim—he took off the hat as he spoke. "Seems they want you." A sandy forelock fell in his eyes. "But getting there counts, not speed." He looked around the group. "I'm leery of shortcuts."

"So it's settled." Lewis swaggered toward George, thumbs in his belt. "No hard feelings." He looked down over his belly at George seated on the ground.

"We'll see how it goes," George answered.

"Pudding is proof," said yellow-haired Sven, his mouth set in a hard line.

Lewis laughed. "You got it backwards."

"Me backward?" Fists up again, Sven's muscles bulged under rolled sleeves.

"Save your strength for the forge." George pulled him to the ground.

Lewis took a breath. "Now see here." Then he saw Joshua.

"Well, Josh, you made it." Lewis pulled him into the circle. "This is my driver, and something of a doctor."

The others stared. "Doctor indeed," someone said, seeing the youngest among them, a skinny kid in a slouch hat, brown hand-me-downs bunched at the ankle.

"We're done, and I'm hungry," Lewis said. "Come meet the wife." He guided Joshua to the wagon. Yes, the biggest.

"Stow your kit. Mess in a few minutes."

"Mess?" Joshua didn't like the sound of that.

Lewis's wife, standing by a small fire, wrinkled her nose.

"She hates military terms," Lewis said. "Mercy's Quaker."

Joshua saw no tremors as she took him in, hat to boots. Well, maybe he could see a slight shudder.

"Even children carry guns out here," she said, and rapped her spoon on the edge of the pot. His knuckles tingled. She may have been small and plump, but her jaw set firm.

"You tend your cooking, Mercy."

"Don't get your hopes up," she said. "I'm new to outside fires." She handed them each a spoon, a tin plate, and ladled-out meat swimming in gravy.

Joshua took a chewy spoonful. "Not a mess," he told her.

"It'll do," Lewis said. He wolfed down his portion. "The kid sleeps under the wagon. And, Josh, we need water." He strutted off.

Joshua fetched a bucketful from the river, and set to with the dishes.

"Took you long enough," Mrs. Lewis said.

"I had to go upstream."

"So far?"

"With all these people, the river's like an open night-jar," he said. So crude, Mama would be upset.

He washed the tin plates. Mrs. Lewis dried in prim silence.

He tried for polite talk. "How long has Captain Lewis been in the army?"

"He commanded a desk. He's not a killer." She drilled Joshua in the eye. "I hope I can say the same for you."

Why answer? She'd never believe he didn't hold with killing.

Even Father, heavy hand on the apple switch, hadn't joined the army. Mama said he couldn't kill, no matter how just the cause; Lincoln could manage without their kind. And Lincoln had.

Lying under the wagon, Joshua listened to Lewis and his wife, voices rising.

"How could you?" she whispered loud as a shout. "He's a ruffian."

"Do you want to drive?" Lewis didn't pretend to whisper.

"You don't know anything about him."

"He's from Pennsylvania like you. He's one of those Plain people."

"I'm more Plain than he is."

At dinner, in her light gray dress, she'd looked Mennonite without a cap. But Joshua got her point.

"His clothes are dark," Lewis said.

"That's dirt, and his hat's the wrong shape. Besides, no Amish carries a gun. He's a fake and a liar. Just look at his face all scruffy and scarred. He could kill us in our bed."

A liar, Joshua had to agree. And maybe a fake too.

From the skin out, he was English. But inside?

Isn't a plucked chicken still a chicken?

Nightmares threaded what was left of the night. He dug through his sins like so much manure: misspent Sabbaths, lies to Mother Biddle, and, worst of all, hitting Father, a sin second only to killing. Repenting often hadn't lessened his guilt.

He woke to overcast dawn and the plop of fresh manure, the captain's horses by the side of the wagon. The weight of last night's dreams hung in his head.

"Harness up," Lewis commanded with a kick at Joshua's bare feet.

Still in his clothes, Joshua pulled on boots, and dragged himself from under the wagon. He packed the holstered pistol in his satchel. Why torture Mrs. Lewis?

He found the harness while Lewis, at the tailgate, scooped oats. "Get the bridles on. I'll see to the nose bags," he said.

Surrounding wagons, hitched and ready, milled around Joshua as he untangled Lewis's straps and forced the stiff new leather into their buckles. Doubletrees with their chains lay spread on the ground, waiting for the horses.

Mrs. Lewis brought bread and cheese. Joshua ate as he worked.

Shadows under her eyes showed she was more bleary than he. He'd finally fallen asleep to the creak of timbers. She must have fretted all night.

Joshua ran the jerk line, a single rein, from the left lead horse back to the last one on the same side. The wheelhorse was the only one of the team with a saddle. Joshua could sit on the seat beside Mrs. Lewis or ride the wheelhorse, or walk by the rear wheel, close to the brake's wood handle. It angled up from a bar under the wagon. A pull on the handle, and the bar clamped wood blocks to the wheels. He tested the brake. The blocks hit the metal cladding, a blessing for steep hills, though none seemed in sight today.

He could walk behind the wagon if he wanted—that's how long the jerk line was—but he didn't know the horses, so he preferred to ride. The magnificent team, six dappled geldings, gray and massive, feathered from hocks to black hooves. At the withers, they stood taller than Mrs. Lewis. They would be daunting to anyone not used to horses.

After finishing the oats, the horses arched their thick necks and pawed the ground. They hated the sight of others pulling ahead.

Lewis's fine-boned mare jigged in place as he hauled his bulk into the saddle. He clutched the horn and took off at a canter. "Line up."

Joshua helped Mrs. Lewis onto the wagon. Riding beside her wasn't inviting, so he chose the wheelhorse. The Percheron stood four hands higher than Lewis's horse. To mount, Joshua reached high, gripped the flat saddle, hopped to the stirrup, and climbed.

At the click of his tongue, the six horses leaned into their harness. Chains rattled. The wheels broke free with a jolt, and the horses surged forward.

Lewis circled back close by the wagon. "Come on, kid, head of the line. Get to it."

The others in their covered wagons and carts watched as he and Lewis passed. Most of them drove a four-horse team. At the tail of the line, George, the would-be leader, rode a horse beside a small ox-drawn cart.

Lewis glared. "Better keep up, George."

"Not to worry, Lewis," George said. "It's a light load."

"That's Captain Lewis to you," he said, and hurried on.

They passed the hothead, Sven, in his cart pulled by a two-mule team. A large yellow dog with a sharp muzzle ran beside them. Sven held a wooden box shaped like a figure eight with a stem. He pressed the box to his chin and sawed the strings with a stick, the sound like screeching cats.

"Quit your racket," said the captain. "No fiddling."

Joshua rubbed his ear. Sven made a sour face and set the box in his cart.

Lewis and Joshua slowed past the pregnant woman. "I'm fine." She nodded to Lewis. Smiling at her husband, she stroked his cheek. But when she stopped talking, her pretty smile faded.

In four more wagons, they came to the chinless father with two daughters. His wife, beside them, sat straight as a pine tree and just as prickly. The daughters looked to be thirteen and fifteen, same as Joshua's middle sisters would be.

An old guy came next, gray beard brushed smooth, white shirt, two rows of silver buttons down his vest. His wife sat beside him, even plumper than he and equally gray, a crinkle of worry around her eyes.

"Hello, Captain," a woman called from the next wagon forward.

"Janie." Lewis tipped his hat.

Janie held a little black dog, its hair as dark and curly as her own. She waved the dog's paw at Lewis. "Say hello to the nice captain, Bootsie."

Her husband beside her chewed on his handlebar mustache. "Please don't do that," he said.

"Aw, Brian, whyever not?" She tossed her hair and waved the paw harder. "Everyone loves Bootsie."

Brian rolled his eyes skyward. Janie's shrill laugh followed them up the line.

Beside the head wagon, Sam, with his little boy perched in front, rode a bay horse. Sam's two daughters sat on the bench next to their mother. She drove the team pulling a small schooner, blue with brighter blue top-boards. A metal brake handle stood within easy reach of the seat, oddly at the opposite end from Lewis's.

Her team jiggled bells attached to their harness. A jolly sound, though Joshua was sure he shouldn't think so, much too fancy.

Sam's wife wore a flowered dress. A bonnet hung down her back by the ties. Joshua touched his hat. She bobbed her head, a smile lighting her plain face. Eyes dancing, her nose crinkled the way his sister Adah's did when she laughed. He liked the woman already.

Lewis tipped his Stetson. "Bella," he said to Sam's wife, then tipped again to each daughter in turn. "Sadie, Frieda."

Bella gave him a tight smile. Sadie and Frieda whispered. The girls were small, about six and seven, much like his middle sisters when he left.

Lewis gave a curt nod. "Sam," his greeting full of authority.

One finger under the brim, Sam pushed his hat up, showing a spatter of freckles thick as the ones Joshua had lost. "Captain," Sam said, as curt as Lewis.

The line spread along the worn trail. Dew from the previous night dried, and dust blew on an east wind. They left a distance of five or six wagons between each, hoping the dust would clear. It merely thinned and sifted through their noses, Joshua's mouth like a gizzard full of grit.

"Come on, boy, let's outrun this stuff." Lewis blew his nose in a white handkerchief. So much for Sam's careful pace.

"Captain," Joshua said. "How far to the next ford?"

"I'll reconnoiter," he answered. "Now get going."

Sun climbed behind them, burning off the morning overcast. Without the captain, Joshua kept a slower pace. He rocked in rhythm with the wheelhorse. The trail rolled into the distance, barren edges giving way to nibbled grass. Nothing within a half mile grew tall enough to hide a woman squatting.

By noon a northwest wind tempered the sun and angled dust from the trail. Joshua took great gulping breaths, glad of clean air and a horse under him, his new home out there somewhere. He could almost see it.

Returning, Lewis called a halt. "Fifteen-minute mess, pass it on."

Joshua pulled his team to the verge. A shout went down the line, and the others pulled off. Mrs. Lewis brought out more bread, hard cheese, a tin cup of water. He bolted his and stretched on the ground. Lewis did the same with a groan, while his wife crawled into the wagon. After about half an hour Joshua said, "Gosh, I wish we had more than fifteen minutes."

Lewis heaved into the saddle. "Toughen up, kid."

By late afternoon, the wheelhorse's gait wasn't as smooth as Joshua first thought. Saddle-weary the first day, not a good sign.

He couldn't think how Mrs. Lewis fared on the wood bench where she sat, gray shoulders rounded, her bonnet lowered against the sun. She held to the seat with white-knuckle hands.

Joshua kicked free of the stirrups and slid off the saddle. The team kept walking. Knees sore, he staggered beside the wagon.

The trail curved, and they descended, the Percherons speeding up going into the swale. "Whoa, boys," he called, and twitched the rein. Instantly, they slowed, a well-trained team. For all that money, Lewis had himself a bargain.

They crested the edge of another swale and Joshua pulled himself to the seat beside Mrs. Lewis. Behind them, the wagon loaded chockablock with a bed set on top, not just the mattress with the head- and footboards laid flat, but the whole thing bolted together, legs running down through the barrels and chests, the wagon looking like a low-ceilinged bedroom. No small job to crawl in, especially for someone heavy as Mrs. Lewis.

He checked beyond the tailgate to the long line of wagons, Westport fading, then settled himself, one foot resting on the front board, the other braced under the bench. Ahead the western sky spread wide and welcoming.

His rump in the blister stage, Joshua sat the bench and wished for quick calluses.

Mrs. Lewis, knees together, feet tucked under, held on tight. She stared hard at the distance. Ruts shook their innards.

"Mrs. Lewis," he said. "You could sit on my satchel. Might ease the ride."

She continued watching the horizon as if praying for her destination to appear.

Time crawled.

Mrs. Lewis sighed.

She sighed again and slid her eyes in his direction. "If you wouldn't mind."

"I'd be glad." He hauled the reins and nipped to the tailgate.

Back on the seat, he beat lumps flat in the satchel and held it out. "I hope this helps." She nodded and settled the bag beneath the spread of her gray dress, and they set off well before Sam's wagon came near.

After another hour of sidelong looks, she said, "I must admit, you have manners."

"It's good of you to say." Joshua ducked his head and couldn't resist a smile. "My mother would be pleased."

The notion of his having a mother seemed to surprise her. She held his eye with hers, brooking no lie, and asked, "Are you Plain?"

"My family's Plain," he told her. "Some would say that makes me Plain, but I don't know. What would you say?"

Her face relaxed. "I'd say it's none of my business."

"But you'll sleep better tonight, won't you?" He kept his eye on the distant trail.

"What an odd young man you are."

The wagon swayed on, their quiet more comfort than not.

The wagon train cut the corner of Kansas and rolled into Nebraska, avoiding Omaha and Lincoln, the pace gentle, about fifteen miles on a good day. A lot less when it rained, what with unpacking, drying, and repacking.

In camp, Joshua hunted firewood. The men and Sven's yellow dog hunted meat. Joshua offered help. He showed them Mr. Biddle's sidearm. "A six-shooter," George said. "That's for varmints and two-legged rattlers."

"A snake with legs?" Joshua had never seen one.

"It's only a matter of time," George told him. And it was.

. . .

Who would have thought weeks of driving could be more tiring than walking? Joshua felt sorry for Mrs. Lewis. She couldn't ride a horse, and was too stiff to walk; her bones had to be rubbed to nubbins.

Through the Sand Hills, a sea of grasses leaned in the wind, seed heads bobbing, and from the depths, cranes startled up, their wings spread wider than Joshua was tall. Their long legs hung behind as they flew.

He thought the land flat until wagons, once in sight, disappeared. Alarming, that moment of feeling completely alone. The wagons reappeared, but the feeling lingered.

Rain and more rain. Joshua and Mrs. Lewis huddled under a shawl of canvas stiff with beeswax and linseed oil, the cloth for patching their wagon's cover.

In places, mud rose thick to the horses' fetlocks, three miles a day a blessing, and with no chance to dry. Everyone in camp grew testy.

Captain Lewis took a shortcut to the Platte River, then Grand Island. The wagons followed the south side; to the north George told of iron-wheeled boxes carrying freight and a few people, no horses needed.

Boxed up? It sounded god-awful.

Four more days of rain and on the fifth, sun. Janie's voice cut the morning. "Oh, Bootsie, can you believe it?" She spun into the center of the circled wagons, dancing and talking with her little black dog.

"Quit playing around and help." Her husband, Brian, spread wet clothes on the ground.

"No time," Lewis said, and mounted his horse. "We'll dry under way."

Grumbling came from every wagon, not so much at Lewis—

everyone knew they had to beat the snow through two sets of mountains. Or else.

Joshua couldn't imagine snow when the sun warmed them. He rolled canvas back to the last bow, exposing Lewis's possessions. A rising wind soon dried the top layer.

With the road still mud, the way slow, many walked the packed verge. A pleasure after sitting crouched for so long. The wagons bunched close. Janie chirped and laughed and turned her face to the sun.

"You better put on a bonnet," Brian said.

"No, the sun's too glorious." She danced in a circle.

"You'll turn brown."

"Sunburn's the problem," Mrs. Lewis said from under her bonnet.

"Doesn't bother me," Janie chirped.

Brian hooked her arm and pushed her toward their wagon.

"Stop it." Janie's voice rose. "Stop it, stop it."

Through dinner, Janie complained. Her face hurt into the night and the whole camp woke to her whimpers. Bella gave her salve. Grateful murmurs went quiet, and they all slept.

The next day, Janie hid blisters in the shadow of her bonnet. The wind increased. Pleasure in the power of drying ended. Without pause, the wind stampeded the grasses, silver and green to the edge of the earth.

The wind howled through the wagons, snapping the canvas. It whipped everyone's clothes, whipped their hair, whipped the horses' manes and tails, assaulted the ears till a body wanted to scream.

And Janie did scream. Joshua leaned around the canvas in time to see her, two wagons back, stand unsteady in front of the seat.

"I hate this. I hate it. I hate *you*," she shrieked at Brian, and jumped from the moving wagon. Bootsie, knocked to the ground, yelped. Brian leapt after, stumbling over the dog. Their wagon rolled slowly on without them, until Joshua stopped, and the line stopped.

Brian grabbed Janie's arm, swung her around, face to his chest, and held her tight. Wild as a greased pig, she flailed free. Bootsie ran circles around their legs, yapping, yapping at their knees. Brian kicked. The yapping grew more frantic. Janie scratched Brian's face.

He caught one wrist, then her free arm, and finally locked her spine to his chest. He bent her forward. The yapping shrilled, and Bootsie sank her teeth in Brian's pant leg. The dog wrenched. His pants tore.

From down the line came a yellow flash, Sven's dog, jaws wide. Bootsie yipped and the yellow dog, mouth full of kicking black fur, veered into the tall grass.

The grasses hummed. Janie's legs folded. She and Brian toppled in the trail.

The others gathered as Sven, his eyes as wild as Janie's, charged after the dog. "No, Thor! Drop it, boy, drop it!"

Sam took off after Sven, tackling him in the first wave of grass. "You'll get lost."

Sven tried to wriggle free. "Thoooor."

Sam held on until Sven rolled flat on his back, hands over his face.

After long minutes they dusted off and walked to the wagons. Sam had him by the arm. Sven, his head bowed, dropped to his knees beside Janie and Brian. "I'm sorry," he said. "Thor's never—"

"Get away from her," Brian snarled. "Just get away."

Wind made Joshua's eyes tear. At night, they stung when he closed them. Mrs. Lewis looked as if she'd been crying.

Rumors flew around the fire after supper. "He set that brute on poor little Bootsie," said the prickly woman with two daughters. Her mouth twitched.

"Prudence, how can you say that?" Sam's wife, Bella, rested a hand on her arm.

"I never liked him," said Prudence. "He talks funny. He's a foreigner." She shook her finger. "You never know what a foreigner might do."

"Come, now," Bella said. "He feels bad about Bootsie."

"He didn't look it, not so much as a crocodile tear."

"You're being unfair. He—"

"I'm surprised you take his side. You have young girls to protect too." Prudence stomped off, skirts billowing.

Later, across camp, she talked with the pregnant woman. Prudence waved her arms and pointed at Sven's cart. The women came over to the fire. "We ought to do something!"

"There's nothing to do," said the old man, stroking his beard. "It was an accident, a sad accident." He threw a log on the fire. Sparks jumped.

"Harold's right," George said, nodding at the old man. "Make no mistake, we'll need each other."

For days and days, Thor didn't return. Stopping each night, Joshua hammered long spikes straight into the ground and tied a rope between, the picket line long enough to attach the Percherons and not get tangled. He and Sven then searched for wood. They called into the distance, stringing out the dog's name. They backtracked, following anything that looked like a trail into the grass. Wolves howled in the distance.

Joshua would've been frantic had Luke been lost in the prairie. He couldn't let Sven go alone, and Sven was bound to go.

One night, after a week, they quit their search as dark settled. They dragged together at the edge of the grass. "We'll find him," Joshua said, and squeezed Sven's muscled arm.

Sven dropped his head on Joshua's shoulder and wept where no one could see. Not knowing what to do, Joshua patted his back as he would one of the Percherons.

Later, at the central fire, Sven swiped at red eyes while talking to Sam. "He's gone." Sven's voice cracked. "With us on the move, he'll never find me."

Brian dropped a log close to Sven's foot. "I hope Bootsie's stuck in his craw."

Near tears again, Sven looked past the wagons and into the dark. "He can't survive alone."

"Good." Brian bit his mustache.

"Come Indian Territory," George said, "you'll think different."

In his dreams, Joshua curled safe in the toolshed beside Luke.

CHAPTER 17

Gulch

F our weeks of Nebraska, the far end in sight, the grasses
shrank, and the earth turned scabby. Without wind, silence
hung heavy and hot.

The land stretched flat, the growth so stunted it couldn't feed
a sheep per acre. The trail shot straight to a dot on the horizon, a
dot that never seemed to move closer.

Lulled by endlessness, Lewis didn't notice the gulch till his
horse balked at the edge, the cut in the earth open and hungry.

Steep banks on both sides dropped away. Water crawled at the
bottom. Lewis held up a pudgy hand, and Joshua stopped. The
wagons bunched.

Sam reined in beside Lewis. George reined in seconds later,
more disheveled than ever. They all looked in the depths. Others
gathered.

Lewis scratched his head. "Sam, you ride south. I'll go north.
Find a better ford."

George close beside Lewis, his voice low, "A waste of time.
This *is* the ford."

"I'll be the judge of that," Lewis snapped for all to hear.

"Look at the trail. *Captain.*" George's voice matched Lewis's. "See how it widens—every train does the same. They gather here and beat the ground to hell. They moan. Those who don't know better waste time riding hither and thither, and in the end they ford right here. The tracks tell you."

Lewis studied the ford. His horse jigged. Sawing on the bit, he reined her in circles. "At least it's shallow," he said. "Not like the Badlands."

"He's never seen the Badlands," Mercy whispered to Joshua.

Lewis wiped his forehead with a red bandanna. "Might as well get started."

One more check at the brink, and he hesitated. "Sam, you first. I'll tell the others." He gave the mare her head, and cantered off.

Sam looked at George. "Chain brakes?"

"No, doesn't look that bad."

"I'll take Mrs. Lewis across first," Joshua said.

"Good, and check the footing."

Joshua stepped down the loose bank. Mrs. Lewis stood uncertain on the lip.

"Take my hand," he said. She leaned forward, hand out, and stepped off. Losing her balance, she fell into him and latched her arms round his neck. With Joshua still standing, they slid to the creek on crumbling dirt.

"Well done," he said. "Are you all right?"

"I think so." She adjusted her dress.

"Ready for the next leg?"

"How do we do that?" She cast a worried eye at the creek.

"Easy." An arm under her knees and one behind her back, he swept her off her feet.

"Oh!" She plastered her face against his ear, a stranglehold with one arm, the other clutching her skirt. She whispered, "Don't drop me. Please don't drop me."

The water came to his knees. He sloshed to the pebbled edge, and clambered up the opposite bank, slipping only twice. She kept her eyes shut tight.

Joshua set her on solid turf. "You're safe now, Mrs. Lewis."

She kept on clinging. He inclined his head and pried at her arms. "We made it, Mrs. Lewis. You'll be fine." Disencumbered, he emptied water from his boots.

"Thank you," she said. "At this point, Joshua, you could call me Mercy."

He did, but it wasn't easy, suspicion still in her wary glances.

On the other side, men and women gathered at the edge of the gulch. Lewis shouted across, "Get back here. Our wagon goes first." Lewis, a man of changeable mind.

Joshua splashed across and up the bank. "I'll check the brake," he said. At the left rear wheel of Lewis's wagon, he gave the handle a pull. The wooden blocks hit the wheels perfectly.

Lewis took the lead horse by its bridle and pulled as he stepped backward over the lip. The dirt gave way. His feet slipped out from under, and he fell on his face, yanking the bridle. The horse threw its head high and came over the edge, front hooves sliding.

Lewis screamed, scuttling out of the way, and pair by pair, the Percherons took to the bank. Front legs stiff, rear legs bunched into their haunches, they skidded, and the front wheels sank over the edge, tipping the wagon forward.

When the rear wheels went over, Joshua hauled on the brake with all his might. The wood blocks rubbed the iron cladding. His whole weight forced the blocks tight. The wheels stopped, but the wagon kept slipping on the bank. Without a good hold in the crumbling dirt, Joshua lost his footing. Legs milling, he swung from the brake handle.

Lewis looked back. "Stop horsing around."

Sam shouted from the bank, "Hang on, Josh."

"You can do it, kid," old Harold boomed. The others joined in shouting encouragement. Sam's son, James, shrilled, "Shosh-wa! Hooray!"

Joshua slid with the wagon into the creek, while Lewis ran, high-stepping through the water, ahead of the horses. He glanced over his shoulder as if the animals chased him.

"Stay straight," George shouted. "Lewis! Stay straight."

Lewis ran at an angle to the creek. The horses followed. Joshua let go the brake and dropped with a splash.

Halfway across, the right lead horse started to sink. The wagon listed to the right.

"Cripe," George shouted. "Bed's gone soft."

Joshua found the jerk line in the water and encouraged the horses to the left, but too late. He yelled at George, "We're mired."

George slid the bank and splashed to the lead horse. He tested the footing. Lewis, on the far bank, slogged up toward the lip. Nearing the top, he snapped at Mercy, "Give me a hand," and he threw his wet leg onto the firm ground. She held to his belt while he hauled the rest of himself after. "A hell of a ford," he yelled at George.

The other men, except old Harold, scrambled down to the mired wagon. Two held to each side, and at the tailgate Sven and Sam, with Joshua in the middle, put their shoulders to the wood. Sweat blotched their shirts.

George straightened the horses on the tongue. "Hup," he called. Chains snapped tight on the doubletrees, and George shouted, "Now, a test of your mettle, boys. Heave."

And they heaved. Mud sucked at their boots. Hooves squelched. Joshua's nose at Sven's neck, Sam's nose at Joshua's, he tasted the stench of effort.

"AND HEAVE."

Joshua could hear the strain bulging cords in George's throat.

Mouths open, the men groaned. Sven's neck and face went purple. Joshua felt his own face swelling, Sam's breath hot on his neck; the wagon inched through the muck to firmer ground.

George called again, "Hup." The horses' hooves crunched on pebbles, and the wagon surged out of the water. Without stopping, the horses took the bank, tipping what felt like the whole wagon on Joshua's shoulders.

"GO! GO!" Lewis shrieked from atop the bank. Ankles bent, feet slipping, Joshua dug for traction. Brian fell on one knee and up again. Their feet churned the dirt.

Horses gaining the crest, the wagon seemed to fly, the men with it for the last few feet. Out of breath, they fell on the turf. They laughed, mud all over. Brian clutched an elbow, George a knee. Joshua sat and banged mud from his boots.

"Oh God," Sven gasped, and whooping with success, they all grinned.

"Nice job," said Lewis, standing over them.

George stumbled to his feet. "Hope you're not too spent." He walked among them, nudging with his boot. One of a team, Joshua flushed, happy and full of mettle.

It took three days to get all the wagons across. Despite exhaustion, Captain Lewis kept up the pace. Time had shortened and nothing suited him. George stayed at the rear out of Lewis's way. Mercy was not so lucky, nor Joshua. Mercy bit her tongue. Joshua bit his, finding it easier to curb a horse than a bad temper.

Lewis rode beside the wagon. "Joshua, earn your keep. You're supposed to drive, not Mercy."

Joshua knew she'd been pleased with her new skill. He'd taught her weeks before, and Lewis knew it. She handed Joshua the rein.

Then in a complete about-face, Lewis said, "I'll drive." With effort, he swung his leg over the high cantle and slid to the ground. "That saddle's a killer."

He walked for a few paces. "Stop, for Christ's sake. I'm not going to walk."

"Sedrick!" Mercy pursed her lips. "Please don't swear."

"You can't call that swearing. You're not Christian." He looked at Joshua. "She says Christ was a prophet; she can't be Christian, right?"

"Please, Sedrick, not that again." She dropped her hands in her gray lap.

"Christian or no, I'm not walking."

"Fine," said Mercy. "Then Josh can ride your horse."

That sounded good to Joshua. He hopped off the wagon.

"Certainly not. Tie her to the tailgate." Lewis handed over the reins. "No one rides her but me. Besides, your clothes are filthy. I don't want you in my saddle."

"Have you looked at yourself?" Mercy asked.

Joshua tied the horse. Mercy could sort Lewis's mood; he'd join Sam.

Bella rode the seat with Sadie and Frieda; Sam on his horse rode behind, holding the jerk line loose in one hand. Four-year-old James ran beside the wagon.

James shouted at his sisters, "Chase me." Sadie, neat in her bonnet and flowered dress, ignored him. Frieda shook her unraveling braids.

"Coooome ooon!" He flounced to a stop, arms hanging at his sides. He spotted Joshua. "Dumb girls," he said. "They never play." Suddenly he perked up. "You could, Shosh-wa. Come on. Chase me." He yanked Joshua's shirttail and veered off in the grass.

At home, Joshua had chased sheep for shearing, chased cows out of the corn, chased chickens to butcher, but what was this chase to no purpose?

He stood in confusion as James roared out of the grass. "Then I'll be IT. You run." He crashed into Joshua with both hands out. "Got-cha!" He spun on his heel and ran. "You're IT! Now you tag me." His eyes danced. "Tag me. It's your turn."

"Ah." Joshua got the gist. "Here I come." James looked over his shoulder as he ran along the track.

"I'm going to get you," Joshua called, hands in talons above his head. Fingers flexing, Joshua wove in the road ahead of Sam's team. "You better hurry. I'm going to eat you up." He gained on James. The boy's backward glance sharpened. He shrieked, delight tinged with fear. Joshua closed the gap. James's eyes stayed on Joshua and not the road, legs in frantic motion getting in his own way.

Nearly on him, Joshua's hands above James's head, James shrieked in true panic. In front of the oncoming horses, he fell in the road, tears streaming. Joshua rolled him to the verge and they sat, out of breath, sage at their backs.

"I wouldn't really eat you, James." He put an arm around the boy's shoulder. "You know that, don't you?"

"I know." He gulped and wiped his eyes. "Again?" he asked, growing bold. He jumped to his feet and shouted, "Again, Shosh-wa. Again." He whapped Joshua's shoulder, and in a burst of speed galloped away.

Sam grinned. "I'll call him off, if you want."

"Don't you dare."

Over and over, they chased each other, until, limp as Rebecca's rag doll, James fell into Joshua's arms. He carried the boy, feather-light, to Sam's wagon and propped him in a pile on the seat beside his mama.

Bella hugged him close, her cheek on top of his head. He nestled into her breast, hidden by puffs at the tops of her tight sleeves.

Joshua's chest ached with a longing he thought he'd outgrown, the ache deep and abiding. He was breathless, his heart thumping; of course, he'd run like a madman all afternoon.

Bella gave a grateful smile. "You tired him out."

"It's the other way round," he told her, grinning like a fool. "He's done *me* in."

"Then the least we can do," said Sam, "is feed you."

One dinner led to another, and Mercy seemed pleased to have him gone.

Bella wasn't as good a cook, but sitting by the fire with her family flooded Joshua's cup.

James's sisters looked on his shenanigans with the patience of wiser beings. Nine-year-old Sadie, serious in her plain-colored dress, hair wrapped in braids around her head. Her hair light brown like her mother's, though not wound as many times.

Frieda, seven, her braids hung to the middle of her back. The girls' gingham dresses, the spit of their mother's with puffed sleeves, gave the look of broad shoulders. The sleeves nipped in at the elbow, narrowed to delicate wrists.

Intent at their jobs, they gathered kindling, washed dishes, and watched their little brother. When it came to bonnets, they weren't so attentive. Sadie's bobbed on her back, the tie in a bow at her throat. Frieda's bonnet hung from her hand and fell to the trail, needing retrieval at least once a day. Her nose peeled.

Rather than play, the girls preferred stories. One wet evening, drizzle made them all cranky. Leaving a smoky fire, Sadie, Frieda, and James changed into dry nightshirts and crammed in the wagon, each nested into a blanket.

"Good night," Joshua said, about to go to his own blanket under Lewis's wagon.

"Don't go," James said. "I'm not sleepy."

"Me either." Frieda wiggled for more room.

Sadie's usual calm snapped. "Stop kicking."

"How about a story?" Bella said. On the seat, she rested against Sam, who leaned against the bow, his arms around her, both protected by the slanted canvas.

"I'm tired of your stories," James said. "I like Shosh-wa's. They're real."

Last week between chases, he'd told James of finding Luke near starvation, how Rebecca sat on Father's knee and persuaded him to keep the dog. James told his sisters, and much to Sam's displeasure, they kept eyes out for a starving dog.

Nevertheless Joshua started in. "You know about Luke, so I'll tell about Goliath in the kitchen." Joshua straddled the bench on the opposite end from Sam and Bella. Despite their occasional crankiness, Joshua could tell how tied together they were. They smiled on the children as they settled. Warm and indulgent, they smiled on Joshua.

"Goliath is king of the farm," he said. "We called him Goli, the lead horse of my father's team. All six big, but Goli's bigger even than Captain Lewis's Percherons, only he's brown with long white fetlocks and a blaze down his nose. He has a black mane, and his tail's so long it whisks flies off his ears, not like the stubby-tailed Percherons." Joshua leaned his arm on one knee. "Well, one night after chores, I forgot to latch Goli's stall. When I left, he must have followed across the dooryard. From inside the kitchen I heard him clopping up the kitchen stairs. The house latch rattled, and there came his nose through the door, followed by big front hooves, then the barrel of his body, and finally his massive rump, the whole horse in the kitchen.

"My father stood up at the head of the table, stunned. Mother clapped a hand to her mouth. 'Great heaven,' she said, stumbling backward. Father slammed his fists on the table, clanging his knife and fork. 'A dog is bad enough—now you've a horse in the house. I forbid it.'

"Goli nearly filled the room, his withers higher than my head, his rump wider than the table. Father could say no all he wanted, but Goli, already there, had no room to turn.

"He nosed Father's loaf of bread on the cutting board, sniffing and snuffling, then lifted his upper lip and took a bite from the middle."

"He should eat his crusts," James said. "We have to."

"You're right." Joshua patted his leg. "Goli sniffed bowls and platters on the table, stopping at sliced roast beef. He sniffed again, threw his head sideways, and blew a soppy breath. His legs shook. He backed into logs stacked by the hearth, and bumping forward knocked over three chairs. With a swift kick, he smashed one against the table, leaving a gouge in the corner.

"His tail slashed the table, and dipped in gravy, it painted everything brown. Another slash swept bowls of squash and potato—crash—on the floor. They splattered everywhere. Finally he gave up and stood shivering.

" 'Get that animal out,' Father roared. Goli rolled his brown eyes at me as if to say, 'Oh please, do as he says.'

"I rubbed his nose, and pressed it to his chest. 'Easy, Goli, easy.' I backed him blindly to the door. He tapped his hoof on the top step, testing each step to the ground.

" 'Wash him good,' Father shouted as he and my sisters sat to their meal. 'Your dinner's on the floor when you finish.'

"I bathed Goli for the second time that day. We shared an apple, and I hugged his huge neck till he stopped shaking.

"He wasn't like you." Joshua poked James. "He didn't want to do it again."

Joshua didn't mention what happened that night in the woodshed.

Sam and Bella laughed and clapped, Sadie and Frieda joining in. James stood on the bench, hands on Joshua's shoulders. "Another. Tell another." He looked at his parents. "Pleeeease?"

"Another night," Bella said. "If we're lucky."

Sam mussed James's hair, then Joshua's.

That night in his blanket under Lewis's wagon, Joshua reminded himself: Mother Biddle liked him well enough, the Baylors too, at least Edith, and where did that end?

Would he be a horse in Sam's house?

No, Joshua knew it in the squeeze of his heart. If only Father had been like Sam.

CHAPTER 18

Breeding

October almost over, the light short, her days long. Thanks to Zeke at the harvest, stub ends of cornstalks lined the front field. Miriam's crop had been weak, the corn crib only half-full, so Zeke said silage would stretch the feed into spring. His cousin Hans, new from Germany, persuaded him to try it at his farm too.

For Miriam, they'd hacked leaves and stalks and threw them in a pit they'd dug under the barn's north side overhang. All morning Zeke had been packing the pit, heavy boots stomping in circles. When Miriam came with a cup of water, he climbed out. Wobbly, he walked a crooked path to take the cup, one hand at his forehead.

"Are you all right?" She held his elbow.

"Hans says fermentation can kill, but an open pit? I thought I'd be safe."

"Kill?"

"Not me. I'm fine, just a little dizzy." He lurched, dropping the cup. She braced him, an arm around the barrel of his solid body,

Zeke, muscled thick where Abraham, these last months, had wasted to angle and bone.

Zeke's warm body against hers, her knees weakened, pressing her to him. Oh, how she missed that solid comfort, that . . .

What was she doing? She should be supporting Zeke, not Zeke supporting her. Had he felt her moment of weakness? *Please, no.* She stiffened her legs.

Yes, she missed the body to body. Abraham's body. But more she missed his loving, missed the husband whose face talked to her, told all without words, his worries over rain, cows calving, a member of his Flock in need, his littles.

She wanted to step away from Zeke's enticing warmth, from the musk of his labor. She lifted her head to check his eyes. "Better?" she asked.

"A bit," he said, his arm around her, his pale face inches from hers. The shoofly pie of his breath sweetened the air as his lips, so heavy and soft, brushed past hers—*Oh!*—and he slid to the ground.

Oh, confusion, how it rattled that instant before his legs had buckled. She rubbed her lips with the back of her hand, quelling the nonsense.

Had her thoughts invited this, her body given him an unintended signal? *No, it was an accident. He would never—she would never—*

But their lips had touched. *Surely he couldn't think she wanted this. She hadn't.*

If only her treacherous body hadn't spoken out of turn.

Knees and hands on the ground, Zeke shook his head, hair dangling. He groaned and, blinking, slowly staggered to his feet. "No more silage today." He studied his boots. *Still dazed or embarrassed? Embarrassed for her?*

"Mmmm," she said, "best not revisit the dizzies." The tops of her ears hot, she drove her fingernails into her palms. *Lordy.*

. . .

The dizzies hit Miriam at the very thought of seeing Zeke. And of all things, there she stood, Abraham beside her, her shoulder like a crutch, the two of them at the white board fence overlooking the breeding of sheep. Twenty ewes milled, their estrus starting, Zeke in the middle, holding a pot of inkberry juice ready to mark each covered ewe.

The ram, having covered one already, rutted the dirt with his back hooves. He eyed the frantic herd as if choosing the next ewe he'd mount. Abraham leaned on the fence. "That one, Zeke," he shouted above the sheep's bleating, pointing at one ewe worming into the woolly pack. "Quick, you'll lose her." He banged his hat on the fence.

Miriam wanted to let the animals sort themselves out. But no, Abraham had to tell Zeke which ewe had been covered and where on the ear he needed to dab as if Zeke had never marked his own sheep.

"He's doing a fine job," she said. "You don't need me here." *Was this purposeful? Had he seen the two of them?*

"Stay," Abraham commanded. "Next year you'll do this yourself, judge the rut as done. You don't want some shy girl breaking before she's properly bred."

The night full of late November cold, Miriam sat on her bedside and smoothed the sheet, this her first time upstairs with Abraham since the fire.

More nervous than a bride, she swung bare feet up and pulled the covers to her chin. Abraham, stretched almost full length on his side, watched.

Over months of his recovery, she'd touched every inch of him, washed and salved the burns, soaped, rinsed, and dried the good skin. She knew and loved every ridge and hollow, the burned and unburned alike. Her Abraham, she'd loved him from the start.

She'd been in girlish wonder the day after service when he'd asked to walk her home. Abraham, the boy known to have God's ear. He believed the way others wanted to believe, not because his parents said he ought. He had a calling, the presence of God in the white light sometimes filling his head. Abraham, the chosen.

And his looks didn't hurt. Strong cheekbones, soft lips with a ridge at the edge. She'd wanted to run a finger along it.

Seeing him gave her a jolt in places best not thought of, especially not at service. He'd singled her out, but why her? His looks far beyond hers, hers of the garden variety.

Her father had said, "It's the wide childbearing hips, sturdy as a plow horse."

She'd proved herself an asset. From ten on, her mama being dead, she'd mothered her brothers, her living sisters all married now and moved to far-reaching families. She'd known the demands on a wife and mother, the expectations, except the nighttime ones, of course. Those duties, her red-faced father would never discuss.

She'd imagined the nights of her future, the mystery enticing, terrifying, and Abraham had pulled back the veil. Gentle Abraham. After they married, his sure lips and tender explorations coaxed her to stunning eruptions he promised weren't sinful, not between husband and wife. Miriam had trusted him. He knew right from wrong.

The weave of the sheets felt rough under her fingers. How much rougher for Abraham's burns? She rolled on her side, her back to the edge. His warmth crossed the space between them, a distance of sheet she'd left on purpose, afraid to knock him in the night, fearing, with a knee or an elbow, she'd nudge a tender spot.

He shifted. The mattress dipped, tilting her toward him. His hand whispered to her along the sheet. "Miriam," he said. "I've missed you."

She clung to his fingers, this simple touch filling her with comfort. She wouldn't disturb this moment. Not with questions. Not tonight.

Snow showers swirled over the fields, whitening foxy brown grasses, softening the edges of dead leaves, obscuring the winter black trees of the distant woods. Hemmed inside, Miriam, weary of crocheting, fretted under the incessant squeak of Abraham's rocker. The rocker could talk, so why not Abraham? His silence grated.

"Abraham, I've been wondering—"

"Mmmm?" he said, and coughed. He lifted his lap quilt, repeatedly coughing into it.

"I want . . ." She persevered.

He held up a stopping hand and shook his head. "Can't you see, I'm—" More coughing cut him off.

"We need . . ."

"Not now, Miriam." He waved a dismissive hand.

She threw down her crocheting and fled to the barn. Animal warmth clouded the windows with moisture. She chose the widest shovel and wheeled the barrow behind the cows. Manure steamed in the gutter. Sliding the shovel under the mounds, she'd barely started when sweat stood on her brow. It wicked to her prayer cap and seeped into her black dress, wetting a circle under her arms. With each loaded shovel, the heavier the better, tendons on her neck stood out; muscles in her arms bunched under long sleeves. Skin of her palms pulling against the wood handle, she slung the mess into the barrow.

The stink filled her nose, stung her eyes, and crawled inside her forehead, work blotting out Abraham and Joshua for seconds at a time. She, at least, had work. Abraham had only his chair and digging at healing burns. Faith alone had to carry him; she should curb her impatience and think of his needs.

She wished her faith could carry her to that place of peace

she'd always maintained in the past, erase these wild fluctuations leading her to say and do the unpardonable. Thank heaven for work and the balm of sweat tiring her to the point of blissful exhaustion, though not really a substitute for faith. And Christmas coming made it all worse. Miriam wanted to blot it out.

What made her think she could blot out Christmas? No, she'd keep the day as it should be, cut the greens. She'd do it for the girls.

Heavier snow coated the fields. Joshua would be tucked under this winter blanket, snug if not warm. Nothing could hurt him now.

Brittle stalks crunched under Miriam's boots as she trudged toward the woods, pruning shears in hand. By the side of the road, she clipped feathery branches from cedars straight and tall as Abraham used to be. Maybe tomorrow, reading the Nativity, she'd feel more Christmassy.

Back in the house Miriam piled the greens on the table. "Mmmm, cedar," Mary said. "Now it smells like Christmas." Emma and Adah wove branches on the mantel and down the center of the dinner table.

Rebecca pushed in beside Joshua's chair and added a branch with berries, blue frosted with white. "Why do we keep his place at the table?" Rebecca asked. "Might he come back after all?"

"It's what we do for the dead." Adah straightened the chair. "The Plain way."

Yes, they kept the place empty, a remembrance. But why? Miriam wasn't likely to forget. She could remove Joshua's chair and hang it on a peg in line with extras, but he wouldn't be any less dead.

"Let's make cookies." Rebecca pulled a long-handled spoon from the crock and hefted a large bowl off its shelf.

"I'll make funnel cake." Emma brought out the biggest bowl. "Mary, you can hold the funnel."

"No that's J—" Rebecca's face turned red, and she threw

herself into Miriam's arms. Face buried in the apron, Rebecca cried, "It's Joshua's job."

True, he'd had the touch. He filled the funnel with batter, working fast so it flowed into the hot fat, making squiggly circles.

"I don't feel like funnel cake." Adah pushed the flour barrel under the worktable.

"When Papa's Flock visits, they won't understand empty plates." Miriam patted Rebecca's head. "We'll do it later."

Christmas Day, the wind howled. Cozy inside, Miriam, with Rebecca in her lap, sat by the hearth and listened beside the others as Abraham read the Nativity. He got as far as "unto the city of David, which is called Bethlehem . . ." and his smoky voice cracked. He pressed on. ". . . Mary his espoused wife, being great with child . . ." He paused for breath.

"What's 'espoused'?" Rebecca asked.

"Joseph's going to marry Mary," said Emma, bright with newly acquired knowledge.

"They aren't yet?" said Rebecca, squirming from Miriam's lap. "How can she have a baby?"

"That's what Joseph wanted to know." Adah covered a giggle with her sleeve.

"Just listen," Abraham croaked.

Miriam lifted the Bible from Abraham's grasp and continued. " 'And so it was . . .' " She gave Rebecca a stern look as she snuggled up to Adah. ". . . Mary 'brought forth her firstborn son, and wrapped him in swaddling clothes, and laid him in a manger.' " Miriam missed the lilt of Joshua's voice, his awe in the story. He accepted all without question, *a shining star she should follow.*

That evening, the Flock dribbled in a few at a time, sipped cider in the parlor, shifting foot to foot. They ate funnel cake, Miriam's honeyed cookies, and Hannah's, before scooting into the raw December night. Miriam was glad to see them go, glad as they seemed to be leaving.

The discomfort, where had it started? Another chicken and egg confusion: which first, their uneasiness around Miriam, or Miriam's uneasiness around them?

Zeke hadn't come with Hannah, and now she stayed late by the kitchen door, ready to go but not going. She held her empty cookie bowl, eyeing the crumbs at the bottom, and took a breath as if about to speak, but thought better.

Miriam cleared plates into the dishpan. To fill the void, she said, "Your walnut cookies went fast." She wanted to ask after Zeke. Was he sick? If only she dared say his name. Did he tell Hannah? Did she blame Miriam?

Hannah shifted the bowl under one arm and reached out with the other hand. "You've changed," she said.

"Oh?" Miriam wiped fingers on her apron. She felt like a child eager for the truth, yet fearing she wouldn't be believed, to the point of making herself look guilty. The harder she worked at control, the more she felt the blush that would read as a lie.

Hannah's hand dropped to her side, her face clouded with reluctance. "You're distant," she said, "as if fending off . . ." Now she held the bowl tight in both hands. "As if your heart . . ." Her reluctance shifted to sorrow and a flicker of disapproval. "No joy," she accused, "in our baby Jesus."

She'd caught Miriam in a mortifying truth, a truth cutting deep in her beliefs, a wavering Hannah would find harder to understand than Zeke's kiss, if it had existed.

After Hannah had gone, Abraham chose to pray in the barn. In bed alone and curled against the cold, Miriam covered her ears. Wind howled at the windows.

CHAPTER 19

Savages

After the gulch, Lewis took to his horse. He surveyed the rolling hills where rocks broke the crests as if the land gave birth to huge spiny creatures.

"You, Josh," he commanded. "Sit beside Mercy."

Erect in the saddle, he scanned south to north and back along the horizon. "I can spot a redskin a mile away," he said. "Sneaky devils wait in the rocks." He pointed ahead. "There." He stretched forward, shielding his eyes. "Those Arapaho turn my stomach. Scalping's bad, but what they do with your privates—necklaces," he said. "Can you beat that? They make necklaces."

Joshua thought he'd chuck up his lunch.

"Right here in Colorado," Lewis said. "Sand Creek Massacre." He grinned.

The terrain grew more barren, the sun higher, the air hotter. Old Harold's lead horse threw a shoe, and the group camped well before dark. It would take the rest of the day to find fuel for the forge. Sven used hardwood, since grass and sage wouldn't burn hot. The search started for abandoned wagon parts, a catastrophe for someone, turned blessing for Sven and Harold.

"Buffalo chips," Lewis said. "They burn well."

"But they're scarce." From his horse, George scanned the terrain. "White hunters slaughtered the herds. Now the Indians starve."

"Don't believe him." Lewis scanned the opposite direction.

George reined in beside Joshua. "You might want your sidearm," he said. "All the men carry."

Joshua swelled. He passed the jerk line to Mercy. "Guess I better."

Not waiting for camp, he rooted in the wagon and strapped on the gun belt. He'd filled out since Mother Biddle punched an extra hole in the strap.

He gripped the pistol's wood handle and pulled. Out came the oily blue-black metal. He turned the thing side to side. Vigor ran up his arm and into his chest. Mercy grimaced, and he slid it back in the holster.

In camp, the weapon like a live thing clung to his leg as he gathered wood. He walked head high, chest out, his legs wide apart. He wanted to crow.

Calvin pushed his two girls aside, giving the space he'd give a bull. Sven, at his chores, raised one eyebrow. "Dang, a cockerel on the loose."

Joshua, feeling giddy, hoped the girls would notice, but when they did, they laughed. Good as cold water dumped on his head. He didn't want their attention ever again. All he needed was two Sylvies picking at him.

Several hours before dark, his chores done, Joshua took time by the fire. He hefted the pistol; pointed it here, pointed there.

"Hey, Josh," George said, "that thing loaded?"

"What?" Joshua looked up.

Slowly, George separated each word. "Are bullets in the cylinder?" He placed a forefinger on the barrel, pressing the tip down till it aimed at the ground. The fat part of the pistol showed six shiny metal crescents.

"Christ!" George grabbed the gun and flipped the cylinder open, pushed a rod, and out popped a handful of shiny metal. He put the bullets in his pocket. "Hey, Mercy," he said. "You got an empty bottle?"

She nodded, and he took Joshua by the sleeve. "If you're going to strut around," George said, and shook the pistol in his face, "it's time you learned bullets."

In a swale far from camp, he set Mercy's bottle on the ground, and took ten paces back with Joshua still in tow. "Watch," he said. With the cylinder open, he held the bullets in the palm of his hand, inserting one after another. "See, rotate the cylinder until each chamber is full." With a flick of his wrist, he snapped it shut.

"Here." He handed over the pistol. "Now, raise your arm even with your shoulder and point."

"Like this?" Joshua asked.

"At the bottle, at the bottle." George wiped sweat from around his mouth. "Don't you ever, *ever* point a pistol at someone," he said, "unless you plan to kill, 'cause that's what a body would think, and he'll shoot you."

"I won't, I promise." Joshua didn't intend to point it at anyone anyhow. He just liked carrying the thing.

George stood behind him, hands on his shoulders, and kicked his feet farther apart. "Now, at the bottle."

With his arm all the way out, Joshua's hand shook.

"Steady now," George said. "Line up the sights."

"The what?"

"The fin at the end of the barrel, line it up with the notch."

The longer Joshua held up his hand, the harder it shook.

"Use both hands," George said.

Even with both hands, the bottle seemed to jump around.

"When you're ready, squeeze the trigger." The bottle came in line with the fin, and before the pistol wandered off target, Joshua jerked the trigger.

The pistol roared, and he found both hands and the pistol high over his head.

"Lucky you didn't knock your teeth out." George looked around. "God knows where the bullet went."

Joshua's ears rang, or was it Sven's hammer working the new horseshoe?

"Okay. Try again," George said.

"What?" Joshua cupped a hand at his ear. "Sounds like wool in there."

"*Squeeeeze* this time."

This time he aimed low, trusting the kick would bring the bullet in line with the target. Feet apart, he faced the bottle. Gripping tight with both hands, he *squeeeeezed*.

The pistol roared. The dirt at their feet exploded.

George hopped. "Shit, kid, I need those toes."

Joshua let the hand with the pistol drop at his side. His forearms twitched. He switched the pistol to his other hand and shook out the cramp.

The next shot actually hit near the bottle. "How 'bout that!"

"Good enough." Relief flooded George's face. "We'll stop on a high note, shall we?" They walked back to camp. "Assuming tomorrow comes, we'll have another go."

"If it's all right with Mercy," Joshua said.

"I'll ask, but believe me, she'll be delighted, and I'll bring more bullets."

Joshua came back to the fire in time for a supper of corn pone and carrots. After they ate, Mercy busy at the pot again, he washed plates and forks.

By then, she could cook outdoors as if she'd done it all her life.

With a few strips of dried meat, sprouted onions, and a hairy carrot, she could tempt the angels.

"It's like cooking at home, but you soak the meat," she said. Drying a piece, she cut across the grain, dredged it in flour, and fried it. "Now add water and simmer. Soaked overnight is best," she said. "Learn to cook and you'll never go hungry."

Rolled in his blanket under the wagon, he mulled the day's lessons and tried not to hear the rising voices from above.

". . . no. I won't have it. Him and his pistol, he could kill us."

"Now, now," Lewis said. "He's a good kid."

"Don't you *now-now* me. I know he's good at heart, but I can't sleep with him down there. We're none of us safe."

Joshua thought himself safe, not knowing how to shoot. But George said ignorance and accident went hand in hand. No guns, no accidents, Mama would say.

In the morning, Joshua took Sam aside. "I need a place to sleep. Mercy's miserable, and it's my fault. She thinks I'll shoot her."

"Would you?" Sam raised both eyebrows. "I'm teasing—of course you can."

"You're sure Bella won't mind?"

"Bella," he shouted. "You mind if Josh sleeps under the wagon?" Joshua cringed in embarrassment as Bella, Sadie, Frieda, and James swarmed around. James whooped. "Say yes, Mama." Sadie and Frieda gave shy smiles and twisted their skirts.

"Just nights. I'll work days for Lewis."

"Have suppers with us and the night," Bella said. "Stow your satchel in our schooner." She gave his cheek a pinch the way she did James's.

Annoyance must have given him away, since in the next breath she said, "Now I'll really feel safe." And she gave him a curtsy. Was she funning? She scrambled his brains.

. . .

Nights under Sam and Bella's wagon, Joshua's body buzzed, an invasion of bees he couldn't quiet, sometimes the tickle of a butterfly wing. Other nights, the Devil's own song hummed loud as a grasshopper plague. An unholy germination.

After a week of lessons, he could hit a mark at thirty paces, no more risk of losing a toe, no cockerel strut. People no longer looked askance, except Mercy.

The day broke clear. George and Lewis ranged ahead, two tiny figures under a cloudless sky. George, thin and straight in the saddle, Lewis, his ponderous self wedged between his saddle's horn and cantle.

By noon, they returned. Sweat beaded Lewis's face, wide stains under the arms, and it wasn't that hot. He wiped his forehead on a sleeve. "Hurry now," he shouted.

"Lewis," George said, his tone stern. "Stay at your wagon and be quiet. You're the captain; stay calm."

"Right. Right."

"George?" Joshua beckoned him close and checked for Mercy's ready ear. "Is it true," he asked in a hoarse whisper, "what Lewis says about Sand Creek, the Indians cutting . . . you know?" Joshua couldn't put words to the necklace of privates.

"Indians!" said George. "More like drunk soldiers under a flag of truce. Four hundred Indians massacred. So you tell me, who's the savage?" He rode off.

Despite George's warning, Lewis stepped up the pace. "Got to hurry, Josh. Camp's miles off."

"Can't come too soon for me." Mercy climbed out onto the seat. "But it's early. What's the hurry?"

"Indians," Lewis said. "They lie in wait on the ridges."

"Those rocks?" Mercy's eyes flitted off the trail where rocks stepped high above.

"Could be," Lewis said. He patted his Winchester. "I . . . I'm ready."

They pressed on over low hillocks. Beneath the blue sky, bluer than blue, slashed with mares' tails, the prairie spread brown and parched except for a skinny line of trees. Scraps of bone testified to those who'd gone before, and from time to time, short pieces of wood scattered the verge, some nailed together still stuck in the ground. Crosses.

"Good firewood," said Lewis. "Josh, get them."

"You can't mean that," Mercy said. "They're markers."

"Not anymore, they're not."

If Lewis wanted them, he'd have to get them himself. Sage would do for the night's fire.

"So many graves," Mercy said. "I'll not think on it."

Joshua knew Mercy thought on the graves. He did too. So many ways to die out there, not just Indians. Thirst, hunger, pestilence. Measles wiped out whole villages; so said George. Between that and the soldiers, no wonder Indians weren't friendly.

The wagons spun dust into the blue like a signal to anyone watching. Joshua rubbed the back of his neck.

Approaching the campsite, they came on mounds of earth like tiny open graves. Between them, a horde of little animals, the color of dead grass, nibbled the inedible. Prairie dogs, little brothers to the New Eden groundhog.

Joshua thought Emma and Adah wouldn't find them cute anymore, but Rebecca would love them. So unconcerned, as if the wagon train didn't exist.

Suddenly, one prairie dog stood on his haunches, erect, front feet bent. It whistled.

Ironclad wheels rumbled closer, a second whistle, and the prairie dogs bolted. Their short legs churned more dust as they scrambled to their tunnels. Each one stopped at a mound and, with a backward glance, dove.

Joshua sheered his wagon off the trail. "Watch the holes," Lewis shouted. The holes lay ready to break a horse's leg. Lewis would kill him if he broke a Percheron. Joshua would be tempted to kill himself.

"Halt," cried down the line. Sam pulled in behind Joshua and, with the others, made a circle in the dog town's dooryard. Horses unhitched and tied, the travelers rolled their wagons by hand, slipping the tongue under the rear axle of another. Except Lewis's, his tongue slanted like a gate, allowing passage in and out.

Prairie dogs popped from their tunnels, peered, and jackknifed with a flick of short tails. Dog for dinner? Too gamy for people, not for wolves loping the skyline.

The critters' antics tickled Joshua as he hunted fuel by the creek. The gleaning sparse, he returned with a small armful where Sam and James bent over a pile of tinder.

"It's back to basics," Sam said. "Our matches are damp." He knelt, a sandy forelock hanging over his pale brown eyes. With one hand, he held a stick set straight in a dented board, the stick surrounded with wood scrapings. He wrapped the string of a bow around the stick, and with a sawing motion, spun it. The pile of fine shavings smoked. James, lying on the ground, pressed his smudged cheek next to the board.

"Easy, James," his father said. "Now, blow." James hiked his rump in the air, took a deep breath, and blew. The shavings scattered.

"Ahhh, James, not so hard." Sam rolled eyes to heaven. He shaved more wood around the stick. "Fourth time," he said.

James took another big breath, expanding his narrow chest. With exaggerated care he blew, and the smolder ignited. "I did it!" He jumped to his feet, waving bird-thin arms and clapping. "I made fire, Mama! Look, look!"

"Four years old," Sam said, "and he has the knack. Finally."

"Good for you," Joshua said. "For that, you can have these." He handed the boy half his bundle of sticks.

"And for that," Sam said, "you'll share the last of our sweet potatoes."

After lighting Mercy's fire, Joshua returned. He wasn't the only one drawn to Sam and Bella. Sven sat at their fire too.

"He's a hopeless cook," Bella said, and handed Joshua a board with a slab of meat. "He brought antelope. It's a bit ripe. Would you cut it?"

Joshua sliced the small piece of meat across the grain. Bella dredged. A pool of rendered fatback spat as she dropped slices in the pot. "Smells better than Mercy's."

"Mercy taught me," Bella said. "She's capable, an odd match to Lewis."

Joshua had noticed and wondered if Edith Baylor and Bart had been suited. And how did one go about finding someone suitable? "You and Sam seem well matched."

"Yes, we're part and parcel, the same person," she said. "I don't know what I'd do without him." Bella looked in the distance above Joshua's head. "Some say there's no such thing as love at first sight." She looked right at him. "Don't you believe it."

The aroma of antelope mixed with other suppers in the circle. Joshua's belly rumbled, nothing in it since bread at breakfast. Waiting for the meat to soften, he rubbed down horses, topped off water barrels, and collected more wood for the night.

George carried a giant armload of sage to the central fire, followed by Sam and Bella, their arms full too, and the girls picked up pieces they'd dropped. Refusing help, James staggered under his own load.

Brian and Janie brought more. Old Harold came empty-handed. Sweat slid down his cheek. His wife, Margaret, holding her skirts in both hands, toiled, her steps unsteady on uneven ground.

"Aren't they long in the tooth for this?" Brian asked. "What's going to happen when we hit the mountains?"

"Bachelors help," said George. "And that means you." He pointed at Joshua.

"James too?"

George nudged Joshua's side. "Give Margaret a hand."

"See what I mean?" Brian said. "And no mountain in sight."

Joshua helped the old woman settle by the fire. The others finished their chores and sat too, the women with legs folded sideways under their skirts. The men crossed legs, or stretched out, propped on an elbow.

Pregnant Rona, looking ready to drop, waddled over, one arm out for balance, her husband firmly attached to the other. She blew a wisp of hair from her face. Bella touched her hand. "How much longer?"

"Two and a half months." Rona sighed as her husband lowered her to the ground. Bella's eyebrows shot up.

"Good heavens, twins?"

Her husband gasped. "Don't say that."

"Come, now, Martin," said Bella. "A big guy like you, scared?"

Margaret joined in. "They grow fast, leading a merry chase."

"Right," Harold said. "Why else would we go to San Francisco?"

While they all talked, Lewis paced the perimeter. He scanned the horizon as wafts off thickening stew filled the air, and a fiery sun dropped behind the horizon. Talk slowed, and the sky went wild with oranges and pinks.

After the colors dimmed, the land went dark, and a new quiet invaded. Prairie dogs kept to their burrows. No night birds chirped.

Unease seeped through the ground. It shivered trees by the creek and slipped between hairs on Joshua's arms, crawled at the back of his skull. The horses on picket swiveled their ears and nickered. Joshua knew the still before thunder, but the sky was a clear blue black.

George turned a slow circle. He examined between the wagons.

The others glanced over their shoulders and stood, knees bent ready in the face of . . . of what?

James pulled Frieda's braid and ran. Sadie tried to catch him, while the older girls whirled willy-nilly. James latched onto one, and they careened past Calvin. "Enough," he said, and they stopped.

The wind shifted. Blood throbbed in Joshua's ears.

Janie stepped forward, stopped, and started again in a different direction. Harold took Margaret's hand, headed for his wagon, then hesitated.

Most on the trail had seen a tame Indian. Joshua had seen many at the livery stable, Indians near white and ones with walnut skin, black hair in braids and feathers; hard-eyed or smiling, they weren't frightening. The invisible ones, *they* were frightening.

"Close the tongue," George shouted at Sam, and ran to the horses. He led the picket line inside the circle. The oxen, unable to fit, awaited their fate outside. Bella grabbed an ax, Prudence an iron frying pan. The rest circled around, their backs to the children, making a fierce pen.

Lewis rushed to George. "Indians. They're out there."

"You saw them?" George crouched, peering from the circled wagons.

"No, but . . ."

"All right, men." George's voice low and smooth. "Under your wagons."

They dove, rifles bristling. Joshua, on his belly, elbow to elbow with Sam, drew his pistol, the taste of dirt in his mouth. They waited.

Sweat dripped off the ends of Joshua's hair and into his collar. Sweat sat damp in the groove of his back. Drops trickled his sides and soaked his shirt to the gun belt.

Sam was rock, his arms steady under the weight of his rifle.

"We're fine," he said, and grinned. "Only the good die young." He knocked Joshua's shoulder. "You're safe."

Watchful as a wolf, Sam scanned the line between earth and sky. Joshua gripped the pistol in both hands. He chewed at short hairs curling over his upper lip. His trigger finger trembled outside the guard, the wagon floor close over their heads.

Movement by a clump of sagebrush raced Joshua's heart. He couldn't shift his finger to the trigger. Sam leveled his rifle, and a rabbit hopped into the open. Sam laughed. "Some Indian!" The animal froze, so like Joshua at breakfast with Father.

He'd sat in his ladder-back chair, happily sniffing at plates of apple fritters, corn bread, and headcheese. When Father came in the door, Joshua stared as if blind, no shift of the eye to draw attention.

It hadn't worked for rabbit kits. They froze in tall grass, and Father had scythed them in half. Not that he meant to; he'd reaped them along with the hay.

Joshua heaved a sigh, and the rabbit ran off. But, had it been an Indian, could Joshua have raised his hand against it? His sweat turned rank. The power of death belonged to God.

Lewis had told him, "The Indian isn't *another*; he's something else entirely. Not of you and me."

George had looked disgusted. "You mean an Indian's a two-legged turnip?"

Joshua's arms cramped. He had to move.

Pistol holstered, he slithered from under Sam's wagon, legged up the front wheel, and stood high on the bench. He held the edge of the canvas top and let his eyes roam.

Stars pierced the night sky. Meat simmered. Only the children ate.

By the fire, Bella kissed her yawning brood and whispered them to sleep in their bedrolls. Calvin left his girls beside them while he and Brian walked the perimeter. Only the children slept.

.   .   .

"Your turn, kid." Lewis kicked Joshua's foot. Leaving Sam, he crawled from under the wagon.

Lewis checked the chamber of his rifle. "Come on, I'll walk with you," he said, his finger still on the trigger. Joshua edged behind him, finger off his trigger.

The women lay next to the children as if in a deadly game of ring-around-the-rosie, a litter of fallen bodies. Bella with James on one side, Sadie and Frieda on the other. She saw Joshua and gave a little wave, dispelling the deathly vision. In the firelight, her eyes spoke trust, not a hint of mockery.

Together, Lewis and Joshua turned from the fire and stepped out of the circle, slow dawn at the edge of the sky.

"Been a long night," Lewis said. His arm sagged, the rifle pointed at the ground, his finger still on the trigger. "And nothing to show."

Behind them, a woman screamed.

"Mercy." Lewis swung his rifle, the barrel arcing over his head and down, knocking his hat as he turned. He leapt the wagon tongue and tripped into the circle, jolting the rifle. It fired.

A prairie dog scrambled from a pile of plates. Mercy, round-eyed, sat with a hand to her mouth. Women threw themselves over their children. The men converged.

In the following silence, Lewis let the rifle butt slide to the ground, his fingers holding the muzzle. Sam, at Bella's side, glared at him. "You might have killed her."

"It's over." George helped Mercy to her feet.

Dragging his gun, Lewis pushed past Sam to the edge of the circle. The hairs Lewis usually brushed across his head hung to one side.

All eyes on his back, he suddenly stiffened. "There!" He pointed. "See. Indians!"

The group crowded beside him, and sure enough, there they were, way out on the rise, a small band lit by early sun. They walked in single file, their heads bowed, two men, four women, five children, and a dog. One man led a packhorse pulling a litter.

Lewis hiked his rifle and took aim at the little band.

"For God's sake." Sam slammed his palm on the barrel. "Women? Children?"

Lewis slumped. He dragged off between the wagons.

"Shall I get him?" Joshua asked Mercy.

"No," she said, watching him go. "Give him a minute. He'll be back."

The children hatched from bedrolls and rubbed their eyes. James pulled at Bella's skirt. "Indians? Let me see."

Frieda started to cry. Sadie's face puckered. Bella held her and stroked her hair.

"We're safe." Sam tightened his grip on Frieda. "They've no quarrel with us."

James craned his neck. "There they are." He scrambled under the tongue and headed for the rise as the band disappeared over it. "Hey, wait for me!"

"James!" Bella shouted, one arm around Sadie. "No!"

Frieda clung to Sam when he tried to stand.

"James!" Joshua ran after him. At the sound of Joshua's voice, the boy looked over his shoulder and shrieked as if Joshua were an Indian, and sped into the prairie.

Hands cupped to his mouth, Joshua called, "You're too fast for me, James. I'll never catch you." Wobbling, he threw his arms in the air. "Save me, James! Save me."

James stopped. Then jumped around facing Joshua, legs spread, hands on his hips. With a last glance at the ridge, he surged toward Joshua. "I'll save you, Shosh."

Joshua swiveled and ran with giant steps that took him nowhere. James almost on him, Joshua wheeled, snatched the boy, and, holding him close, carried him into the circle. "This yours, Sam?"

Sam wrapped his arms around them both.

"Oh, Joshua!" Bella set her wet face in his shoulder. Sadie and Frieda clutched his legs and hers, one big hug.

They were all things to him. Sam the father, brother, and friend. Bella the one whose trust made him feel tall. He wanted to protect them. He would suffer anything if it meant they didn't have to. He would have given his life.

"You'll make a good father," Sam said.

Joshua's cup full beyond measure, joy overflowed. James in his arms so light and laughing, the boy might float away, and in that moment, a terrible fear gripped Joshua's heart. Was this a father's burden, this joy laced with terror?

CHAPTER 20

Budding into Spring

Christmas blessedly over, January stretched cold without the warm Sunday visits of Januarys past. Even Miriam's refuge at Hannah's, just the two of them, had fallen off. Hannah's disappointment in Miriam had fed Miriam's reticence, curbing her tongue to the point of tears.

The turmoil she desperately needed to share bubbled and festered until one Sunday afternoon she could stand it no more. *She'd do it.* Go visiting. Sunday the natural time. Interrupting the flow of Adah reading psalms, she abandoned her chair by the hearth. The girls glanced up from their folded hands.

"Where are you going?" Emma asked.

"It's Sunday," she said. "I'll be back later."

"I'll come too." Adah, rising, tripped on Emma's darning basket, unused on this day of unrestful rest.

"Maybe next time." Miriam swung on her cloak and donned her black bonnet.

"Who . . . ?" said Abraham, rousing from his silent prayers.

Miriam clicked the latch. "We'll make bread pudding for

supper when I get back." Wind blasted into the parlor. A chorus of squawks erupted.

"Quick," Adah commanded. "Shut the door."

And Miriam did.

As she raced through the dooryard, a waft of woodsmoke made her wish for her place by the fire, though not enough to turn back.

She strapped Goli into the traces, her fingers stiff with cold, and set out down the lane. Sleet ticked at the buggy's top.

They could think what they liked; she hadn't lied. With no other refuge possible, she headed through the woods to Susan Jackson.

Herr Jackson waved from the barn as she passed. *He* could work on Sunday, not fidget in his chair knowing the next day harbored a mountain of labor.

In the house, she and Susan settled by the fire. Miriam cradled a cup of tea in her hands. Warmth seeped into her stiff fingers, up her arms, and with each sip the dark liquid, nothing bitter about it, filled her innards with comfort.

"Still no word?" Susan asked. "I can't imagine how you manage."

"Not as I should." Miriam sank into the curved back of the soft chair and let her turmoil flow gently into Susan's ready ear.

To confide, could it be a sin just because the ear was English? *She wears no bauble, tells me no godless tales. Yes, she eases my heart, and is this sin?* She'd think on it. For now, peace almost seemed possible, somewhere in the dim by-and-by.

The quiet of January seemed a luxury as February set in with the advent of spring lambing. Miriam could hardly call it spring, snow still patching the ground. The lambs didn't care; they came anyway.

She had no time to dwell on chill creeping up her nightdress as she ran to the barn in the middle of the night. Here was life and death she could do something about: sleepless nights, yes, bleary days, mostly ending with little lambs, noses at their mothers' teats, their haunches high, tails wriggling. A small corner of faith came into bud.

Her shawl flying, she cornered twenty ewes in the inside pen. One ewe—the widest, with twins, possibly triplets—bleated, repeatedly extending her black tongue.

"Come on, Jez." Miriam's irritation came out more curt than she'd intended. "Your pen awaits." The ewe squeezed in among the others, seemingly wanting help but afraid to come forward. Every year the same. *You'd think she'd know how this works.* The ewe thrust her head toward Miriam, again bleating, mouth stringy with saliva.

"I'm trying to help." Miriam stamped her foot, and with much rushing and feinting, she tried to cut Jez from the shifting flock. This made catching her for shearing look easy. At shearing, all Miriam had to do was wedge her against the wall, pounce, and drag her to the platform. Doing that now? She shivered at thoughts of rupture.

"I'll help," Abraham said as he climbed clumsily into the pen. Arms almost extended, his nightshirt long over black pants, he waved his hands, keeping the other sheep cornered while Miriam feinted at Jez. The ewe dashed left, bulges wobbling.

Miriam let her pass, and once started, Jez knew the way. Miriam followed her to a small pen in the warmest part of the barn, and closed her in. Jez breathed heavily. The straining had begun.

Abraham joined them, raspy as Jezebel.

"I'll keep watch," Miriam said. "You look knackered."

"I'll lay out grain for tomorrow." Abraham headed for the grain bins. "Shorten the morning chores." She heard a clatter. He must have stumbled over the pitchforks.

"You all right?" she called. He grunted in answer.

Jez panted. Miriam worried at the chance of triplets. The third, often a runt, would have to be bottle-fed in the kitchen, a delight to the girls. The shaky lambs would click around the wood floor, their little cleft hooves hardening each day.

Lambing, an exhausting time, a time of renewal. Something to savor, and Miriam would when she had time.

Jez's lambs born and nursing, Miriam retreated to the house. She mounted the stairs, candle high, and found Abraham awake. She gathered the hem of her nightdress.

"Triplets?" he asked from his pillow.

She pried off her boots. "Twins," she said, and slid in beside him.

His feet nibbled hers. "Burr," he said.

"Winter does that." Her words light, a hint of teasing. His feet wrapped around hers, and he took her in his stiff arms, carefully, gently.

She'd longed for this moment. She wanted to fall into his comfort, confide face-to-face, see the old love swimming in his good eye. He rubbed the hooded one with the back of his wrist as if to clear it.

He held her to his chest, and through layers of nightclothes, she felt his leathery skin. "It's time," he said. He ran his finger down her nose and kissed the tip, and with that, his sharp breath hit her. The sickness. Oh God—how could his weakened body fight sickness?

"Miriam, are you listening? It's time."

"Time?" she asked.

"We're failing," he said.

Ignoring the poison breath, she took his gnarled hands in hers. Finally they'd clear the fog between them. "Tell me," she said, soft and entreating.

Unburdening himself, he'd return to her, and be the Abraham she loved. Eager to welcome him back, she could feel her own defenses melting.

"Our Lord says"—Abraham nuzzled below her ear—"be fruitful." His wooden member poked her leg. "The staff of life." This time, *his* words teased.

She stiffened. "This isn't . . ."

"The Lord demands it," he said, gripping her raised forearms. "We need a son."

A son? We have a son. A great well opened, swallowed her, and the waters closed over her head.

"Miriam?" He took her cheeks in his hands. From deep in her well, she saw his wavery face above her.

How could her withered heart hold another child?

Too many nights filled with lambing and worry over Abraham's sickness left Miriam wrung out. From her dealing with Jez's fears she took a lesson, so when Hannah came to the door offering assistance, Miriam accepted.

In the barn, Hannah sat on a stool milking the brown cow; Miriam milked the Banded Swiss, both cows tied to the manger. Milk bubbled white in the pail, and with each pull of a teat, the bubbles increased.

"Funny," Hannah said, "how someone else's work doesn't feel like work."

"The giving feels good." Miriam resettled herself on the stool. "Accepting is harder."

"A farm this big"—Hannah flexed her arms and changed teats—"you need more hands."

"That's what Abraham says." Miriam sighed.

Milk hissed into the pail.

"Is he . . . able?"

"That way?" Of course, Miriam knew what she meant. Only

Hannah would ask outright, though she studied the stream of milk.

"Yes, but he has a sickness." Miriam flicked the string of her prayer cap.

"Beyond burns?"

"It comes and goes." With the back of her hand, she itched her nose. "He's had it before, a lurching, red-eyed sickness. His breath could choke a vulture." She leaned her head against the cow's side. "I shouldn't make fun—it could infect another child."

"It sounds like too much Communion wine." Hannah laughed.

Miriam laughed too. Abraham allowed no wine at service. None of his Flock imbibed. In fact, Miriam had never seen it or smelled it. "How do you know such things?" she asked.

"Zeke," she said without a ripple of discomfort. "He says English make drink beyond the grape. Applejack has them blathering; moonshine causes a killing sickness."

"Thank heaven, Abraham wouldn't have that."

That night, his prayer in the barn mercifully short, Abraham came to bed, his breath the breath of a bloating sheep. He scratched at the scars crimping his inner elbow.

Miriam winced. "Don't," she said. It gave her the shivers, his nails pulling at the tender new skin.

His eye darted around her covered breasts, and he touched her shoulder the way she would touch a hot frying pan. Wary. Testing.

"Not another child," Miriam said before he could speak. "How can I? I'm worn to a shred already, and Zeke does most of the work."

"I've had enough of Zeke," he said. "This is my place. I'll be doing it."

"But you can't, and the girls and I can't do it alone. You should be thankful."

"I should have a son."

"Son or no," Miriam said, "we need hands now."

Abraham fell back on his pillow.

"We can't take and take," she said. "And you're sick. This smell of bloat, you might pass it on."

He kept his eye on the ceiling. "I won't."

"How do you know?" She leaned up on one elbow.

He rubbed where his beard used to be. "Because," he said, and rolled over, his back to her.

"That's not an answer."

He curled his knees. "Because it's the back side of cider."

"Cider?" She pushed at his spine. "Foolishness!"

"Drink, Miriam." He flung himself over to face her, his mouth taut. "Drink," he barked.

She scooched away to the edge of the bed. Stiff-armed, she leaned, hands flat to the mattress, and stared at him. He furrowed his brow.

"Never." She whispered her disbelief. "You'd never." If she said it enough, would she make it true? Disappointment flooded in with certainty.

He sank back and crossed an arm over his eyes. His mouth twisted open, lips moving, his tongue too, working at words he couldn't catch.

"How?" Her voice stayed low. "You wouldn't allow it, even at service!" Then louder, "Other Flocks, yes." She smacked the sheet with her palm, and now shouting, "But not yours!"

"I've failed them," he mumbled. "I'm no longer *the salt and light of the earth.*" With his knuckle, he scrubbed at his forehead. "A sip of Communion cider brings light."

"Surely more than a sip." But if that was all—at least this wasn't sickness. So much sickness without chance of a cure or even knowing what it might be. This could be fixed. He could stop and all would be well. Surely.

"But you repent," she said, half question, half statement.

He crossed his other arm over the first. She knelt on the bed, leaned in close, and, taking his wrists, uncovered his face. "You have to." She crossed his limp hands over his privates. "Or no more sons."

March. Early morning, Zeke and his sons with a team of horses clopped into the dooryard. Zeke harnessed Goli and Sampson. "We'll ready the garden," he said when Miriam waved from the front door. The garden was a gift, not part of their agreement.

The land on loan for a cut of the harvest, she could walk it, kneel, and touch the richness. Her land, but not hers.

In some way, she felt closer to Joshua than the land. Gone though he was, she folded him to her, his every detail etched in her heart, his smooth apple cheeks framed in silky hair, his lamby smell. Her boy. Hers forever.

Another son couldn't change that. Should the next be a boy, it wouldn't be any different from loving her four girls. She could do this. Abraham hadn't had a bout of sickness for weeks.

She preferred to call it sickness. Drink brought the image of devils feasting on him, turning him to their purpose. With sickness, recovery seemed possible, and she could forgive him, welcome him to the marriage bed, not just the mattress.

In the past, she'd been in the Devil's grip herself, and he'd forgiven her lapse. Her ears grew hot at the thought, the shame of it.

Before marriage, she and Abraham had lain side by side one afternoon in the hayloft. Dressed in fall clothes, he in long jacket and pants, she with a heavy shawl, dress, and black stockings, their legs out straight, boot toes pointed at the overhead beams.

Dark with age, the timbers had held strong over a hundred years, but that afternoon, they creaked in the crisp wind whistling at the corners of the barn. The scent of dead leaves seeped into the summer warmth lingering in the hay beneath them.

Lost in thoughts of their coming wedding, she felt a tickle at her neck below her black prayer cap. Soon she'd change to the white of a married woman. She brushed at the tickling frond, and to her surprise knocked Abraham's hand. Their eyes met. In his, she saw herself reflected, not as she'd seen her face in the watering trough. In the water her face showed plain and capable, making her frown. She didn't bother to look again.

In Abraham's eyes, this girl—no, this young woman seemed tender, near radiant.

He grinned and ran the frond under the neck of her dress. It slid down one breast, where it found her teat, and a yeasty explosion filled her body, breasts to nethers, to her toes, swelling her, not the slow rise of dough in the pan, but dough leaping its confines and into the sky. A squeak escaped with a catch in her breath. He folded her in his arms.

"I wish I could be that piece of hay," he said, his breath warm in her ear.

Her toes curled. "I wish it too." And all on its own, her body arched against his own risen flesh, want blotting out every ounce of ingrained decorum.

That instant, his arms went slack. "But we can't," he said. His words, more reproof than regret, doused her.

He'd saved her. A man committed to his beliefs and to her. He'd loved her despite her lapse, as she must now love him.

Another watchful week passed. This wasn't right. To truly forgive him, she had to stop this hawkeyed suspicion. He might not be the irreproachable shepherd she'd believed him to be, but she did love him, the one whose touch filled her with hope and joy. Since his burns, she'd missed the closeness he brought her. Now she could rekindle this small light.

Now, tonight, no matter how late he came from checking the animals. Tonight.

. . .

The drop of his boots woke her. She'd drifted off, and half-awake, she felt the dip of their mattress as he sat and slipped carefully under the covers. His cold toes touched her ankle; then the heat of his body pressed against her side.

His fingers, awkward at the neck of her nightdress, pulled the cloth aside. She hadn't sewn the opening shut against winter's chill.

His way made easy, he elbowed aside the blankets and sheet. She lay before him, exposed, her nipples at attention.

He cupped the farthest breast in a bent-fingered embrace. "My Miriam," he breathed.

She bolted up. "No!" She yanked the sheet over her breasts. "Did you think I wouldn't notice?"

"The Lord demands—," he intoned.

"Don't you dare say what the Lord demands! You with your red eye, the stink of the Devil on every word."

"But you said—"

"I said repentance, then forgiveness. Good intentions don't count."

"I tried." He bowed his head.

"Try harder." She stared him in the eye. "You've shunned men for less."

"Help me," he said. "It's got me by the throat." For the first time since she could remember, the real Abraham sat beside her, drowning as she watched. She'd do anything to save the real Abraham.

She'd forced liquids on him after the fire. He was the patient then, not her husband. He had to obey *her*. Chestnut tea saved his life; she wouldn't let this other liquid steal it. But how?

The pressroom, she'd been there before; she could do it again. The person who forbade entrance wasn't her true husband. He had no right to her obedience, and she had no obligation.

Clutching her nightdress, she abandoned the bed, no time to dress. She pulled on her boots, in a rush before he knew her mind.

"What are you doing?" he asked.

"You sleep," she said, and on tiptoes hurried passed the girls' bedroom, down, and out, racing to the toolshed. Luke jumped circles around her. "No, Luke, just a shovel, go to bed." She latched him in and turning for the barn, she saw a candle come to life in the kitchen. Abraham.

With the shovel, she ran into the barn, her nightdress flapping open. Inside, she lit a lantern, and found the pressroom latch. It wouldn't open. She brought the lamp to bear on the handle. A padlock hung below it.

She heard the kitchen door slam. "Miriam," Abraham bellowed.

With the edge of the shovel, she hacked on the latch until the door split. Latch and lock fell to the floor, and she entered the room, shovel handle in both hands. She swung it. No time to pick and choose, she whaled the flat of the blade across every table, jugs and jars smashing, glass flying, the floor littered with shards.

"Miriam!" Abraham in a rage at the door. "No!" He rushed her. As he grabbed for the shovel, his anger turned to shrieks louder with every barefoot step.

Howling, he dove out the door. She'd wounded the one unscathed part of him.

The next morning, Abraham, with his feet in white bandages, crawled on hands and knees from the reinstalled pallet to his rocker. Miriam's anger turned to guilt. In her attempt to save him, she'd made things worse. For the moment, she told herself, only for the moment, and helped him to his chair at the breakfast table.

Day upon day his hands shook less. She'd made a shambles of the pressroom, and now all she had to do was wait for her true husband to return, not this man who craned his neck and raked at his scars as if he'd rolled in poison ivy.

She prayed for him the way she'd once prayed for Joshua's return. Unscathed, the both of them, go back to what life had been. Childish wishes even God couldn't answer.

If they turned back time ten months? It would all happen again. There had to be some lesson. A reason.

She prayed instead to face the man Abraham would be, to have God grant her the patience to understand him. If she couldn't quell her doubts, they could never return to who they were, and she knew she'd never be the wife and mother she ought to be.

Or maybe, they weren't those people to begin with.

She had to try. She *would* have the next child. That much she could do.

CHAPTER 21

The Rockies

Four weeks and August ended. They were late. George talked of wintering over after the Rockies, the Sierra Nevadas saved for next spring.

"No need," Lewis said. "We'll make time through the pass." His map showed a shortcut.

Joshua drove Lewis's wagon, but every free minute, he stayed close to Sam and the family. He was full to bursting as they shared fire and food and traded hopes of land, animals, a house, a barn. Sam knew cattle; Joshua knew sheep, horses, and pigs. Sam knew lumber. Joshua could forge the nails. Evenings, they drew plans in the dirt.

"California," Sam said. "Your Monte Rey sounds perfect. We'll plant apples and pears, and every kind of vegetable you can imagine."

"How will we find it?" Joshua asked.

"First the Rockies, then the desert, go over the Sierras, and west to the sea."

"And the house?" Bella planted herself behind Sam and looked over his shoulder as he drew. "The kitchen needs room for a stove, not just a fireplace," she said.

"A bathing room," Joshua offered, "with pipes bringing in water."

Sam laughed. "That's a bit far-fetched." Joshua's face flared.

"Maybe one day," Bella said, "when we're old and rich." Bella, always kind.

"Sadie and Frieda can share a room."

"I'll share with Josh-wa." James spoke up, his slur fading.

"We'll see," said Sam. "He may want a room of his own."

With those few words, Sam opened a new world.

Two weeks of wheels rolling over the flat brown land, the sameness chafed.

"Whenever will we get there?" Mercy asked. She took the jerk line from Joshua. "Let me drive. I need something to do."

"Soon enough," said Lewis. "Look." A black line spread south to north along the horizon. "That's a hell of a storm. We're in for it."

"The Laramie Mountains," said George. "And you're right, we're in for it."

Daily, their supplies dwindling, the black line swelled until peaks blotted the sky. "A terrible beauty," said Mercy as they followed metal tracks toward town and its fort nestled small in the mountains' shadow.

From a distance, the water tower with its hooked spout looked like a giant bird standing among the tracks. Offshoots went to the fort. Sidings held freight cars for loading and unloading. Bells clanged; whistles warned away people like Joshua who stood openmouthed. The screech of metal on metal pierced his head. So many people, so much noise after the quiet of the prairie.

Low on food and eager to restock, they camped on the outskirts of town. Sam and Lewis gathered lists from each wagon and rode to Laramie. Money being short, the lists stayed small, what with flour at a dollar a pint and sugar for a dollar fifty. The next afternoon supplies would be delivered.

"We'll feast on vegetables when we're over the Rockies," Lewis said. "They'll wring us dry, here."

Bellies full, spirits soared, beans themselves a celebration. Sven brought out his fiddle. He danced with the older girls, one after another, spinning them with his bow hand, their cheeks bright red, eyes shining, their parents hawkeyed on the sidelines. The girls couldn't stop the giggles. Most everyone clapped along, even Mercy.

After dark, the children tucked in their bedding, Bella and Sam danced by the dying fire. They didn't lock elbows and spin. They held each other face-to-face, Sam smiling with his eyes even more than his mouth, Bella's eyes half-shut.

She settled her face against Sam's neck. He kissed her hair, the two of them sewn together with invisible thread. Their happiness made Joshua happy, made him covetous in a greedy corner of his heart.

Bella caught his eye over Sam's shoulder. She whispered in Sam's ear. They separated and became their everyday selves. Sam motioned Joshua over, and they each took a hand. They danced him in a circle until he laughed. "You should've seen your face," Bella said. "What were you thinking?"

"I can't remember."

Lewis tapped Sam on his shoulder. "You want a belt?" He held out a bottle.

"On the other side." Sam pointed over the highest mountain. "Dutch courage won't help tomorrow."

"Sleep will," Bella said. "I'm turning in."

In a canvas bag Bella had sewn, Joshua snugged under Sam's wagon.

. . .

Up and up, they pressed into the trees, the mountains dim under layered clouds. From time to time a ray of sun broke through, lighting rocks covered in green and gray lichen. The group slogged in a slow line up one crest, sank in a trough, and climbed the next. When they gained the first real peak, trees looked like climbers stranded in scrub. Joshua stopped the wagon, crisp air thin in his lungs, the horses sweaty and breathless.

This had to be God's dooryard, and he hadn't been invited. None of them had. Joshua could hear His voice:

> *I will destroy*
> *man whom I have created*
> *. . . both man, and beast . . .*
> *for it repenteth me*
> *that I have made them.*

Joshua crossed his arms and squeezed. Was he what God repented?

Reining in beside Lewis and Joshua, Sam leaned back in his saddle. "Praise be!" he said, surveying the valley dropping away, hazy peaks fading into the distance.

Lewis, on his horse, threw open his arms. "I'm Captain of the World."

"Shhh!" Joshua hunched his shoulders. "He'll hear you."

An answer came from across the next valley. "I'm Captain . . ."

"You see." Joshua put a finger to his lips.

Lewis laughed. "It's an echo." He spat on the trail.

"Maybe so, but—"

"Let's see this God of yours." Lewis shouted louder, "Show Yourself!"

Mercy, on the bench, pursed her mouth. "Leave the boy be."

They descended to a small valley, and up again, steeper this time. Lewis's horse, slender legs, white stockings above small hooves, picked its way through the rubble. Lewis dug spurs in the animal's sides.

The mare stumbled. Lewis dragged himself out of the saddle. Reins thrown over her head, he yanked at the bit. "Come on."

The way grew hard. Joshua, jerk line in hand, trudged beside Lewis and the loaded wagon.

"I have it all here," Lewis said. "A seven-room house." He patted the top-board. "From the biggest wagon to the biggest house."

Pride, thought Joshua. *Pride goeth before destruction.*

He worried for himself too, standing next to Lewis. Joshua hadn't that kind of pride, but he had other evils, and God might see it as smiting two birds with one stone.

The rubble underfoot grew worse as the mountain tilted at their faces. The air hurried their lungs. Joshua took deep breaths. Lewis puffed and braced his hands on wide thighs, throwing his whole body into each lumbering step.

A switchback hid Sam, as if they were alone, no one to hear or help.

Joshua fretted about old Margaret and Harold, hoping they still rode their wagon. Could they walk if they had to? He had doubts.

Down again, and the trail wound through forest. Antelope stared from deep in the trees, and Joshua wondered what else watched their wagons.

The sky filled with mountain, glory beyond glory, God had to be near. In the trees, Joshua heard Him sigh, and knew every step was trespass.

The hairs on his neck stirred. He'd been thinking Lewis would bring God's wrath, but what if Lewis was the second bird when God stoned Joshua? Joshua, who hadn't stayed separate, who raised a hand against Father. Joshua, who coveted another man's family. Everyone would do well to keep his distance.

Leading his horse, Lewis sweated and groaned as he toiled up the trail. Each peak higher, he leaned to one side and retched.

Joshua offered a hand. Lewis knocked his arm and snatched the jerk line. "I'm fine."

"You want water?"

"I said"—Lewis gasped for breath—"I'm fine. Go!"

Joshua retreated to the verge. As Lewis moved on, Sam's schooner came abreast, harness bells ringing with every labored step. From the bench, Bella and the girls waved, while James rode double with Sam.

The valley had gone dark, but sun slanted on the pines, their needles a sharp green. The scrub rustled, alive with unseen hurry.

Ahead, the trail became a steep rock pasture. Lewis urged his team as it slowed. "Get up, you lazy buggers." Loose stones rolled under their hooves.

The lead horse balked and Joshua moved forward. Lewis took up a whip from under the seat. *Crack*, and the Percherons surged, a mighty effort before the lead horse stumbled. He went down hard on the condyles of his knees, bone grinding the rock.

The horse, head down, seemed to kneel to the mountain. Then with a grunt, he arched his neck, threw one hoof forward, then the other, front legs out stiff. The muscles of his flanks bulged. He staggered up, gray knees oozing red.

Lewis cracked the whip again.

"Good Lord," Sam said, coming forward. "What's he thinking?"

Lewis's team, lathered white under their harness, faltered a few more steps before the wheels stopped.

Heads low, the horses pawed the trail. They flinched at the

whip. Again *pop*. "Go, damn you." Lewis laid the whip across the wheelhorse's rump.

"Hey!" Sam shouted. "Cut that out."

"They won't move." Lewis glared at Sam.

"They can't."

George rode up as the other wagons bunched to a stop. "Chock your wheels," he called down the line. A few men gathered.

"What's the holdup?"

Lewis leaned on a front wheel, head on his arm, his face pale. Mercy climbed down. "What's the matter?"

"I can't keep—" Lewis took a breath. "Walking like this."

"Give me the whip," said Sam, and through his teeth, "I'll help you along."

George checked inside Lewis's wagon. "Better lighten the load."

"No," Lewis snapped.

Mercy's hands fluttered. "There's nothing to lighten."

Sam shook his head. "Then this is home."

"That's impossible."

Sam kicked at a stone. "We're wasting time."

Lewis slammed his hat on the wheel. "Can't we rest the horses?"

George tipped his head at the sky. "See those clouds? Snow's coming."

Lewis grabbed a cheek strap on the lead horse and pushed. The horses eased back, rolling the wagon out of line. "Give me a hand, will ya, Josh?"

Joshua hunted two proper stones. He wedged them under the rear wheels.

"The top things go," said Lewis.

They all pitched in.

"No, not the bed," Mercy cried.

Lewis plucked her by the sleeve. "Are you deaf? We can't keep it."

Three of them lifted the bed all of a piece, and passed the head out to George. They set the bed on the ground, leaned the mattress beside the wagon, and went for more.

"The chest stays," Lewis said. "It was my mother's."

"It's heavier than the bed," said Mercy. "Take it out."

"Not on your life." Lewis tried to stand in the way.

Sven carried a bonnet-top cradle, Joshua a chair.

"No, no." Mercy hammered Sven's shoulder with her fists. "You can't."

Sven set the cradle down and raised his hands, palms out. "I won't touch it," he said.

"Enough." George turned on his heel. "Work it out, then catch us up." Heads shaking, they all returned to their wagons.

"You'll get left behind," Joshua said.

"Don't meddle," Lewis snarled.

Joshua looked to Mercy. "Go," she said. "We'll figure it out."

By the time they'd all mounted their wagons, and Sam's schooner passed, Lewis was still rummaging. Mercy stood forlorn, surveying their whole bedroom, so small under the wide sky.

Sam's six horses made light work of his modest possessions packed below the bright blue top-boards. The bells on the harness jingled. They sounded like celebration.

The pass loomed over their heads, a giant gateway. Beyond, Joshua knew the promised land would make every tribulation a minor stone in the road. They redoubled their efforts, sparing no muscle in the final push.

A bitter wind chilled them, though summer hadn't ended. Bella brought out blankets and quilts and sheets and sweaters and rags, anything to stay warm. She bundled James first, then the girls, blankets over their bonnets.

Frieda held a rag doll to her chest as Bella wrapped her. "I'll keep Molly inside my blanket."

The littles looked plump, the size of bear cubs.

Joshua's turn came next. He added an extra sweater, wrapped a quilt around his head and shoulders, strapping it at his hips with the gun belt. The corners snapped in the wind, beating his icy thighs.

He boosted Sam, bundled to papa-bear size, as he hauled himself up and perched on the saddle. Walking, Joshua kept just below a sweat as the wind sneaked in.

"Bella," Sam called. "Bundle up." She wrapped rags around her neck, and a yellow blanket over her flowered bonnet, crossing it at her chest.

The strain steady on the doubletrees, Sam's team plodded forward. The wagon creaked, a bug crawling toward God's fingers.

From nowhere, a snow squall howled down the narrow track, blinding them, Joshua's only guide the harness bells. He trusted the horses until sight returned, showing white veins of snow scoured into the cliffs. Between them the trail crested, and like poor men entering heaven, they threaded the needle's eye.

Sun dazzled at the crest. James whooped, "We made it!"

Sam unwound his blanket and dismounted. He breathed deep through his nose, big grins all around.

Ahead, the trail dipped into the mountain, their promised land somewhere down there close enough to smell.

"Everyone out," Sam called. "We'll set chain brakes."

Sam and Joshua ran icy links through the rear spokes and hooked the ends to the wagon. Their hands stiff with cold, work went slowly, the links giving a cheery rattle.

On the narrow trail, a cliff wall rose on the right. Sam mounted and rode behind the wagon. He stayed left, close to the drop-off, guiding his team by the jerk line. The others followed, hugging the rock wall. Joshua held James's hand. Bella walked with Frieda and Sadie.

Sam clicked his tongue at the horses. The rear wheels began to turn, then stopped and slid, locked by the chain. Small stones chattered and bounced over the outside cliff, falling down and down, and disappeared in silence.

Sam's horse lurched on the steep trail, her front legs straight. Sam swayed easy in the saddle, his boots in hooded stirrups.

The wagon hiccuped over more stones, shifting wooden bows side to side under the canvas until the grade between switchbacks gentled.

"Ready to ride?" Sam swung out of the saddle. He and Joshua pulled the chains and stowed them. They took off their wraps, Bella and the littles crowding onto the bench. James shoved the girls for more space, his skinny body needing little. Bella kept her hand on the brake, an easy reach from the bench. Joshua waited on the trail while they settled.

"You're all elbows and knees!" Sadie fended off James. Frieda brought out her doll. "See, Molly, we're safe."

Everyone in a good mood. From his horse, Sam whooped and threw his hat in the air. James caught it. "It's mine," he said, and put it on. The hat floated over his ears.

Bella lifted the brim from his eyes. "Yours until we camp."

With relaxed rein, Sam rode behind the wagon. "Thank that God of yours," he said to Joshua, "our new life is at hand." He liked to tease, but Joshua knew they shared the same God.

As they descended, Joshua's toes jammed in his boots, his knees strained, steps speeding. He overtook the wagon and waved to Bella and the littles. Neck and neck, they grinned at each other.

The wagon rolled faster. Bella stood to the brake, two hands on the metal lever. The doubletrees tilted with lumps in the road. Cheering came as Brian and Janie rounded the upper switchback, jouncing fast.

They gained on Sam's wagon. His horses increased speed.

Sam, with one eye on the trail and one on the following wagon, avoided a rock by the front wheel, only to catch it on the rear. With a bone-jarring lurch, the wagon tipped toward the rock wall rising overhead.

Sam spurred forward between the cliff wall on the right and the wagon, coming abreast of the horses. "We're fine," Bella called. But the load shifted, the sound soft as a whispered secret, and compacted against the right side.

The raised wheel jolting off the rock, the load slid to the left side, skidding the rear wheels toward the drop-off, and spat an avalanche of small stones over the edge.

Bella, standing to the brake, knocked her yellow blanket to the ground. She pulled the lever. The blocks bit, and the wheels shuddered as she strained, arms straight, back arched. Her bonnet blew off.

Caught by the ties around her neck, it flapped like a tethered bird. She braced a foot on the front board and hauled with her whole being. Sam yanked the jerk line.

The wagon slewed. Its left rear wheel skirted the cliff edge.

"Sam?" Bella called. The edge gave, and the wheel sank to its axle, the wagon tipping backward. The right front wheel lifted.

"Sam!" Bella's voice cracked, and slow as dreamtime, her grip on the handle lost, Bella's hands rose above her head. Her body, suspended under the canvas arch, then settled to the seat, her side resting against the wooden bow. Her legs blocked James as he slid against her, followed by Sadie and Frieda, buttock to buttock, the four in a knot, their mouths open ovals.

Enormous eyes all turned to Sam.

The wagon hung on its rear axle for the space of a breath no one could take before the front wheel, under Bella, sank. She and the littles pitched forward, hands clutching the front board. A gust of wind floated Sam's hat off James's head and over the brink.

Stiff-legged in stirrups, Sam stretched his arms wide. The wagon teetered.

Their six horses scrabbled, hauling against the wagon's slip.

Sam leaned back in his saddle as if to counter the balance. A sound like a rifle hit Joshua's ear, and the wagon lurched, the rear axle broken. The tailgate dangled over the edge. Sam's mouth round and soundless, he seemed to twist the very fibers of his mind as if he could splice a shank mighty enough to pull his family back.

The rein attached to the lead horse whipped from Sam's outstretched hand.

The only sound, horse breath. The huff before tumble.

Huff before the horses, white-eyed and rearing, screamed. And screamed as the wood wagon they'd pulled for hundreds of miles came alive and hauled them backward over the cliff.

End over end, they galloped the sky, the wagon releasing its precious cargo. Wingless birds, they grew smaller and smaller, until, lost in the trees, they entered the Promised Land.

CHAPTER 22

Salt

Sunstruck, the day glittered. Bella's yellow blanket lay in a heap at the edge of the cliff. The skin under Joshua's eyes twitched like a horse shaking off greenheads. He couldn't feel his fingers, nor the ground under his feet.

Sam collapsed into his saddle. Slow and boneless, he dismounted. Joshua reached a steadying hand. Sam's head jerked, his cheek muscles clenched.

Joshua wanted to wake up yesterday, wanted Sam to wake up yesterday and tell his unholy dream. They would laugh. Instead a strangled sound twisted from Sam's throat as he led his horse to the cliff.

The animal threw its head high, yanking the reins free. Joshua grabbed and missed as the horse, empty stirrups flying, galloped down the mountain.

"Sam." Joshua hooked his arm, the cliff edge too close. Far below, trees made a dark pool, the surface dotted with blue as if the sky had fallen.

Gently, Joshua tugged on Sam's sleeve. He twisted, arms up in defense, staring as if he'd been attacked, when a clatter sounded, and Brian's wagon careened toward them, horses wild in the traces. Janie gripped the front board with both hands. Brian hauled on the brake and checked over his shoulder. The old couple, now clear of the switchback, bore down behind them.

As they passed, their eyes darted from Sam to the trail; any hesitation and they too would find the same reward.

And how was it they survived? Or did this punishment belong to Joshua? Sam and his family, God's instrument?

The others came one after the next around the switchback, not knowing they missed the burial. No Bible. No time for solace. Godspeed, Bella and Frieda. Sadie and James, Godspeed.

The late arrivals looked with wonder as they passed. For all they knew, Sam and Joshua, standing by the cliff, admired God's handiwork.

George and his oxen slowed as they came abreast, but Lewis's Percherons barreled around the switchback behind him. Lewis shouted, "No palavering, go!"

George thrashed his rein and yelled. Lewis screamed, "Whoa," his horses skidding close on George's tailgate as they disappeared around the next curve. Sam shivered in the sun.

"Take my hat," said Joshua.

He set it on Sam's head and folded the yellow blanket over his shoulders. Arm in arm, weaving like old men, they descended into the timber.

After dark George found them. He carried a dim taper and guided them toward camp. The others could be heard around a switchback, their voices in broken hymn, "Nearer . . . nearer . . . my God to Thee." How near was it safe to get?

Ahead, a great fire glowed, showing the wagons in a line on a narrow piece of verge, only partially off the trail.

"Oh, Sam." They all came to their feet, and, one after the other, wrapped their arms around him. Brian and Janie must have broken the news, and Joshua was grateful. Where would he have started?

Mercy led Sam to the fire. He stared at nothing as if head-struck, his hair in tufts. She spooned mush on a tin plate. Janie added bread. Margaret offered a strip of soaked jerky. Sam turned away.

"Please, sit here." Joshua tugged his arm. His knees gave, and he sat on the ground by the fire, legs crossed. "Take the plate."

Mercy put it in his hand. His arm sagged until it hit the dirt. Lewis bustled behind him, and clapped him on the shoulder, then moved around front. "I know how you feel," he said. "But buck up, man, you need to eat."

Sam opened his mouth, head falling back. He raised his arms, and hands clamped to his hair, he closed his fingers and yanked.

Lewis backed off with a grimace. Even Mercy, looking helpless, stood at a distance. Sam belonged to Joshua.

After the others settled, Joshua curled cold in a loaned quilt, his blanket gone along with the satchel. Sam sweated through the night under Bella's blanket. He thrashed with visions Joshua tried not to imagine. He wanted to help lighten Sam's load, but Sam didn't seem to see him, leaving Joshua alone with his failings.

Sam's breakfast, like dinner, stayed on the plate untouched. Mercy said, "You eat it, Josh." He forced down the mush, knowing the blessing shouldn't be squandered.

"Wagons, ho!" The group made a fast start, their teams having been left harnessed through the night. No one wanted to linger so close on the trail.

Sam and Joshua, behind again, walked the valleys between timbered peaks. Sam's feet dragged. He veered, a man cut loose. Beyond widower, what could hold him?

He tripped, and Joshua caught him when he fell. Sam pulled away as if the touch scalded him. He had no words, no tears.

. . .

A week, and Sam no longer resisted Joshua's hand. Sam, no better than an animal, its leg in a trap, the jaws grating bone. Red eyes, gashes in his gray face.

At night Joshua swaddled him in Bella's blanket. He trembled, Job in the flesh.

And Joshua, not widower, not bereaved father or son or brother, or even second cousin, had no recognized name for what ripped his heart, and no time to tend it.

By the fire one night, Lewis ignored Sam and flopped next to Joshua. "You're lucky—you do what you want," Lewis said. "Footloose and fancy-free."

And how free was fancy? Was he free of Father? Of Mama's arms, free of his sisters' laughter? Free of Bella and the littles? These freedoms, Joshua could do without.

What he had out there somewhere was land, a place where he could work off his sins. Land with its promise of resurrection. He and Sam needed that promise, and to get there, they had to push on. If nothing else, they had to have faith in the land.

Behind them, the mountains disappeared. Rough outcrops rose above their heads as they held to the valleys.

The wagons raised a wall of dust. Sam and Joshua walked through it, the earth hard and melting hot under their boots. By night, they rolled in blankets, cold enough to chatter their teeth.

Though everyone helped, Sam sat blind to their charity. Without thanks they continued, for this was their offering to God, that they might never walk in Sam's boots.

Joshua, on the other hand, accepted whatever they offered. In exchange, he cooked, washed clothes, gathered firewood. Work a balm Mama had taught him.

In sleep, he retreated to New Eden spring, the earth glistening with overnight dew, the plowed furrows rich and brown. Robins stretched the early worm, and he walked his horses to the barn. Swallows dove; geese snapped at frogs in the marsh. He listened for Mama's call. Weeping willows turned yellow by the creek.

Joshua wore the Lord like a too-tight shirt, pinched in the shoulders. He wore Him like dirt he'd sooner wash off, but God remained, a habit persistent as sickness.

On waking, he walked again with Sam in the dry Wyoming basin, alkali in the dust stinging the lining of his nose. Better than Sam, at least Joshua could feel the sting.

Sven's mules didn't seem to care, cropping the salt grass at every chance, and when none grew, they walked on, bellies empty.

Bunched together, the wagons moved at a crawl. Lewis rode off the trail, first one side, then the other. "Watch for water." Shading his eyes, he stood high in his stirrups. "There's supposed to be a stream."

He waved his map as he approached George's cart, then stabbed the paper with his finger. "Water's right here."

"Well, it's not," George said.

"Has to be. The army says so." He held out the map. "See?"

"Where'd this come from?"

Lewis tapped the lettering. "U.S. A-R-M-Y. Bought it off a soldier."

George examined the paper. "That's hand-lettered."

"What's your point?"

"You got suckered," George said. "The man drew it himself."

Lewis snatched the map. "It worked so far."

"Dumb luck, Captain."

The day hot for October, Joshua blessed the falling night and his turnip supper. Water dripped through his prayers.

Full light, and the sun lay like an egg broken for frying. The camp woke under a batter sky, early heat rippling the parched land. Stones in the road looked like bread.

Their bones cooked, and the sun rose to a hard circle. Sweat ran into Joshua's eyes, thirst pasty on his tongue. Sam unheeding.

They walked faster than the sluggish animals, and coming on Calvin's tailgate, Joshua heard one of the girls plead for water.

"We're all thirsty," said Prudence. She climbed off the moving wagon and dipped half a ladle from the barrel's bottom. "Take a sip, no more."

"It's brown," the girl said. She took a sip. "And hot."

"Be glad you have it." Prudence caught Joshua watching. Not wanting to seem to ask, he busied himself gouging dirt from his nails.

"Josh," she said to his back. "A small sip?"

"Thanks, I'm not thirsty." He kept his back to her. He knew she could hear the saliva thick on his tongue.

She laughed and brought over the ladle. "Liar."

He sipped. The smallest trickle, brown and hot, slid down his throat. It tasted of the barrel, and he savored every drop.

Without asking, Prudence tipped the ladle to Sam's cracked lips. His mouth took the water, but he wasn't there.

"Water!" Lewis shouted. They all shaded their eyes. A line of grass ran in a zigzag. Pale blades, not the lush green Joshua expected.

Lewis galloped for the stream.

"No," George yelled. But too late, Lewis's horse dunked its nose and drank. Lewis, sliding from the saddle, stooped to the stream.

"Don't!" George ran. He shoved Lewis, snatched the reins, and yanked.

Lewis spat. "It's salt."

"Right, and your horse just drank a bellyful." George hauled his lead ox by the ring in its nose. "Everyone away from the water. Get on picket."

Joshua stretched the rope for the picket as Mercy struggled with the Percherons.

"What a madhouse," said Sven as he tied his mules to the line.

When the group gathered, George said, "Half a bucket is all a horse can manage."

Sven carried water to his mules, and more for Harold's horses. George tapped him on the shoulder. "Help Lewis."

"I've had enough of him."

"Do it for Mercy."

"She's no better." Sven turned away.

"We threw out her cradle," Joshua said, and went for the water himself. A good excuse to leave Sam where he stood.

But Sam wandered, and later Joshua caught him squatting at the stream.

"Stop." He knocked Sam's hands. He'd have drunk his fill, the burning in his throat of no concern, just another reason to vomit.

By nightfall, after another dinner of turnip and weevily bread, they all sat around a meager fire. Groans came from the picket line. On checking, Joshua found Lewis's horse fidgeting. He ran his hand under her swollen belly. She humped her back and a tremor went through her.

Her head dropped. She swayed. Her legs buckled, and Joshua jumped back as she fell. The other horses on picket shied, yanking the line tight.

"Lewis!" Joshua untied her tether. "Get over here."

The horse, on her side, breathed heavily. Lewis, Brian, Sven, and Joshua, each on a leg, struggled to pull her free of the tightened rope.

Through hours, she strained. She and Sam moaned, he in his snatches of sleep. Surely she had none.

Sam threw an arm across his face, hiding his eyes above hollowed cheeks, the cheekbones sharp enough to cut his sallow skin. Joshua couldn't see Sam in that face.

Which was worse, Joshua didn't know, the moan of Sam's sleep or Sam staring into the dark when awake. Joshua wrapped himself in a blanket and paced the camp. Groans from the horse welled out of the dark. He covered his ears.

Thirsty for a moment of peace, he walked the prairie. Night creatures scuttled softly about their business as he took in the cool air and felt disloyal taking the respite Sam could never have.

The horse had no respite either. Lying on her side, she arched her neck, her legs working along the ground.

Joshua returned to Sam and tried to sleep, fingers in his ears. But no use, the horse tore at him, and he rose, leaving Sam curled under his blanket.

Murmurings filled the camp.

Joshua went to Lewis's wagon and found him asleep on the ground. He rubbed his eyes and sat up at Joshua's approach.

"I need my bed." Lewis stretched his neck. "Mercy says be with the horse."

Joshua stood over him. "She's right."

"It's just a bellyache."

"It's not." Joshua ground the heel of his boot in the dirt. "Lewis, do something."

"Don't tell me what to do, boy."

Joshua's tongue sharpened. "She'll be dead by morning."

Lewis shrugged. "If you're so smart, you fix her."

"She's beyond fixing." Joshua gritted his teeth. "Shoot her, or I will."

"You can't. That's an expensive horse."

At that moment, he'd rather have shot Lewis than the horse. Joshua put his boot to Lewis's chest and shoved him over, resisting a good kick. He'd leave the smiting to God.

Grumbling, Lewis gathered his rifle, and headed for the horse.

In the cold moonlight, he leaned over the cramping animal. George joined them, and murmurs in the camp stopped.

With a ratcheting sound, Lewis pumped a shell into the

chamber and waited. The horse arched into another groan. "Now," Joshua hissed. "Goddamn it, now."

Lewis fired. The other horses shied, yanking at their tethers.

"At least we'll have meat," George said, and pulled his knife.

An odd way to answer a prayer, but this was truly a gift horse.

As dark faded to gray, Joshua hunted for Sam. Breakfast bubbled on the fire. Sam's yellow blanket lay heaped by the wheel where Joshua had last seen him, but no Sam. He'd left the hat on top of the blanket.

Joshua walked the perimeter expecting to find him sitting alone, cross-legged on a rock. Joshua checked the stream.

Farther out he looked for Sam squatting in what was left of the grass. Maybe loose bowels had taken him away from camp. Joshua climbed on a wagon seat and looked in every direction, sage and sage and smatterings of salt grass. No Sam.

Heart thumping his chest, he called Sam's name, turning and turning. Gone, but where? He had no direction, nowhere to return to. Joshua, who had nothing, had more than Sam. Everyone searched.

"Harness up," Lewis called.

"What about Sam?"

"The Sierras won't wait." Lewis threw his saddle in the wagon. "We go."

"Without him?"

"No choice. We're late as it is."

"Lewis, we're too late already," George said, standing with the others. "A few more hours won't make a difference."

Lewis raised his voice. "I said, harness up."

All eyes turned to George. "Get horses," he said, "workhorse, saddle horse, doesn't matter. Harold, stay with the women; you too, Josh." George mounted. "Fan out, men. You have two hours." Everyone scattered.

Lewis stood alone in the center of the circled wagons. Joshua led in his wheelhorse. Hands cupped at Lewis's knee, Joshua hiked him to the flat saddle, and Lewis rode slowly after the others. The women packed for the trail.

Three hours later George, with the last man, straggled in. "No sight of Sam, but there's water half a day off." A cheer rose and quickly died as they remembered what had taken them searching.

They found clear water, and a settlement for supplies, but thoughts of Sam cramped Joshua's belly. When he closed his eyes, he saw Sam wandering hatless in the noon, saw his bones in a cluster under a clump of sagebrush. Joshua told himself that Sam would be happier with Bella. He'd carry James on his shoulders, tickle Sadie and Frieda. Blessings be upon him.

The Devil offered this bread. And God help him, Joshua ate.

CHAPTER 23

October

Months of morning sickness passed and Miriam swelled. Could a child conceived under duress be loving?

Of course this child could be loving. Look at the animals. Born out of instinct. Look at Goli, his capacity as great as any person's. Look at Luke: he loved everyone, though no one as much since Joshua.

Abraham pushed his plate to the center of the table. "I'm not hungry."

"Just one more bite," she said. "You're withering away." She reached over her enormous belly and cut his chicken in smaller pieces. If only her belly were the biggest thing between them.

The baby near due, and too much still unsaid, Miriam straightened and wiped her hands on her apron. *Just ask.*

Impatient, he shoved from the table and stepped out on the porch. "Your lettuce bolted," he accused. "Tall as my knee."

She came onto the porch and surveyed the garden she'd been neglecting. "It's no horse," she said. "I can't catch it." But he was right. Centers of the heads had shot up, the leaves too bitter to eat. A mess. She should have pulled them.

"I'll do it myself." He labored off the porch, his breath short. Halfway to the garden, a coughing fit took him. He bent, hands on his knees, until his breathing slowed. He dragged back into the house. "Joshua knew better. Why don't you?"

She followed him inside, and stopping short, he turned. They collided. Off-balance, they clutched each other.

His eyes swam. "I didn't want God to have him," he said, a catch in his breath, truth in the pit of his eye.

"Dear Abraham." She held him, her cheek to his.

"Yes, I threw him from the fire," he said, resting his forehead on her shoulder. "All the same, the Lord took him."

She rubbed his back in gentle circles. Abraham had been close enough to save him, yet he couldn't. Helpless, he had seen what Miriam could only imagine. Without complaint, he lived with it. His loneliness wrung her heart.

"Tell me," she said, her voice soft. "Let me help."

"We were—" He writhed the way he did that first night, burns reeking of cooked meat. "The flames blue across the floor, I couldn't—" His shoulders shook. "Too fast."

He pulled away. A sob took his words, and he shuffled for the stairs.

His burns a testament to what happened to Joshua, why make him talk? Miriam could see the fire all too clearly, snaking blue and terrible.

She waited for relief. But why blue? Why so fast?

November, Miriam carted her belly around the house. She stuffed rags where drafts testified to coming winter, made extra bread, checked the cellar, recounting hams and sausage. Zeke, true to his word, had kept them supplied.

She'd laid by the usual pickled vegetables, and this year five jars of persimmon jam on top of strawberry, raspberry, and plum.

She'd spread straw on the garden, so why did she wonder what she'd forgotten?

Miriam bathed close by the hearth. Orange flames threaded among logs stacked against the andirons after dinner, the warm room still rich with the smell of pork shoulder, fried potatoes, parsnips, and carrots.

She stood naked in the wash pan, the baby straining the confines of her belly. Hot water to her ankles, she soaped over the bulge with a wad of sheep's wool, and around her belly, the indent now pushed out like a third nipple.

Firelight played across the shiny surface as she lifted each spreading breast, soaped beneath and up the cleft, breastbone to clavicles, across, and, chin up, around her neck.

Ready for bed, Abraham watched from his rocker. "I'll wash your back," he said. Her body blocking the fire, he soaped her shoulders and down over her rump. Dropping the wool, he ran his hands around to her belly, and the baby kicked.

How loving he'd been this last month, almost like his old self, his brow less cringing, his breath sweet. Her forgiveness? The baby? Perhaps less worry with sheep settled in the barn, windows and doors closed, grain bins full, all nailed down for winter.

"A feisty boy, we have," Abraham said, and drummed her taut skin with his fingers. He moved his hands higher, cupped her breasts. She tipped her head and kissed his scarred arm. "Maybe," she said. "Remember Rebecca? You were sure then."

He kissed her neck. "It's a boy, it will be."

She squirmed under his half beard. "You'll get all soapy."

"Makes no nevermind to me." He tightened his grip. The front of his nightshirt soaked water from her back, and his member, turning wooden, pressed against her.

She grunted and arched.

"Aha," he said.

She pushed him off. "The baby!"

For Miriam, the birth came fast; not so for Abraham, who knocked at the door, five, six, seven times. "Is he here yet?"

And finally the midwife said, "A fine son, you have." She left the bedroom, and Abraham strode as best he could to the bed and lifted the yellow-haired boy.

"Isaac, my son," he said, his head bent to the infant's red face.

"But we agreed on Daniel." Miriam reached for the baby.

Abraham rocked the boy in his arms and carried him to the window. "Isaac," he said, the crook of his elbow high. "This will all be yours, fields, the barns, bigger herds."

Miriam had this same path in mind, the barns painted to the highest roof, no more peeling, thirty lambs in the pastures, pigs again in their pens, cows with their calves, two teams of horses, and a saddle horse for everyone. Something to strive for.

What difference did a name make? She rather liked the name Isaac.

Abraham's arms sagged as if carrying a boulder. With a look of panic, he held the baby to his chest and shuffled quickly to the bed. "He's hungry. You best take him."

Relieved of Isaac, he flexed his arms.

"Afraid you'll hurt him?" she teased.

The months flew by with Isaac in the bonnet-topped cradle by Abraham's side of their bed. Abraham hardly slept for listening, picking him up at the slightest peep. He watched her swaddle him, pointing at wrinkles that could chafe, adjusting his legs in her arms as the infant nursed.

By March, Abraham's picky insistence through the nights made Miriam cranky.

"Enough," she said. "Isaac's not sleeping and neither are you, and certainly I'm not."

Leaving Abraham downstairs after breakfast, she and Adah carried the cradle to Joshua's room. They set it next to the bed, but being in the room felt like intrusion.

Miriam had kept it ready for Joshua's return, floor swept, the bed made, bureau and chest at the end of the bed dusted. Intrusion or not, it had to be.

Miriam lifted Isaac and laid him gurgling on the bed. She changed his swaddling. Beside her, Joshua all too real and ready to help, as if he might hold Isaac's exuberant legs kicking loose the fresh bands.

Such a little father Joshua had been to his sisters, especially Rebecca, dressing her for the night, tucking her into the cradle, rocking her until she fell asleep.

Joshua would be torn if he were holding Isaac. Would he rock him or read to him? *Oh, that boy with his books.* He did read the Bible, his devotion beyond question, yet Abraham held to tradition: no other books, no school beyond eighth grade. Joshua never got to eighth grade. He'd have been upset had he still been home.

Abraham hadn't budged, and Frau Lentz had taken the brunt. She'd been a good teacher. The children missed her. Never the same with Herr Lusk. His briar cane scared Mary and Emma. Rebecca just rolled her eyes. "Him and his wispy fringe," she'd said.

Sitting on the bed, Miriam lifted Isaac to her breast, her arms clamped as if he might slip away. This had to be what Abraham felt.

Isaac cried, wriggling in her grip. Afraid he'd fall, she gripped harder. He shrieked into her breast.

Stop with the bear trap, she scolded. As she settled onto the pillows, her arms relaxed, and immediately Isaac took to her nipple.

He wouldn't slip away. He wasn't Joshua.

For Isaac's sake, she had to let Joshua go. Bury him deep in her heart.

By summer, Isaac, his fat legs churning, scooched naked across the kitchen floor. A breeze came in the open windows.

Knees and palms thumping the dark boards, he buzzed straight to the hearth. Short of the stone, Miriam swooped him up, his arms and legs crawling the air, and set him in the parlor.

He rocked on all fours, gave her a two-toothed smile, and veered for the front door, now open to the porch. At the jamb, he rolled on his haunch and, looking back at Miriam, waited, eyes sparkling, mouth in open anticipation.

The minute she moved, he bolted. And before he could roll down the steps to the yard, Abraham, sitting outside, locked him in scissoring legs. Abraham grimaced and grinned at the same time. His pleasure won over the pain, and he lifted Isaac, squirming, onto his lap.

"Emma," Miriam called toward the garden where the girls pulled weeds. "Come watch Isaac."

"Me, I will." Mary dropped an armful of feathery greens. She ran, the strings of her prayer cap waving.

"No, it's my turn." Rebecca brushed dirt from her black dress and ran for the porch.

"You'll all have a chance. Emma first."

"He's mine now," Abraham crowed. Squashing Isaac in his arms, Abraham waggled the boy until giggling shrieks poured, the two of them breathless.

In Abraham's hug, the boy stilled. Miriam tousled his sunny hair. This beautiful boy she'd been afraid to have, afraid to love, he had all their hearts firmly gripped in his pudgy fingers. Abraham's most of all.

. . .

"Happy birthday, Isaac." The morning bright and clear and warm for November, the girls in nightdresses crowded Isaac's room. He knelt on the mattress, holding to the sideboard Miriam had drilled and pegged to Joshua's bed, bouncing, bouncing with their excitement, no idea what a birthday could mean.

"Get him dressed," Miriam said. "I've started johnnycakes." The aroma wafted up the stairs. "They need turning." She hurried down to the hearth. In the iron pan five circles of white batter crisped at the edges, their centers dotted with bursting bubbles. She flipped them, counted to ten, and stacked them on a plate she set close to the fire.

By the time Miriam had stacked six plates, Adah, with Isaac riding her shoulders, herded the black-clad littles to the table.

"I want real cake," Rebecca said. No prayer cap, she bobbed on her rump.

"Is it *your* birthday," Miriam asked, "oh little Fräulein Not-quite-dressed?" She doled out a plate at each place.

"No, but Isaac wants carrot cake with walnuts."

"And a gingerbread boy for the birthday boy," said Abraham as he sat at the head of the table. Adah plopped Isaac in the high chair beside him. Abraham patted the boy's cheek and forked johnnycake, dripping syrup, into his bird-wide mouth.

Surprise flashed as Isaac gummed the treat, and with both hands he attacked his plate, dimpled fists cramming his mouth full. Abraham laughed.

"You wouldn't laugh if I did that," said Mary.

"Syrup and johnnycake all over on your face?" Rebecca said. "I would."

Isaac clapped sticky hands on his head, and they all laughed, Miriam too. She swabbed him with a wet cloth and cleared his plate. Rinsing her hands at the washtub, she caught a glimpse of yellow by the barn door. She dropped the dishrag, her chest tight.

It wasn't Joshua. She knew, so why the feeling she'd left him in the cold?

She meant to keep him close inside her, not wandering the dooryard. But even inside her, where he belonged, she needed him separate. She couldn't live in a world where she saw him and couldn't touch.

She had to wall him off, stone by rough stone, even block the cracks where his pale visage leaked through. No more comparisons with Isaac. The boy would grow into himself, Isaac in his own right.

Miriam wrung the dishrag and hung it by the fire to dry. "Who wants to make carrot cake?"

PART III

The Devil's Bowel

CHAPTER 24

Learning Whisky

Late October, and the Sierras too distant for comfort, Joshua's toes sprouted through his boots. The group camped on the outskirts of Easton.

Evening by the fire, Rona rested in a chair, hands spread on her huge belly. So large she couldn't bend easily. "My chest burns." She propped swollen legs on the wagon tongue.

Her husband, Martin, collected wood. Joshua built a fire and cooked their dinner.

The night quiet, Sven had walked to Easton. He returned early. "Can't get drunk on a dollar." He flopped by the fire where the others huddled from the chill.

"We can't go on," Martin announced.

George rested his elbows on his knees. "A little further," he said. "Short of the Sierras we'll stop."

"No." Rona answered for Martin. "We stay in Easton till the baby comes."

"Wait for Utah," George said. "Ogden has a doctor."

"You've got to hang on," Brian pleaded. "There's safety in numbers."

Janie, hands on her hips, confronted Rona. "You can't leave us."

"We have to," Martin said. "Rona bleeds."

"Hush, Martin." She slapped his arm.

"They have to know."

Old Margaret got slowly to her feet and put an arm around Rona's shoulder. "I wish *we* could stop. *I'd* like to turn back."

"Not me," Harold said. "I wouldn't go through the Rockies again, never."

Sven clapped him on the back. "Barkeep says if we liked the Rockies, we'll love the Salt Desert."

"May as well winter in Ogden," George said, disappointment written in the slump of his shoulders. "Early spring, we cross the desert and Sierras after snowmelt."

"Sounds right to me." Lewis spoke up for the first time since he'd lost command. "No Donner party for us."

"I'd rather eat rock stew than you," Sven said with a harsh laugh. Joshua guessed Sven had had more to drink than he thought.

"A rock is all any of us can afford," Mercy said.

"Gila monster is what we'll eat in the desert."

No one had a morsel to spare, and they willingly shared with Joshua. His talents of little use off the trail, how could he add to their woes?

He needed money, the key to survival in the outside world. Only three dollars left of Mrs. Biddle's present.

"It's best if I stay here too," he said. If he went to Ogden with them, they'd feel the weight of his need, and he'd be tempted by their charity. He had to find work.

Camped by the Bear River, their plans in order, the others stayed a few nights in Easton persuading Rona and Martin toward Ogden and the doctor.

With separation coming, tempers cooled, making it harder for

Joshua to leave. They'd weathered so much, and like it or not, he was tied to each one.

Morning came, the sky overcast. His friends crowded round and promised a welcome when he reached California, as if California was a small town where everyone knew everyone. He could only hope.

"You should join me." Sven pounded Joshua's back. "Got me a secret land deal," he whispered. "Get some money. The saloon, maybe."

"Jokester," Joshua said, and pounded him in return.

"No joke," he said, and again whispering, "We close next summer. Davenport, by the ocean, be there."

As the group prepared to leave, Lewis gave Joshua a curt handshake. Mercy kissed his cheek and said, "Get rid of that gun. You're a good boy."

George spurned his hand and wrapped him in a bear hug. George's eye on Mercy, he whispered in Joshua's ear, "Remember, don't point till you're ready to kill."

After much hand pumping, a few scattered kisses from the women, Joshua watched the group head for Ogden. He shouldered Bella's blanket, the only possession he wasn't wearing.

Most likely he'd never see these people again. The tie between them would fray, but they would always be with him, Sam, Bella, and the littles too, the closest Flock he'd found this side of New Eden.

But in their hearts, had they found relief when Sam disappeared? After all, what would they have done with him? What would Joshua have done with him?

Maybe Joshua was the one relieved, not having Sam's grief on top of his own. But their plan remained. Monte Rey, and to get there, Joshua needed money.

. . .

Neither a borrower nor a lender be. Joshua had been a thief, and never again.

"You've got schooling," George had said. "Try the newspaper." The *Easton Age*, in the center of town, not Joshua's first choice, but considering the poor land around Easton, no farmer could afford him. Trading work for food wouldn't get him to Monte Rey.

Pistol at his side, he walked the main street, some twenty buildings long, flat fronts all joined together by a board walkway. He looked in each window for the *Age*. As he passed what must be Sven's saloon, the swinging doors burst open and a man in black flew out, crashing into Joshua.

Back on his feet, Joshua reached a hand to the other cowering on the walkway, fear in his slanted eyes. In black jacket and pants, he almost looked Plain, except for the long braid and yellowish face.

Still uncertain, the man finally grasped Joshua's hand as a crowd of men poured from the saloon. "Hey, Chink lover." One of them grabbed Joshua's neck.

His new friend in black screamed. Head low, he plowed into the grabber, careening them all through the plate glass window.

On the floor inside the saloon, Joshua thrashed under the other men. He heard thwacking and painful yips, as they rolled off. A heavyset man with a cane stood over him.

"That window don't come cheap," he said. "Your little friend beat it, so you're on the hook."

"I'm what?" From the floor, Joshua cocked his head.

"You're the body what broke it, you're the body what pays." California paled. "But—"

"Up and at 'em, kid." He raised his cane, swollen knuckles on the crook.

In a small town with nowhere to run, Joshua had little choice. "Guess I could give you a hand," he said.

"No guess about it." The man lowered his cane and tapped the floor. "I'll take the hand," he said. "And I could use a leg too. You got extra?"

"No sir, but both mine work."

He gave Joshua a hard stare.

"Hey, Frank," said a fellow at a far table. "A baby gunslinger you got there."

"I don't reckon." Frank brushed through the crowd and hung his cane behind the bar. "Sweep," he said, holding up a broom. "Outside and in, and no glass in the street."

"Yes, sir."

Joshua finished the steps and boardwalk, moved inside, and dumped the slivers in a bucket behind the bar. Frank called from the back room, "Kid, get in here."

In the storeroom, Frank counted bottles, touching the top of each with a bent forefinger. He shuffled along a line of dusty crates, leaning heavily on his cane. He swore as he shoved at an empty. Joshua hopped out of the way. "What do you want, kid? What? What? I'm busy."

"You called."

"Oh, yeah, here." He tapped a full crate with his cane. "Take these, bottom shelf behind the bar." Joshua hefted the crate into the other room and, bending, his head level with the bar, lined bottles on the bottom shelf.

A dirty arm reached across the bar and yanked his hair. The grizzled face behind the arm leered. "Glass's empty, kid."

And thwack, Frank's cane hit the arm. "Stub's looking for a handout. He'll drink the spittoon if you let him." Joshua rubbed his smarting scalp.

"Room, board, ten cents a day," said Frank, "till you pay for the window. Room's at the end of the hall, upstairs to the right." He pointed. "And stash that pistol. I don't want you shot."

Joshua frowned.

"All it takes is some jackass looking to better his reputation. Get rid of it."

"Yes, sir."

"The name's Frank." He took Stub's glass. "And mind you don't bother Rosie."

"Who . . . ?"

"Tarnation, kid, do your job and don't worry the woman."

Upstairs, his room was a hair bigger than a closet, raw board walls, hooks nailed in, a rusty bed with one remaining brass knob crammed under the eaves. Next to the bed a pitcher and bowl sat on a washstand. So he could wash every week, Frank told him. No need for more. Sweeping wouldn't raise a sweat. The room, more plain than Plain, was a palace compared with sleeping under a wagon. Joshua hung Mr. Biddle's pistol on the bedstead, and through his one window studied open land down to the river.

Downstairs, while Frank cleaned glasses without benefit of water or soap, Joshua worked the other side of the bar, avoiding the drinkers' feet as he swept street dirt and eggshells from under the brass rail. At either end, he checked the spittoons. A little sludge shimmered in the bottom. Stub must have been sipping.

He moved on to the rest of the big room, the floor smaller than a Pennsylvania way station's, the ceiling higher, and enough room for three round tables. More windows let in more light.

"Wash the spittoons," Frank called.

Couldn't be worse than a night-jar. Joshua ended up doing that too.

November, and Frank closed the saloon's solid door against the cold, trapping the stink of tobacco and sweat. After a month of, "Excuse me, please," when sweeping, he poked a cowboy with the broom handle.

"Hey!" The man, his breath a blast of whisky, swung around.

By the time he wobbled to a stop, Joshua had already pushed the next guy aside.

The regulars cocked one boot on the rail, and leaned an elbow on the bar. Worse than sows at the trough, they grunted and hunkered in close to their glasses. All the drinkers did.

Joshua knew the regulars by their boots, horse soldiers in shiny black to the knee, cowboys' curled at the pointed toe. Ranchers walked carefully in fancy leather, oiled brown or green or red or all sewn together. Haulers' boots laced on hooks, the laces broken and knotted. Joshua's boots, from the Baylors, were rounder toed and too tight, the leather cracked, a hole worn near through the bottom left. His clothes didn't look much better.

Rosie, the one he shouldn't bother, bothered him: a blast of red he couldn't get used to. He stared, bug-eyed. Even the streets of Gomorrah didn't hold the likes of her.

She passed fearfully close. The white skin of her breast glowed in the midst of red ruffles. At the floor, her skirts whispered to the boards, the skirts wide as a barrel, and big enough to hide a multitude of devilment. She lifted the hem, exposing high-buttoned slippers with sticks at the heels. You couldn't call them shoes. God only knew how she walked.

Joshua blinked past her chest to peachy cheeks and piles of chestnut curls, tendrils dropping below her ears, where baubles hung. Her eyelids bluer than her eyes, she had to be sin on the hoof.

She caught him staring and raised an already arched eyebrow, shut one blue lid, and opened it again. He couldn't move, couldn't breathe.

"Rosie," Frank yelled from the bar. "Cut that out. He's s'posed to be working." Then at Joshua, "She is too. Get out the way."

Joshua hadn't seen her work at anything except the back of a fancy man's neck. Smoother than a farm cat, she sashayed round the table where men fooled with little pieces of paper, money piled in the middle. Rosie's dress swished.

"Silk, sweetie," she said a month later when he got up the nerve to talk to her. A woman of Gomorrah, maybe, but he saw nothing evil beyond the dress and the face paint. Oh, yes, the baubles. Her voice low and soft, she never swore.

Mostly she didn't seem to see him. If he got in her way, she'd cuff him like a mother cat keeping kittens in line. The drunks fared worse, her claws out.

Seven months of long days, and by midnight, dinner and bed came as a blessing. But, oh, the dreams. They'd have been good dreams if they didn't cut to the bone. Joshua still too thin-skinned for his own good. He heard Sam calling, words riding on warm air through the window, *Hurry, Joshua. Spring's coming. Get plowing.*

And Bella in the kitchen, the littles holding bowls of stew. *Sure you don't want more?* She held up the dripping ladle.

He wanted to say, *Yes, yes, please,* but she closed the pot and smiled, satisfied she'd fed him well. The kitchen turned to fields, the same as New Eden, but with an ocean at the back of the back forty. Sam said, "Oh, Josh, it's everything we hoped."

Waking in his rusted bed, Joshua rubbed his eyes. He sat up and cracked his head on the slanted eave.

Joshua eighteen, and four years gone from Sylvie, she seeped in his mind no matter how hard he pushed her away. He couldn't believe what had happened.

No, he couldn't believe what *hadn't* happened. Nothing in the bedrooms where they opened the beds and stripped sheets to the ticking. Not in the barn, her hip grinding against him while he tried to milk. "You're good," she'd said. "Good with teats, huh?"

Sylvie's scent followed him. She lingered in his nose, the smell of yeast, the bite of lye soap, her buttery breath. His growing hunger fed on her spicy sweat.

He didn't think on Edith, the touch of her lips an accident drowned by thoughts of Sylvie purring nightly on his pillow. Where once he pushed her away, now with all his might he reached for her. Too late, his arms too short, or they'd lock in ice, or the heat of her would bubble his skin. And in the morning, wet as an infant, he bit his pillow.

After Frank gave several raises, Joshua paid off the window. Frank got a boot out of what Joshua didn't know and taught him the business, though he said he wouldn't be staying. Still, time unfolded, and not a step toward California.

With winter coming on, and no word from Sven, Joshua figured he'd been talking through his hat, so why not stay in Easton? Food aplenty, days and nights in the warmth, and Frank needed Joshua's house skills. Frank had none, and neither did Rosie.

Joshua washed the sheets for every third overnight patron. That gave him a good month between. He scrubbed Frank's clothes and his own more often. Rosie lived out and saw to herself.

A year and some, he'd watched Rosie from a distance, and felt no ill effect. He got bolder. She came down the stairs in her high heels, wide skirts, one of many red dresses lower on the bosom. Her breasts enthralled him.

She glanced round the room, squinting slightly, and caught him staring. She locked his eye, his face hot. Older than he, no doubt she could read a lustful soul.

"Ain't he cute, Frank?" She snickered. "Gotta love that blush." She stepped down the last stair, crossed to the piano, and dragged her fingers over the keys.

"She's a beauty," said Frank. "Bought her cheap."

"Really?"

He poked Joshua with his cane. "The piano, fool." The ill-used keys clicked sour notes, and Rosie drifted on to the gamblers' table.

But, oh, how she got under Joshua's skin. Her voice, all incense and oil, poured in his ear. His head overflowed.

Not even a message arriving from Sven could cut through the soup. He'd addressed it: *Joshua Amish c/o the Easton Saloon.*

"It's on the bar," Frank said. Joshua put it in his pocket.

"Could be important. Better read it."

He did, aloud: "Land deal closes september 15 davenport post office stop partners yes stop bring $100 stop sven."

"Where the hell's Davenport?" said Frank.

With more wages Joshua could take the horseless train. Plenty of time. Joshua would think on it later. He returned the letter to his pocket.

Frank snorted. "You in a fog, kid?"

In Joshua's mind Rosie's leg pressed his; he felt her tug on his arm as he stocked bottles on shelves in the back room; her fingers stroked his neck while he wiped glasses free of lip and fingerprints. As he swept the bedrooms, he could feel her behind him, arms around his arms, holding the broom as if giving him lessons.

Rosie pushed Sylvie aside, and purred through his dreams. Falling into his arms, she turned into the Devil himself, hot fingers digging. Joshua screamed and woke, the bed damp, his pent-up juices boiling.

He had to wash every day, and felt the sudden need for a change of clothes. With California money in his pocket, he ventured out in the cold in search of a new shirt and pants. The general store offered canned goods and clothes, tools of every kind, in one small room with a potbellied stove. A group of men sat smoking around the stove. "More palaver than buying," said the man behind the counter. "You're a nice change of pace."

Joshua knew he should buy black clothes, but he didn't see any.

"That's Chink stuff," the store man said.

Joshua bought a blue shirt and brown pants—a pair of boots or he'd have to cut off his toes before California.

His new boots on, the clothes wrapped in paper and string, he ambled through the town. The newspaper office clacked its disapproval as he passed; he should have worked there, but if he had, he'd never have met Rosie.

Off the end of the boardwalk, he walked to the railway station. The Ogden weekly waited by the brick building, workers filling the locomotive's water tank. Two well-dressed men boarded. Travelers didn't ride threadbare—it wouldn't do—and Joshua was happy to find his new clothes justified.

When he got back to the saloon, he washed, put on the shirt, and slicked wet hair out of his face.

" 'Bout time," Frank said, "and a shave wouldn't hurt—you look like Stub. Take my razor."

Seeing himself in Frank's mirror, he did look like Stub. All scraggy. His hair had gone dark. If Baylor's posse happened by, they'd keep right on going.

An hour and too much blood later, he came downstairs, and there was Rosie.

"What a dandy," she said, and put a hand over her mouth. He fingered the bigger nicks on his face.

"Don't worry, kid. You'll get the hang of it."

The winter crowd thinning, their talk grew big. "Come spring, I'm getting outta here. Goin' west. 'There's gold in them thar hills.' " The same words over and over from different men.

"Fools," Frank said. "Can't be an ounce left. Near twenty years of gold rush, them hills gotta be panned out."

"Forget gold," a cowboy said. "Land's the thing. If I had a better horse, I'd cross the Sierras, get myself a ranch."

"You keep drinking," said Rosie, "you won't make it past Ogden."

"Land, it's true," a hauler added his two cents. "Perfect pasture. And cheap."

Joshua's ears pricked. The sleepy pull of California awoke.

"Na," said Stub. "Nothin' beats gold." Stub, the biggest talker of all, in his constant shirt and stained pants, a ratty jacket in the heat of summer or sitting close to the woodstove.

He wore one round-toed boot; the other had a cutout for his toes. "Don't sweep my foot," he yelled as Joshua attacked dried mud with his broom. Stub went right on talking. ". . . never the same after she caved," he said, a sad eye on his foot.

He pulled Joshua close, tipping into the cowboy on his left. The cowboy shoved him. "Get away, you old goat. You stink."

"He hasn't washed since his mine caved in," Rosie said. "Fifteen years."

"Not so." With a huff, Stub pulled his jacket closed.

"Caved in?" a new drinker asked.

"Oh, bucko, now you've done it," said Rosie.

"Here we go again." Joshua covered his ears. No stopping him, Stub could bore the hind leg off a dog.

"Fifteen years," Stub said. "Seems less." He rubbed his strawberry nose. "I was this close." He held up thumb and forefinger near touching. "Gold, I smelled it."

"You couldn't smell past yourself," said Rosie.

"Oh, a temptress she was," said Stub. "And I loved her. She give me a nugget now and again, leading me deeper, then *whoosh*." Stub gulped from his glass. "A rock got my foot, and she piled on, dirt and stone to the neck. Broke every rib." He labored with each breath. The others pushed away down the bar.

"I'm not up for the pus," said Joshua.

Stub, enjoying his pus and pain, downed another drink. His Adam's apple bobbed, sharp in the wattles of his skinny neck. Another shot, and he threw his arm around Joshua's shoulder, swamping him in a ferret smell. His lips wet to Joshua's ear, he said, "You remind me of me at eighteen."

Now, that scared Joshua. No doubt Stub had been eighteen, though hard to imagine. He might have been a runaway. He was running from something, all right.

"I had a kid brother once." Stub tightened his grip on Joshua's shoulder. "A lot like you." Stub breathed into Joshua's face. "We're family now, you and me, and this is our land of opportunity." He held his glass high. "Our land, and I intend to drink her dry."

"You've got a good start," Rosie said.

The land may have been his, but it wasn't Joshua's, and he wasn't Stub's brother.

Stub snagged a fistful of Joshua's shirt. "Do me the honor, boy. A drink."

"No, Stub."

"It's on me." He had Joshua's arm pinched. "I've money," he said, and pulled coins from his pocket. Joshua couldn't fathom where he got money.

"See. Just one teeny-weeny drink, warm you right up."

"Yeah, firewater, I know." Joshua didn't serve Indians even if they paid double, and sure enough no Chinamen, though they laid track for the railroad. Once in a while a Negro came. Joshua still thought of burned angels, and if no one saw, he'd served out the back door.

Whisky, two bits a glass, or a dollar for the best, it was all the same to him. Maybe if he liked the taste, it would have been different, but the scent took him back to Father and God's word taught with an apple switch. "I prefer sarsaparilla," he said.

"That sissy stuff? That'll wilt your willy faster than you can say Aunt Molly. Whisky, that's a man's drink." Stub kissed his glass. "Grows you a tail in front. It'll wag you good." He rocked back and forth. Wheezing, he let go Joshua's shirt and gave him a weak punch to his freshly shaved chin. "Come on, kid, it'll keep the hair coming."

"Yeah, come on." A cowboy, on Joshua's other side, elbowed his ribs. All down the bar, one after another, the men came to life, banging their glasses on the wood. "Drink. Drink. Drink." They packed around him, pushing and laughing. A glass pressed in his hand, Joshua took a sip. He coughed.

"Hold your breath and down it," Rosie whispered in his ear, and he did.

"Another. Another," they chorused, and pressed another in his hand. He'd heard this chant before. He could see the Pittsburgh boys, smell the river, taste blood. Nothing good had followed, but these men wouldn't be denied. And then there was Rosie.

The broom and Pittsburgh faded in a warm haze. A third glass banged on the bar. Liquid shimmered. Warmth flooded his stomach. He grinned in the faces grinning around him. He'd never noticed how friendly they all were. His upper lip tickled, and most unexpected, he grew light on his feet. If he didn't sit, he might rise to the ceiling. Great God, he downed the third glass. Not a cough. Not a hiccup. He held on to the bar.

"Ain't he the man now?" He hoped Rosie heard that.

"Enough," said Frank. "You'll make him sick."

"I don't feel sick. I feel—I feel—happy." Deliciously, gloriously happy. Happier than ever in his whole life.

From there on, things got a mite fuzzy, and before he knew it, he was no more.

Oh sullen day. Birds shouted. Bedsprings shrieked. Buttons on Joshua's shirt stuttered, the world so bright, he couldn't open his eyes, his teeth furry in the desert of his mouth.

Downstairs, he swept the floor. His broom's usual whisper

grated inside his head. Frank grinned from behind the bar. "Tar-nation, lad, some fun last night."

Joshua put a hand over his ear.

"Hair of the dog?" Frank said. "That'll set you right."

Joshua's stomach took a turn. "Feels like I ate the whole dog already."

By dinner, Joshua's stomach still in a roil, Frank said, "Try a raw egg."

Rosie flounced down the steps into the main room. She looked hard in Joshua's face. "Another month and you'll be just like Stub."

"Not him," Joshua said. "No, not another drink, not as long as I live."

This was why Father dunked his head, why he scrubbed with a bristle brush. But why do it again and again?

"Never?" said Rosie. "Ha!" and she stalked off, high heels clicking. She made him want to lick his wounds in private.

Rosie, an iron flower that bloomed at night. She smelled like a flower too. Joshua couldn't take his eyes off her. He wanted to touch her.

All those months with Sylvie, he'd never thought to press fingers in her flesh, savor her smell. How had he been so brainless?

He knew about animals, the ram and the ewe, mares and stal-lions, but there his knowledge ended. As far as he'd known, his mother came from his father's rib. He hadn't thought about how sisters came to be, or himself for that matter. They just got begat.

Now God had opened his eyes and offered another chance. Be she angel or devil, Rosie possessed him.

The first night of no storm door, spring air filled the saloon. Rosie looked good enough to eat, in her low-cut dress, low enough to show her creamy breasts cleaving together. Those breasts cinched high, the tops curved bare. Heart-stopping flesh. With every tap of her heels, the curves jiggled.

Before this, the most he'd seen of a woman's body was Mrs. Biddle's collarbone. He'd seen nothing of Mama. To him, breast was a warm pillow covered in black, where his head rested in comfort. A place where the world was safe and Mama-scented.

Gamblers sat at the biggest table, money in the center. Rosie glided behind each man in turn, the rancher in a clean shirt, a hauler dirty from his hair to his boots, a cowboy still in his hat. The rank farmer chewed his nails, and Silas the dandy smoothed his frilled shirt. Slick and clean, he pulled a fresh deck from his pocket, separating it in two sections, and made the cards fly together three times before he flicked them around the table.

The players fanned their cards, and Rosie slid a red fingernail behind a farmer's ear. Joshua could feel that finger behind his own ear.

Taking another card, the farmer squirmed in his seat and grinned, showing a mouth full of uneven teeth. His free hand wandered.

The hauler in the next chair swatted him. "That'll cost you, bub."

"She ain't yers, so shut yer yap. 'Sides, I got money."

"Not enough, you haven't." She snapped his ear with her fingernail. "No one does." *Hands off,* Joshua wanted to say, *she's mine.*

All the men laughed and pointed at the farmer. "Hey, kid," he slurred. "Whisky." The others snickered and checked their cards. The pot grew.

The farmer put in his last eagle. "Gotta win this one or Bonnie'll kill me."

As Joshua came back with the glass, Silas fumbled the deck.

"Oh no, you don't!" The farmer grabbed his wrist and went for his pistol. Cards sprayed the floor. Chairs tipped over, and the players scrambled for coins.

Joshua stood back, but Frank jumped fast for a gimp and, with his cane, slashed the farmer's knee. He crumpled before his pistol cleared the holster. "Son of a bitch." Rolling on the floor, he clutched his leg.

The hauler, beside Joshua, pulled his pistol. With his broomstick, Joshua whacked the barrel. The pistol flew. Frank grinned, "Good job, lad."

Joshua couldn't resist a grin. He and Frank were a team.

The gamblers righted their chairs and sat. They rubbed their bruises. "Deal," the cowboy said with a curl of his lip.

Rosie crossed Joshua's path to the bar. "Some pleased with yourself," she said. "Broom Boy besting a gun." One eyebrow arched, she flipped her hair.

How like Sylvie. And Joshua thought he knew just what to do.

CHAPTER 25

Splinters

Into his fourth year, Isaac raced through every corner of the house and barn. With delicate touch, he put the tip of his first finger on a dragonfly's wing when it foolishly lit nearby on a fence post. He chased bumblebees—not to catch, no, that would hurt them. Like them, he put his nose in every flower or he followed Luke to the front mound of groundhog homes, then hunted up the escape hatch at the other end. Miriam and the girls had to hustle or he'd find a steaming cow pie and squish it with both hands. So hard to get work done.

Miriam had come from the garden, an early morning trip to rescue a basket of tomatoes. The groundhogs were greedy that summer. Best to pick tomatoes greenish. She set them to ripen on the windowsill.

"Mama," Adah called from upstairs. "Isaac needs help."

Half-dressed, he sat cross-legged on the floor by his bed. "It hurts," he said, shielding his hand with his body.

Miriam knelt beside him. "Let me see."

"Don't touch it."

The fleshy pad at the heel of his hand had turned an angry red. "It's infected," she said. "A splinter?"

"I pulled it myself." He snuffled.

"Not all of it." A dark sliver burrowed deep under the skin. Miriam led him down to a stool by the hearth.

Abraham shut his Bible. He tipped forward in the rocker. "Problems?" he asked.

"His hand's bad." She poured hot water from the kettle into a bowl and soaked a cloth, making him a compress. Isaac drew a breath through his teeth as the warm cloth touched his wound.

"You have to keep it on." Miriam pushed his other hand out of the way.

One-handed, Isaac gripped the stool.

"Come to me," Abraham said, his arms out. "I know it hurts."

While Miriam reheated the compress, Abraham slid the boy onto his lap.

After the soaking, Miriam dried his palm. She sat on the stool beside Abraham, Isaac's hand in hers, a plate beside her on the floor.

"What's that for?" Isaac looked at her sideways. He nodded at the plate, holding a fire-blackened needle and Abraham's razor.

"I'll try the needle first, but it looks deep."

"Then what?" Isaac squirmed.

"Papa's razor."

"She'll cut off your hand," said Abraham, a lilt to his words.

Isaac craned his head to see his father's face. Abraham grinned, hugged him, and kissed his ear.

"Perhaps a finger or two," Miriam said with a tickle. "You'll never miss them." Isaac giggled.

"Here comes the needle."

The boy squeezed the arm of Abraham's rocker and arched, his face turned into his father's neck.

A firm grip on Isaac's fingers, Miriam probed. He hiccuped and held his breath.

She could feel the splinter's end. "It's no good." Miriam wiped the needle and returned it to the sewing box. She unfolded the razor's straight blade.

"No," said Isaac. "Not my hand."

"Not even your little finger. A tiny nick, less hurt than the needle."

Isaac stifled a whimper.

"No harm in crying," Abraham whispered. "We all do."

"You do?" Isaac's eyes went wide.

"Some things can't be borne." Abraham tightened the boy against his chest. "All over soon. You'll see, Mama makes everything better."

She hoped so. At least with Isaac, she could see the splinter and knew how to remove it.

With Abraham, only God knew what his splinter could be. She read the hurt in his closed face, the eye that wouldn't meet hers. She saw it in the clench of his jaw, in the red scratches across his neck and down his sides, and in the anger flaring for no reason.

That night Abraham thrashed in his sleep, pulling the quilt to his chest, rocking, rocking. Miriam lit a candle. "Abraham." She tugged at the quilt. He cried out, anguish from that unspeakable place.

Leaping from bed, he hurled the quilt at the window and, turning, shielded himself from the candle. His eye wild around the room, his bare legs shook. He flattened his back against the wall and rolled his head. "God, oh God, I didn't mean to. I didn't."

"Abraham," Miriam commanded. "Wake up." Slowly, her hands out as they would to a cornered dog, she said, "It's all right."

Sobs hitched in his throat. She reached for his wrists and brought his arms down. "A nightmare, it's over." She slid an arm around his waist and guided him to the bed.

"I can't." He cringed as if the bed had burst into flames. "The candle, it keeps falling. We're on fire." He clamped both arms over his head, elbows together. "All my fault, God help me."

"Candles fall." She shook him. "An accident, you said so yourself." He swayed. "You did the best you could." She pulled him to the bed. They sank to the edge, and he collapsed across her lap, gripping her legs.

"He's with God," she whispered. After snuffing the light on the bedside table, she bent over him, and arms around him, she rested her head on his back.

In the morning, she stretched and found him awake, knuckles grinding at his eyes. "Abraham." She pressed herself against him.

She thought last night she'd found the shard plaguing his sleep and pulled it. Yet this morning his pain seemed worse, and no razor to excise the wound.

The passing days should have brought clarity; instead, the fabric of their Plain life seemed to unravel more. Answers only brought confusion.

Miriam wished she had someone to talk to. Adah wouldn't do. Though she was close to nineteen, this wasn't her burden.

Not Hannah either, or anyone of the Flock—they held Abraham in too high esteem. No one could fathom a cloud on his soul.

Besides, whom could she trust with this secret—a secret so awful he couldn't entrust it to *her*, to Miriam, who loved him and would forgive him anything—this hurt so much deeper and darker than his worst burns?

He couldn't seem to broach it with God, who'd always had his interest at heart. And Miriam couldn't approach God, expect Him to hear much less listen, and certainly not answer. All her crying in the night over Joshua had already proved her unworthy.

. . .

Rebecca ran up the porch steps with a basket of peas to be hulled, startling Miriam from her slough. She coughed, covering her face lest the child see her inner thoughts escaping.

A hand came onto her shoulders, Adah's hand. "You're jumpy as a jackrabbit," she said. "A visit would do you good. It's been forever."

A visit, the very thought stiffened Miriam's shoulders. "It's not Sunday."

"Just go."

"I'll watch Isaac," said Mary.

"Papa needs you *here*." Emma stood in the doorway, hands on her hips. "He's by himself in the kitchen."

"If you're so concerned," Adah said to Emma, "you hold his hand." She dragged Miriam off the porch, her voice rising. "Mama's going visiting."

In the buggy, Miriam gathered the reins, and as Goli started, Adah hopped in beside her.

"I haven't seen Hannah in ages."

"Well, I . . ." Miriam swallowed hard. "You see, I wasn't . . ." She certainly wasn't going to Hannah's, to sit with hands folded, pretending nothing had changed. She couldn't.

Miriam's unsteady hands twitched the reins as she checked ahead for anyone on the road. Goli took it as encouragement and trotted faster. He made the turn at the bottom of the lane, striking out for the woods toward Susan's house.

He'd made the decision. *Good.* She didn't like secrets, though what would Adah think? They'd find out soon enough.

"Where are we going?"

"You know those cookies Isaac likes . . . ?"

Adah stole a scandalized glance at Miriam, Goli taking the road without direction.

Susan swept them into the house. With a kiss on Miriam's cheek, she asked, "Who's this beauty?"

Adah blushed.

"Must be Joshua's sister." How Miriam loved the flow of his name, so natural on Susan's lips.

"What's that delicious smell?" Miriam asked. The scent sweet, but different from other visits.

"I'm making bread, *squash* bread."

"You put squash in bread?" Standing by the worktable, Adah shot an incredulous eye at Miriam.

"Shhh, don't tell my husband." Susan laughed as she stirred a large bowl heavy with shreds of green and white. "It's his favorite, and if he knew . . ." She handed Adah a long green squash. "Here, you can help shred. These days I put it in everything, porridge, mashed potatoes, mixed with tomatoes and onions. But the bread, that's Henry's favorite."

"He has no idea?" Miriam couldn't help smiling.

"No, none." Susan grinned at Adah. "Can you imagine?"

They worked for two hours, eating and laughing over Henry, then on to Isaac's antics, how much he reminded them of Joshua when he was little, all the while comparing how they cooked the fruits of their farms.

"Come back soon." Susan kissed them both. "I wish I had a daughter like you." She gave Adah an extra hug before loading her down with three loaves of the fragrant bread. "I'll be making more tomorrow and tomorrow. You're doing me a favor."

"Are all English like that?" Adah asked, Goli trotting home into the gathering dark.

The next month, Miriam sat by the creek, a warm August evening. Isaac, beside her, slept spread-eagle on a blanket, sweat at the back of his neck soaking into his black shirt.

On the bank, Miriam had taken advantage of the quiet afternoon and now continued to drop a worm-covered hook in the deepest pool. Grass tickled her legs. A swarm of hatchlings skimmed the water. She pulled the sultry air deep in her lungs and cast her line the way Joshua used to do, whipping it underhand to the middle of the creek. He never did catch the old catfish.

Last year, at three and some, Isaac had learned the same method. A quick learner, he threaded the worm himself, though the first few casts had landed short of the water, his worm wriggling in the dirt.

Legs bent, she leaned between her knees and threw her line again. The hook sank in green shadows, and she thought she saw the flick of the whiskered fish. No, that codger wouldn't rise to her bait. Clever old thing, he stayed content with small nibbles, while the greedy swallowed her hook. A quick gulp of her worm, and their imagined happiness ended in a frying pan.

By the time she'd caught seven, Isaac woke. Her Isaac more than a nibble of happiness, he rolled to his back, kicking bare legs. He whooped at swallows cutting the darkening sky, and greedy for more laughter, Miriam tickled his belly.

"I'm hungry," he said.

"So am I." Her fish in the creel, the blanket under her arm, they walked hand in hand to the house.

CHAPTER 26

Oh, Rosie

Joshua snatched Rosie's hand and swung her to him, the move he'd practiced in dreams. The thing he should have done to Sylvie. What Sylvie wanted.

Latching his other arm around Rosie's waist, he pulled her close. He *was* pleased with himself, besting the gun with a broom-stick, and now this.

"What the hell," she snarled. "Get off me, you little turd." She bounced both fists off his chest. "You're just like the others."

"I—I thought—"

"What? What did you think?"

Hot with shame, he'd have crawled under the bar if he could. "I thought you wanted—"

"Wanted?" she bellowed two inches from his face. "Why? Because I serve drinks in a filthy saloon, you think this gives you the right?" She spun on her heel.

He fell back against the bar and Frank put a hand on his shoulder. "She's here to tempt, not touch. Many have paid mightily for that mistake." Frank gave him a look as if they understood each other. If only they had.

Joshua's heart banged in his chest, filling his face with blood. He retrieved another bottle from behind the bar and watched Rosie work her table. "Go easy on her," Frank said. "Times are hard. Her pa ran off, ma's broke down, two little brothers and a dog all on her, and she's not seen twenty-three."

At dinner Rosie ignored Joshua. His cheeks flamed.

Ready to leave for the night, Rosie took her shawl from a hook in the storeroom. He stopped her at the back door, and looking above her hair, he said, "Thought your dog might like a treat." He handed her a pot of leftover stew.

Next evening she came in with it empty and shined like new.

"Licked clean," he said. "He must have liked it."

"My brothers beat him to it," she said.

It had crossed his mind that might happen.

"They thank you," she said, and unwrapped her shawl, hung it on the hook, and headed into the big room. Stopping at the door, she said, "Joshua, I take it back. You're not like the others."

After two weeks, though they didn't talk much, Rosie seemed easy with him, like a sister. Joshua didn't want another sister, but he kept his eyes to himself, his hands and his thoughts too.

One night while he sorted empties in the storeroom, Rosie came in and collapsed on a crate. "God, I'm tired," she said. "Will this night never end?" She stretched white-stocking legs from under her skirts. "Standing makes my legs ache, and sitting's no better."

"Business is slow," he said. "Let's sneak out."

"Too cold."

"It's almost April. Come on, here, use my coat." A castoff of Frank's.

They ducked out the back door to open land near the river. Looking back, he saw lights in the upstairs windows of the other buildings, the false fronts outlined black against the deepening dark. Stars speckled into the distance.

Rosie walked, arms out for balance. "My heels sink," she said, and pulled the right one out of the ground, as the left one cut deeper. She hooked his arm.

"See where the stars end?" He pointed across the river. "I'm going there."

"Not me." She shivered and chafed her arm. "All rock and desert."

"There, yes, but beyond, it's summer year-round."

She wrinkled her nose. "That's garbage."

"No, really," he said. "In California. Every sunrise, I come here and plan." A lie. He hadn't for months, his mind taken with Rosie, Rosie, Rosie.

"At my place," she said, "I sleep in."

"Your place, isn't that the coffin maker's?"

"He's a carpenter."

"Is he your husband?"

"Never had one, never want one. Brothers are better than a husband. We live upstairs, saving for a house." She stretched. "I'm cold. Let's go."

"Where've you been?" Frank with his hands on his hips.

"Out canoodling, that's where," a new hauler shouted. "Now get me a drink, 'fore I die a thirst."

"Looks like you've had enough already," Rosie said.

Frank cuffed Joshua's head.

"We weren't canoodling," he said.

"I know, lad. Now get to work."

Rosie carried a bottle and four glasses, a finger in each, to another table of gamblers. As she poured, the hauler stood, square as Mrs. Biddle's icebox. His black hair hung greasy in his face. "A honey like you shouldn't mess with little boys," he said. "You need a man."

"Like you, I suppose," she sneered.

"You bet." With that, he clamped his arms around her waist, picked her up, and buried his stubbled face between her breasts.

Rosie hit the heels of her hands against his shoulders, stiffening her arms. "In a pig's eye." She brought her red silk-covered shin fast between his legs. Bellowing, he dropped her and doubled over.

Eyes slit, mouth hard, she adjusted her dress. "Don't you ever—"

He lifted his head and roared, "Biiiiitch." He dove at her, butting her across the room onto the piano's open keyboard. Like a rutting bull, his legs kept moving, pressing Rosie under him, scraping her with his boots. He tore at her dress.

She beat his face with her fists. The piano clashed tuneless music, and Joshua vaulted across the bar, clean glasses flying. He leapt on the hauler's back, wrenching the slippery hair.

A second later, Frank smashed a bottle over the hauler's head, and the three of them fell in a pile on the floor. A crowd circled. The hauler out cold, blood oozed from his head. His friends broke through the ogling ring and dragged him by his heels. Out the swinging doors, they left a smear of whisky and blood.

Rosie sat up, clutching pieces of dress to her bosom. Joshua lifted her in his arms, swept through the crowd, and carried her upstairs. His room closest, he laid her on the bed. "Be still," he told her.

Little dots of blood speckled her face. Glass glinted in her hair. The hauler had torn her dress from neck to skirt and shredded her stockings with the hooks on his boots.

Joshua perched beside her and picked glass from her face and hair. Thank heaven, much of the blood on her face seemed to be the hauler's.

Frank came in the room, his arms full. He carried a bottle of whisky. "Wash her cuts, a couple of swigs first—not you! Here, take the towel. Salve too. Rosie," he said, "are you all right?"

"A bit shaken is all."

Frank leaned over the bed. "You sure you're all right?"

"With Joshua?" she said. "Of course."

"Good, 'cause I'm going to kill that guy." He slammed the door and stomped down the stairs.

"That's the last of the glass," Joshua said. "Now for the cuts and scrapes."

"Ooh, it's going to hurt."

"Salve should help."

He started with her face, trying not to look lower. With every dab of whisky, she sucked air through her teeth. She dug fingernails in his leg, sending up ripples of pain—pain, he told himself. He crossed his legs and squeezed. He smoothed a dollop of salve on her face, down her neck, over her shoulder, and stopped.

The torn dress showed her collarbone, her right shoulder, a swath of pale flesh, and a tear in her white underthings. Shallow red scratches ran beneath the white.

"The scrapes . . . ," he said, and gulped, the sound probably heard downstairs.

She widened the tear, exposing more breast. He held his gasp and dabbed with the whisky.

"It stings!"

He worked across the breastbone as gently as he could, stroking the smooth paste over the upper curve of her breast. His hand trembled.

Even this gentle touch made her breath ragged. "I'm hurting you." He shifted off the bed. Nearly unable to stand, he moved to her legs, where he unbuttoned the boots and stripped her shredded stocking. Again he washed, her ankle first, and salved the red streaks, gliding his fingers around her kneecap and up, up the inside of her thigh. The worst scratch buried itself under the frill of her torn knickers.

She moaned and put her hand on his.

"I'm sorry." His voice shook. "I'll stop."

She raised her head off the pillow and buried her face in his neck. "Don't," she whispered, and guided his hand under the frills. "Don't stop."

Joshua had sipped the Holy Grail. Oh, Rosie. She'd taken him to paradise.

She, his true Beatrice, and he loved her beyond measure.

Rosie stayed home for three days, leaving him wild to see her. On the third day, Joshua said, "I'm going over."

Frank laid a hand on his arm. "Not uninvited."

"But she's—"

"I don't care what she is. You can't."

He and Frank wiped glasses behind the bar. "Poor lad," Frank said, and patted his shoulder. "I know that look, but she's not the one. Believe me, lad, I know."

"She is!" Joshua knew it down to his toes.

"There's lots to choose from."

"Then where's yours?" Joshua turned on Frank. "I don't see a wife."

"I had one once."

"You?" Joshua tipped his head. "Where is she?"

"Got me a mail-order bride. Tricky business, that. I made myself sound a right good prospect." He banged a clean glass on the bar. "Said I owned a hotel. Didn't mention the saloon. Didn't mention the leg."

"What was said about her?"

"Company told me she wanted America; she'd marry for the price of a ticket. One of those Swedish girls, long yellow hair. Hardworking, they said. I couldn't wait."

"And?"

Frank gave him a lopsided smile. "Well, she was more hard-worked than hardworking. Had yellow hair, *once*. Below the gray

I could see the ends knotted behind her scrawny neck. Red hands, pinched face, a real sight as she got off the stage."

"What'd she think of you?"

"One look, and she wanted back on board."

"But you married?"

"Yes. Neither of us had money to get her back east, much less home. Lasted till she ran off with a soldier passing through. Longest year of my life."

"And then?"

"After a few years of Dry Willy, I tried again. This time I spelled it out: 'Corpulent'—I looked it up in the dictionary— 'Corpulent man in his fifties, ready to wed Jane with no calamity.' They sent me an all-American Rose." Frank's eyes softened. "She thought I was a corporal but didn't mind I wasn't.

"Off that stage, pretty as a picture, younger than you are now and skittish as a doe. Her mother and little brothers with her. I thought they were through-passengers stretching their legs." He laughed. "I told her I couldn't marry a child. Rosie said I had to, I'd promised. It was a blessing when the preacher told me he wouldn't, what with me being married already. I told her I'd set her up over the coffin maker, and she could work for me; she'd be a draw. Flies to honey, and she hates them all. Six years now and I'm the only man she trusts."

Joshua breathed a cloud on the glass and toweled it. "She can trust me. I'd take care of her."

"It's not that easy, lad. You're better off west."

Joshua flung the towel over his shoulder and stacked the clean glasses. "I want a family, and all I have is you."

"That's pathetic," Frank said. At the same time he looked pleased.

Frank might have cracked skulls with a bottle, yet he hadn't a mean bone. Father could've learned from Frank. But smart as he was, Frank didn't know everything.

"Rosie loves me." Joshua put a fist to his heart. "And I love her. That's all that matters."

The one minute Joshua's eye came off the door, in she walked, because there she stood in a high-necked dress by the bar. Even with scabs on her face, a more beautiful woman had never walked this earth. He couldn't wait to get her alone, bursting to tell her— to have her tell him—

He waited another half hour before he saw her head for the storeroom. He followed.

The door closed. Among the boxes, she wheeled on him. "Stop doggin' me," she spat.

His mouth went dry. "I—"

Her hands fisted at her side. "I said you weren't like the others? Well, you are!"

His head filled with noise. He thought he might throw up. "Ro-Rosie," he said. "You don't understand. I—I love you. I want to marry you." He reached for her.

She retreated. "Marry?" she said.

"I'll protect you. We'll go west together."

"I know how it works." Spittle flew. "A couple of kids and you'd be gone. Besides, there's Mama and my brothers."

"We'd all go. We'd be family. We'd buy land."

"Oooh! So that's it." She shook a finger at him. "It's not me, not even my body. You want my money. You're worse than the others."

"No, Rosie, it's you. I love *you*."

Her eyes narrowed. "You don't know love."

"I do, I do. I'll love you forever."

"Forever! That's not forever-love." She stamped her spiky shoe. "That's pecker-love."

He stared at her, mouth sagging open. Unable to move, he blocked the door, his arms hanging at his sides.

"Do you hear me?" she bellowed. "Pecker-love, for you and for me. Now get out of the way." And she slapped him, a whack that hurt more than all of Father's whippings.

Joshua faltered out the back door. He ran, ran and ran until he couldn't run any farther, and threw himself on the riverbank. He'd rather have thrown himself in the river than go back to the saloon.

Drowning would be a blessing, the way Father did with unwanted kittens, in a sack with rocks. Joshua looked at the water, black ripples against the mud shore. He couldn't live without her.

She'll be sorry—he beat the ground with his fists—*when they find me bloated downriver.* He could see her kneeling by his body, tearing her hair, saying, *Why, why did I turn him away? He wasn't the same as the others. We could have had a life together.*

The bite of first love festered all night by the river, and with the dawn, his usual early morning hopes stared him in the face, the scales already washing from swollen eyes.

The simple life, *ha. He was the simple one*; imagine, Rosie and Joshua standing before the Elders, he in black, Rosie in red for their wedding. Rosie kneading bread like his mother at the kitchen table, flour spilling down her wide skirts, or in her heels picking her way around cow patties in the field, or forking hay under the August sun, her red ruffles wilted, white chest glistening with sweat. The glistening part, now that made sense.

The night's chill had needled him. Not like the night before when cold meant nothing.

He slunk back to the saloon.

CHAPTER 27

Marked for the Bludgeon

His foolish heart crushed, Joshua wallowed for days. Women—
a world of hurt.

Father would rejoice. He'd count Joshua's misdeeds—covet-
ousness, liquor, and lust—a boy deserving of pain.

Frank sprawled in his chair, a five-day stubble on cheeks and
chin, slovenly as his saloon. And God help him, Joshua cared for the
man. But he'd turn as others had, and soon; so said Joshua's bones.

It didn't matter. Nothing did. Rosie wouldn't love him, and he
couldn't bear to see her lay a finger on another man, the pain hotter
than the woodshed fire, worse than insects nibbling his burned
legs. Those burns healed. He didn't think these would.

And yet, he had to stay, be close to her. She'd change her
mind—he could see it happening in the curve of her lip the few
times she looked at him.

Frank shook his head. "That's a sneer, you dumb-bone."

Still, he couldn't leave.

It took a month and Frank said, "You slink around like a sick
chicken. This can't go on."

Joshua felt like a sick chicken, everyone taking a peck, and he pecked back.

Another week and Frank shook him by the shoulders. "Dumb's bad enough—now you're nasty. You make Rosie nasty, and that's bad for business. Take Sven's land deal." He pounded his cane on the floor. "We don't need you," he said, and swiped a rag at nonexistent spills on the bar.

Not being wanted in Gomorrah had horrified Joshua. Not wanted at Frank's was worse, love and sin all mixed up. Money figured in too. No one used money in New Eden; they traded, like Sven's suggestion in his second letter tossed somewhere in Joshua's room. The train west took money.

"Don't be a dunce—you have wages. You're done here."

He wanted to argue, but Frank was right.

Come morning, Joshua stomped to the swinging doors. Pistol packing, his new shirt and pants on under his coat, old clothes in a carpetbag along with Bella's blanket, he couldn't just walk out the door.

Rosie wasn't due for hours. Frank, at the bar, cleaned glasses with a dirty towel. He faced the other way. Joshua knew Frank heard him. He wanted Frank to say something, so he kicked the doors open and waited.

Frank didn't turn. If Joshua spoke, he knew his voice would crack.

Nothing for it, he stepped over the threshold and threw the doors shut. They snapped back, bang on his rump, good as a swift kick.

Fine, he told himself, *good riddance, Frank. Good riddance, Rosie.*

He walked past the last houses and over the ground where Rosie's heels had sunk. Those heels still stuck in his heart, he bought a ticket to Roseville and waited for the train.

Swallows swooped in and out of the station rafters. He could have bought a ticket to Sacramento, a little closer to Davenport, but he'd have no money left. He'd sewn the land payment into his shirt, enough in his pocket for food and emergencies only.

He had six days and nights on the train—the man behind the cage said so—and a week's walk to the sea. He wished he were a swallow. He'd fly.

The train arrived, a locomotive hooked to a long wooden box with windows. Could have been a church on wheels. Benches lined either side of an aisle, a door out the back, the travelers combed and brushed and in their best. They stared into the middle distance.

The train lurched forward. Joshua watched Easton slipping past, and there across the field stood Frank in back of the saloon. He blew his nose on a red kerchief.

Joshua wrenched open the window. It banged against the casement, and he leaned out. "Fraaaank!"

Frank swung the handkerchief in slow arcs above his head. Joshua, out the window to his waist, arms high and frantic, waved back at Frank as he and the bit of red cloth grew smaller and smaller. A bend in the track finally cut him off.

Frank, the closest Joshua had come to the father he wanted.

The wheels clackety-clacked.

As they streaked across the Great Salt Lake, the bridge was invisible below the train. It looked like they rode on water. He expected to sink at any moment.

When the water ended, the train entered an endless white, the Salt Desert, and Great it was, glaring at the sun. The sun glared back.

The train rumbled on, the locomotive refueling every seven hours or so. It stopped for meals, if you could call them that. He'd have had more satisfaction eating the dollar fifty each meal cost.

Head on the seat back, Joshua slept.

. . .

Palisade, Battle Mountain, Hazen, Reno, Truckee. By turns, he was sore, stiff, windblown, and bored. The Sierras froze his heart with their ungodly peaks quilted in snow. More beautiful than the Rockies. More terrible.

He concentrated on the land beyond, his eye on the promise. His land, green forever, somewhere just shy of the sea.

"Roooooseville." He hobbled off the train.

A week or so west to the sea, the stationmaster told him, plenty of time to get to Davenport if he moved along smartly. Joshua set off on a maze of roads through forest and field, valley to mountain settlements and camps, glad to be walking instead of sitting. The nights cool for July; the days perfect. Air fresh with the scent of growth, his spirits lifted even as his legs complained at the pitch of rough roads. He'd grown soft from saloon work.

Climbing higher, he followed a stream and came on three prospectors up to their knees in the water. They wore ragged shirts tucked in threadbare pants and swirled sandy water in wide pans.

Joshua drew closer. "Any luck?" he asked.

"What the hell!" One whipped out a pistol.

"Got us a jumper." The others scrambled, rifles pulled from their gear.

George's words rang: *aim to kill.* Joshua had no doubt they did, and stepped slowly back—one step, a second—then turned and ran. A shot rang, and he stumbled.

Felled by fright, Joshua rolled the steep hill, rump over head, unable to stop. He landed gasping, banged and twisted among rocks at the bottom. The men out of sight, Joshua lay still, his knocked-out breath squeaking into his lungs.

Breathing took care of itself, but a twisted ankle reduced him to Frank's hobbling pace. There'd be no walk to the sea, and he'd be out of luck if he couldn't barter a ride.

. . .

In the next valley, Joshua limped into a sprawl of tents hard by a ramshackle building, a hotel built into the hillside. It overlooked the ill-used land with one skinny tree in the midst of hummocks and mud puddles. He could see a quarter mile out, weeds taking hold, and in another quarter, the trees thickened to woods. His ankle hurt too much to go on, and he hoped this wasn't camp for those trigger-happy prospectors.

The thought of a bed hurried him up the hotel steps, a speed his ankle regretted. The first floor housed a store full of miners' shovels, buckets, cauldrons, canvas, and pans. The clerk ran both store and reservations.

"I'd like a room," Joshua said. "And I'm looking to work."

"No work and no room. We rent beds," said the clerk. "You want day or night?"

Joshua must have looked as confused as he felt.

"Men sleep in shifts, your choice, day or night. Cost a buck."

Either one was uninviting and too expensive without finding work. He'd have to use his savings and he couldn't. To make his money make money, he bought canvas for a makeshift tent, rope, and the smallest cauldron in the store.

Outfitted, he limped off to snare dinner.

For many nights, Joshua bedded close among the prospectors. Gold a stale hope in their eyes, little found for their pockets.

These men, guns loaded, a hundred or more, lived pinioned to the beaten land. They walked the mud paths, and Joshua's rabbit stew drew them to his fire. They had no time or inclination to cook, and the two women who haunted camp tended a different sort of hunger.

Young to be so fair a cook, or so the prospectors said, and Joshua asked little enough to keep them grateful. Soon he'd have a mule. Better than the horses he'd seen in camp, a mule and he could work with Sven. Their land only a few days off, a sure thing. For minutes, Joshua's certainty drowned the taste of Rosie's kisses.

On the land, he'd never again be a runaway looking in other people's kitchen windows, covetous of a glowing hearth. No more chewing the inside of his cheek as he watched families at dinner, warm bread passed by kind hands, a kiss from gentle lips.

He'd be farmer and father, raise a family he'd protect with his life.

All this so close, and then the Ringmaster rode into camp.

Sundown, he appeared slick at a distance, he in his red jacket, shoulders dripping gold braid, blue pants striped white and tucked in high boots. A bear followed, bent and shambling at the end of a long chain. Mother Biddle's circus, Joshua figured.

"Circus! You're wet behind the ears, ain't ya?" a fellow sprawler said, and nodded to his neighbor. They gave knowing grins and shifted their eyes as the pair approached.

From a squat on skinny legs, Joshua left off stirring his cauldron. He adjusted his gun belt.

The bear sniffed, coming close to pulling the Ringmaster from his saddle.

"Killer's got a nose for meat," the man said, and dismounted. He lifted his chin toward the pot. "I'll take it all, kid."

"It's paid for. And the name's Joshua."

The bear rubbed its face on Joshua's arm in a most unkillerlike fashion. The Ringmaster yanked its chain. "I'll pay double," he said.

Joshua scratched at the thickened hairs on his chin.

"Well?" The Ringmaster hurried him.

The sooner Joshua bought a mule, the sooner he'd leave this godforsaken camp. "Can't," he said. "Not tonight."

"You drive a hard bargain, Jo-shu-a." Master smiled, his teeth streaked brown. "Tomorrow, then."

Joshua wasn't so sure. But double, how could he resist? He could get a horse and a mule.

Master smiled bigger, divining Joshua's answer, he supposed. "You'll work for me, kid, only me."

And what would that mean? Joshua didn't stop to think.

Master wangled a hotel spot that night for himself and the bear. The next day he staked his tent site, never mind the space under the camp's one spindly tree was occupied. He pinioned the bear by the man's tent and poked the animal with a stick. The bear gaped wide, mouth red and toothy, a yawn of distress Joshua came to know.

The tent flap lifted. A pale face appeared, and Master poked the bear harder. It roared.

Joshua helped Master settle in, carting a table, a cot, and a chair. That evening, they sat by his fire, Master with a bottle in hand, tipping his chair on two legs. Joshua added logs to the fire and stirred dinner. The bear leaned close at the end of its taut chain, clapped its paws, and held them out. Joshua lifted his hands, an instinct from patty-cake with Rebecca years ago. Thinking better, he pulled them from the bear's reach. Once more, the bear clapped and offered its paws. Joshua curled his hands close at his chest.

A half bottle into the evening, dinner done, Master tilted his chair again. "Damn bear," he said between swallows. "Won her at blackjack." With his thumb, he scrubbed a drop from his nose. "Useless cub. What could I do with a one-trick bear named Daisy?"

The bottle empty, he threw it, just missing the bear's head. "Cute don't pay." He fell forward, slapped his thighs, and cackled. "With a name like Killer, who's gonna check if he's a she?" He adjusted his own bulge. "Trained her like a wife."

"How's that?" Joshua asked.

"Stupid boy." The words slurred like Father's in the woodshed.

"Beat her till she crawled," Master bragged. "Then dogs, kid, there's where the money is, fighting dogs." The pinion holding the bear let loose, and Daisy scooted low against Joshua's leg. He hardly dared move.

Looking into his eyes, she laid her scarred head on his lap and licked his hand. She almost purred, and after a hesitation or two, he smoothed the fur above her nose with one finger.

Master didn't notice. With his mossy teeth, he worked the cork from a full bottle.

"Come one, come all, riches can be yours. Don't dig in the dirt. Challenge the bear." Joshua rode Master's horse, on his head a three-peaked hat with bells, his hands cupped at his mouth. "Bring a dog or fight him yourself!"

Down the paths between tents, he barked the message. Many showed, but no challenge came. The few dogs in camp couldn't start a fight, much less finish one.

"Louder, kid." Master, in his fancy clothes, roostered down the path and pushed Joshua from the saddle. "I'll show you." With a chaw deep in his cheek, he spat a stream of black juice, wiped his lips on the back of his hand, and with each breath seemed to pull air from Joshua's lungs.

From his horse, Master led Daisy by the chain shackled to her neck. Her shoulders stooped as though under a burden, her skin loose like a child in a shaggy coat.

Master yanked her up on hind legs, her head lifted. "Come one, come all! Win a fortune!" He sounded like Father of a Sunday gathering his Flock.

Joshua limped back to his tent.

Every evening after a dinner of beans, Daisy and Joshua escaped to the creek, where he fed her heads, entrails, and bones of whatever he'd caught and cooked. Feeding her any more went against orders. Master wanted her hungry, eager for the pit.

But two weeks passed, and no one came. Lucky for Joshua, Master paid wages anyway. Close to the price of a mule, Joshua figured he'd be leaving soon. A mule and his muscle together with Sven on their land, Joshua could barter for everything else. Just like home.

Master laughed when Joshua confessed his plan. "Not in this world, kid. Your hundred and his won't buy jack."

Though Joshua believed in Sven's deal, Master's words niggled at him. Daisy would cock her head and nudge Joshua as he sat glum by the creek, until one night before bed, Master tempted him from his slough.

Joshua staked Daisy on her chain and stretched by the cook fire. Master, three-quarters into his bottle, yelled from his tipped chair, "Stop moping." He passed his bottle. "Here, have a swig."

Joshua sniffed. Good whisky, better than Frank's.

"It's happy juice. Hold your nose."

"I know what it is."

Master kicked at him. "Drink."

Joshua didn't balk. "Bottoms up." He drew in a mouthful and returned the bottle. Master drained it, belched, and brushed himself off, before ducking into his tent. Returning, he spat a cork he'd pulled from a new bottle and held it out. "More?" he said, his tone friendlier.

Joshua knew better, but his gloom began to lift.

"That's more like it," Master said. Joshua grinned.

Next payday, cash for the bottle came out of Joshua's wages. That and the day-after headache cut into his lifted spirits.

Supper after payday, he served Master by his tent, a plate on his lap. Joshua scraped the edge of the pot, rasping the wooden spoon on iron sides, and banged the last onto the plate. In a show of cleaning the spoon with his fork, Joshua left a healthy portion in the bottom. Meat for Daisy and himself; he wondered, would God punish him?

He and Daisy ate by the creek. They shared the spoon, one lick for her, her tongue like a shovel, a mouthful for him. When he hit the bottom for real, she peered in the pot, then tipped her head, eyes beseeching.

"Empty," he told her. She cocked her head the other way.

"No loaves, no fishes, old girl."

In the cold water, he washed the pot, Master's plate, his tin cup. Daisy and Joshua sat on a rock in the buzz of midges, the sound of home with his sisters after a long day scything. He stretched his legs, leaned on his elbows, thoughts of Mama at her bread, oh, the yeasty sweetness, a quick hug warming him. He sat up.

He didn't need Mama's encouraging hugs. They came with Father's rage.

Joshua had his own land coming, something to offer the right woman. He could see her: Rosie in Mrs. Baylor's clothes, a full-breasted woman with Mother Biddle's kindness. Another life awaited, a life where he'd do right, follow the Ordnung, and never raise a hand against another.

Daisy pressed her arm to his sleeve and rubbed greasy lips on his shoulder. He rubbed his face in her fur. What he wanted in sight, why blink away tears?

That Wednesday afternoon, a surly man with a surlier dog hollered outside Master's tent. "Hey, you with the bear."

Jenks and his dog looked to have been in the pit before, both of them. Now, that would draw a crowd.

Daisy and Joshua hung back behind a neighboring tent. Crouching, they sneaked a look. Master folded open the tent flap. The dog growled, massive head lowered, its lips crimped. Black tongue working, he slavered. Master retreated. Daisy shifted her feet.

"Easy, King." The man circled the dog's rope around one thick forearm. His other hand gripped the line. He braced against the lunge, the dog rising on its hind legs. "Down, King." And Master sidestepped out of the tent.

Solid through shoulders and haunches, King had a light brown coat rippled with scars. Jenks, equally solid and scarred, ran a hand over his bald head. He retightened his hold. "Two rounds, three minutes each, King'll take your pussycat."

"Yer all mouth." Master stood his ground. "Let's see the money."

"Saturday."

Three days. Daisy had to be ready, but how?

CHAPTER 28

The Sugary Slope

Miriam's September apples had been abundant, pie for breakfast, cobbler at dinner and supper. All through the winter, the apples' sweet scent lingered.

"Cat got your appetite?" Miriam asked. She sat, her chair between Abraham's rocker and the fire. "You hardly ate."

"I resigned as Deacon," he said, staring past her. "Zeke took the letter."

She twisted her chair to face his, her palms on his knees. "Why?"

"I haven't the strength." He tipped the rocker back, his knees out from under her hands, and turned his blind side.

"I don't believe you." She hitched her chair closer and tapped his thigh. "Whatever it is, you can't carry this burden alone."

His hazy eye told her nothing. "We need a funeral," he said.

"But he's not . . ."

"You see." He turned on her, pinned her with the pupil of his good eye. "This is why we need a funeral." His fist pinched her fingers. "He's dead. No matter how many times I relive that night, I can't change the end." He pushed her hands off his legs. "Believe

in Lazarus all you like; you can't bring him back. Joshua Is Dead."
He heaved to his feet. "We have to think of Isaac and the girls," he
said, as if Miriam didn't.

A funeral. The outward and visible sign might stop her sliding
her eye over hedgerows, stop the glimpses of Joshua's corn silk
hair. She knew he was dead. A stone would mark the end.

"When?"

He stopped at the bottom of the stairs. "Get Hubler. He'll
carve it."

"He uses money now." More and more other Amish had
turned to money, their names whispered at dinner after the Old
Order service.

"Then I'll do it myself."

Again, *when* was the question.

It wasn't just the stone; Miriam needed money for milling flour,
metal for horseshoes, salt. With nothing to trade, all came dear.
Zeke's prediction had come to pass. Money didn't seem right when
he sold the wool, yet Miriam had used it, and now the need grew
worse.

Adah had figured it out as Miriam conserved salt. "I'll work
for Frau Jackson," Adah insisted. "She's asked before."

"Work outside the Fold?" Abraham would never allow it.

Visiting had led to this. Another Ordnung rule trampled.
Miriam in her selfishness had let this happen. Nice as Susan was,
Miriam had put not only herself at risk, but Adah.

A week later, before the others were up, Miriam and Adah whispered in the kitchen. Miriam wrapped Adah's breakfast in a basket.
"This isn't right."

"Don't worry, Mama. Frau Jackson lives as Plain as we do. She
won't hurt me."

"Of course she won't, but—"

"I *have* to go." Adah tied a bonnet over her prayer cap.

Miriam listened for Abraham on the stairs. She didn't want him asking where Adah headed.

Though she hated the secrecy, it seemed to Miriam a necessary evil now that a touch of whitewash wasn't enough to patch the barn, its boards flaking down to gray. And weeds threatened the garden. They choked the dooryard and along the fences too. The garden came before all else, and putting up the harvest. Without the garden, come winter, there'd be little for supper. They needed help.

"Once Emma marries, we'll have one less mouth to feed." Adah paused at the door.

"And two fewer hands." The proposed marriage a year away, Miriam hadn't let Emma's announcement seep in. At that, the child would be less than eighteen.

"Hans is going to have himself a handful." Adah smirked.

Miriam kissed Adah's cheek. "I wish you didn't have to go."

"If wishes were fishes, I wouldn't." Adah wrapped her shawl around her shoulders. "This way, Isaac will have more of Frau Jackson's cookies."

Miriam should never have brought sugar cookies home. Truth to tell, her mistake came earlier. She should never have searched beyond the woods, shouldn't have talked to English, or let Susan Jackson's kindness turn into friendship.

Stay separate. This was *the way*, and *this* was why. One broken rule led to another and the whole system could crumble.

But if Adah didn't work for Susan, the family might crumble, and for Miriam, feeding her littles came first. Her easy comfort in the Ordnung had gone, and now nothing seemed sure, her unshakable structure cracking.

"You best hurry. If your papa knew—"

"Knew what?" Isaac hopped off the last step, ran through the parlor and into the kitchen.

"Knew what a gorgeous day it was, he'd—" Adah slipped out the door.

"He'd be down now." Miriam finished the thought as the latch clicked.

"More cookies?" Isaac said with a sly grin at the empty cookie jar. Nothing escaped him; he knew who made those treats.

"Cookies?" Emma stomped into the kitchen. She sat at the table and knotted the strings of her prayer cap tight under her chin. At sixteen she increasingly knew her mind and made it known. "You shouldn't eat them." She glared at Isaac.

"And, Mama, you shouldn't let him." Mary slid into the chair beside Emma, the two with matching scowls.

"We make our own," Emma said. "No need of English interference."

"They're a gift, not interference." Miriam set bowls of porridge before all three and called upstairs. "Rebecca, breakfast."

"What's Adah doing with English?"

"Working," Isaac piped up.

"So you heard, did you?"

Emma dropped her spoon. It clanked on the bowl. "She can't— it's not right."

"No," Miriam said, "it's *not* right." She stirred her gray porridge.

"English cookies are better than Mama's." Isaac scooped up more honey.

How slippery the sugary slope.

A funeral after seven years could only stir the ashes, and Miriam didn't want renewed condolence nor the sight of her neighbors' raised eyebrows. They were sure to follow. The Flock had mourned and long ago returned to the rhythm of sowing, cultivation, and the satisfactions of harvest. The grieving Miriam intended to end would begin anew if others took part.

"Just us," Abraham agreed. "No one else."

With a trickle of relief, she leaned against him, her head at the ridge of his collarbone.

Buds on the trees had begun unfurling, the green haze greener by the day. Zeke came on Abraham and Miriam cutting a small stone in the field. With chisel and hammer, Abraham worked only a few minutes at a time before he gave Miriam the tools.

"I'll finish," Zeke said. "What inscription?"

Early morning, two days later, most neighbors at chores in their barns, Hannah came to the house. She made no comment, offered no condolence, only food for the family service and a warm sense of forgiveness, Miriam surely returning to the Fold.

Zeke harnessed Goli to the dragger, lifted Joshua's stone to the flatbed, and led the group through the dooryard. The road hard under their feet, they made a procession of nine in black. Miriam, with a deep bonnet over her prayer cap, walked slowly arm in arm with Abraham. He pulled his hat low on his head.

A chill wind blew the ties of the girls' bonnets as they wrapped their cloaks closer, Adah beside Mary, Emma with Rebecca. At the end of the line, Hannah held Isaac's hand as he bobbed and swung his arm, his wide-brimmed hat askew.

Beside the stones of their ancients, Abraham pointed, and Zeke dug a hole deep enough to keep the new stone from tipping. He tamped in the footing and stood beside Hannah. They all circled, Isaac latching an arm around his father's leg.

"Beloved boy," Abraham started the sermon. His voice shook. He pinched the bridge of his nose.

"Yes, Papa," Isaac said. "I'm here." He tilted his face toward his father, his hat falling.

"As you should be." Abraham patted the boy's pale hair, his eye soft and loving. His chin gnarled. He took a deep breath. "May

Joshua be at peace." He squeezed Miriam's arm. "May we all be at peace."

"Amen," she said.

It rained for days after the funeral. Joshua dead and buried as best they could, Miriam waited for peace to descend.

Try as she might, the slice of acceptance she found couldn't stop her questions digging silently at Abraham. This wasn't the peace she'd hoped for, though a hollow quiet reigned in the house.

On the third day, the afternoon wore on. Abraham, in his chair, jittered his foot. He stared out the window while Miriam filled the quiet with incessant scrubbing on high shelves and down to hard-to-reach corners at the baseboards. Rebecca and Isaac helped, the others having gone to the barn.

Miriam attacked the kitchen window Abraham found so compelling, and wiped the small panes with a vinegar-dampened rag. "Rebecca," she said, "more rinse water."

Abraham's boot began tapping the floor, the sound of a distant woodpecker drilling. She glanced over.

He wasn't staring *out* the window. His eye landed to the right on a crack in the plaster. She'd noticed it before, a hairline, the movement unseen, yet it grew in a jagged slant across the wall, like a spider's leg widening at the hip, the delicate end reaching for the doorframe.

"Papa?" said Rebecca. Abraham startled, but didn't respond.

Miriam slid up the window sash with a bang.

"Don't," Abraham growled. "It's too cold."

"It's spring. We need the air. *Everything* needs airing." Miriam matched him scowl for scowl. The bottom sash at the top, she pulled down the upper, and wiped the first pane.

"Stop slamming." He squirmed in his chair. "You'll bring the house down."

"Papa, what's wrong?" Isaac rested a hand on his shoulder.

Without a word, Abraham pulled him onto his lap, buried his nose in the boy's smooth young neck, and inhaled.

"Your mama can't leave well enough alone."

Isaac hopped off his lap. "Why would you—"

Miriam slammed both sashes shut, marched to the door, and flung it open. "Window or door, we'll have air."

The breeze came in and with it a faint ticking followed by a sharp snap.

"Look," said Rebecca, pointing at the crack. "The wall broke."

The hairline gaped, exposing the plaster's horsehairy edge and a sliver of lath beneath.

Isaac clutched Abraham. "Will the house really fall down?"

Abraham smoothed the boy's hair, and with his eye hard on Miriam he said, "Now see what you've done."

CHAPTER 29

The Pit

"Kid," Master called, "barking time. Take Killer. All bets at the tent."

Jenks and King roamed the camp too. Daisy and Joshua slipped behind the hotel, staying out of sight, their time to hatch a plan. They brooded and brooded and hatched nothing.

Master wanted her mean. Not Daisy, this pet walking on hind feet. Joshua and the bear tiptoed between tents. His tender ankle complaining, they turned for the creek, and there stood Master.

"What the hell, kid?" He shoved Joshua back among the tents. "Let's hear it."

"Come—" Joshua's voice croaked.

Master, with a hand to his ear, singsonged, "I can't hear you."

Joshua cleared his throat. "Come one, come all!"

Cranky wouldn't do it. Daisy had to be fitter than fit.

Not enough meat in his snares, Joshua bought extra off a hunter. His own money—he'd have to stay extra days.

When evening came, Jenks tied King in sight of Daisy. Their noisy show of temper and teeth gladdened the growing crowd.

Bets mounted, and Joshua's worries mounted with them. Sweet Daisy.

"She'll take him," Master said. "It's not like I took her claws. I didn't pull her teeth. They used to, you know."

More bets rolled in. Master grinned and gave extra with Joshua's pay. The money, like dead leaves, crinkled in his pocket. Blood money. He hated it, but that night, he added to the stash sewn in his shirt. Not his boot, it gave him blisters.

After another long day barking, Daisy and Joshua escaped to the creek. By themselves, they reveled in a quail dinner, four, stewed tender, not that she cared about tender. The last bones cracked for their marrow, she leaned against him, her eyes on his, weaving boy and bear together. He tickled behind her jaw the way he tickled Rebecca, and walked his fingers down her spine. She groaned, and pressing her head to his chest, she suddenly lifted her nose. Catching him under one arm, she spilled him into the creek.

He splashed to shore and clutched her chain. Scooping water at her, he roared, "You beast." He clutched her fur, and they rolled in the shallows.

What was he doing? This play wouldn't help in the pit.

Saturday came, Daisy well fed, but Joshua had done little else by way of protection. He and Jenks dug a wide circle two feet deep. With a sledge, he pounded a post in the center.

Master poked Daisy to snarls. "Unhook the pinion," he said.

Joshua did and, guilty as Judas, led her through the gathering crowd.

At the pit edge, he stopped.

"The post," Master shouted.

Joshua hooked her chain to a ring on top, and Jenks jumped in the circle with King. Daisy swung to face him. Jenks unsnapped King's leash. For a second, the dog stood eyeing Daisy at the post.

"Kid, get out." The fight had started, Daisy on her chain.

"Out." Joshua hopped from the pit as King advanced at a crouch, lip raised, teeth white. King was the Killer, not Daisy. Still crouched, the dog circled.

Daisy reared on her hind legs, hulking over King. Her movements practiced, she feinted left, struck right, never taking her eyes off the dog as he dodged. She roared for real. She knew the ring, the chain and its length. She knew dogs.

He rushed her hind leg. With one paw, she swatted his ribs and knocked him flat amidst the scrambling crowd. Up in an instant at the edge of the pit, King heaved for breath. Hisses and boos swept the men.

"Sic 'em, King!" Jenks, in a fury, waved the dog on. King gathered his haunches and, from the edge, leapt at Daisy's muzzle. She swatted him again, a glancing blow that brought him down at her feet, where he sprang straight up between her front legs and sank his teeth in her nose. His jaws locked.

She arched and threw her head high, his hindquarters lifting in the air. Blood spurted, flooding his sides, spraying the crowd as they screamed in delight.

The dog still latched to her nose, Daisy swung him down and up higher, tail above her head. As he came down, her arms spread, and with a clap, she slammed him between her paws. Air woofed out. The dog's mouth opened, and he fell at her feet.

"Come on, King, get up." The screams mixed with others yelling at Daisy, "Kill, kill him." Daisy pounced, and with one swift bite snapped the dog's neck.

"Hey, Jenks," a man yelled. "Who's the pussycat now?"

So like his dog, Jenks lifted his lip. He lunged. "You're the pussy." The losing men beat him to the ground, as winners, their hands out for money, swarmed the Ringmaster.

"Spoils to the victor," he crowed, and worked through the crowd.

In a welter of blood, Daisy—no, not Daisy—Killer consumed the dog.

Joshua's gorge rose, and he ran for the creek, stripped his clothes, and plunged in the cold water. Had he not seen her, he wouldn't have believed it. His Daisy.

Dressed and still feeling sick, he made for the woods. He'd check his snares, though Daisy wouldn't need dinner, and Master could rot for all Joshua cared.

When he returned, he dropped a small rabbit at Master's feet, too nauseous to gut it.

"Don't just stand there." Master kicked the rabbit. "Cook it. I'm hungry. And don't bother Killer. Leave him bloody. It's good for business."

Killer's nose healed slowly, and she melted into the bear Joshua loved, a few more scars the only evidence. Their days easy with no new challenges, Daisy's bovine eyes knit him to her again, sweet ties comforting as a full belly.

Growing testy, Master withheld wages. He kept watch as Joshua went about his work and arranged to buy the mule. But he was short of cash.

"At the next fight," Master said. "Wages and more." Joshua had no choice; he had to wait. He needed the mule, though his ankle was almost sound.

That night at the end of dinner, Master tipped the stew pot for a better look. He scowled and swatted Joshua's head. "Give me that." The saved portion scooped onto Master's plate left none for Daisy or Joshua.

"Gotta have a goddamned dog," Master said. "They won't come to me, I'll go to them." The following morning he packed his saddlebags.

When Joshua brought him his horse, Master planted himself toe to Joshua's toe, their noses near touching. "I'll be a few days. Don't feed Killer." Deliberate and slow, Master took a fistful of Joshua's shirt. "You do," he said, and latched his other hand hard on Joshua's privates, "I'll have your oysters for breakfast."

He squeezed. Joshua yelped.

For two weeks without Master, Joshua and Daisy spent mornings poking at fish in the creek. After snaring dinner, they basked away the afternoons, the rabbits stewing. Maybe Master wouldn't find a dog. If he did, no dog came bigger or meaner than King. Daisy would be fine, and Joshua would get his wages in time to make the closing. He had ten days; Master better hurry.

Their last morning by the creek, Daisy rolled on her back, legs waving, mouth open, hairy belly exposed for a tickle. Her mouth wide, Joshua put his head right between her teeth. Daniel and his lion had nothing on them.

"Get yourself up here," Master called from the road. "Now."

Remembering Master's threat as he left, Joshua's privates twitched.

"Heat water," Master said. "Let's get this over with."

What over?

"A rag and bucket," he ordered. "Get it."

Buckets of warm water, that's what men had brought in the house on St. Michael's Communion Day. They'd washed one another's feet and dried them.

He shuddered. Wash Master's feet? His shirt, yes. His socks, maybe. Not his feet. Joshua pinioned Daisy.

In the tent, Master unbuttoned his red jacket and threw it on the cot, then unbuckled his belt and pushed his pants to his knees, exposing the thighs of his gray union suit. He sat on a stool.

"Bath," he said.

Washing just his feet suddenly seemed easy.

"Don't gawp, kid."

But where to start?

"Boots, kid. My boots."

Joshua squatted and pulled. The reek near knocked him over.

Master pushed his pants to the ground, anchored the pile with one foot, and yanked the other free. There he sat in his stained underdrawers, working the buttons from neck to crotch. He bent the collar open. "Start at the shoulder."

With his fingers, Joshua gingerly peeled the thin cloth. He tugged at a stuck place.

"Don't skin me," Master snarled as he stood for Joshua to continue.

At arm's length, Joshua held the top of the union suit between two fingers and eased the cloth down Master's back, over his buttock, wetting stubborn scabs, and soon his hands came coated with Master's corruption.

The drawers finally in a heap at his feet, Master stepped into a bucket of warm water. "Now wash," he said.

Over the next twenty minutes, Joshua rinsed scabs and yellow seep, down to raw mottle.

"Now the salve, kid."

And he did, but never again, he told himself. Money or no money. Never.

That afternoon, the heavens opened, washing the camp as if ready for some momentous event. When evening came under scattered clouds, Joshua laid a table for one in front of the tent, the table's slender legs forced into the muck. With a flourish of his white handkerchief, Master sat.

A circle of dirt-covered men gathered to the smell of frying elk, a treat from Master's trip. Meat drew men faster than barking. To what purpose, Joshua didn't know.

Master tucked the handkerchief in the collar of his red jacket and steadied the meat with a fork in his fist. Drawing a knife through the brown crust, he laid open the bloody center. The crowd couldn't take their eyes away.

He cut a small piece. Fork switched to the other hand, he speared the morsel, and lifted. "Oh, so genteel," he smirked, and sucked the dripping glob from the tines. He chewed, his mouth open, tongue sliding the morsel side to side, every brown molar given a chance. Whisky from a tin cup washed the meat down.

Daisy, pinioned beside him, chewed at her long claws and quietly reverted to patty-cake, when a mule-drawn cart rumbled into camp. The crowd parted. Daisy yawned and turned away.

Master smiled. "Geeeeentlemen," he said, his mouth full. "My dogs." Two haulers unhitched the flatbed with its large metal cage stuffed too full to show more than fur. The men rolled the cart to the side of the road.

"Half mastiff, half wolf." Master's smile widened. He tossed a piece of meat between the top bars. The cage erupted in a flash of snapping teeth. The crowd gasped.

The beasts settled, ears flat to their heads. Hackles down, their yellow eyes smoldered at the now-jeering crowd. Master glowered. He hit the cage with a stick, bringing the dogs to a slavering boil.

"Gentlemen, lay your bets." He patted the table. "Tomorrow, three dogs, and not one of 'em man's best friend." He gave a meat-filled grin. "Will Killer kill or be killed?"

Daisy opened her mouth wide, all teeth, her long tongue out. Silence buzzed in Joshua's ears. The crowd seemed a distant mumble.

More money fluttered on the table. Master's lips moved. "Tomorrow," he mouthed. Without hearing, Joshua saw the words on his lips. "Who do you fancy?"

Men crowded the table, eager to put money on a sure thing. Three at once, what possessed him?

"Clean up, kid." The Master pushed his plate on the ground.

The clang brought hearing back. "Make room for the money," Master said.

Joshua reached under his elbows, clearing the cup and fork. The knife went in Master's belt beside the key to Daisy's shackle. He stuffed money and gold in a sack between his legs. "By this time Sunday, you'll have your wages and more."

Tomorrow with its promise of blood, Joshua couldn't think of wages.

Daisy rolled, rubbing her spine on the ground, and pulled her hind foot to her mouth like a baby. She licked between her back toes. Master couldn't stop smiling. "Take Killer, and wash up," he ordered.

Joshua led Daisy to the stream. Talking softly, he held one paw at a time and pulled off the shedding husks. The points glistened brown and sharp. Sharp enough to take on three? He didn't think so.

King had been easy, not that he'd thought so then. Even at her best, Daisy couldn't take on three. This wasn't a contest. What could Master gain?

Not that it mattered. Either way, Daisy would die.

Joshua mulled. Already a thief of Master's food, why not steal Daisy? Horse thieves got hung, but Daisy wasn't a horse.

Three on a bear? Master should hang.

Joshua couldn't be part of murder. But how could he walk away?

The next day would bring riches. If not riches, then the promise of blood. This meant that if he stole Daisy, he would steal from every man and boy in camp.

Was it theft to set her free?

Master stole Daisy's freedom, and if she fought the dogs, he'd steal her life. Master was the thief.

. . .

Late that night, clouds breaking to an occasional moon, Joshua crept to Master's tent, boots squelching on the quiet road. Daisy, already on her feet, rattled her chain as she shook off dew. She butted Joshua's chest. He held her head in his hands and whispered, "Hush now."

A low growl came from the cage. Joshua pushed Daisy to the side of the tent, praying the dogs wouldn't erupt. He caught a line of candlelight at the flap. Oh, God, Master couldn't still be up.

Joshua peeked in through the line. There, sprawled on a cot, was Master with his mouth open, the money sack nestled in the crook of one arm. Despite his bath, the place stank.

Joshua slipped in and squatted beside him. One hand fisted against his chest, Joshua extended his other arm and, with two fingers and a thumb, pulled the tail of Master's jacket away from the belt. Joshua reached with the other hand for the key to Daisy's collar.

Outside, her chain clanked. The Master shifted. Joshua pulled his hand away, still holding the coat, in case by dropping it Master would wake.

Stretching one leg for a quick getaway, Joshua held his breath and reached again for the key. Master coughed and opened one eye, the pupil staring into Joshua's. He couldn't move. Master's eye rolled back. The lid dropping, he lay quiet.

After a minute to unfreeze, Joshua tucked his little finger in the circle topping the key. Gently, he eased the key up till the shank appeared above Master's belt.

The key in his fist, he shifted to the runaway leg and, silent as a ghost, slipped through the tent flap. Daisy shook her chain. Joshua fumbled at her shackle, sliding it around her neck until his fingers touched the keyhole.

Loud as a screech owl, the key grated in the rusted hole. It wouldn't turn.

Harder, he twisted harder, fearing he'd break the shaft, and all would be lost. He couldn't free a bear dragging a chain. He kept one eye to his task, the other on the tent.

Daisy tucked her head, trying to see. "Keep your head up." He twisted back and forth until the lock clicked, tumbling the shackle, and they raced for the woods, splashing in leftover rain. Under the sometimes moon, his pants wet to the knees, he and Daisy headed out the road. At the path to the creek, Daisy veered.

"Come on, girl, not this time." He patted his hands on his thighs. "Come on." She slapped her thighs and clapped her paws. "No, I'm not playing." Reluctant, she followed slowly, perhaps missing the stew. He had no treat to encourage her.

After what felt like miles of hard breathing, the road well away from camp, the sky leaked dawn. Time to strike into the woods. Without a path, he felt his way among the trees, grateful for the growing light.

Daisy glided. He stumbled. She'd have been a better leader.

At full light, deep in the woods, they came on a clearing filled with raspberries. Their long canes arced heavy with soft red fruit, and by the handful, seeds crunching, he swallowed a feast. Daisy nibbled one raspberry at a time with delicate black lips. She bumped him from her patch. He pushed her head and reached behind her, but she wasn't fooled. She gave him her best open-mouthed roar, breath sweet, tongue red with mashed berries. She shouldered him out of the way and continued her careful picking.

"A bear is missing," he told her. "I have to report." He had to lead the search.

"You're free, Daisy." He kissed her scarred nose. She continued munching. "You'll be happy."

Joshua wished he could take her to the coast, but how could he hide a bear on the road? Master would find them in a matter of hours. She was better off in the woods, her real home. The place she belonged. He jammed his hands in his pockets and stepped out of the clearing. Her big head swung toward him, and she dropped on all fours.

"No, girl. You stay." On her haunches, she cocked her head, watching as he left.

As soon as she was out of sight, he missed her. Had Mama missed him? He tried to outrun tears. What kind of man cried over a bear? Besides, she was free. She'd find other bears. She'd have cubs. She'd be what God intended.

By now Master would be in a froth. Joshua dodged trees, ducked under branches, swamp soaking his feet.

He gained the road. Drizzle came along with a badger of questions. What was free? In the woods when he first ran, had he been free? Yes, free to starve. And what did Daisy know of the woods, she a newborn when the hunter took her?

Ahead, in increasing rain, a throng clamored where the Master's tent had been. The men raised fists in the air, some with rifles. They stomped a pile of canvas into the mud, the table and chair smashed to kindling.

The cage of dogs sat on the cart, silence within as tempers rose nearby. Mounds of wet fur pressed against the bars. Joshua squinted. The cage leaked red onto the cart, where it mixed with rain and flowed over the edge.

Shot, his guess. The shooters ranged-up for more.

Next to the cage, a black-haired man, not Master, held Daisy's chain above his head. "He's loose," the man shouted. Heads shifted. Eyes checking every direction landed on Joshua.

"Hey, the kid, grab him." And they did, by the collar, by the hair, by his belt. His feet came off the ground, his pistol lifted from its holster.

"Where's he at?" A voice from the crowd.

"I don't know."

The mob moved like water, swimming him past the cage, to

the spindly tree. He squirmed, afraid they'd drop him. Afraid they wouldn't.

"Tell us."

"Honest, I don't know."

"He's got our money. Tell us or—"

"He owes me too," he said to the sky, as they joggled him along. No lie, though at that point he'd have said anything.

"Hang him," another shouted from the crowd.

"Yeah." A chorus on all sides. "Hang him." Stomach in his throat, Joshua gasped.

"Tree's too scrawny."

"The woods."

"Ya, the woods."

The mob surged onto the road, Joshua held aloft, face high, arms spread. He begged; he pleaded; he squirmed in terror. He pissed his pants.

They passed him hand to hand, about to fall, and never falling. Hands under his neck, more in his pockets, under his rump, under his knees, tearing his shirt, his shoulders tipping. "Money," someone shouted. Bills floated in the air, and a scuffle followed, his legs scissoring someone's head, but they didn't drop him, and turning as one, they retraced his steps.

"Please." His voice rose to a shriek. "NOOOOOO!"

The crowd swelled to a blood frenzy, no way to stand down should they want to.

Three of them swam him out ahead of the crowd. Their leader walked backward, hands high, one shaking a rope, the other a rifle. "Almost there, come on."

Joshua hammered at them.

"Someone get a horse."

In his battle, he craned his head upside down and fear for himself vanished.

"Bear!" The cry went up. The men beneath him splintered.

He dropped on the ground. And there she shambled. "Daisy, go back. Go."

His yelling lost in the crowd's panic, Daisy paid no attention. Stoop-shouldered, her fur flattened in the rain, she looked less a killer and more like a heavyset prospector down on his luck. She raised her head as if seeing the crowd for the first time. She shook her wet pelt, her fur fluffing large, mouth open and toothy in her widest yawn of distress.

Joshua ran, arms imploring. "Daisy," he called.

A shot rang from behind him. Daisy reared, front paws reaching. Men, running in every direction, stopped and fired a torrent of bullets.

Daisy batted the air as if bothered by flies. She staggered under another barrage, walked on her knees, and arms high in surrender, she fell on her face.

Before he could reach her, the mob descended, knives waving, Daisy lost under the crowd.

"Mine," the men shouted. "He's mine. I shot him."

Joshua ran for the foothills as the black-haired man raised his rifle. He sighted on Joshua, and a hiss passed his ear before he heard the report, and followed the bullet into the westward woods.

CHAPTER 30

To the Sea

On the road, his neck cramped from looking over his shoulder. At every approaching horse and rider he readied for a fight. At empty cabins, his right hand didn't speak to his left. He took what he needed, a knife for the knife he'd lost, blanket for blanket, flint and steel. A pair of pants with a belt, his pants soiled beyond redemption. A near lynching will do that.

He ran west by habit. Hate stalked him: faceless, shadowy, behind trees, inside the cabins he ransacked. Hate, more deadly than a following posse.

He woke in one cabin, the owner off. Hours fishing, weeks panning, he didn't care, too sick with visions of Daisy in the road: "No—" whispered, shouted; she raised shaggy arms, hugged him, buried him in her fur. Smothered him.

Another cabin, the latchstring left out, he accepted the invitation. Not that he needed one—he'd have gladly kicked down the door. Hate, sharper than hunger, shook him, dog on a rat. He opened closed containers, scattered contents on the floor, flour brown and dusty as he flung it, an empty sugar jar, empty coffee, empty cracker tin.

He groped under the rucked-up bed. Nothing. Even if he found food, it would stick in his craw. And finally on a high shelf, on top of a Bible, whisky. He closed his fist on the bottle's neck, careless of the book. It flapped, bird shot, to the floor, printed wings spread. He left it.

Bottle in both hands, he pulled the cork with his teeth, fumes eating his nose. He toasted Hate with a tip of the bottle and sat at the table. The first long pull seared him, tongue to gullet, a fleabite compared with visions of Bella and Sam, of Daisy holding Frieda by the hand, James climbing Daisy's back. He washed them with whisky, swallowing until the burn receded. He battered his fists on the table, kicked the square legs. "More whisky," he roared.

But where was the glow? The happy lightness of Frank's bar refused to bloom. Joshua's fingers tingled, legs loose enough to dance, and no desire.

"Ha," he barked at himself. More drink. Ha, ha! Laughter should be catching.

In a rage, he lurched to his feet, kicked the stool aside, and turned over the table. Casting about, he stripped covers off the bed and whirled them across the shelves, tools and utensils crashing to the floor.

Hate clogged his head. The room spun, and he found a dog's-eye view of tumbled furniture, his cheek slammed to the rough floor. *More whisky.* He crawled after the empty bottle.

Seven days on, Joshua walked toward the land he had no money to buy, the paper bills sewn into his shirt having floated free. Now a day and a half to find Sven, to offer work. To plead, to beg. To let Sven down. To have Sven let him down.

Joshua had turned one cheek, then another, and had no more to turn. Why would he trust Sven or God? Or himself for that matter.

He came on a forest of giant trees, red trunks wider than a barn door, the canopy high as Mother Biddle's cathedral. The tarnish of hate black on his soul, he curled in a stolen blanket and waited for God to squash him.

He woke to the last day for finding Davenport. Sun through the canopy dappled the ferns. The blanket slung over his shoulder, a scrap of hope pushed his legs.

His belly grumbled. At a creek, he drank. A fish jumped. He missed Daisy. A bear that ate with a spoon; he could have taught her about fish, and honey in hollow trees.

She'd trusted him, and he tricked her with soft words, abandoned her as he'd abandoned Mama and his sisters. No better than Master.

Master had promised her nothing. Joshua was worse. He'd offered Daisy life. He'd offered love.

What did he know of either in this world?

Love, tender and terrible, he'd buried it, but Daisy with careful black lips had unwrapped the shroud, and Master had crushed what lay beneath. Joshua hated him, a hate that overshadowed pain and guilt and love alike. Hate gave him strength.

Damn the Ringmaster. As if he were there, Joshua spat in his eye, punched him, tore his gold braid, ripped buttons off his union suit, beat his head with a stick, and watched both eyes go black. Joshua dined on beating him till he fell.

Ah, blood, yes. And Master down, Joshua kicked him, stomped him, first with one foot, and when that one tired, he stomped with the other, then squeezed his scabby neck till his bulging eyes knew Joshua's. Squeezed until Master's legs galloped to a crawl and stopped.

Out of the woods, Joshua walked brown hills, his head aching as if he'd stared at the sun. Davenport had to be over the next rise, or the one after. But where was the green, the constant summer?

Collywobbles threatened, and he ate what he knew, a few wild onions, burdock, and purslane. He looked for ginger and sorrel. None.

He pushed on, sun rolling across a cloudless sky, the afternoon waning. Sven would be closing on the land. Joshua hurried, his breath shortening.

But why bother? He'd miss it, and with no money to offer, what good was he anyway?

Arriving in Davenport, Joshua had found a clerk locking the office. "Too bad," the man said. "Nice parcel, close on the ocean." He'd pointed toward a ridge of stunted trees cutting the late afternoon sun. "Take a look—another parcel might come up."

Joshua followed a narrow track, much like a sheep path over a grass-covered hill, the grass pale and dry as straw. Nothing of promise about it.

He climbed to the trees, their gnarled branches studded with dark needles, and came on a rock ledge. Below him, the land dropped to water and water, immense to the edge of the sky.

He stood, legs spread. Hands hanging at his side, his knees shook as the sun, red and round, slid into the ocean, the surface battered into white ridges.

Damn Sven, another trickster. Damn the saloon liars. Damn Frau Lentz's brother for putting the dream in Joshua's head. Eight years striving, come to naught.

And damning them, Joshua broke pieces of dead tree. He threw sticks on the ledge, anger better than emptiness in his chest.

Evening damp off the water spoke of coming winter, and Joshua heaped the broken branches, piled tinder, and lit them. Blanket over his shoulders, he warmed his hands.

Above the sound of waves, hooves clopped near. Out of the dusk, a burly man on a mule made his way to the fire. Joshua didn't bother to move.

The man a young coot in dirty overalls, a sack over his shoulder, legs hanging halfway to the ground. Whiskers hid his face. "You're a sorry sight," he said. "Want company?"

"Suit yourself." Joshua watched small flames licking the broken branches.

The mule halted. "A cheery fire you've got." The man slid to the ground. "Can't say the same for you, brother."

Joshua looked up. "You're not much to look at yourself." But on closer inspection . . . "Sven?"

Sven gave Joshua a gap-toothed stare. "Shit," he said, elbows akimbo. "Where the devil were you? You made me lose . . ." He spread his arms wide to the land.

"I got myself robbed." Joshua gave the fire an angry poke. "A hundred sewn in my shirt, and more owed. Enough for a mule."

"Christ." Sven opened his sack. "You need a drink as bad as me."

He pulled out a jar, amber liquid close to the brim. "Want a snort?"

"Why not?" The catch of want tightened Joshua's chest.

Sven folded his legs, his rump landing beside Joshua, thumbs working at the wide cork. It popped to the ground, and he took a swallow. "Here, this'll help," he said.

Joshua gulped. The liquor flashed in his stomach. "Aaahhh, heaven." He took another, and Sven unloaded his years of struggle, ending with the loss of the land.

Well into the jar, warmth took hold. "The liquid of visions," Joshua said. "I could use one about now."

"Still God-fearing, are you?"

"I was, before I slipped the hangman's noose." And once Joshua started, his story tumbled out. He led Sven through nights on the farm, told of the woodshed and how he'd run.

"I'll drink to that." Sven lifted the jar.

They both drank and laughed over Joshua's burned angels.

"What?" Sven poked him. "Raised in the heart of the Civil

War, and you never saw a darky?" He made fun of Joshua's guilt those first months pilfering gardens. "And look at you now, ha! A hairy man worth hanging."

He hooted at the boys under the bridge. "You a yellow-haired girl? Hard to believe, wild-eyed you, the matted beard?" He rocked back and forth. "Wish I'd been there. Prissy, stupid little you." His eyes glittered. "What'd they do, bugger you good? Tell me."

Joshua told him Sylvie was yet to come, and Rosie.

Sven hurried him through tears over Mother Biddle. "Yeah, yeah, yeah, tell about Sylvie. Did she—" He wanted every finger and tongue of Sylvie's touch, of Rosie's. The jar near drunk, Joshua obliged. Both men on their own grew hard and ecstatic.

Another jar from the sack. Joshua uncorked it, along with his love of Sam and the family.

"No kidding, all that time and you were a dirty little boy!"

"No, not like that. *Love.*" And he uncorked Daisy. He poured hatred for Master.

"Lover-boy and a bear." Sven laughed. "Now, that's lonely."

Hate bloomed anew, shiny as an Indian-head penny.

Woozy by the fire, Joshua hated Sven's insinuating eyes, and as he glared, Sven became two, overlapping himself, his too many eyes mocking.

The heads shook. "A bear. Why am I surprised? You look animal yourself, brother."

"Shut your mouth, and don't call me brother. I'm not your brother."

"See the water?" Sven said. "Go drown yourself. You don't deserve this sweet ocean air." He slurped from the jar, swallowed, and wiped his mouth on the back of his hand. "Why would angels save you? You're not half the man Sam was."

He pushed Joshua in the chest. "You left your mother to take the beatings, and you didn't warn her. Or your sisters. Even now, he might kill them."

"He wouldn't. No, Father hated me, not them."

"You just don't care. At least Mommy Biddle had a son who did." Sven leaned back on his elbows and crossed his ankles. "Sure got rid of you. Smart woman. I bet Daisy wishes she'd done the like. Poor thing, swatting at bullets while you hightailed it." He punched Joshua's thigh, a laugh low in his throat. "You're spoiled—" He took another gulp and worked at a loose tooth. "You're a softy"—he kicked Joshua's leg—"scared silly by a jackass father spouting hocus-pocus."

"It's not hocus-pocus." Spit flew from Joshua's mouth. "And he's not a jackass." Joshua couldn't believe those words on his own tongue. He returned Sven's kick and hit the fire, scattering burned sticks off the rock.

Two Svens shied to their feet, and Joshua kicked again.

"If land and family mean all," Sven sneered, "why be here?" He whacked the top of Joshua's head. "You buggered up the family God gave you. You don't deserve another." He pushed Joshua over in the dirt. "You're nothing but a sniveling brat." The three of him laughed, heads thrown back.

All teeth and rage, Joshua flung his arms around Sven's knees and felled him. The mule skittered into the dark as they rolled over the dead fire, flailing at each other's faces. Joshua snatched up a stick and hit him, hit the ground, hit Sven's back, hit his own head in a full-liquored frenzy. And finally spent, they fell apart, Joshua's eyes afloat in the nether reaches of his head.

He woke in a scatter of broken glass, his mouth a swamp of leftover whisky. Head too heavy to lift, he moaned. Was this how Father woke, those mornings in the woodshed? Had he chased the glow, his demons ever-resurrecting? Demons Joshua had somehow caused.

He rubbed his clogged nose with the back of his hand. The hand, crusty, brown, and scratchy, hurt the swollen flesh. Blood dribbled. Father had scrubbed himself clean and pretty with a pig bristle brush.

Pretty is as pretty does. Mother Biddle's words sat him up. And dear God, how pretty was he, dried blood all over his hands and down his shirt.

As dawn lit the eastern sky, he climbed down to the ocean, gingerly touching for wounds. He splashed his face in salt water. The sting stopped him. He probed his nose. Even bleeding its worst, could it account for all that blood?

Pretty is as pretty does, and what had he done? On the ledge, smeared ash marked the scuffle with Sven, the half-burned sticks flung in every direction, but Joshua found nothing more. Had he wounded Sven? Killed him?

Joshua searched among the shore's boulders and inland a mile through grasses in every direction.

At a clear stream, he peered down to its floor. No body, but floating on the surface, face-to-face, he saw himself. "My God," he breathed, shock at the sight of those eyes shot with blood, dark hair tangled to his shoulders. Shorter, redder hair matted his jaw and upper lip, around his mouth the remains of things his stomach wouldn't tolerate. He touched his blood-darkened cheek, the scar running under his eye in a line through his beard to his ear.

A breeze riffled the image. A lock on his forehead shifted, the touch soft as Mama's hand. Would Mama know him? And worse, would she care to know a man who could wrong his friend, beat him, perhaps kill him?

Though Joshua had no house, he had a door where the wrong, whatever it might be, lay like a carcass. Sven was better without him, better as the blacksmith he'd been.

Joshua scrubbed his face, creek sand uncovering pits in his sallow skin. How could he ask if Mama would know him? He didn't know himself.

After drinking his fill, he returned to the ledge. He stood in a rising wind and looked to the sea. Water endless and undrinkable ran to the horizon. He'd run out of west.

His dark angels had sung of a Sinner Man. *On that day,* they sang, *the sea'll be a-boiling.* And the sea before him did boil among the rocks. His private judgment day.

Even if he'd found land as green as New Eden summer, what crop would grow, the seeds sown with hate?

What crop would he reap? His soul, more pitted than his face, had grown worse as he blamed his sins on others, starting and ending with Father.

Always Father, hulking in black, Joshua ever eleven and small. Father honing the blade of his scythe, his reach long and arcing.

Joshua crouched on the ledge, arms around his knees. He stared at the white-capped water. Father hadn't put Joshua's soul at risk; Joshua had. His body had taken swiftly to Mr. Biddle's clothes, buttons and all, not so much as a flinch. The hand that lifted the whisky had lifted the stick. He held his hand in front of his face, fingers spread. Joshua had done it with his own hand. Done it with intent.

He turned his back to the ocean.

Eleven no more, he had one remaining hope. He wanted to hug Mama and his sisters. He wanted to see a crocus reach for the spring sun, wanted to watch downy mallards waddle pond to creek, the hatchling chicks turn pinfeather wings into flight.

He wanted to sweat in midsummer heat, drive himself to exhaustion the way he had his last day at home, and lie in bed the way he had then, hands behind his head, listening to peepers, their song drifting through his window. He'd savored the sweet ache in hardworked arms and legs, every bite of supper earned. He hadn't wanted that feeling to end. He'd fought his drooping eyelids as the rain lulled him to sleep.

Now he wanted to pitch hay in a race with the rain, fall into his own bed on his own land, that place of peace where no man raised a hand against his neighbor. Even Father never hit a neighbor.

Full of resolve, and ready to beard Father in his lair, Joshua walked into the morning sun.

In the heat of the day he submerged himself, clothes and all, in a stream. He soaked until mats in his hair softened and he could drag his knife like a one-tooth comb through dark tangles. No prize pig at the end, but better than he was. Good enough to muck out someone's barn for a meal, or stand behind a bar and pour.

He poured, though his hand shook. When asked to join the drinkers, he touched the scar across his cheek and declined.

Through the fall, in settlements and towns, some offered a place for the night, a slab of bread. Everyone offered advice. An embarrassment of riches in the face of earlier theft.

It seemed many carried a fondness for the East. They heard Joshua's purpose with envy, and he traveled high on their hopes for his future as he worked and walked Santa Rosa to Sacramento, Roseville to Truckee, to Reno, and around the Great Salt Desert, Ogden to Easton.

He dreamed of Father dressed in gold shoulder boards and the Ringmaster's striped pants. Joshua needed a drink, and there came the Lord in white robes, glass in hand. Joshua stared woolly eyed. The Lord laughed, and Joshua caught a glimpse of cloven hooves.

The anticipation of seeing Rosie and Frank beat in his chest.

CHAPTER 31

Shepherd No More

Miriam walked up Hannah's lane, the late afternoon air full of summer balm, the same kind of balm her friendship with Hannah used to bring her. Miriam had to nurture it back to life.

"When you're ready, come see me," Hannah had said after the funeral. She meant when Miriam collected herself, accepted an end to her pining. Only then would the stiffening between them disappear completely.

She trudged through the dooryard and up stone steps to the heavy oak door. Where was the lightness of renewal she'd come to find?

She knocked and waited. Why not tap and walk right in as she always had? Hannah opened the door, and seeing Miriam, she beamed.

"You've come," she said, her arms taking Miriam into the warmth of a bosomy hug. "I'm so glad."

She gave off a forgiveness Miriam knew she didn't deserve, and the stiff shoulders she expected from Hannah turned out to be her own.

Hannah's arms dropped. "You can't do it, can you?"

"I want to," Miriam said. "Believe me."

"All-accepting is who we are." Hannah turned and busied herself at the table cutting green and yellow squash in thick rounds. "It's the only way to still a troubled heart."

Miriam, standing by the door, wrung her apron in a tight twist. "I can't. I don't know why. I just can't." She felt for the door behind her and retreated through it. Her last sight of Hannah, her wintry back, the bare neck and neatly rolled hair at the base of her white prayer cap.

Miriam lifted her skirts and ran down the lane. If she could, she'd run to Susan's house, the only place free of judgment. But what good would it do? No matter where she ran, Miriam's own judgment would follow, berating her for this unpardonable lapse, hers as a friend, hers as a baptized Amish woman committed to the Flock. Not their fault. They had tried and tried to keep her with them. She had crafted this aloneness herself.

The next morning, early sun through the parlor window cast a slow-moving pattern on the floor. With Isaac's help, Abraham hitched his chair as the sun spot moved. He stayed in the center the way a cat would, looking content, Isaac in his lap, the mullion shadows crossing them in warped squares.

Miriam called from the kitchen, "Isaac."

Abraham went rigid.

"Come along, it's time you learned milking."

Abraham tightened his embrace around the boy.

"I'll be right back," said Isaac, extracting his pinned arms. "It won't take long. I've done it before."

"Then you don't need to go." Abraham waggled him back and forth.

"He needs practice, and I need help mucking the gutter."

"Let Adah help." Abraham kept his hold on the boy.

"The girls are weeding the garden," she said. "Isaac, now."

Abraham loosened his arms and Isaac slipped off his lap.

In the barn, she sat him on the three-legged stool, his knees near touching Bovina's udder. Bovina, the oldest and most patient of their cows. The young ones had a way of kicking an inexperienced milker off his stool.

"Hat's in the way," she said, tipping it onto the straw.

He ran his hands gently over the cow's side and under the belly to her fully expanded bag. Miriam sat beside him on another stool. "Now . . ."

He massaged the bag with both hands. "I know," he said. "Rub, or she won't let down her milk."

"Good. Then . . ."

"I can do it. Adah showed me." He gripped a teat in his right hand, pressed thumb and forefinger together up near the bag and closed each finger in order, forcing the milk out into the pail. More like a dribble than a hissing stream, but he had the idea.

Isaac relaxed his hand and the teat filled with milk from the bag. Squeeze by squeeze, he worked into a slow rhythm.

"So, Herr Know-it-all"—Miriam elbowed him in the ribs— "let's see you do it with both hands." He grinned at her. "You'll be faster than me in no time."

Before Isaac could synchronize, Abraham, with his halting walk, made his way to the horse stalls. "Enough milking. I'll teach you horse sense."

"When he's finished here," Miriam said with a hand on Isaac's arm.

"He's finished now." Abraham opened Goli's stall. "A good brushing and we'll saddle up."

Isaac gave Miriam a pleading look.

"Now." There was no mistaking Abraham's tone to her, and Miriam wouldn't have Isaac torn in the middle. She should be glad of the love they shared, so much more evident than his feelings for

Joshua. Perhaps making up for past mistakes, his love sharpened by loss.

"Go," she whispered. "I'll lift the saddle when you're ready." He ran for the box of currycombs and brushes, while she slid onto his stool and flowed smoothly into the rhythm of milking.

A good thing Miriam wasn't a cow—her milk would never come down. Abraham had been right: she could bring the house down. And whom would that serve? Joshua was dead, so what difference did answers make? They wouldn't bring him back.

She couldn't wait for peace. She had to make it happen.

A year later, Isaac straddled Abraham's lap and leaned back against his chest as he did most evenings while listening to psalms his father said by heart. The whole family listened, a time of contentment Miriam loved.

The boy's size didn't matter at three and four years old. Abraham managed even at five, but at six and some, Isaac's splayed legs hung to the floor, the boy's ear close to his father's mouth.

Miriam heard the catch in Abraham's voice when Isaac shifted his weight. She saw Abraham tense as the psalms came to an end, tense anticipating Isaac's pivot for a loving hug. Despite the pain she read on his face, she knew Abraham wouldn't give up the enfolding.

Isaac raised his arms and shifted. Abraham's legs crumpled. He cried out, and Isaac fell to the floor. The boy scrambled to his feet, and surprise turned anguish as he took in Abraham's body writhing over the arm of his rocker.

"Papa," he wailed. In that instant, father and son in tears, Isaac became the comforter, the protector.

From then on, he saw to Abraham's every need, heated his bath, washed his back. Cane and crutch needed or not, Isaac stood ready and he brooked no interference. Age seven, he learned the art of shaving his father's unburned cheek and above his upper lip, trimmed what was left of his hair at the good earlobe.

By then, Abraham seemed to have found more corners of peace. He'd lost the haunted shift of his eye, and Miriam blessed the solace he and Isaac found in each other.

And so it continued until Isaac, reading the Bible aloud one evening, chose the near sacrifice of his namesake.

The cook fire settling, they all gathered in the parlor, windows open to a warm breeze. Isaac stood by Abraham's chair and the others sat to listen. As the story unfolded, Abraham's face went grim, and when Old Testament Abraham raised the knife to slay his son—

"No," Abraham shouted, and struggled to his feet. "No more." Tears ran down his face. He crushed Isaac to his chest. "Upstairs now." He pushed his son away. "I've prayers in the barn."

"I'll come," said Isaac. "We'll pray together." He took his father's arm.

Miriam rose. "No," she said, "pray here." A ripple of unease ran through her.

"The Lord calls." Abraham opened the door.

"You might need me," said Isaac.

"I do. More than you know." And off they went.

He'd promised, and for years, Miriam trusted Abraham. No more dark side of cider. He wouldn't break his word and certainly not in front of Isaac.

In bed, she curled in a ball. The back of her neck itched. She rubbed it, stretched flat, then curled to her other side.

Fall, the year Isaac turned seven, storms swelled the night with sound. Miriam listened to thunder roll down the valley when a brilliant flash brought the night whiter than white, brighter than noon ever imagined. And fast as the lightning came, the dark closed over her. Worried, she felt her way to Isaac's room.

Rain hammered the windows. The girls crowded behind her. No Isaac.

The kitchen latch clacked. Miriam heard the door slam open against the wall. She dashed for the stairs, the girls following, and felt her way down to the dim kitchen.

A candle guttered as Abraham and Isaac, drenched and bent, hands on their knees, caught their breath. Abraham coughed and coughed, his protective arm over Isaac.

"He'll not—" Abraham gasped. "He'll not have you." He pulled the boy closer as if God might snatch him.

Isaac eased his father to a chair. "We're safe," Isaac said. And alight with fearful excitement, he turned to Miriam. "Mama, did you see? The chestnut's down—it near killed us."

Before Miriam could close the door, another flash lit the dooryard whirling with leaves, the splintered trunk scattering the lane with pieces big as a man's body. Miriam latched the door.

"Damn God," Abraham snarled. His eye red and swollen, he glared out the window. "Take the tree, fine, but You'll not have my son." He thumped a fist on his knee. "And no beatings, not so much as a hair on his head." His grip on the boy tightened.

"Abraham!" Miriam squinted. "Cider again?" She wanted to scream.

"Bed," Abraham roared. "All of you."

Isaac's chin trembled. Miriam unlatched him from his father's clasp and, with a candle, led the way upstairs. She gave him a dry nightshirt, turned down his bed, and plumped the pillow while he changed.

"Come," she said. "You know his temper. It's nothing to do with you. His soul—"

"—is in torment, I know." Isaac crawled into bed. "I hear him. In the barn, he begs, 'Dear God, don't forsake me.' And what can I do?"

Miriam swept the sun white hair from Isaac's brow and with

her thumb smoothed the anxious creases. "You can't fix this," she said. "Now sleep, sweet Isaac." And she kissed each freckled cheek.

Abraham's shuffle sounded on the stairs, with the *shush shush* of his shoulder against plaster. Balance had been a problem even without his god-awful cider. She didn't want to talk to him, raving as he was, but a storm brewed in her innards.

She marched after him into their bedroom. Abraham stood under the line of pegs where he'd hung his jacket. Hanging on to the jacket, his back to the room, he pressed his forehead against the wall. Gray hair on one side of his head snarled loose, scars on the other, white and shiny.

Miriam shut the door. She seethed behind him, her hands in fists. "How could you?"

"The Lord will never be my shepherd," he said into his jacket.

"And whose fault is that?"

He rolled his back to the wall, and banged his head, once, twice.

"You and your drink." She spat the accusation in his face.

"Not drink," he said. "Only a collection of moth and rust."

She stepped closer. His eye, red and awash with tears, said otherwise. She took another step closer, and still no bloated breath.

"If not drink, what's this babble? What beatings?"

He groaned and slid down the wall. Out of instinct, she reached to support him, and they both sank to the floor, he on his rump, she kneeling between his bent knees.

He averted his face, his melted ear toward her. "Joshua, I couldn't give—," he said, and stopped. "Beating him seemed—" His mouth opened and no more words came out.

She rocked forward, dug her fingers into his upper arms, and pulled his back off the wall. "Look at me," she hissed. He looked from under his one bushy eyebrow.

He couldn't mean what she thought she'd heard. "Did you—"

He nodded. "Yes, I did. I beat him."

She wrenched his arms. Shoving him, she stumbled to her feet, every fiber trembling.

He flopped on his side, head pulled in, arms and legs drawn close. She stood over him, her breath ragged.

"I couldn't do it," he said into his curled arms.

"Do what?" Her lips tightened against her teeth. "You could *beat* him, but couldn't do . . . *what*?"

He slid an imploring hand along the floor, fingers inching toward her shoe. Spidery fingers reaching. "Please," he said.

Revulsion grew hot, her whole body a gorge rising. Forgiveness, in a great pyre, burned to ash. And if she truly let loose, she'd burn the barn, the house, and her family in it.

Abraham had done enough damage; she had to rein herself in, encase her anger, tamp it, make silage of it. She fled.

Miriam rose rumpled and stiff from the night in her kitchen chair. She wore the same clothes from yesterday, and in a haze beat cornmeal, milk, eggs, and butter with a wooden spoon, the pan set to bake.

She saw again his fingers inching the floor. So close to her boot, they'd tempted her. She wanted to stomp them. Her rage ready to spill, she'd fled, in her mouth the taste of blood.

Outside, Indian summer reigned glorious. Inside a chill beyond winter filled the room. She hadn't rekindled the fire, and her yellow batter stayed flat and raw.

She jabbed the buried coals with tongs and slammed logs on top. Flames sprang to life.

Retrieving sausages from the cellar, she slapped them in a frying pan. The skins sizzled, and she stabbed them with a fork, up one side, down the other, stabbing, stabbing.

"Vengeance is mine . . ." She wanted vengeance for Joshua. For herself.

"Mine, saith the Lord." She said it aloud to better heed His word and flung the sausage and frying pan into the fire. *Damn Abraham.* In his burns, she'd agonized for him. He'd eked forgiveness from her, one admission at a time. She'd held him. She'd forgiven him with her whole heart. And all that time—

His words had followed her as she fled down the stairs. "I couldn't," he'd said louder and louder as if this last admission could make everything right. What could be worse than what he'd done?

Vengeance. God claimed the right, and she must leave Him to it. She wouldn't let Abraham drag her into his pit.

She'd turn her back. Lost soul that he was, grovel though he might, she would give no succor. Vigilance would be hers. For the sake of her children and her soul. Vigilance.

From then on, Luke slept on Isaac's bed. This treat thrilled him and served as a safeguard, allowing Miriam a chance at sleep.

Most nights, Abraham retreated to the barn. If not, Miriam slept with her back turned to his side of the bed. He didn't exist.

Three weeks later, Miriam tucked the girls into bed. They were never too old, though Emma claimed to be as she planned for her wedding.

"You haven't talked to Papa for days," Rebecca said as Miriam folded the quilt up to her chin.

So she'd noticed, and if she did, so did the others. Miriam had seen their sidelong glances, yet hadn't dared mention it. The shun belonged to Miriam alone. He had shattered her faith; she wouldn't shatter theirs.

"Why?" Mary asked.

Peepers kept a steady thrum in the quiet.

She couldn't tell them.

"You don't serve his dinner," accused Emma.

"Isaac likes to," Adah answered.

"You move if he comes near." Emma rose on her elbows. "You won't look at him."

"This is for Papa and me to sort out." Miriam gave a quick kiss to Rebecca, moved on to Adah, then Mary.

Emma turned from Miriam. "How can you be so mean to poor Papa?" She hunkered under the covers away from Miriam's kiss.

"I love you all more than you'll ever know."

"But what about Papa?" Mary said. "Why?"

"Leave Mama be," Adah said. "She'll tell when it's time."

"When will that be?" said Rebecca.

Hopefully never.

CHAPTER 32

A Kick and a Kiss

Joshua arrived at the saloon, expecting Frank at a table with his foot up, banging his cane, cranky and demanding. He imagined the dinner he might lay out, most likely the closest Joshua would come to a fatted calf.

Instead, he found a skinny man in Frank's chair, his face clean-shaven, pouchy under the eyes. Lines of hard use creased his forehead and cheeks. He squinted, something familiar in the nose, bumpy as an old strawberry.

"Yeah, what?" the fellow said, and stood. With the man's feet out from under the table, Joshua knew him despite his new boots, the left one sewn short.

"Stub, what happened?" Joshua said. "You cleaned up."

"Who the hell are you, bucko?" Stub squinted at him.

"It's Josh—don't you know me?" Joshua shook Stub's hand, a two-handed shake.

"Jeez, kid." Stub eyed him up and down. "A year, and you're a hairy mess."

"Yeah, well, I'm cleaner than I was, and dry. You too?"

"Can't do business drunk." Stub sat to his papers at the table.

"Where's Frank?"

"Up the golden stair," Stub said. "Bought him out a month shy of the funeral."

"You had money?"

"Nuggets in a gopher hole. Frank turned sick, couldn't work. He figured you wouldn't be back. That last month Rosie didn't leave his side."

"Where *is* Rosie?" Joshua wasn't sure he wanted to know.

"Got a high-collar gent," Stub said. "Sundays, he's a priest, nights at blackjack. Luck of the Devil, not the Irish he claimed."

"So where is she?"

"Took off, mother and brothers too. A gift horse she wouldn't look in the mouth."

Joshua had been no gift, and still he roamed the room, grinding his teeth.

"So what's your pleasure, Joshua?"

"A bath for starters."

"And about time too."

How easy it was falling into old habits, a comfort in familiar surroundings. Better money than any other job—he'd put his pay toward a horse and saddle, the cheapest way to speed him east. Every day he struggled pouring for others and not himself. He missed the glow, but mornings with no headache had merit.

From behind the bar, he recognized a few regulars. The dandy at the high-stakes table was different, his dark hair parted down the middle.

Charlie from the Bar-Q came Saturday nights. His boys were new, though their boots had the same worn heels and curled toes.

A year walking already and another winter passed in the saloon. Deep into spring Joshua chafed to get going, afraid of what havoc God might wreak on his family.

He grew short with drunken antics, and one night, a cowboy

he hadn't seen before set him off. The cowboy leaned across the bar. "You ain't pretty as Rosie," he said. "What tits, coulda sipped all night." He raised his glass. "To Rosie!"

"Shut your gob, bucko." And Joshua slammed Frank's cane across the cowboy's upraised hand. The glass shattered, shards and whisky splashing across the bar. The cowboy howled. Joshua threw the cane across the room.

"Damn," said Stub. "What's eatin' you?"

While he and Joshua cleaned up that night, Stub said, "You had no call breakin' his hand."

"I'm sorry." More sorry than Joshua could say. The person he wanted to be still seemed out of reach. "I've got to get home."

"If Frank were alive, he'd get you a horse, give you a kiss, and kick you in the pants. So I'll give you money, no kisses. You can pay me back later."

When he left, Joshua kissed Stub on the lips.

Joshua took the train toward Omaha. He'd get a horse there. At first he slept on his seat. Then wakeful, he couldn't help watching for Sam.

The train clattered through the Rockies, wind shrieking around the cars, and all his unshed tears came. His head pressed against the train's cold window, finally, he let himself mourn for Bella, Sadie, Frieda, and James.

Omaha. He rode out on a strawberry roan, the saddle a castoff from the cavalry, rounded pommel and cantle, an opening down the middle to ease the horse's spine. A bedroll from the same source hung from rings at the back of the saddle, jerky in his saddlebags, water in a canteen, a few dollars still in his pocket.

The thrill of seeing Mama and his sisters overshadowed the fears of Father as Joshua rode at an intermittent lope. He'd have preferred a gallop, hurry pumping his blood. A thousand miles to

Pittsburgh, a couple hundred more to the farm, he needed the horse in good shape if he expected to reach New Eden before snow made the mountains a misery. Alleghenys, the Tuscarora, they were nothing like the Rockies, but miserable enough.

The closer Joshua came to home, the more he worried. The barn could be charred beams, the house a shell of crumbled field-stones, chimneys blackened. One careless match, who would survive?

Short of breath, and almost as frantic as when he left, he rode the steep trails.

God had taken so many, He could easily take the rest. After all, He had a poor history with His own son.

And if they lived, Joshua feared for their suffering. He didn't dare think how they might greet him.

Imaginings slipped in unwanted, and he twisted the scene to wide-eyed surprise, Mama's boy back in her arms. Or, like Mother Biddle greeting Robert, a splash of irritation, then smiles that would overtake everything, his sisters crowding around.

And Father. Joshua would be bigger and stronger. Father wouldn't scythe him down.

He pressed on through woods glimmering with red, yellow, and brown leaves, time growing short. And money shorter, the roan and he lived off what little the trailside families could spare, both the horse and himself worn thin. The roan flagged under his constant urging.

By the time he reached New Eden, tired and dirty and hungry, the roan favored her right front leg. He urged her up the final hill and reined in at the graveyard, letting her graze among the head-stones. One among them, not yet covered with lichen, drew him to the chiseled name. *Joshua, Beloved Boy.* He shouldn't have been surprised.

Yet disquiet held him, and he lingered, taking in the spreading patchwork of corn shocks, hay stubble, and raw earth sown with winter wheat. Green shoots pushed toward the sun. A breath of fresh loam and dead leaves filled the air.

Down the road, white board fences lined the way to immaculate houses and barns. And there was Joshua's farm, first at the base of the hill.

The stone house stood firm, the chimneys straight, his sisters' dormer, his dormer, the white barn, and a rebuilt woodshed. The creek ran under the milk house and wound along the property line. All of it worn, but unscathed.

He pulled the scent of fresh earth deep in his lungs. After ten years, nothing could hold a candle to this place. Yet he hesitated. In the adjoining field, he dismounted and sifted earth through his fingers. Had he really come this far, to go no farther?

At twenty-one, he looked a man, yet inside, the boy he once was shivered. He wanted to pick the boy up as he'd picked up James, carry him down the road, and return him to his family.

A moth fluttered in his belly. Hunger, he told himself.

Miriam dried the last breakfast dish and set it on the shelf. From the window she caught movement on the hill, a rider in the graveyard. English, she thought, bedraggled, the worst of their kind. She leaned the heels of her hands on the worktable and watched.

Had Joshua lived, he might have known such a person. She pressed a hand against her cheek. *No crying.*

She wiped her eyes, but couldn't wipe away images of Joshua, his smooth skin, the silky hair, freckles, and his laugh when she'd teased him those last days. And, oh God, the torment she'd missed. How possibly? All that time, Abraham . . .

Anger flooded her, and she banged the pot as she set dinner cooking. Even as she shunned him, Abraham dragged her down.

She must shore the walls. There'd be no changing what had happened, only what might come.

In from outside, Isaac strained under an armload of logs. "We have a visitor," he said, and kicked the door shut. "At the creek."

He stacked his load by the hearth. Miriam cracked the door and peeked out. English, yes. Filthy, yes, and the creek hadn't helped.

No kin to English she knew. And into her dooryard he boded nothing good.

Just shut the door.

CHAPTER 33

The Prodigal

The roan fidgets. Joshua eases the reins. Her favored leg gone to a limp, she jolts down the hard-packed road. He stops her at the lane and checks her hoof. The sole is soft, the smell rancid.

He leads her to where the creek crosses under a plank bridge. The roan drinks. He splashes his sun-dark face. Water drips from his beard, breaking the reflection, warping the crooked nose, the pitted cheeks and twisted brow. He runs fingers through his knife-cut hair and starts up the lane. Passing the garden, pumpkins clinging on withered vines, he focuses on the door to the house, another needle's eye he must navigate.

The door opens a crack as he enters the dooryard. It closes, then opens again wider to a woman in black. Hands on her hips, she stands in the frame, watching him. She's wrinkled, more like Oma than Mama. Her hair slips gray from under her white prayer cap. She draws a shawl close around her shoulders, her face full of suspicion.

The moth in his belly rises from its gnawing as if a flame ignites and brings the wings to frenzy. Time to harvest what he has sown.

His boots heavy, Joshua draws closer, and a young boy steps

in front of Mama. She rests her hands on his shoulders. His clothes are the usual black, his hatless head a mass of straw-colored cowlicks. Freckles sprinkle his nose and cheeks. He can't be more than eight or nine. Wiry. He has a curious tilt to his head.

They watch as Joshua ties his horse to the fence and steps on the stone walk. Sweat soaks his shirt. He stares at the boy's high-colored cheeks, his smile of anticipation.

"Milk's in the springhouse," Mama says. She takes measure of the weathered man before her, never looking in his eyes. "Help yourself," she says. "I've work if you're looking."

How can he say who he is? He has to say something. "Is the Deacon home?"

"Isaac," she says, shaking the boy's shoulders. "Fetch your father; he's on the porch."

Isaac. The moth in Joshua's belly bursts into flame as he looks to the rebuilt woodshed.

"Few ask after the Deacon." She looks a little closer, and Joshua knows what she sees: the bit of dark face not covered in hair, the dust made mud in his attempt at washing. The nose that speaks of drink and brawling, and not the least hint of the boy she'd lost. She shakes her head. "Do you know him?" she asks.

Here's his chance, and he hears himself say, "Better than most." Oh yes, Joshua knows him, and more, as he's come to know himself. "How old is Isaac?" he asks.

"Almost nine is what he'd tell you," Mama says. She smiles as she watches him run around to the porch.

"He looks a fine boy."

"Yes." She talks low, more to herself than to Joshua. "He's a sweet arrow in my heart. A cherished apple in all our eyes."

Isaac brings an old man around the corner of the house, a firm hold on his elbow. The man shuffles. His gait is stiff, his arms cocked in the sleeves of his black jacket.

This can't be Father. A few thin wisps of white hair fall beneath his wide-brimmed hat. They scatter over a melted ear. Joshua sees again Father in flames as he lunged from the burning woodshed. *Dear God, this is my doing.*

The skin on one side of Father's face swirls like a spring stream, the flow broken by tufts of hair. His eyelid pulls, hooding a blue haze, but the other eye . . . that eye stares steady and brown, taking Joshua in.

Inside this frail man, Father's iron will crouches strong as ever. It's all Joshua can do not to retreat.

"English, is it?" Father says in a smoke-torn voice. "God save us."

"It's God has sent him," Mama says, and to Isaac, "You take him for milk, then chores."

Isaac leads him to the milk house, its low roof in need of repair. They duck through the small door set in the fieldstone wall. Two large cans sit in the channeled floor, up to their shoulders in cold water. Joshua raises a can, takes off the top, and pours a tin cup full. In ten years, milk never tasted so good.

Isaac takes the roan and Joshua to the stable. "We're down to Sampson and Goli," he says. "They're too old to work. Besides, Herr Kauffman and his sons farm the fields." He guides Joshua's horse into an empty stall, and takes off the saddle. "What a strange saddle," he says.

"Came with the horse," Joshua tells him. *Military* seems the wrong thing to say. Isaac throws the saddle over the partition, then unbuckles the bridle. He drags the leather over the roan's ears. The bit drops from the horse's mouth.

Joshua and Isaac go up to the wide threshing floor, one side stacked with straw, the other hay. They shove bedding down the trapdoor to the stalls below, followed by hay thrown in the manger. Joshua gathers great armfuls. Isaac wields a three-tined fork much taller than he is and, when he's done, jams the tines into the floorboards. The long handle leans, ready for the morning. They go back down to finish the stalls.

"If Kauffman does the fields," Joshua asks, "who does the rest?"

"Mama, my sisters Mary and Rebecca, and me," Isaac says. "We manage. Father directs from the porch; his lungs are wet."

Isaac brings a carrot from his pocket, breaks it in four, and hands two to Joshua. "Here, they like carrots. This is Goli. Goli, this is . . . What's your name?"

"Josh," says Joshua. Goli leans his head over the stall door and nickers. Joshua strokes his neck, the carrot offered on the flat of his hand. The horse nickers again and rubs his nose on Joshua's arm.

"You know horses," the boy says. "He likes you."

"All my life, the farm and overland on the trail, always horses. And books."

"You're a farmer?"

"I was once," Joshua says. "Do you read?"

"The Bible, morning and night."

"Other books?"

"Others?" Isaac looks confused.

"From school."

"Mama taught me reading; I don't go to school."

Again, this is Joshua's doing. Had he been there, shouldered his part, Isaac would have been schooled.

"It would mean a lot if you'd stay a while." Isaac feeds his carrots to Sampson, the roan left out. "You like what you see, I can tell."

"I'd like to stay, but . . ."

"Father's tongue is sharp. You mustn't mind. He hates to see work undone, and him not as able as he was. Mama says he's not the same since we lost my brother." Isaac moves easily around the horses, brushing their shiny coats. "The fire made Father what he is. Mother says, beyond that, he's chewed on the inside. She makes allowances."

Turns a blind eye. That's how they came to this pass, and nothing has changed. Joshua's blood rises to a simmer.

He searches Isaac's eyes. No haunted look, no flinching.

"Stay where you are," Isaac says. "We need another pitchfork."

"I'll get it." Joshua heads to the toolshed.

Isaac follows. "How did—"

A great barking from behind the shed, and a dog lunges at Joshua. He's knocked to the ground, the dog all over him.

"Luke, off, boy!" Isaac's brow creases. "Luke's old bones never moved so fast. It's like he knows you."

"Mmmm," is all Joshua can say, his mouth closed on a laugh as Luke's pink tongue slurps his face.

Isaac tries to pull Luke off, but in the end rolls on the ground too. His laugh bubbles from deep inside. He's so like James, easy in his laughter, trusting.

Joshua revels in his flash of delight, yet he fears what terrors might fester unseen.

They pick themselves up, and with one final rub of Luke's ears, they attend the job at hand. Luke keeps watch as Isaac, deft with the fork, loads the five tines almost as heavy as Joshua does. They pitch manure from the stalls into the spreader.

"We'll take it to the garden tomorrow. Rebecca will help."

"And what of your other sisters?"

"Emma's married, and Adah, she works for English over the ridge. Father doesn't know—don't say a word. He'd be angry."

"What does he do when he's angry?"

"He's not angry often, but when he is, he's silent. Then he prays in the hayloft. He stays there most nights now."

"Do you pray with him?"

"Sometimes. Sometimes he sleeps. I don't wake him."

Joshua flexes his fingers. He steps close and peers down Isaac's collar for sight of a stray scar. He sees nothing. Joshua's scars couldn't be seen either.

He can't stand to think of Father and his unholy prayer. Has he learned nothing? And Mama. How can she not see?

And what do his sisters see? They must know the mornings after. They knew, back when they were littles frozen in their chairs, knew the result if not the cause. By now they must have figured it out.

"Mama says Father prays to ease a tear in his soul," says Isaac. "She says he has no respite after losing my brother, and we must know his temper for what it is."

"And what is that?"

"Just a tempest in his head." Isaac flinches as if caught in a lie.

I've been lashed in that tempest, Joshua wants to say. *And I bet you have too.* They continue working in silence. Then Isaac says, "I tell you these things because you mustn't let Father's tongue drive you away."

The sun drops. Joshua puts Luke in the shed. The dog scratches and whines. Isaac gives Joshua an appraising look. "Luke stays in the house," he says.

Inside along with Luke, Isaac and Joshua carry buckets of water to the kitchen. They replenish the pot Mama has emptied for Father's bath.

"Ready, Father?" Isaac says. And to Joshua, "Set a stool by the fire. Not too close—his scars feel the heat yet." Joshua sets the stool off the stone, backs away, and stands by the parlor door. Father sits.

Isaac pulls looped threads from Father's shirtfront and tenderly removes it. Then come the pants and white underdrawers, until Father sits, back bent, naked on the stool. The old man is a mass of scarring except for his feet.

He leans into Isaac as Isaac gently rubs him with a wad of lathered lamb's wool. He swabs over Father's face, the closed eyes, and slips into every crevice of the crunkled ear. With equal care he rinses. Clear water runs down Father's body to the smooth skin on his feet.

Father rests his head on the boy's chest. Isaac dries his shoulders and back.

"You are the lamb and the shepherd," Father says to Isaac, "and I love you with all my soul."

Joshua's arms prickle at his words. Beyond a small bite of jealousy, he is wild with a terror that pulls every hair on his body to attention.

Terror for Isaac. Isaac, this serious, respectful, loving boy, loved by his father beyond all else. Isaac, the true test of Father's devotion to God.

"It's our turn," Isaac says. "Wake up." He passes Joshua a bucket of warm water. "Out by the pump."

Outside, Isaac strips off his pants and shirt and soaps himself. Joshua hesitates, then does the same, standing so Isaac can't see his back. The skin on the front of Isaac's body is pale and firm and perfect. Not a mark to be seen. Joshua waits for him to turn. He has to know.

The brown block of soap shoots from Isaac's grasp and lands in the dirt. He leans to pick it up. Joshua steels himself for the sight of the boy's back.

"Oh, Isaac," escapes Joshua's mouth. His eyes sting. The skin on Isaac's back is covered in freckles.

Isaac straightens. "You've got soap in your eyes," he says. "The burn'll stop soon. Rebecca and I used too little lye."

"You work at everything, don't you?" Joshua says. "Your father would be lost without you."

"The fire crippled his body. His soul too, Mama says. Ten years this past spring. The day is fresh in his mind."

As Joshua puts on his dirty shirt and pants, Isaac glances at his legs. "You're burned too," he says.

"Yes, a painful business. I can only imagine what your father went through." Joshua says no more. He's taking advantage of Isaac's trust.

The boy runs a towel over his back and down his slender legs. "Mary says Joshua did the work of two men every day. Joshua, that's my brother's name, same as yours, isn't it?"

"Yes. My name is Joshua." The words strangle in his throat as he works to push out more.

Isaac looks into Joshua's eyes and says, "I'm told my brother likely died of his burns. Adah says Father's Flock searched, everyone from the smallest child to the oldest Elder. When they gave up, Mama and Papa kept on. But I don't think he died."

"You don't?"

"No. I think *you* are my brother. You are, aren't you?"

Joshua stands shivering before this small incarnation of himself, this fair boy a reminder of what they lost, but he is much wiser. Might he despise Joshua's cowardice? Denounce him?

Isaac's eyes shine with excitement. He struggles into his clothes, a smile playing across his face. He claps his hands, his laugh triumphant. "I knew it, I knew it. Goli nudging you, then Luke, and when I saw the burns, it had to be."

He hops from one foot to the other. "I can't wait to see their faces. Let's tell them now."

Joshua's steps drag gallows slow, and Isaac tugs him across the dooryard. "Come on."

CHAPTER 34

Sifting the Wreckage

Into the house, Isaac and Joshua enter the scent of oak beams, beeswax, and woodsmoke mixed with browned chicken, onions, carrots, potatoes. This, the smell of home.

Mama stands at the hearth. She stirs the cauldron. Mary and Rebecca sit on one side of the table. Adah, home from work, sits on the other side, Father, in his usual place at the head. He's wrapped in talk of the day. He doesn't look up. Joshua is the hired hand, after all. The girls, in their black prayer caps, lean toward Father. They listen with care to his rasping.

Mary glances at Isaac jigging with excitement. She frowns and lays down her fork. Rebecca looks up, looks at Mary, then back to Isaac. All forks down. Father is the last, except Mama, who's still on the hearth, filling a bowl from the cauldron.

"There's a bit more if you finish this," she says, and turns to pass Joshua the bowl. His hands touch hers as he takes it. Their eyes meet. She steps back with a quick inward breath.

Her mouth opens and closes. She gives her head the tiniest shake as if trying to clear her vision, and slips into her chair at the table. Hands trembling, she whispers, "You must be hungry."

She blinks, adjusting the napkin in her lap. Her breath in short bursts, she stands again, napkin falling to the floor. She looks around as if she doesn't know where she is, wanders into the parlor, and drops slowly into an armchair by the window. Her eyes stray to the distant hedgerow.

In the parlor, Miriam's heart knocks. Seeing her boy in a glint of sunlight is one thing, but in this ruffian's face—? She must be un-hinged; Frau Gruber is right.

"What the devil is this?" Father squints his one good eye.

"No devil," Isaac says. He takes the man's elbow and pushes him to the empty chair next to Rebecca. Isaac is alight like she's never seen him.

He spreads his arms toward the man. "This . . . is Joshua!"

Blood surges in her every vessel. *Oh, Isaac, no.* Her ever-hopeful Isaac wanting to make dreams come true. It's hard enough shoring walls against her own ghosts; now Isaac batters those walls. On the arms of her chair her hands shake. Her lips tremble.

The man sits stiff at the table, his face gone bloodless. No one says anything.

The girls turn to Abraham. It's not clear if he grasps what Isaac has said or if he even heard.

"Joshua!" Isaac says louder. "My brother!"

Adah looks into the parlor, her face full of sorrow. No one else seems to know where to look.

"Eat," Father commands. "Not another word."

Miriam can't move.

At the end of the meal Father stands and throws his napkin on the table. "Joshua is dead," he says, his good eye fierce on each in turn, including Miriam. He storms through the kitchen door.

Mary stands and stacks plates. She elbows Isaac. "What a mean thing to do," she says, and busies herself over at the dishpan.

Crestfallen, Isaac slumps in his chair. "But—"

"Why would you say that?" Mary near tears. "He"—she points while keeping her back to the man—"is dark. Dark hair, dark skin. Joshua was fair like you." She follows Abraham outside before Isaac can answer. Plucking at her sleeve, Rebecca follows.

Adah comes into the parlor, kneels by Miriam's chair, and folds her into a gentle embrace.

Joshua spends the night in the barn, shades of living at the Baylors'. The forkful of stew he managed to gag down sits in his belly like a stone. He can't bear the hurt in their eyes. He should leave. The Father in his head rises, scythe in hand, swinging.

But Father's not that man, and Joshua isn't that boy. *I won't be driven off. No.*

At dawn he mucks the gutter behind the remaining cow. Isaac brings in the horses, waters them, and Joshua measures their ration of oats.

"Come on," Isaac says, "breakfast."

How could Joshua face them, much less eat? A ghost in the family house, he would rather stay in the barn.

At the table, his own family concentrates on their plates, more suspicious than Sylvie's uncles, colder than Mercy that first day on the wagon. She called him a fake, an impostor.

For sure, he isn't the son Mama lost. A person, yes, but in this house, he is *other*, like Captain Lewis's Indian, as good as a two-legged turnip.

They eat in silence, and he's a boy again, frozen in his chair, smelling the fried scrapple and corn bread he loves. Isaac spoons a great dollop of blackberry jam from the crock at the center of the table, one spoonful for himself and one for Joshua, sitting beside him.

The seeds crunch as Joshua eats, and he can't go on. The last berries he shared were with Daisy before the end. Could this be another? The end of all hopes?

"If you're finished," says Isaac, "we have chores."

All day, Joshua works beside Isaac the way he worked with his sisters when they were little, the rest of the feeding and mucking. With three horses, it takes half the time. He splits wood. Isaac helps carry the logs. Fourteen-year-old Rebecca collects eggs. Cows, all but one, are gone, and the sheep.

At the end of the day, Joshua squats clipping overgrown grass under the dooryard fence. Isaac kneels using a sickle, its blade so sharp, it slices thick weeds as it would the tenderest grass. Luke lies beside Joshua. Rebecca pauses to watch. She frowns as Luke crawls along after Joshua, moving together down the fence line.

"Why's he doing that?" Rebecca says. She suddenly claps hands over her mouth.

"Yes!" Isaac jumps, jubilant feet off the ground. "And his legs, look." He pulls at Joshua's pant leg. "Scars like Papa!"

She flings herself at Joshua. "You are, you really are."

He holds her, and the stones in his belly melt.

"We've got to show Mama." Once more, Isaac tugs him toward the house.

"No, wait," Rebecca says. "That beard. He can't go like this." She runs to the house and returns with a razor, a bowl of warm water, and something white over her arm. "A clean shirt," she says.

Joshua scratches deep in his five years of wiry beard, this hair a part of him. If he's clean-shaven, others will see him as the unmarried man he is, but he will see himself unmasked. A frightening prospect.

He works at the long strands with his knife, starting in front of his left ear. Isaac runs into the house for scissors. "Here." He pushes Joshua's hands from his face. "I do it for Papa, all the time."

"You? Not your mother?"

"He allows only me."

In the middle of the lane, Joshua sits on the chestnut's wide stump, Isaac beside him, their feet in leafy vines. Isaac cuts, and Joshua watches clumps of reddish beard fall.

Rebecca holds the bowl of water. "Now soap it," she says.

"While it softens, I'll cut your hair." With the *shlick-shlick* of scissors, he trims just below Joshua's ear, a kinder job than Fingers' under the bridge. "Now, that's as should be."

"Ah, yes," Joshua says, "the Ordnung."

Isaac lays a towel around his chest, and unfolds the razor from its bone handle. He flexes his arms. "Ready?" He sets the edge to Joshua's cheek.

"Soon you'll look the Amish man you are."

When Joshua comes in the kitchen with Isaac and Rebecca, Mama, Adah, and Mary wait by the hearth. Mary sidles to him, her head bowed. She stands close but leans away, shy and suddenly tongue-tied. She whispers with a hint of accusation, "You don't look like him."

"He's gone," Joshua says, "and I'm what's left."

He takes off his boots and sets them by the door. Mama comes from the hearth. She reaches, three fingers touching lightly on his breastbone. Her lips tremble. She clamps them closed. Her chin crinkles.

She gives him a careful hug as if he might break. As if she might break. Her jaw works, and she takes a breath, about to speak when Father comes in from the porch. She turns away.

"Dinner's ready," she says, and hurries to the bubbling pot.

They all sit straight in ladder-back chairs. Father concentrates on the bowl Isaac sets before him. No one speaks. It doesn't matter; they believe him. Father doesn't count.

That night, the songs of crickets and frogs fill the house. Beams tick. Joshua's sisters whisper in their room, things he can't quite hear from down the hall. He sleeps in his old room, a mattress on the floor. Isaac and Luke sleep on the bed.

The murmur of prayer floats from farther down the hall. The difference comes in the softly closing door, followed by quiet steps bypassing his room. They go downstairs, through the kitchen, and outside. Isaac, curled into his pillow, breathes even and deep.

The night turns cold.

Isaac stirs. The boy sits up in bed, lights the bedside candle, and takes a quilt from the blanket chest. "Stay," he says to Luke. "Father will be cold," he whispers, and goes out the door.

"No, Isaac." Joshua throws off his blanket. "Let me." He pulls on boots and rushes to the hall, and there's Mama at her door, a candle held high. "Since you're up," she says, and beckons.

In her room, the candle set on the bedside table, she sits on the edge of the bed. For long moments, she looks into the flame.

"I haven't dared hope," she says, twisting her fingers in the lap of her white nightdress. She looks Joshua in the eye for the first time, and crosses her arms over her breasts, gray hair braided down her back. The chill allows for shaking, though hers is a deeper shiver. The shiver of someone walking over a grave. "Can this really be you?"

She touches his cheek. Her eyes brim. Her other hand hesitates. "I'm afraid you'll disappear."

"Not this time," he says. But Isaac, he's alone with Father in the barn.

"I know your father believes it." Hands clasped in her lap, she rubs her knuckles. "I know, by the way he digs at his scars."

The candle gutters, its reflection licking around bubbles in the window's glass. Distortion spreads the dancing flame.

A night bird cries in the distance, and Joshua cocks his head. Luke howls, and Mama's face knots, too painful to behold.

"Isaac," Joshua shouts, and down the stairs three at a time, he's through the kitchen and out.

Screams echo in Miriam's ears, the screams she ignored ten years past. She rushes after Joshua. Her girls in white nightdresses pour from their room. Barefoot, pale, and questioning, they clog the hall.

Miriam corrals them in the kitchen. She won't have them go to the barn. Joshua will do what he must, and they needn't witness God's will.

But Isaac. What of Isaac?

She prays God will spare him and leave whole the love he has for his father.

Out into the chill, across the lane, Joshua leaps at the barnyard gate and, falling on the other side, rolls to his feet. He yanks the barn's side door.

Luke makes a run at the gate, but falls short, his old legs not strong enough. He howls.

The horses nicker. A hoof bangs at the stall. Isaac's voice wails from the loft. "No," high and frantic, "you can't. Please, Papa, no!"

In the dark, Joshua sprints up the stairs, bouncing off the wall, dashes into the big room past the grain bins, and onto the threshing floor. His knee knocks the pitchfork Isaac left jammed in the floorboards.

At the other end of the room, two lamplit figures struggle, their long shadows thrashing on hay piled behind them. Isaac in his nightshirt, arms above his head, grips Father's wrist. A sickle's blade glints in Father's hand. His wet lungs gurgle.

"Help me!" Isaac in a panic.

Wrenching the pitchfork from the floorboards, Joshua runs, long stride dream-slow, the fork's shaft in one hand, the tines aimed at Father's back.

A roaring fills Joshua's head, growing louder as he runs, and nearly there, he lunges, the shaft in both hands high above his head, poised for the downward stroke.

"Nooooo!" The thin wail breaks through the roar as Isaac wrestles Father for the sickle.

Wrong, wrong. The sickle's honed blade curves at Father's neck. And in that instant, Father twists toward Joshua, spreads his arms, and bears his chest to the oncoming fork as if he too wants the tines buried in his body.

Joshua, beyond stopping, thrusts the fork aside and slams into

Father, who falls on Isaac, the three of them knocked to the floor. The sickle clatters. Joshua snatches the blade and throws it into the dark.

Isaac chokes. "Father." His eyes stream. Kneeling, he presses fists to his cheeks. "Joshua, help him."

Joshua slides one arm under Father's shoulders, one under his legs, and lifts him off the floor. Isaac rolls open the big barn door, and they run out, Isaac shouting, "Mama, Mama."

Luke runs ahead across the lane to the house. Mama and the girls swing wide the door, their faces anxious. Light streaks the lane.

"Hurry," Isaac whispers.

They all follow Joshua. He lays Father on the table, slipping his arm carefully out from under. Father doesn't move.

"I hit him," Joshua says. He could still feel his body slam into Father, the collapse of old bones.

For a moment, the girls hold one another in a silent gaggle. Mama surprisingly calm.

Isaac removes Father's boots. Adah and Rebecca undo his jacket. Mary holds the bowl while Joshua bathes the wispy head.

Father's breath rumbles. Joshua finds no acrid bite.

"Take him upstairs," Mama says.

Bedded in his nightshirt, Father squints at the ceiling, his face gray, beard spindly. He picks at the quilt Isaac drew to his chest. Isaac turns down the lamp on the table, the gathered family in nightclothes caught in a soft orange glow. He kneels beside Joshua at the head of the bed.

Father groans. Joshua takes his hand, Mama on her knees at his other side. Her forearms rest on the mattress.

His eyes running with tears, Father covers Joshua's wrist with crooked fingers. "I couldn't do it." The words rasp in his throat.

"Do what, Father?"

He rolls his head to face Joshua. "Give you"—his fingers squeeze—"give you to God."

Mama's lips go thin, a white line.

The girls kneel at the other side of the bed, hair awry without caps. Their eyes wider with every word. A sob breaks from Isaac.

Father's good eye holds Joshua's. "I loved the Lord," he says. "But not enough." Phlegm rattles.

"Shh, don't talk."

Father lifts his head from the pillow. "I couldn't fool Him," he says, clinging higher on Joshua's arm. "I beat you and still He knew. He knew I loved you best."

Joshua's head fills with glittering minnows. Knees gone soft, he sways.

Abraham sinks back on the pillow. Miriam presses fists tight to her temples. "What love is that?" She reaches across Abraham's chest. Again fists, she crumples the neck of his nightshirt.

Joshua rests a gentle hand on her shoulder. Her boy. Her scarred boy.

She should have saved him. So close in the woodshed all those nights—she *could* have saved him.

Her head slumps between her arms, fingers loosening. *As we harrow the land, so God harrows us. To what purpose? Tell me, Jesus, to what purpose?*

If she'd been burned like Abraham, she'd rip her scars till they bled.

Crouching next to Mama, Joshua shakes off the minnows. By his head, the bedclothes shift. Father gasps, and around the bed, all movement stops.

His body stiffens. Both eyelids fly open, his brown eye focused beyond the footboard to the room's darkest corner.

A late cricket falters in rusty song. Father's legs ease. A slow breath seeps out, and his face goes slack.

CHAPTER 35

The Iron Gate

I n the morning, their three horses graze the front-twenty as if nothing has happened. They swirl the grass with upper lip and crop it short. They chew slow and rhythmic.

Father lies gray, washed, and cold in his bed. Sounds of Mama rattle up from the kitchen. Joshua sits on the side of Isaac's bed, Isaac in it. The day is bright, crisp and blue. A breeze from the barely open window smells of dead leaves blowing in the dooryard.

"You didn't kill him," Isaac says for the third time.

Joshua watches the horses work their way to a greener section. "May as well," he says. "I wanted to. I intended to."

In the name of deliverance, or was it vengeance? And all the time, this festered love. Joshua's stomach heaves.

He must dress for the funeral. Mama has left him Father's Sunday jacket and pants, his hat. Wearing underdrawers, black socks, and a white shirt, he sits on the chest at the end of Isaac's bed, and fingers the black material. In good conscience, can he wear the sign of this faith?

As if he has spoken aloud, Mama says, "Joshua." She stands in the doorway. "Wear them for me."

"For you, Mama," he says, "I will."

Through service in their house, the new Deacon speaks of Father, the best Deacon in living memory, while Father, in white jacket and pants, lies in the parlor, his coffin open.

In the men's section, seated between Emma's husband and Isaac, Joshua rolls his shoulders cramped in Father's jacket. His neck aches. The tight pants ride up, showing his socks and a strip of skin. He rooches around worse than the smallest boy there.

Ordinarily one could say this is Father's service; no one will notice. But Joshua's an attraction like Daisy in the pit, she and he in ill-fitting skin. Those around him whisper behind a hand. He doesn't need to hear; he knows their doubts.

On the hill, Father's Flock gathers at his grave. Joshua concentrates on what he was, at best a shepherd true to his sheep, teaching the Word as he understood it. At worst, a cornered rabbit baring its teeth.

Joshua and a few stalwart Elders lower Father into the ground, hand by hand on ropes, until the coffin rests. With a tug, the ropes slide out.

At the graveside, Emma leans her head against her husband's chest. Adah, Mary, and Rebecca, their eyes hidden under deep bonnets, throw a handful of dirt on the coffin. They touch Joshua's sleeve as they pass.

Mama takes her turn and steps away from the open earth. Isaac won't go near. Inconsolable, he clings to Mama, who clings to him. His hat gone, yellow hair presses against her black dress. She takes Joshua's hand for balance.

Returning to the house, Zeke and Hannah guide Miriam, she with her arm around Isaac. The girls follow in a cluster, and the rest of the Flock waits for a moment before filing into the house.

They crowd the kitchen and parlor, serving themselves from plates of fried potato, chicken legs, corn bread, green beans with sugar, and pies and pies and pies. Between forkfuls they whisper one to the other.

At her approach, they stop, and Miriam accepts their gentle embraces, pretending not to notice their attentions wandering over her shoulder, all watching for Joshua. Of course they're wary. He no longer fits among them, part Lazarus, part prodigal, his ten years a bone they can't leave off chewing. How much more would they gnaw if they knew of happenings in the barn?

And they too pretend, ignoring for today how poorly she fits in their Plain fabric, not just a thread out of place, but a warped log in the woodpile, throwing the whole into disarray.

Through many tomorrows, she'll sort herself out. Today and today and today, Joshua is home.

She nods and accepts compliments on her shoofly pie.

Joshua stays on the hill. He's loath to enter the throng crowding his house with condolence.

Night settles. A slice of moon breaches the horizon. With his fingers, he rakes scattered earth onto Father's mound, restoring the bent grass as best he can.

He lingers, and overhead the moon climbs. Three-quarter and cold, it shows the patchwork fields dotted with white barns and stone houses. And like his mother, he sees a straw-colored head by the barn. He sees a boy and his dog at the creek fishing. He sees the untarnished man he expected to be.

Kneeling at his own headstone, he traces the inscription, *Beloved Boy, 1872*. He'd like to strike the date, but 1872 marks the start of his death, and try though he might, for him, there can be no resurrection. Yet this land speaks a constant promise—after winter comes spring, seedtime and harvest, these seasons his without end.

He rises, brushes dirt from his knees, and girds himself. Guided by the candlelit window, he heads for the house.

STONES
IN THE ROAD

E. B. Moore

A CONVERSATION
WITH E. B. MOORE

Q. Your previous book was based on an experience of your grand-mother. Is Stones in the Road *also based on a family story?*

A. Yes, the story is loosely based on my grandfather's early life when he ran away from home at age eleven, after being repeatedly beaten. He made it across the country on his own and, after ten years, returned with a notch in one ear from a stray bullet.

His story came to me through my mother, who, as a child, sat on his knee, soaking up the little he was willing to share. Unfortunately, he died long before I was born, giving me no chance to get more than the bones of what happened. I did learn enough about running away to think it a poor choice, yet I gave it a try the summer I turned five. Sure to wear boots, with a sweater around the waist of my jeans, I tied necessities in a red bandanna—my arrowhead collection and three wedges of pecan pie. Halfway down the lane, pie innards dripped through the cloth, and my mother distracted me with the promise of fresh peach ice cream.

Q. *What kind of research did you have to do?*

A. My research began when I traveled the route of the Overland Trail west from Nebraska. I couldn't believe how impossible the terrain must have been for a covered wagon, and how startling to see the Devil's Tower and the Badlands. Imagining this through the eyes of a young runaway led me to start the book. After that, I read histories of towns along the trail as well as journals of men who made the trek.

Q. *Unlike your first book, this one has both a male and a female point of view. Were there any special difficulties in writing from a male point of view?*

A. As a kid I was a tomboy growing up on a farm like Joshua's, so I felt comfortable fitting into his skin, except for the sex part. For that, I had to ask a lot of questions, and believe me, there aren't many men who are willing to have their boyhood bodies researched.

Q. *Did you find writing your second novel easier than writing the first?*

A. "Easy" isn't a word I would use when it comes to writing. For me it's a compulsion I can't and don't want to resist. I get snarky if I'm away from it for any length of time. But these two books did help each other, since I'd written half of *Stones in the Road* before I wrote *An Unseemly Wife*. Both were started in poetry form and then morphed into prose. I loved the writing process, attempting to become each character and letting them lead me to unexpected reactions.

Q. You're a professional sculptor. Does that skill play any part in your writing?

A. The process is remarkably similar. In sculpture you have to look from every angle to be sure the piece works as a whole. In writing, if you don't do the same, you end up with flat characters or a disjointed plot. Also, my love of tools made its way into many chapters. These implements now hang unused on beams in my loft, so writing them into stories gives me a chance to relive my other life.

Q. Do you need peace and quiet to write? What would be a typical writing day for you?

A. I live alone, so most of the time, my working hours remain quiet. But not on vacation. Noise made me cut those weeks short, but deprivation set in, and I learned to work in the midst of a crowded living room, participating in passing conversations or ducking Ping-Pong balls during exuberant tournaments.

On these weeks, my days start between four and five a.m. (not by design). I eat lunch while everyone else has breakfast, then welcome a second lunch at noon. Napping is a necessity, followed by edits and a much-needed walk. By late afternoon I don't trust anything I write, so a martini and cooking with friends round out the evening. Staying awake till ten proves a challenge.

At home, interruptions demand greater attention: the call of laundry, organizing maintenance of the converted factory where I'm a trustee, culling my freezer for lost chocolates. The ubiquitous Facebook.

Q. What are you working on now?

A. I'm working on a novel set in the current day, about an elderly woman on the lam in the Boston Garden. Slipping from reality, she escapes her children's loving clutches, running away from the hospital dressed in a johnny, a mink coat tied with a telephone cord, and a pair of goggley-eyed slippers given by her youngest grandchild.

QUESTIONS

FOR DISCUSSION

1. Did you think of Miriam as naive when it comes to Abraham?

2. After the fire and Joshua's disappearance, Miriam takes many steps outside her normal boundaries. Which one did you find most significant?

3. How would you say Joshua's faith evolves over the course of the book?

4. After he leaves home, Joshua encounters various mother and father figures in the book. Whom do you think has the most impact on him, whether positive or negative?

5. Several times, Abraham's helplessness is compared to that of a child. In what ways is this apt or not?

6. Is there a "villain" in the book? If so, who is it?

7. Why do you think Abraham resists the idea that Joshua has returned?

8. Could you find sympathy for Abraham by the end of the novel?

9. What are the "stones" in Joshua's or Miriam's road?